Too Rich, Too Thin

For a matter of a second, to Maudie Grant's affronted eye, the young man lying there in bed, jacked up on one elbow, exchanging with her look for aghast look, was not distinct from but mere part of this rough-house, no more out of place than the single capsized stiletto sandal, the black and lacy brassière which strangled a chair leg, the litter of empty envelopes, debris of so many mornings' mail.

'It's not what you think,' offered Caroline in a tiny, childish, pathetic voice, standing at Maudie's elbow, still clutching the waving plant, a housewarming present (as if this house were not already fugged enough with heat). And it wasn't of course – it was not at all what Maudie thought. It was far more serious than she could even hazard.

Rose Shepherd is a *Sunday Times* journalist and writes for numerous magazines including *Marie Claire, Company, Options, Women's Journal* and *Good Housekeeping*. *Too Rich Too Thin* was her first novel; her second, *Happy Ever After*, will soon be available in hardback from Heinemann.

Also by Rose Shepherd

Happy Ever After

Rose Shepherd

———— · ————

Too Rich,
Too Thin

Mandarin

A Mandarin Paperback
TOO RICH, TOO THIN

First published in Great Britain 1992
by William Heinemann Ltd
This edition published 1993
by Mandarin Paperbacks
an imprint of Reed Consumer Books Ltd
Michelin House, 81 Fulham Road, London SW3 6RB
and Auckland, Melbourne, Singapore and Toronto

Reprinted 1993

Copyright © Rose Shepherd 1992
The author has asserted her moral rights

A CIP catalogue record for this title
is available from the British Library

ISBN 0 7493 1098 7

Typeset by Deltatype Ltd, Ellesmere Port
Printed and bound in Great Britain
by Cox & Wyman Ltd, Reading, Berks

Summer 1988

CHAPTER

———— • ————

1

'Who. . . ?'

Sweet-scented and rosy and rustly in satin, Caroline emerged from her bathroom, summoned by a peremptory knock on her bedroom door.

It would be Elizabeth, she supposed, with the dress. And, as she padded across the pale expanse of Chinese carpet, as her plump, pink reflection came and went in the cheval glass, her chagrin was suddenly so acute that she doubled at the waist, hugging herself to hold in the pain.

She was a pretty girl with the look of a child still, with large brown eyes, wispy blonde hair, a warm, susceptible heart, and thin, pale skin, beneath which the blood seemed in constant flux. Now her face was washed with colour at the memory of the humiliation of yesterday.

'Everything will be fine,' Elizabeth had promised her, a shade desperately, through a mouthful of pins. And, her smooth brow suddenly a mass of little pleats, she had tweaked and plucked at the taut delphinium silk crepe, hitched up the hem to frown at the neatly stitched, ungiving seam, making a rapid professional assessment of the possible, looking for leeway, for margin, for so much as a centimetre of slack. 'A few minor alterations, the work of moments, *non c'è problema*.'

'A damage limitation exercise, more like,' Caroline had told herself wretchedly, as Elizabeth tried once more, vainly, to close the zip. Hopeless, hopeless. Craning her neck, she had glimpsed over her shoulder a big wedge of flesh where fabric refused to meet fabric. 'A matter of making the best of a bad job.'

Not, of course, that it was the job, the dress that was at fault. The responsibility lay squarely with the wearer, with Caroline herself.

These things were to be expected, Elizabeth had assured her then, lightly, laughing with sisterly understanding. She had one client who could gain inches, *inches*, overnight. Yes, she would positively *balloon*. 'We ladies have these little ups and downs, we have our cycles.'

And it had been left to Laura – who but Laura? – to put into words the stark truth that Caroline had gained half a stone since her last fitting, because she lacked the willpower, the self-discipline, to stick to a diet.

There was a second sharp rap on the door, and before Caroline could shout 'Come!', someone came – for Maudie Grant, her maternal grandmother, was not a woman to be kept waiting. Maudie's knock said, not 'May I?', but 'Stand by!' It said 'Stand back!'

At seventy she was an uncompromisingly slim and smart woman, with a style of her own, a sort of austere chic, at once expensive and severe. Beneath a rigidly tailored suit in her beloved navy blue, she wore a cream blouse with – for this was a day of celebration – a frivolous, floppy bow at the neck. Not one inch of her five feet ten was sacrificed to poor posture: Caroline had to stand on tiptoe to touch her lips to the cheek which was offered for a kiss, and which was dusted pink, as powdery and pliant as marshmallow.

'Hello Granny. How lovely to see you!' she murmured with that mixture of genuine affection and creeping apprehension which Maudie always inspired in her.

'Many happy returns, darling.' Maudie afforded her flustered granddaughter the merest smile. But then, she had never been big on smiles, which were known to cause crows' feet and 'laughter lines' (as though lines were ever a laughing matter).

'I'm afraid you caught me . . .' Caroline flapped one distracted hand in apology, indicating her state of undress, which rendered her more than usually vulnerable. She was all at once very conscious of her damp skin beneath the thin robe, which attached to her like cling-film to cheese. 'I wasn't expecting anyone quite yet.'

The guests had been invited for one o'clock. The final preparations were scarcely underway. The staff were only now erecting trestles on the west terrace, draping them with starched damask cloths, decking them with flowers. The band had just begun setting up – every so often there would be the screech of feedback through a microphone, or a deep, disembodied voice would boom out across the rollered lawns of Hartwell, testing, testing.

'I had the car come for me at eight,' Maudie told her with the insufferable briskness of the early riser, peeling off her gloves, flexing her long fingers, each one tipped with a perfectly shaped and lacquered nail. 'It's really quite a tolerable drive from town if you make sure to be on the road before the morning rush. We had a slight snarl-up outside Shaftesbury, more of those never-ending roadworks – if half-a-dozen layabouts leaning on their spades can be described as "working" – but otherwise it was plain sailing all the way.'

And with that she went, uninvited, to sit ramrod straight on the window seat in the tall bay, patting the cushion beside her with a smooth, ringed hand, motioning to Caroline to join her there. 'In any case, I wanted the opportunity of a little chat with you before we all let our hair down.'

Acquiescent, Caroline parked herself, stifling a jittery smile at the very idea of Maudie with a single hair of her ruthlessly disciplined head either literally or figuratively 'down'. She felt uncomfortable and clammy, and desperately wished that she might be delivered from this interview. Whatever her grandmother meant to say to her – and her portentous manner suggested that some kind of prepared speech was impending – she did not care to hear it.

The worry was that Maudie would bestow upon her one of those 'kindnesses' which were a speciality. She might, for instance, be preparing to tell her of this marvellous little man about whom everyone was talking, and who might finally have the answer to her 'problem'.

Over the years, at Maudie's insistence and not inconsiderable expense, Caroline had been paraded in her pants and bra before a succession of eminent nutritionists, doctors, diet gurus and quacks. She had been despatched to health hydros to sweat it out in steam bath and sauna, had been smeared with stinking seaweed slime, hosed with brine, oiled and wrapped in plastic, bubbled in a *bain bouillant*, Blitzgussed, body scrubbed and salt rubbed, slapped with mud, lapped in plankton . . . and always she had emerged, to her grandmother's perplexity, the same old Caroline, simply not sylph material.

The process was, Caroline considered, like putting a garment repeatedly through the boil wash, in the vain hope that it might shrink. It would never work, but nor would Maudie admit defeat.

Still, at least her grandmother did not actually blame her for her shape, whereas Laura, Caroline's mother, tended to the view that she did it on purpose, to be awkward. She regarded her daughter's fatness as a gesture, as disobedience, evidence of her irreverence, of her anarchic humour, her highly developed sense of the absurd, which was actually, above all else, Caroline's salvation, a sort of psychological ballast.

Caroline had tried to look at it from Laura's point of view. It was possible, she supposed, that she had 'chosen' to be big, that the flab was an outward manifestation of some deep-buried inner resentment. A metaphor for mother-daughter animus. A symbol of rebellion or a perverse form of rivalry.

But she had come at last to the conclusion that her biochemistry was to blame. She supposed she must simply have fat genes. And whereas she would have infinitely preferred to have inherited her mother's body architecture – her implausibly long legs, her narrow hips, her high cheekbones, not to mention the flame-red hair, the vivid green eyes, the face that had been Laura's fortune – it had been Caroline's fate to take after her natural father ('That *dreadful* man,' as Maudie referred to him; 'That shit,' as Laura would have it).

Now she wished only to forget about weight, to be free to get on with her life, to address more important issues, to make something of herself. She wanted a career, she wanted to use the keen mind with which she had been blessed and which, she would argue, was surely, when all was said and done, every bit as important as appearance.

Laura, however, would never be persuaded. In her estimation, if you could not go about in a figure-hugging Lycra body and a pair of Azzedine Alaia shorts, if you could not bare a provocative inch of taut midriff, if you did not have suntanned legs up to your bum, then really you might as well write yourself off.

'Aren't the gardens looking lovely?' ventured Caroline fatuously, gazing out upon the lake, upon the soupy water, in which the blue sky, the reeds, the weeping willows appeared teasingly inverted. 'Weekes says he's never seen the roses do so well, though he's been here man and boy for more than half a century.'

'You are eighteen years old today,' said Maudie importantly, refusing to be deflected by some piece of servants' tattle. It was Weekes's job to tend the roses, not to talk about them.

'Yes,' acknowledged Caroline, 'I know.'

'The age of majority.'

'Old enough to vote.' Caroline made what she hoped was suitable response. Then, as she experienced one of those inexplicable surges of mirth for which she had so often been in trouble at school, she added, 'Or to marry whom I please. Or to sue, or be sued. Or to fight for my country – in the unlikely event that I should be called upon to do so.' And she dissolved in laughter at the notion, at the vision of herself in khaki.

'Well, quite.' Maudie's face momentarily betrayed her exasperation. Eyebrow tilted with eyebrow at the bridge of her beaky nose. Caroline was her flesh and blood. She was fond of the girl, she'd not deny it. But there were times when she frankly failed to comprehend her. At this moment, for instance, what on earth did she find so amusing? One thing – almost the only thing – she would say for Laura: at least she was not given to bouts of unaccountable hilarity.

'I'm sorry, Granny,' Caroline hastily apologised. 'I'm just so excited about today. Really nervous, you know?'

'Ah, I see.' That made sense of a sort to Maudie. She knew about nervousness. It was a well-documented phenomenon which, she understood, afflicted others, although she'd never herself had an intimation of it. 'About the party. Of course. Your big day. Well, you mustn't worry' – she laid a kindly hand on Caroline's arm – 'I'm quite sure you will be the belle of the ball.'

'I very much doubt that,' Caroline replied before she could bite back the words.

'Oh, come, that's not the attitude, is it? You simply lack confidence, even now, although why you should, I couldn't say.'

A lack of poise had been identified, along with overweight, as a handicap for Caroline. And, in the belief that external solutions might be found for all such ills – that anything, even self-esteem, might be bought at a price – Maudie had urged that she be sent for finishing, to be rounded off, imbued with social graces.

Thus Caroline knew how to dress for point-to-pointing, how to address an earl. She knew about dinner party procedures, who to sit where and which wines to serve with what. She knew never to push her plate away or to use it as an ashtray; how to eat artichoke and escargots. She had learned to execute a neat little curtsey, to extricate herself from a Lamborghini without showing her knickers. And still sometimes she died inside with shyness; still she must do daily battle with her own humility.

'It's to be a grand affair, I gather?' Maudie quizzed.

'Quite a large do, certainly,' Caroline allowed. 'But I don't know that "grand" is the word for it. It's supposed to be pretty informal. There'll be lots of family friends, of course. And a few of my old school chums. And a number of "names", probably, who Mummy's managed to rope in for the occasion.'

At Laura's behest, indeed, a number of the famous and the infamous would be showing their faces. She had many contacts even today in the fashion business – agents, photographers, designers – as well as old flames from the sixties, rock stars, restaurateurs, entrepreneurs. Laura had moved up in the world since her wild days, she had moved on. Yet, while she was thrilled to be Lady Charteris and to call Hartwell her home, she still craved notoriety, longed for the limelight, fancied herself to be more of the jet than of the county set.

'How lovely!' responded Maudie with evident distaste. She had always taken a poor view of the riffraff, the rascals, with whom Laura chose to consort, but now and then their society was simply unavoidable. If she found herself thrown together with them, she would make a supreme effort, make small talk as common courtesy demanded, though her aversion to them would be comically apparent, and she clearly regarded them as something other than human. (Caroline had once watched Maudie petting a Persian cat in much the same manner. The animal had jumped on to her knee and, not the least chary of its affections, had tramped, purring, up and down the inhospitable lap, shedding long, white hair, and snagging the Jean Muir skirt. 'How lovely!' Maudie had said then, with just such transparent insincerity, sooner than offend her distinguished host, the animal's devoted owner. 'How sweet!')

'I think we've invited about a hundred in all.'

'Quite a gathering. Now, my dear, pay attention, do. I think the time has come for you to have this.' Maudie dipped into her handbag, extracted a slim leather case, weighed it in her hand, deliberated. 'Can you be trusted, I wonder? Yes, I fancy you can.' With some ceremony she handed over the case. 'Very many happy returns of the day, Caroline, darling.'

'What is it?' asked Caroline stupidly.

'Well, take a look and see.' Maudie affected a twinkle, although twinkling was not really within her repertoire, and there was a trace of impatience in her tone.

Caroline fumbled with the clasp. Then, 'Oh, my heavens!' she said as she prised open the lid. 'Goodness, gracious!' For there, couched on oyster silk, lay a Victorian necklace, diamonds like white fire, big lozenges of emerald, bright as boiled sweets, an heir-loom, which had been Maudie's mother's, and her mother's before that. 'Crikey!'

In many ways, and particularly since her mother's marriage to Sir John Charteris, Caroline had been out-rageously, materially spoilt. This very morning she had come down to breakfast to find a key on a leather tag by her place at the table. 'Outside the front door,' her stepfather had told her over his *Telegraph* with a pretence of nonchalance, sounding mightily pleased with himself. And there on the gravelled drive had been her parents' gift to her, a little red Fiat with a targa top. 'Your own runabout,' John Charteris had smiled, at which Caroline had been so overcome that she'd had to hurry away to the stables, to breathe the reassuring, sour-sweet smell of bedding straw, to give Freckles the pony a hug, and to weep with wordless gratitude against his woolly neck.

She had so much now, so much of everything, she could hardly believe it could all be meant for her. Surely it had come to the wrong address!

'I only hope you can handle it,' Laura had remarked when she came gliding down in her dressing gown an hour later. 'Don't you go writing it off inside a week.' But even she had seemed almost indulgent as she bent to stamp her daughter's cheek with a perfunctory kiss, as with the official insignia of maternal love.

A car of her own! Such extravagance! Yet the gift of the necklace was far more lavish.

'It's too much,' Caroline protested with a hint of panic, unable to raise her eyes, to look into Maudie's face. 'I don't . . . I can't . . . I mean, I never expected anything so . . .'

So expensive? So valuable? So *onerous*. It was more than she wanted. More than generous. In fact, she instinctively knew, something other than pure generosity was at work here. She felt her face burning with distress as she groped in vain for the right words.

She was spared, however, from uttering them, by the arrival at that instant of Laura, who slammed in reeking of Fendi and foul temper, with her head swathed in a towel, and with the shimmering blue dress slung over her arm. 'Well, Elizabeth has done her best, but even she can't work miracles. We shall just have to hope that she's been able to save the day.'

Laura never merely entered a room, but she burst upon it. She was calamitously attractive. She created around her a kind of abstraction, a sexual vacuum, like a gasp she stole from the very air. And wherever she went, a rush of male lust filled the void in her wake. 'Try this on quickly,' she ordered, 'we'll see if we can shoe-horn you into it.' Then, seeing that Caroline was not alone, she added, 'Oh, hello, *you're* here. No one told me you'd arrived.'

'I had Stevens show me up,' Maudie responded frostily. 'I wanted a little word in private with my granddaughter.'

'Well, you're having one, aren't you? Caro, go on now, take this into your dressing room and find out if it fits. You wouldn't *believe* it, Mother, the trouble we've had with Miss Piggy here, and her ever-expanding waistline.'

'Oh, don't,' Caroline silently exhorted. 'Today of all days, just *don't*.' The tears sprang. How she hated her own lack of self-control. But Laura had always been able to affect her this way, to reduce her to emotional jelly. And the stupid thing was, she didn't mean to. Not really. She simply did not think. She so lacked imagination, she hadn't an inkling of how it felt to be Caroline – or indeed to be anyone but Laura Grant. She was constitutionally incapable of empathy with her fellow human beings.

'Now, what are you blubbing about?' Laura scolded. 'Look, don't just sit there. Get your skates on. Nicky will be here any second to fix our hair.' She unwound her makeshift turban, swung her head so her auburn locks swished this way, that way, and began to towel them vigorously.

'I'm sure our little girl will do us proud,' said Maudie in a distant, anodyne way.

'Oh, I dare say she'll pass.'

The two older women, mother and daughter, traded looks of distrust.

'I . . .' began Caroline. She had been thinking to say that she would prefer to do her own hair, but hesitated lest she be branded an ingrate.

'Yes?' Laura gave her, for the first time, her full attention –and for the first time she focused on the open case, on the necklace, in Caroline's possession. Glancing down at it, Caroline wondered at the brilliance of the diamonds, at the depth and colour of the emeralds which would have looked so ravishing at Laura's pale throat, with Laura's vitreous green eyes.

That was it! From there sprang her unease. The necklace should have passed not to her but to Laura. Why should it skip a generation?

Lifting her head, she read the signals that flashed

between Maudie and Laura, the messages telegraphed back and forth. Oh, mischievous Maudie!

'I should have guessed,' thought Caroline, feeling suddenly very wise, all-knowing, and full of woe. 'This is not for me. It's just her way of telling Mummy. She hasn't really forgiven her, even now. After all these years, she still hasn't redeemed herself. I don't suppose she ever will.'

———— • ————

'Oh, he's really *outrageous*. He just doesn't care. I never know what he'll come out with next.'

As Nicky ran expert fingers through Laura's hair, massaging her scalp with a gentle, circular motion, kneading her temples with his thumbs, she eased back in the chair and let his inconsequential chatter – some story about his friend Jamie, a fellow of apparently infinite jest – run off her.

His touch was soothing, his voice strangely soporific. She practised her deep respiration technique, saying 'calm' to herself with every out breath, and waited for the tension to seep away as promised through her fingers and toes. She tried to discover that still centre of herself which, on the good authority of Dmitri, her personal trainer, the man charged with her physical and spiritual well-being, must be in there somewhere, but which she had yet to plumb. And, in spite of all, she seethed. Her heart felt squeezed like a lemon; the sour juices seeped into her veins.

I am not going to let them ruin it for me, she silently

vowed. For this was to have been, as she had conceived
it, very much 'her' day. She had been impatiently looking
forward to seeing friends, to flirting discreetly as befitted
her status, to being as ever the centre of attention. She
had pictured herself, a vision of loveliness, in a flouncy,
off-the-shoulder, floral-print, chiné taffeta dress. She
had imagined her hair swinging about her honeyed
shoulders in delicious red-gold coils, with the glossy,
sauvage, slightly windblown look that only true artistry
and a good styling mousse can achieve. She might make
Tatler, make *Harper's*, make Jennifer's Diary. 'I simply
cannot allow Maudie, that mean-spirited old bitch, to
spoil it with her nonsense.'

At issue, after all, was a mere necklace, a bauble, a
thing. Wasn't that what people said? 'So I broke your
priceless vase. Ha, ha. Never mind, now. Who cares? It's
only a *thing*.' But such rationalisation just would not
work for Laura, who came at life much as a bargain
hunter comes at the January sales, in a state of high
anxiety lest she miss out. Laura, to whom things were,
well, *everything*.

In any case, there was more to it than that. There were
implications. There was spite at work. There was retribution of a kind, her mother even now trying to punish her.
And it was utterly unjust. 'That necklace belonged to my
grandmother,' Laura told herself righteously, 'and to my
great-grandmother before her. It wasn't for my mother to
give it away. She was holding it in trust. She was holding
it for *me*.'

'We have a few split ends,' Nicky told her, snip-
snipping busily.

'Uh-huh,' she responded distractedly. She was accustomed to his 'we', to his 'our'. He had been her stylist for many years – she did not care to think *how* many – since they first met on a photographic session. He was the only one she trusted to take the scissors to her head. So it was hardly surprising if he took a proprietorial interest in her hair.

Then, 'Whoops!' he exclaimed. And, 'What do I spy?'

'What is it?' she demanded, suddenly alert, and her eyes flicked open in alarm. Split ends were one thing, but . . .

'A silver thread among the gold,' he crooned. 'You have a white hair, lovey.'

It was as though he had put a match to a firework. Laura experienced one of her flashes of temper, a sudden explosion of anger that whooshed through her and left her winded. How dare he, how bloody *dare* he, be so crass? 'What are you saying?' Her voice shook with emotion.

'It's only one little white hair, ducks. No need to get in such a twist.'

'Are you sure about it?'

'Of course I'm sure. I should know, shouldn't I? Or I'm in the wrong business.'

'Pull it out,' she commanded him urgently. And 'Ouch!' she protested as he complied.

'There now,' he reassured her. 'All gone.' Bending, he pressed his cheek against hers, so that she might see in the glass his smiling face beside her stricken one. The smell of Antaeus filled her nostrils. 'It happens to the best of us, dear heart,' he offered. '*Anno Domini* and all that.

Do you know, Jamie is getting quite bald. I told him last night, "You're getting quite bald." '

'Oh, shut up about Jamie,' she snapped, thrilled by her own nastiness. 'I'm sick of hearing about your faggot friends.'

'Well!' Nicky backed off, folded his arms across his chest, huffed in indignation. 'Thank *you*. That's very nice, I must say. Perhaps I had better leave. I mean, if I'm getting on her ladyship's nerves. If she would prefer to do her own hair.'

'No!' She twisted in the seat to entreat him. He couldn't desert her. Not now. Not like this. For, harsh though she often was to him, he was part of her life-support system, one of the band of people who sustained her. 'Don't go. I'm sorry, darling, that was unforgivable. It's just . . .'

And he knew, of course, what the 'just' was. He knew that for her this 'just' was enormous.

Laura Charteris was thirty-eight years old. She had had many lovers, two of whom she had married. She was a mother: her body had been forced to make the unreasonable adaptation to pregnancy, even as she, after years of sex and drugs and rock and roll, had made the expedient adaptation to respectability. And, especially now that her daughter was officially an adult, certain facts might have to be faced.

It crashed in on her that she was no longer nineteen-year-old Laura Grant, that she no longer had it all before her. How had it happened? She simply could not account for it. Someone, somewhere must be to blame. The years had been stolen from her, knocked off while her back was turned.

Then, growing older was one thing; *appearing* older, another. She would walk in beauty like the night, or, she felt, she would take to her bed and never get up again. For when that beauty was gone she would be as other women. And to be as other women, in Laura's canon, was to be as nothing. She had premised her life on her looks; now, more and more, she terrified herself with the realisation of how weak a premise this was.

Intuitive, kind-hearted Nicky, absolving her, caressed her neck. Slowly she began to relax. What was one stray white hair when all was said and done? No need to over-react.

Presently he asked, 'What's this I've been hearing about you doing a cover for *Finesse*?'

'Who told you about that?'

'Who told me? Why darling, *le tout Londre* is buzzing with the news. But is it true?'

'I've been approached,' she confessed, and she indulged an impulse to smile. 'It depends if they can afford me.'

'But that's marvellous! The launch issue. You the quintessence of finesse.'

'I'm still in demand, you see, Nicky.'

'Well, of course. There's no one to touch you.'

'This new generation, kids just out of school, they're so *unformed*, I find.'

'Dearest, don't tell me.' He rolled his eyes. 'I mean, I *meet* them. I *work* with them.'

'Sort of half-finished.'

'No character.'

'Vapid.'

'The very word for it.'

'It's the coming thing, you know,' she informed him. 'Greater maturity. That's the new ideal. The woman in her thirties is going to be *it*.'

'Laura, you were always *it*. No one else has your *je ne sais quoi*.'

'No, I suppose you're right.' Laura felt suddenly, miraculously, recovered. It was as though she had woken from a bad dream to find that everything was as it should be. The sense of relief was so huge that it threatened to overwhelm her. Had she been one for weeping, she would have wept. Beyond the window, she noticed, the sun was bobbing like a yellow balloon in the shimmering sky.

'A little more fullness at the sides, I think Nicky,' she told him bossily. 'A little more height at the front.'

Down in the main drawing-room, half an hour later, Laura found Tobias, the younger of her two stepsons, ensconced in a deep leather armchair, cleaning one of his guns, with Pasha the labrador and Pee Wee the Jack Russell basking in a stripe of sunlight at his feet.

Tobias was a strapping lad of twenty, with sandy hair, a big, open face and an amiable disposition. Unlike his elder brother, the elegant, cerebral Jasper, he had never given Laura any real trouble. 'Hello, wicked step-mother,' he greeted her heartily, snapping open the lethal-looking 12-bore and peering down the barrel, as Pasha, ingratiating, drummed his tail on the floor.

'Would you put that away please, Toby. You know I can't abide firearms around the house.'

'Don't worry, it's not loaded.'

'That's not the point.' For it wasn't the potential danger that bothered her, the remote risk of mishap, of stray shot peppering the damask-hung walls, or embedding itself in a sofa, or shattering some piece of Dresden. Rather, it was that guns put her unhappily in mind of rugged, outdoor pursuits.

Once upon a time, when she had set her sights on Sir John, when he – sweet man – had fondly imagined he was wooing her, she had supposed it might be a bit of a lark to go creaking around in a waxed Barbour, with an adoring dog weaving at her heels. She had pictured herself on horseback, in skin-tight jodhpurs, going flat out, with her hair streaming like a silken banner behind her. Or at the wheel of a Land Rover, off on some fishing trip, or to a point-to-point, with a champagne picnic in a hamper in the back. She had fancied herself in *Country Life*.

But the reality had been disillusioning. The sporty outdoors meant weathering wind and rain, getting soaked to the skin and frozen to the bone. It meant broken veins and a runny nose and rats' tails. It involved hauling yourself up on to some fidgety hunter, at least a hundred and fifty hands high, which snorted at one end and farted at the other, and felt decidedly rocky in the middle; or hanging about on the bank of the bloated river, with your green wellies all squelchy, and mud on your backside where you'd just gone arse over tit.

Laura had first visited Hartwell in the summertime, when the trees were boiling with birdlife, and the golden Bath stone house was bleached by sunshine. She had marvelled at the richly patterned Persian carpets, at the paintings of grouse and gun dogs, of hare and hounds and finely muscled horses, at dark portraits of disfranchised forebears, past incumbents now enjoying the cold comforts of the family crypt at St Luke's.

She had thought then, 'I want this, I *want* it!' And she had never guessed how the draughts would whistle in the plastered passageways, nosing under all the doors, in and out of doggy-smelling sitting rooms, upstairs, downstairs, and in the vast, dusty spaces under the roof, where it lifted the slates to let in grey squares of sky. Or how those paintings would come so soon to oppress her.

Most oppressive of all, of course, was the portrait which hung above the splendid Adam fireplace, of her predecessor, the boys' mother, the sainted Jane.

The first Lady Charteris had been killed in a motor accident with a friend, when Tobias was seven and Jasper nine. The face that smiled serenely down from above the mantelpiece was that of a good woman, the sort who sat on committees, who ran church bazaars, who saved old greetings cards and tin foil to help the disadvantaged. She had a comely and a kindly aspect. She seemed to epitomise all the wifely, motherly virtues. And it irked Laura half to death to think that this person had set so impossible a precedent.

For Laura was not the type to hold open days for charity, to sell flags door to door or to organise a bring-and-buy for Ethiopia. She was ravishing, she was exotic, she was famous –that would have to be enough, since she had nothing more to give.

'*Alora*, Laura.' Tobias set the gun aside. 'Your wish is my command.'

'Thank you.'

She walked to the tall French windows and stood there a moment, staring out. All that green-and-pleasantness. All that peace and quiet. I miss London, she told herself. I ache and ache for it. I feel so trapped, out in the sticks. I'm only half alive here. I must take myself up to town for a few days, she decided. Do some catching up there.

Presently, without turning, she spoke. 'Toby?'

'Over here.'

'Do you . . .' But she could not, when it came to it, frame the question. It was just a feeling, really, a rare moment of self-doubt, having to do with her position at Hartwell, in the household, in their affections, their esteem.

'I'm sure I do,' Toby told her equably, 'whatever it is.'

'Well, I hope so.' She crossed the room to sit facing him, smiled at him. 'Where's John, do you know?'

'With Stevens, I think, sorting out about the bubbly for today's bash.'

'Ah, yes, the fizz.' It was a heartening prospect. 'Do you suppose we should have some now? A livener?'

'Don't see why not.' He jumped up with alacrity to ring for service. 'The cup that not only cheers, but better still inebriates. We should get some down Caro before the hordes descend. She'll need to be braced for the big event.'

'She's having her hair done at the moment,' Laura told him. 'Her grandmother was with her when I went up to her. She arrived early, astride her broomstick. Bearing gifts.'

'Such is the custom on these occasions, I'm told.'

'So I believe.'

She would have liked to tell him about the necklace, about her mother's awfulness. 'It's not the stupid trinket,' she would have said dismissively, dishonestly. 'Heavens, no, a little thing like that wouldn't bother me. It's the thought behind it, the sheer nastiness.' But her relationship with her stepsons was a strange, ambiguous one, sustainable only so long as they maintained a certain distance.

From the outset she had made it clear: she was too young to play mummy to two hefty lads in long trousers. They must respect her authority, but they might not look to her for cuddles. She would be a wife to Sir John, but not a parent to his children – and on these terms he had married her.

Well, it wasn't as if they had wanted for mothering. What were domestics for, after all, if not to wash cricket whites, and to iron adhesive name tags into umpteen pairs of underpants? Why did schools employ matrons if not to bathe the boys' cuts and to ask them if they'd been? Why employ house masters, if not to warn of the evils of masturbation? Let these people cope. Because she as sure as hell could not.

In truth, Laura had been more than merely nervous of John's sons; she had been positively squeamish. Boys in general, she believed, were a kind of noisy, grubby, smelly-socked sub-species. She could not relate to them, had no idea how to get close to them. And she found something profoundly distasteful about their pubescence.

But now Tobias and Jasper were grown, they were men, which was a further complication. Because Laura had this compulsion, around men, to check out her sexuality. Their eyes were the mirror in which she might see that she was still so heart-stoppingly attractive. Their reactions were a true reflection of her abiding charms. And almost unconsciously she would emit her firefly signals, flash her lights at them, in certain hope that she would catch them winking back at her.

Only it wasn't on, frankly, to engage in sexual semaphore with one's stepchildren, to flirt with one's husband's sons. Even Laura, with her loose grasp of fair play, could see this wouldn't be cricket. So partly it was scruple which prevented her from so doing. But, more than that, it was a sneaking uncertainty, a secret fear that she might find in them no response, that she might actually leave them cold.

They were too young for her, of course (this was how she would express it: they, not she, were the 'wrong' age). And in any case, they both had girlfriends – Tobias a string of lusty Camillas and Cornelias from agricultural college; Jasper a fellow student from university, some kind of Trotskyite, a busty girl with jumbled teeth, a strident manner and a lamentable lack of dress sense. But if she could not come on to them sexually, she could not come on to them at all. Hence a certain awkwardness must always attend their encounters.

'I bet she's a bag of nerves, our birthday girl,' Tobias remarked. Both boys had teased Caroline mercilessly since the day she arrived, calling her Dumpling, calling her Pudding, taking great delight in making her blush.

But over the years they had grown fond of her, as she, in her awkward way, was fond of them. 'Ah, Stevens, there you are! We are crying out for refreshment here, our throats unslaked, our black lips baked. Could you spirit a bottle of some cheeky little effervescent number from your bottomless cellar? That would be most agreeable. Thank you so much.'

'She was in a bit of tizzy,' Laura told Toby, reflecting on her daughter's wretched state, remembering how Caroline's face had crumpled, simply because she had been a tiny bit brisk with her in the matter of the dress. And she felt a familiar discomfort, that unwelcome drag on her emotions which was her experience of maternal love.

It was not a pleasant sensation; it was an affliction of a kind, for which there was no cure; it was an imposition. A daughter was like a damaged limb, it seemed to her, a source of pain and mortification. If Laura could not feel *for* Caroline, she could at least feel *about* her.

'So this is where you've been hiding.' Sir John Charteris stood in the doorway, smiling benignly at his wife. At fifty he was still unknowingly handsome, tall, with a slight, apologetic stoop which lent him the misleading air of a good listener. He was a genuinely kind man, mild, tolerant and irredeemably vague. Family mythology even had it that he once absent-mindedly wolfed down the dogs' dinner in mistake for his own, with great relish, a half bottle of Brouilly, and no evident ill-effects. (What Pee Wee and Pasha made of the *faisan à la Normande* which fell to them that day was not recorded.)

'Hardly "hiding",' Laura corrected him, and, making buffers of her hands as he bore down upon her for a kiss, she chastely offered him a cheek. 'Don't smudge my lips. You'll crush my dress. Oh, do mind my hair.'

'You look absolutely sensational.' He spoke with a slight stammer which some people apparently found appealing, but which tied him in knots of embarrassment.

'That's sweet of you,' said Laura, appreciating the sentiment, if not the halting delivery. 'We were just about to have some champagne. Ah, look, here it is. You do the honours, John, there's a sweetheart.'

As Sir John received from Stevens the smoking bottle and filled the glasses, all Bollinger and *bonhomie*, Laura, watching, wished that she could yet find him even slightly sexy. For she had fancied him like mad when first she met him; she had been attracted to the man and not merely to his title. There had been something about his nerviness, his long limbs, his loping gait. He went in for bear hugs and exuberant wet kisses. He was large and awkward. He would be, she had somehow known, an enthusiastic and inexpert lover. He would cover her comprehensively, all legs and arms and a great weight of torso. He would worship her with his body. He would be awed by her beauty.

For Laura, making love was a supreme act of self-worship. A man must be weak with lust for her, then speechless with gratitude to her. He must gaze in wonderment upon her, and grope for words to express the inexpressible. He must murmur that he had never, never . . . that this was more than he had ever hoped,

ever dreamed he might . . . that she was quite the most
. . . that she was absolutely . . .

Reverential, inarticulate, John had lived up to her
every expectation. But she had wearied some years ago
of his puppyishness. And more and more she found
herself secretly longing for a change. She must, she
decided, take a lover; that was the only thing that would
make her feel renewed.

'Hello, everyone.' Caroline had slipped almost un-
noticed into the room and was in their midst, slightly
sheepish, shyly smiling, in the new blue dress, and with
her hair newly washed and shiny.

'Caro,' yelled Tobias, 'you look good enough to eat.'

'Thank you,' said Caroline, flushing crimson.

'Yes, very nice.' Laura, still inwardly seething, twirled
a champagne flute between her fingers, musing on the
suicidal rush of bubbles, refusing to spare so much as a
glance, though she felt her daughter's brown eyes upon
her and sensed that her approval was sought.

Well, the hell with it! Why should she – why bloody
should she – indulge the spoilt child? Was it not enough
that she had arranged this party? Enough that she had
taken so much time and trouble to ensure, as far as it was
within her power, that everything would be perfect on
the day?

But then she experienced again that disagreeable draw
on her affections. She felt as she had felt with a baby at
her breast, as if something of her essential self were being
leeched from her. And she reminded herself angrily,
only really to assuage the feeling, that it was not her
daughter's fault about the gift. She must not take it out on

the girl. Rather, the minute she saw the back of her mother, once Maudie had left again for London, she would have a quiet word in Caroline's ear, explain the rights and wrongs of the situation, and propose that she 'borrow' the necklace for the time being. That way not only would honour be satisfied, but she would have the last laugh on Maudie, who, having parted with the beastly thing, would be in no position to protest.

She knew just how those precious stones would look at her throat. Laura had an eye for what would suit her. Emeralds, diamonds, they suited her fine.

Delighted to have hit upon so simple a solution, she turned to speak to Caroline, to offer some more fulsome congratulations.

But what she saw then so shocked her that the words died on her lips. For tight around her short neck, Caroline was wearing the priceless collar, while on her face she wore an expression, not of supplication or of ingratiation, but of brave defiance.

———————— • ————————

Jasper Charteris sat alone in the fountain garden, gazing moodily through a gauze of tiny insects at green water pregnant with pond life. The surface was dark and smooth as a table, spread with lily leaves large as dinner plates, with white flowers like fancy, folded napkins.

Not that Jasper saw any of this, so deep was he within himself, so deeply, deeply Jasper. He remained quite motionless as the breeze played with his dark forelock, fluffing the fine hair, sweeping it back, then fanning it over his face. He wore a loose shirt of the thinnest white cotton, and an expression of soul-felt regret, each of them cut to fit, the shirt to flatter his lithe physique, the expression to point up his exquisite physiognomy.

To the fat stone cherubs who regarded him with wall-eyed indifference from their little island at the centre of the pond, he would have appeared to be doing nothing. But if to be is to do, he was doing it with every fibre; he was doing being.

Mrs Bastable, matron at the old school, his Alma Mater, would have said he looked peaky, looked green around the gills. She'd have popped a thermometer in his mouth and packed him off to bed soon as look at him. But in his own mind's eye he presented a more tragic figure, not so much off colour as interestingly pale, wan, spectral.

He was in torment, his heart in tatters. He thought, 'Now, more than ever, seems it rich to die,' and in that instant, almost, *almost* believed it.

I've been idiotic, he told himself. Then, because that barely seemed to meet the case, I've been a bloody fool, a moron, I've been a . . .

'Wanker!'

The memory was horribly vivid, of Hilary as he had last seen her, her features sort of bunched with hatred, badmouthing him, calling him all the bastards under the sun, over the polyester bedsheets, which she had hauled up to her chin in self-protection. 'This is just a game to you, isn't it, Jasper? A kind of class adventure. You thought you'd get some spurious street cred, rubbing shoulders with the hoi polloi, having it off with a pleb,

slumming, and all the time thinking yourself so sodding
superior. I'm your bit of rough, aren't I? Well, *aren't* I,
you patronising pillock?'

'Hilly, that's not fair.' Feeling horribly disadvantaged –
for there is none so naked, so raw, as one exposed to a
lover's scorn, when all romance is suddenly stripped
away – Jasper had reached for his Armani sweater, for his
leather waistcoat, for the green tweed trousers which
had set him back a couple of hundred at Gianfranco
Ferré, and which spoke to him of the simple, rustic life, of
dance and Provençal song and sunburnt mirth.

Jasper loved Nature, loved the countryside, at least as
a concept. He loved the earthiness of it all, though he
preferred that it didn't get under his fingernails. And, it
was true, he also had a fascination with the very
otherness of other people's lives. Hilary Martin was so
different from the girls in his milieu, she might have
come from another planet.

In fact she came from Walsall, where she had grown up
in an untidy semi, with a mother who wore jeans, who
wore T-shirts emblazoned with bossy admonishments
(Stop This! Save That! Say No To The Other!), and who
taught children with learning difficulties; a father with a
Zapata moustache, who smoked roll-ups and worked for
British Telecom. Intelligent, articulate parents, active
members of trades unions, they played their Led
Zeppelin records very loud, until the people next door
hammered on the walls.

The Martin home had held for Jasper Charteris the
charm of a dolls' house, and had seemed to him to have
been built to the same dimensions. You could have fitted

the entire place – gardens as well, back and front – into the drawing room at Hartwell. And yet it was liveable in, it had its own logic, it all worked. You sat down to a meal at the kitchen table, within ketchup-passing distance of the person opposite, and you tucked your long, long legs under you, lest you inadvertently kick your neighbours.

A butler, a Stevens, endeavouring to top up glasses in the close confines of the Martin residence, would have been forced to squeeze between chairback and cooker. His dignity would have been sorely tested as he eased between Geoff Martin and the pine dresser, between Maureen Martin and the Creda washer-drier. But of course the very notion of a butler, of domestics, was hilarious to these people. They looked out for themselves. They had an independence, a freedom after which some small part of Jasper (who was not otherwise known for his small parts) hankered.

Oh, and in other ways, it had been just the job. Jasper, accepting a can of Pils from Geoff, pulling the ring, inhaling the yeasty vapour, had rejoiced at finding himself in the bosom of a working-class family, where all the while he could make mental notes, research for his novel – some work of gritty realism soon to be begun, which would be hailed as the publishing sensation of the decade, a fine exemplar of the writer's art, a stark illumination of the human condition, with rigorous psychological development, authenticity of detail and unimpeachable integrity.

Hilary, in her turn, when she'd motored down with him to Hartwell to meet his folks, had found the house completely over the top. Beautiful, she had allowed, but still both anachronistic and obscene. Folding her arms across her chest so that her breasts were bundled under her sweater, she had surveyed the ancestral pile with disapproval, squinting up at the gracious facade the way a dubious builder might before sucking his teeth and pronouncing, 'It'll cost yer.' Then the squelch of her Doc Martens on the stone flags, the clump-clump of her footsteps on the sweeping oak staircase, had expressed more eloquently than words her disgust with the iniquitous system under which Sir John Charteris and his ilk so prospered.

At dinner she'd been defensive, surly, slurping her wine and making challenging remarks about capitalism, which according to her was bound to self-destruct, pulled to bits by its own internal contradictions. To this John Charteris had responded with his usual unfailing courtesy, while Laura had rolled her eyes and looked pained; Caroline had squirmed, and Toby had grinned hugely, as though it were all the most tremendous sport.

Jasper had shot her several warning glances ('Shut up, Hilary,' his look had plainly said), but she'd been a little drunk, not a little belligerent, and had refused to be deflected.

'Did you have to?' he'd asked her later, crawling in beside her between the crackling, lavender-scented linen.

'Have to what? Hey, how come I'm not sharing *your* room? Don't tell me they don't know we sleep together.'

'Guests always have their own bedroom. Of course they know we sleep together. Did you have to be so bloody at dinner?'

'You were ashamed of me,' she'd accused then, with malicious glee.

'No, no, not ashamed. I was just . . . well, it was all a bit awkward, don't you see?'

'Not really. They didn't mind. Your dad was fine, he was listening, he was genuinely interested.'

'My father is too well bred – '

'You believe in all that, don't you? That breeding crap? You think you lot are of better stock than the rest of us. Come on, admit it.'

'I don't. Of course I don't. I'm talking about upbringing. About good manners. The stuff we have dinned into us from the day we're born.'

'*Noblesse oblige*?'

'If you want to put it that way. Besides which, he's a nice man. It's not in his nature to think badly of people. In any case, it's not him that bothers me.'

'Then who?'

Then who?

Clasping one of her breasts, wondering at the way the veins showed blue through the luminous white skin, Jasper had pondered the question.

He didn't give a fig for Caroline's opinion. She had a place in his affections, but she didn't exactly count. And frankly he couldn't care less about Toby, though he was sure to have a field day, to make much of his brother's leftie girlfriend. But Laura. . . ?

Jasper still had a profound inner conflict over his stepmother, which was nowhere near resolution.

This is how he recollected it: there had been his mother, a kind and comely woman, with brown hair and reassuring crinkles at the corners of her eyes – then, suddenly, well, there she'd not been. And so soon after, in her place, had come this other person, who had a sharp tongue and showy hair, and whose manner was awfully abrasive.

God, how he had hated Laura from the moment she set foot in Hartwell! He had never encountered a human being with so many hard edges; there was nothing soft, nothing tender or tractable about her. What his father saw in this female, he had not been able to fathom, any more than he could forgive him for installing her in their lives. And that Toby seemed able to accept their step-mother with such equanimity had seemed to Jasper to compound the treachery.

Yet, perversely, even as he'd made it his boyhood mission to undermine her, Jasper had craved her approval, her benediction. He had died inside when she laughed or sneered, as she so readily did. And the uneasy truce which existed today, the limited accommodation they had made for one another, was no more than that. The peace between the two of them was very tenuously maintained.

'I just didn't want things to turn nasty, that was all.'

'Well, they didn't.' Hilary had snuggled up against him, giggling. 'I never *saw* such a big bed, let alone slept in one.'

'Laura can be a bitch you know.'

'I can imagine.'

'It wouldn't do to cross her.'

'Why not? What's it to me?'

'It's what it is to *me*, Hilly. That's what I'm talking about.'

'Then, what *is* it to you?'

What *was* it to him?

He'd moved on top of her and slid his hands under her flattened buttocks. He had loved her lumpy body, which she wore with glorious unconcern like a garment chosen for comfort rather than style. He found her so much more substantial, somehow, than all the decorative Amandas, the Lucindas and the Sarah-Janes who peopled his world, with their Chanel smell, their glossy hair and all-year suntans, their aura of health, of wealth, their smooth, well-nourished complexions.

'Your bum's freezing,' he had told her, with a conscious effort, forgiving her for her indiscretions.

'Soon get warm,' she had assured him cheerfully.

But nothing would have warmed her on that last night together, in her rented room, where she'd called him a wanker and got all screwed up with loathing, making a face like a balled-up paper bag.

He had known, of course, for some while – certainly since their weekend at Hartwell, if not from the beginning – that their relationship was not for ever. Like the capitalist system, it would be pulled to bits by its own internal contradictions. In Hilary's very unsuitability, indeed, lay her appeal for him. Marriage was simply out of the question. When Toby joked – as Toby could not resist doing – about 'Lady Hilary', about 'the next Lady Charteris', Jasper could not deny the patent absurdity of that proposition. Hilly could no more make Hartwell her home than he could turn his back on his birthright.

Did that mean it was fair, did it mean it was right, for her to call him all those names, to lob insults at him from behind the barricades? For didn't it take two to make a mismatch? And hadn't she been just as tickled as he by the improbability of the thing? As intrigued as he to see how the other half lived?

All right, he had been somewhat of a voyeur on his visits to Walsall, a fly on the wall in the Martin household. All right, he had been attracted to Hilary *because* she was so unlikely a girlfriend for him. And, yes, it had pleased him to imagine how people must speculate about them, how they must wonder what he saw in her. But did that give her the right to say he was so sodding superior? To call him a patronising pillock? Did that axiomatically make him a wanker?

'You think you're so damn good looking,' Hilary's words came back to him now. 'You think you're God's gift.'

His own face stared woefully up at him from the unbroken surface of the pond. And, yes, it was a good-looking face, it had a rare, pared-down beauty, just this side of gaunt. He had a long, straight nose with flared nostrils, soft grey eyes flecked with gold beneath the supercilious arcs of his brows. The flesh between his nose and upper lip was deeply grooved, and there was a small indentation in his chin. His ears lay nicely flat, unlike Tobias's, which were sticky-out and glowed red in bright sunlight. Nor had he Tobias's hammy hands or ruddy cheeks.

All in all, he congratulated himself, though he might not be so robust as his brother, or so good at rugger, he was far more favoured in the looks department. It was as though the most refined qualities had been used up first time, so that Tobias, the second son, had had to make do with the leavings.

Jasper thought of Narcissus, the mythical boy, who had been besotted with his reflection and had died staring into his own eyes. Such vanity seemed to him not entirely beyond reason. Then he thought of Hilary's ungainly walk, the way her inner thighs rubbed together, the irritating scrape of denim against denim. She wasn't fat the way Caroline was fat, a little waif suffocating in her own flesh, but she had a wobbly bottom. And she could have done more with her face. And the expression she wore at times, of sheer contumely, the 'I'm right, you're wrong' set of her features, was enough to drive a sensitive fellow such as Jasper to distraction.

He was practised at doing this – at thinking himself into his sorrows, following a twisty-turny route through them, and then finally, with ego miraculously intact, coming out the other side.

If he were honest, what irked him was not so much that Hilary had misjudged him, as that she had judged him altogether too acutely. But there was no place for such ruthless honesty in his internal debate, the purpose of which was to console, to cheer him, to restore him to himself.

And, as the sounds of preparation for a party drifted on the summer air, as he remembered that today was a big day – notionally for Caroline, but in his mind very much for him, an opportunity for him to cut a dash – he set off for the house, for his suite of rooms. There, a sprauncy ensemble – jacket and trousers from Issey

Miyake, shirt from Luciano Soprani – would by now have
been laid out to await him.

——————— • ———————

From her kitchen window Doris Fairchild could watch
the traffic, the Saturday trippers speeding to the coast, to
Brighton, Hove, Shoreham-by-Sea; and more ambitious
travellers bound for Gatwick, presently to pass overhead
in droning silver planes. She could watch the do-it-
yourselfers shuttling to and from Payless on the Purley
Way, or from Home Base, Texas, B&Q, their car boots
dipping, suspension straining under the weight of
plaster and paint pots, modular shelving, track lighting,
mixer taps, shower curtains, vinyl wall coverings,
Vanitary units . . .

Very little had been done in her own home by way of
improvements. Still, it was all right for the moment; it
would tide her over until . . .

She had bought it in 1964 with the money from the sale
of her father's mean little Victorian terrace house in
Anerley. Nice and modern it had seemed then, and
spacious and light, with its pale brick exterior, its sliding
steel-framed windows, its fluorescent strips and low-
level bathroom suite. But the place was jerry-built, no
doubt about that, and was slowly coming apart at the
seams. The wind whistled through gaps and cracks. It
needed infilling. It needed pointing and puttying.
Though if anyone imagined she could pay for those
things on a pensioner's mite, they had another think
coming.

The electric kettle came to the boil an instant before the pop-up toaster presented her with two gilded slices of Mother's Pride. She found this synchronism very pleasing, it gave her a sense of order, a feeling of having things nicely under control. While the tea infused, she could butter the toast, and spread it with Marmite, then take this lunch to her sitting room, to be enjoyed along with the Saturday paper.

Doris was, by most people's standards, poor. It was a struggle to make ends meet. And she minded, after a lifetime of struggle, having so meagre a reward. Yet she had moments such as this of supreme richness, quiet times when she might gloat over her 'investment', her little insurance for the future which any day now might mature.

Not that money made people happy. Not that pots and pots of the stuff ever seemed to be enough for the so-called beautiful people, for your international playboys and celebrities and whatsname yuppies. And this was the thing. If Doris had her way, it would be the poor who got the wealth. Because, frankly, on the available evidence, it was wasted on the rich.

You had only to turn to the gossip columns to see it. Princesses had marital problems. Pop stars died of drugs overdoses. Cabinet ministers cavorted with call girls. Actors became alcoholics. The children of film stars found themselves pulled this way, that way, between their acrimonious parents. Starlets kissed and told of their three-in-a-bed romps with soccer players. Which in Doris's view only went to prove, if proof were needed, that money invariably fell into the wrong hands.

It was a wicked old world all right. As she turned the pages of the *Mirror*, the stories she read set her tut-tut-tutting. This was the age of crack and of bimbos, of palimony, Aids, of rent boys, toy boys, all kinds of funny ideas that had simply not been thought of when she was a girl. It ought not to be allowed. Muggers, they should put a stop to their lark, lock 'em up and throw away the key. And rapists. Hanging was too good for them, she always said.

She was shipping a raft of toast to her mouth when an item in Gibb's Gossip, a snippet of tittle-tattle caught her eye. Laura Grant (now Lady Charteris), former model, famous socialite and – as the caption story had it – Face of the Sixties, was tipped to make a comeback. Her photograph would adorn the cover of the launch issue of *Finesse*, 'the magazine for the woman of style and substance'.

Lady Charteris indeed! Lady Muck, more like! A stuck-up little madam, as Doris remembered her, and no better than she should be.

Oh, Doris knew about Laura Charteris. She knew things about Laura Charteris that even Laura Charteris did not know.

The thought was a peculiarly pleasing and sustaining one. Doris set the paper aside, folded her hands in her lap, and nodded off. And even as she dozed, and as her face slackened, there was about her lips the ghost of a smile, a hint of some profound and private satisfaction . . .

'You were talking in your sleep.'

'Hmmm?' said Doris crossly. When she opened her eyes, the girl was there, standing in front of her, tall and leggy, wearing only an outsize Snoopy T-shirt and a pair of thong sandals.

'Sorry to wake you.'

'I *was* awake. I was just resting my eyes.'

'I finished early.'

'So I see.'

'It was one of those quiet days. Lots of cancellations. Jules said I could go early. Special treat. Shall I make tea?'

'I just had a cup.' But at that instant the carriage clock chimed two. She must have been out for the count for a couple of hours. 'Oh, go on then. I'll have another with you.'

'All right.'

'I got a cake.'

'That's nice.'

'For *you* I bought it.'

'That was sweet of you. Thanks.' The girl stooped to kiss her cheek. Picked up Doris's empty teacup, the plate of toast crusts, gnawed like chop bones.

'Ugh,' said Doris, 'you smell like a brothel.'

'Don't you like it? It's called Coco.'

'Like the drink?'

'Like the person.'

'Coco the clown?'

'Coco Chanel.'

'It gets up my nose.'

'It's delicious. A present from the others at the salon.'

'Very nice of them, I'm sure. Nice to have friends.'

'It wasn't cheap, you know. It costs a bomb.'

'What doesn't, these days?'

Doris sat a moment, considering her granddaughter, commending herself for her foresight, thinking with gratification that it had all come good, everything as she'd hoped. There had been times, it was true, when she had had cause to wonder, moments when she had been filled with doubt, when panic crashed inside her like cold waves breaking around her heart, leaving her shocked and gasping.

At one stage the child had been something other than pretty, too tall for her years, graceless and gangling. Her hands and feet had appeared at least one size too big. Her clothes would not hang right on a frame that had seemed all skin and bone and disproportion, so that however you dressed her she had had the look of an urchin in someone else's cast-offs. Her hair, too, had been disappointing, neither one colour nor another, straight and wispy, stubbornly refusing to take a curl, or to accommodate the clips and slides and bows with which Doris had tried to deck it.

But at least she had never been plain. And now her body had matured, softened with womanhood, though she remained rangy and deceptively athletic-looking; with those legs she should have been a sprinter, yet she moved with a curious lethargy, simply floating through life, as if through water, always dreamy, sometimes sighing with the effort of it all. Her hair was thicker, too, and richer, a tangle of chestnut, of copper and gold, framing a heart-shaped face, with ivory skin, and enormous pewter eyes, into which men might look and lose their reason.

'Beautiful, beautiful . . .' thought Doris with a strength of emotion that quite rattled her, a complication with which she had never reckoned.

There would be, she had supposed in the beginning, a certain satisfaction in caring for this unwanted scrap. It was to be expected. But that she should find love in her heart for the girl, and a fierce, possessive pride, had been something for which she'd been ill-prepared. While the idea that she should be loved in return – that anyone should be so affectionate – was more than she had ever bargained for.

'We'll manage,' she'd told Dawn, her daughter, after the birth. Meaning, of course, that *she*, Doris, would manage, she would take charge.

No one had mentioned adoption, though the word had been there unspoken between them, like the mystery object in a game of I-Spy – something beginning with A, just asking to be named.

Indeed, Dawn had said nothing about anything, but had stared at her mother, with blotchy-eyed hostility, then had turned her face to the wall. And in that instant Doris had made a most extraordinary decision. How to explain it now? It was as though . . . well, as though a door had opened suddenly upon a world of possibilities. Then, just as suddenly that door had slammed, though not before Doris had glimpsed the future. Not before she had seen what she would do. Not before she had seen how things would be.

'She can stay with me till you get yourself sorted.' She had addressed the offer to a breathing mound of blankets, to a mat of unwashed hair, an angry, unrepentant back. And God only knows how she had kept her voice steady, with all that she was feeling, with all the thoughts that were running through her mind, as she bent over the crib and coochie coochie cooed . . .

'So are you just going to stand there, or are you making that tea?'

'I'm on my way.' The girl moved in her languid fashion towards the kitchen.

'The cake is in the tin. In the cupboard. There are candles, too.'

'Sweet.' She had a voice dark as liquorice, sugary enough to coat the tongue.

It took her for ever, of course, to fill the kettle, to rinse the pot, to set the tray. With slight irritation Doris listened to the desultory preparations, chink, clink, ting. . . . If I had a heart attack, she told herself grimly, if I said 'Run, quick, and fetch a doctor,' I'd be stone dead before she'd got herself to the front door.

Increasingly these days, thoughts of her own demise preoccupied her. Not that she was in poor health. But nor was she, let's face it, in the first flush of youth. And we've all got to go sometime, haven't we? That is the awful truth which we only ever half believe. Even Doris only half believed it, never mind that she had buried her husband years ago, never mind that . . .

Her eyes were drawn to Dawn – to the photograph in its silver frame, taken at that awkward age, fourteen, fifteen, when young girls, adjusting to their new identity, their burgeoning sexuality, with hormones flooding their systems, are commonly difficult, temperamental, irrational (and Dawn had been more difficult, more temperamental, more irrational than most).

They never had got on, had they, mother and daughter? Never did see eye to eye. All the same, Doris reflected, it was not on the whole a good idea to outlive your child. It left you feeling, ever after, that you were here under false pretences, that by rights you ought not still to be about.

'This is lovely.' The girl brought in the cake, a white-iced confection with blue piping, on its silver-coated cardboard base, which she set on the floor. Kneeling, she poked the candles into the holders, counting as she did so, one for every year since her birth.

'I thought you'd like it.'

'Yes I do.' She sat back on her heels. Her bare thighs, bulging tautly under the weight of her upper body, were tanned, and were thinly furred with gold. When she bent her head her scalp showed white at the parting, a path through the enchanted forest of hair.

She was amiable and biddable, if sometimes a little remote, and had never been the bother Dawn had been. But then, Dawn was always very bright, very brainy, which is not altogether a blessing – well, is it? – especially in a girl. For no one, after all, likes a smarty boots.

Yes, thank goodness, this one was different. She hadn't that restlessness of spirit, or that rapacious appetite for knowledge, but could sit for hours, staring at the television – could sit for hours, full stop. Now and then she would pick up a paperback, some romance or other, and her eyes would mist, going through one of their sea changes so they appeared more sage green than grey, and her prettily shaped lips would be moving as she turned the pages. But she never devoured books the way Dawn had done, with a kind of desperation, as though the very meaning of life were in there somewhere.

'The kettle will boil dry.'

'I'm just going, aren't I?'

'Bring the matches, will you ducks?'

'It's all right, I've got a lighter in my bag.'

'You shouldn't smoke.'

'I don't. It isn't mine. I'm looking after it for someone.'

'What nonsense you do talk.'

When the candles were lit they threw out a flickering glow, lending an illusory animation to that lovely face. The whites of the girl's eyes were opalescent, moist as scallop flesh. Smiling up she asked, 'Shall I be mother?'

And that, in so many words, was what Doris herself had asked, all that time ago. Should she be mother?

She'd acted for the good of everyone, she reminded herself fiercely; she'd had the highest motives. Everything had been for the best, as she had seen it, in the best of all possible worlds. The girl would understand – of course she would – when everything was properly explained. Doris dwelt on her secret, which was precious to her still, although increasingly in the way that a pearl is precious to an oyster; it was something priceless, but it gave her endless pain.

'You'll have some, won't you?' The girl cut a neat wedge of yellow sponge, a 45-degree segment, and eased it out.

'All right, my darling.'

First there would have to be explanations. There might also be recriminations. Then they would reach some kind of new accord. And at last they could start to make their plans.

Doris thought, 'The time has come, I have to tell her *today*.' It would be a relief, at long last to unburden herself.

But she funked it. When she accepted the plate that the girl passed to her, her hand dipped involuntarily. 'Whoopsie daisy!' she said, on the edge of hysteria.

She took a bite, worked over the dry and crumbly mixture, swallowed with some difficulty, decided 'Yes!'; only then her courage failed.

After all, it didn't have to be right now. Tomorrow, perhaps, or the day after, she would tell all.

CHAPTER

•

2

'Now,' said Sir John Charteris, who stood looped like a question mark over Caroline, beaming down at her.

He had never quite grasped the convention of dialogue which says that you do not take this kind of initiative unless you can follow through. With a brisk 'Right', a 'Well then', or a 'Now', he would raise expectations in his audience, only to fail to deliver. Some people use the telephone in such a manner: they ring you when really they have nothing to communicate, and suddenly the onus is all on you, so you find yourself busking it, vamping, while you wait in desperation for the caller to get to the point.

Caroline, of course, had come to know her stepfather. She was accustomed to his little foibles. But she had often witnessed in social situations, on the faces of the uninitiated, expressions of interest and anticipation, fading to confusion, finally to be eclipsed by panic as they cast around for an escape. Politely raised eyebrows would knit with perplexity. A smile would curdle and turn cheesy. Excuses would be mouthed ('I must get myself a top-up of this delicious Sancerre/go and powder my nose/rescue poor darling Giles from that frightful little man from the *Mail*').

'Hello,' she said fondly, touched by this way Sir John had of putting himself out to tender, by his unfailing trust that the other chap would come back with a bid for his society. For minutes they stood in companionable silence, looking on as the event gathered momentum. Useless scraps of chit-chat blew about them like discarded sweet wrappers: 'Manolo Blahnik . . . *bresaola* . . . off-shore company . . . September in San Gim . . . ringworm, spavins . . . simply cannot get the staff . . .'

Julia Fairfax, in an ill-judged shade of fuchsia, ambled by with Arabella Claridge, boasting about her new Italian lover, who could apparently go like a train all night on the energy provided by a single plate of spaghetti vongole.

The band was playing, but softly, in deference to people for whom there is no music so sweet as the sound of their own braying voices. From somewhere could be heard Laura's patently false, flirtatious laugh. And there *was* Laura, sitting on the stone balustrade, with one bare leg slung in an attitude of studied carelessness across the other, smiling at Rick Sharkey, bass guitarist with Unfit to Plead, who had an alligator face, lidless amber eyes, sharp little teeth, ill-nourished skin, and who was rolling a joint the size of a Monte Cristo cigar.

Twenty years ago, the two had been lovers – at least according to the newspapers, the cuttings from gossip columns which Laura kept to this day, pasted up in a scrapbook, and which she would still read as avidly as the morning's newspapers or the latest issue of *Vogue*, one smooth hand stroking the page. She and Sharkey had been sighted around town together – dining at

Alvaro, at San Lorenzo, dancing at Samantha's, at the
New Pheasantry, the Bag o' Nails – and were assumed to
have slept together, the way people did in those far-off
days of supposedly free love, almost as a means of
getting acquainted. There was indeed, even now, an air
of complicity between them which Caroline found unwholesome.

At once she averted her gaze, fearful that Sir John
might follow it, and she very deliberately drew his
attention elsewhere. Panning with her hand across the
crowd, the knots of people cluttering the terrace and
spilling over on to the striped carpet of grass, she told
him, 'I am so enjoying this.'

Well, what else was she to say? That to her mind a
party – *any* party, but most especially one in her honour,
of which she must be a focus – was not an occasion for fun
but an ordeal to be endured? That she had no higher
hope than to get through this afternoon and evening, to
get it over with? That dread, dismay and despondency
had been her dour companions in the long weeks of
preparation for this day?

'I don't really want . . .' she had protested to Laura,
when the idea was first mooted. And, 'I'd be much
happier if . . . . You know, honestly, there's no need to
go to so much . . .'

'Nonsense,' Laura had told her, gazing not at her but
past her, to engage with her reflection, with the Laura in
the mirror, who inclined her head to right then to left,
twinkling conspiratorially all the while. 'You have to do
the thing properly. You can't *not*.'

'Why not?'

'Caroline, darling, I do hate that mulish look of yours.' Making combs of her fingers, Laura had raked back her hair, clamping it with her thumbs above her ears, musing a moment on the matter of high cheekbones, which were surely a prerequisite of pure, patrician beauty. 'You remind me of . . . but never mind that now.'

Go on, say it, why don't you? Caroline had nerved herself to retort, but though there was anger at work in her face, twitching at her mouth, the words had got dammed up between her brain and her tongue, so she could not actually utter them. I remind you of my father, she had articulated in her head. Well, is that so surprising? I dare say I have a bit of him in me. But then *you* had a bit of him in *you*, didn't you? Wasn't that where it all started? Where I started? With you and him in bed? And how am I to blame for any of it? I never even met the rotten man.

'We're trying to give you a treat,' Laura had persisted. 'We want this to be the birthday of a lifetime. For *your* sake, Caroline, and with no expense spared. But what do we get in return? "I don't want a party. Stuff you and your party." '

'I never said that. I never said stuff it.'

'Well, as good as.'

'You're always going on at me,' Caroline had accused.

Then, 'You're always going on at me,' her mother had mimicked her aggrieved tone.

This habit Laura had of mocking her, of doing voices, pulling faces, Caroline had always found grotesque. Leave me alone, she had wanted to shout then. Or, I hate you. I think you're foul. But that would have been to invite further parody. For Laura could keep it up indefinitely, parroting her words, shrilling them back at her, amplifying and distorting them, turning up the treble, glaring and gerning, until Caroline felt she would explode, quite literally blow apart, with rage and frustration (they'd be scraping shreds and tatters of her off the four walls).

So in the end she'd said yes to the party. And please and thank you. She'd said how much she appreciated it. And if she could not actually revel in it, she was resolved to put a brave face on it, particularly for her stepfather, whose impulses were always generous, and whose motives were never base.

'We couldn't have asked for better weather, what?' Sir John was one of the few people Caroline had met who used the interrogative expletive, the comical final 'what?', which was a kind of verbal tic, a posh form of 'innit?'

'Mmm.' She squinted up at the cloudless blue sky, at the brash and bullying sun. If she were being objective, she would have had to allow that the weather had turned up trumps for them. She could not have taken issue with the guests who greeted her with murmurs of 'gorgeous', and 'too, too perfect', and 'sheer bliss'. It was the kind of flower-scented, bee-buzzy, honeyed summer's day that burns itself into the memory and is recalled in later years with all the senses, obliterating the many other times when rain stopped play, when tennis matches were washed out, gymkhanas abandoned, when everyone retreated to a fuggy tea tent, to complain about the British climate above the drumming of drizzle on canvas. But it is hard to be objective in the here and now, when your skin is nettled by the heat, and you feel fluttery and agitated, exhausted of small talk, and when you've been packaged in a dress a size too small for you.

She slugged back some champagne and felt the beginnings of a headache.

'Quite a turnout, too, what?'

'Mmm,' she agreed again, thinking, And thick and fast they came at last, and more and more and more. The number of people who'd shown up today was no index of her own popularity. In truth most of them were here for Laura, or were relatives, or those sundry acquaintances which attach to titled families. Many of them she knew only by sight; many more she knew not at all.

'Isn't that that photographer pal of Laura's?' Sir John wondered. 'Buffy, is it? Or Dailey or something?' He nodded towards a stocky, dark-haired man, who was holding fast to a glass, holding forth ('. . . so Diana Vreeland said to me, "Darling, I don't need to explain to *you* what's wrong with this picture. Look at the *mouth*. There is nothing rapacious about that mouth" ').

'Yes, I think it's someone like that,' said Caroline distractedly, glancing now at Maudie, who was standing a little apart, aloof, and who, having accepted from a waitress some kind of friable filo pastry parcel, was eyeing the confection with suspicion (it might be filled with Sevruga caviar, her expression read, but it might equally be filled with tin tacks).

'Hey, Caro mia, how is it for you?' Tobias was hanging about with Jasper, within hearty shouting distance. He waved at her and, when she smiled, they drifted over, up to mischief, in search of some little divertissement.

'Doesn't she look a picture?'

'Oh, absolutely,' Jasper agreed. 'A Picasso, perhaps.'

'Or a Stubbs.'

'Thanks a lot,' said Caroline, who felt far too raw right now to put up with this kind of ribbing.

'Only joking, my sweet,' Toby assured her, slipping an arm about her waist, drawing her to him and planting an exuberant kiss on her cheek, which instantly flared as if it had been torched.

'Yes, I do realise that,' she responded, going rigid, refusing to bend to him, to acknowledge his body with hers, holding her breath lest it mix with his and by some mysterious alchemy combust. She was suddenly sensitised to her own femaleness, uncomfortably aware of her spongy flesh, which seemed somehow to have absorbed her general distress, to be throbbing with it. Her hands flitted to her throat, to toy fretfully with the emerald necklace, which she had decided in a fit of bravado to wear, and which now threatened to throttle her in horrible retribution. To herself she said firmly, Come along now, you're over all that.

She had in mind the secret passion she'd felt, first for Jasper, then for Tobias, both of whom had figured for a while in her rudest, wildest fantasies. Now she thanked the Lord that she had never declared herself, never revealed her torment to a living soul. Mercifully, they might never know how, in the darkest hours of the dreaming night, she had brought all her adolescent ardour and inexperience to bear on making love with each in his turn.

Nor would they ever know of, ever guess at, the enormous effort of will she had made in talking herself out of such silliness. For in the end you had to be realistic, didn't you? This was how she'd looked at it. You couldn't set your sights too high. There was Jasper, after all, not just handsome in his father's mould, but with so much style, such presence, such prodigious talent (he was writing a novel, he had revealed, though with un-characteristic reticence he refused to tell what it was about, hinting only that it would be epoch-making, a work of breadth and depth, of wit and wisdom, to take the literary establishment by storm).

There, too, was Toby, in whom, it had to be said, the Charteris good looks had been sort of botched. His features were slightly ill-defined, as though they had been rubbed out and drawn in again a number of times by an increasingly impatient hand. But though his face was more rough and ready than Jasper's, though it lacked a certain refinement, he was awfully appealing and personable just the same.

Then, there, also, of course, were their various girl-friends, with whom she could not hope to compete. Golden girls with knobby shoulders and strong teeth and sleek, streaked hair. Or undergraduates, intellectual young women such as that one of Jasper's, who had been brave and talkative and terrifying, and who had got tiddly at dinner and dared to hint that their capitalist days were numbered.

'Is Hilary coming?' asked Caroline politely now.

'No,' Jasper told her shortly.

'Oops,' said Toby, 'sore point.'

'Is it? Oh, I'm sorry.' She was blushing again.

'That's all right. You weren't to know.' Jasper, with his hands plunged nonchalantly into the pockets of his elegant suit, gave a small, restrained smile, a little shrug, acting out his chagrin. 'She and I are no longer an item.'

'She dumped him,' volunteered Tobias.

'We parted by mutual – '

'Because he wasn't ideologically sound.'

'Oh, do shut it, little brother. What do you know about it?'

'Which is why he's so touchy on the subject.'

'I see,' responded Caroline awkwardly. And again, 'I'm sorry Jasper.'

'It was all perfectly amicable.'

'Look at him, he's a broken man.'

'We're still the best of friends.'

'I'll tell you what,' Tobias continued, with blithe disregard for his brother's finer feelings, 'I quite liked old Class War, didn't you, Caro? I thought she was a laugh.'

'*Hilary*,' stressed Jasper. 'Her name is Hilary.'

'Great sense of humour, manifested in her dress sense.'

'Oh, do stop it, Toby,' scolded Caroline. 'In any case, *you* can talk. Your shirt's hanging out at the back. And red is really not your colour.'

'Now, *I* know that, and *you* know that,' Toby grinned, 'but sadly Ophelia doesn't.'

'Ophelia Deverose brought the shirt for you?'

'Protanopia.'

'A bridal outfitters?'

'Not Pronuptia, Pudding. Protanopia.'

'Colour blindness,' Jasper translated for her. 'Like all of my brother's young lady friends, the Hon Ophelia Deverose has defective vision.'

'In the matter of her Hon,' Tobias persisted, 'she is pretty easy come, easy go. The shirt, indeed, was a sort of thank-you-for-having-me present. She is under the impression that it's green. And her eyes, I will have you know, are in every other respect A1. Twenty-twenty.'

'Then, like her namesake, she must be out of her tree.'

'I thought colour blindness was like baldness,' Caroline said. 'You know, very much a male thing.'

'But, my dear Caro,' Toby reminded her, calling upon his knowledge of animal husbandry, of scientific tinkering with the DNA, of the breeding of super-pigs, 'you do get bald women. And you get colour-blind women. It's when the X chromosome carries a recessive allele.'

'Oh, I can never understand about genes.'

'Exactly,' said Jasper, whose thoughts had momentarily strayed. Turning to Tobias, he added, 'You could have made more of an effort, you scruffy oik. I mean, jeans are hardly the thing.'

'These are the original 501s,' Tobias informed him, slapping his thigh as if to attest to the quality of the denim, 'bought for me by Deborah Jessop. For servicings rendered.'

'You're head to foot in hand-outs. You're like a walking Oxfam shop.'

'On whose rails,' beamed Tobias, 'these garments will before too long hang. Or they will find themselves in the rummage box, priced at 50p or under. But today I feel bound to wear them. I cannot disappoint my public.'

'You're a slag, you know that?'

'I prefer "gay Lothario",' said Tobias. 'Gay as in larky. Merry as a cricket. Happy-go-lucky. Debonair.'

'You just can't see hay without rolling in it.'

'Yoo-hoo, Caroline, how lovely! What a treat this is!' A tall, rather gawky girl in a short skirt and floppy, flowered hat came teetering over, scarifying the turf with her stilettos. Lavinia Pine. The name had always suggested to Caroline something you used in the bathroom for cleaning under the rim and around the hidden bend. Lavinia was a slightly preposterous, conceited young woman, who would at times try the patience of a saint. ('I have perfect pitch,' she would proclaim. Or, 'I'm a natural artist.' Or, in a silly, baby voice, 'I never get spots, I don't know why, I suppose I'm just lucky that way.') But she was also, as she had been throughout their school years, Caroline's closest friend, for which fact Caroline had been grateful, taking the view that it was essential to have at least one friend, someone to sit by you, and to partner you in ballroom dancing.

And she didn't easily strike up friendships. The few she had were desultory in their nature, on-off, take-it-or-leave-it relationships with scant commitment on either side.

The two girls went through the usual kissy-kissy routine, an exchange of lipsticks, and Lavinia pressed upon her a gift-wrapped box of soaps, Penhaligon's Victorian Posy. 'Honestly,' she gushed, 'I don't know if I'm coming or going at the moment. Here I am, in deepest Dorset for your party. And this evening I have to be in Hertfordshire for a big ball.'

'Lavinia likes big balls,' said Tobias, flagging down a passing waitress, a small girl with the round, un-blemished face of a doll, who in real life, out of uniform, was Emily, a niece of Mrs Dowdeswell from the village, and who for a small consideration had agreed to be drafted in for the afternoon.

'Ooh, I say.' Lavinia helped herself from Emily's tray to a plover's egg, which she examined uncertainly. 'Isn't it pretty? Do you eat the shell as well, or what?'

'Oh, absolutely.' Tobias took an egg and popped it in his mouth.

'Don't!' cautioned Caroline as Lavinia made to follow suit. 'Take no notice of him, it's his idea of a joke. Of course you don't eat the shell.'

'You're a spoilsport, Caro.' Tobias gobbed the egg back into his palm and began to peel it. 'You won't let a fellow have his bit of fun.'

'Well, you never do know,' Lavinia said defensively. 'I mean, there's a certain sort of crab that you eat with the shell on.'

'Quite right,' Tobias agreed. 'I once ate fish and chips with a hat on.'

'Oh, *you*.' Lavinia gave him a playful push. 'I do believe you're sending me up?'

Tobias laid a hand on his heart and raised his eyes to the heavens, as if appealing for a reference to some higher authority. What *me*? he seemed to be saying. As God is my witness, I would never do such a thing.

'Such masses of people,' Lavinia remarked, crinkling her eyes, squinting into the sun, scanning the crowd for familiar faces.

'All the world and his Y-fronts,' Tobias agreed.

'Who's the blond guy over by the gazebo? The one with the wing collar and the five o'clock shadow?'

'That, my dear, is designer stubble,' said Jasper to Lavinia. And, to Tobias, 'I think she means Hugo. Old Hugo First, as we used to call him in our schooldays. If ever there was a hint of danger, he'd always lead from the rear.'

'Well, he looks like a film star.'

'He's a belted earl,' Jasper told her with a touch of peevishness (if anyone looked like a film star, it was surely he).

'Yes, it was I who belted him,' Tobias recalled. 'For some very ungallant remark he made to Sophie Picton.'

'At the village summer fair,' remembered Jasper.

'The annual fete worse than death.'

'There was morris dancing.'

'I don't know what Morris has got to be so happy about.'

'I say, that's pretty,' said Lavinia, reaching out to finger Caroline's necklace. 'Are they. . .?'

'Paste,' said Caroline quickly, for she always had to deprecate. I am worthless, her demeanour suggested. That which is mine is worthless.

'I was going to *say*,' said Lavinia.

'What?' asked Tobias.

'What?' said Lavinia.

'*What* were you going to say?'

'Well, you know.'

'No.'

'Well, I mean, if they *were* real they'd be worth a fortune.'

'I suppose they would,' said Caroline.

'Let's all have a sharpener,' proposed Tobias as a waiter brought champagne. 'Here, Lavinia, this will put the roses back in your cheeks.'

'Ooh, lovely.' Lavinia accepted a glass. 'Chin chin everybody.'

'Double chin.'

'Mind you, I mustn't drink too much,' said Lavinia, 'or I'll get silly.'

'How will we tell?' Tobias wanted to know.

A great gust of merriment swept through Caroline, billowed in her midriff, blew out her chest as she stifled a laugh. And, 'Oh, goodness!' she wailed. 'Oh, no!', as, with a pop-pop-pop-pop of stitches, the ill-fated frock literally burst at the seam. She suffered in that instant a kind of absence spasm, an unpleasant time-out-of-time sensation, as if she had slipped into another dimension. The sounds of music, laughter, chatter were muted, as by distance. Everything seemed very bright and whirly and weird.

Then, just as suddenly, she was returned to herself, to the moment, to a reality more acutely embarrassing than any she could remember. Wrapping her arms protectively about herself, she backed off a pace or two. 'I just . . .' she offered, gazing wildly around, focusing on nothing, on no one, just forming a vague impression of blob-white faces and gaping mouths. 'I have to . . .' With which she turned and fled, blundering across the terrace in search of some place to hide.

The fuzz of heat which hung over the grounds did not follow her through the French windows into the drawing room, where everything felt soothingly familiar and strangely inert. The stillness within was sweet after the frenzy without. Sunlight slanting through tall panes of glass had warmed the woodwork, teasing out the smells of linseed oil and of lavender polish. The velvet drapes, the carpets, the ancient sofas shed minute hairs which floated in the ochre-tinged air.

Caroline folded up into an armchair, which gave a little outbreath, a sort of sigh, as if it were sleeping, dreaming (she might now be a feature of that dream). She was shaking, and her mind was racing. 'What do I do?' she asked herself. 'Oh, what am I to *do*?'

There was, of course, a simple answer. She could go to her room and select one of the dozen or more dresses which hung in her wardrobe, ready to wear, immaculately laundered and pressed – loose-fitting garments; garments that gave. She would be thankful, indeed, to get out of this dress, which might have been conceived as a punishment, designed both to prickle and to restrain her. She would happily slip into something that stretched.

But what . . . this was the real worry . . . what would Laura say? Because Laura was sure to say *something*. It was she who had paid for the dress ('It will be *my* present to you,' she had decided). It was she who had discussed with Elizabeth the design; she who had chosen the fabric.

Perhaps. . . ? Caroline raised one arm, crooked at the elbow and, like someone surreptitiously sniffing for body odour, ducked awkwardly to peer under it, to try to determine the extent of the problem. It was not a pretty sight. If it had been simply the stitching that had come apart, she might have been able to sew it. But the silky material itself had ripped and frayed – thin filaments of it clung to her moist skin. No quick needle-and-thread job, this. It would take a skill she did not possess to repair the damage, and the bodice would be tighter than ever, it would be unbearably, unwearably strait.

Well, then, there was no help for it. Caroline extricated herself from the leathery embrace of the armchair and went quickly out of the room, down the hall and up the stairs, all the while turning over in her mind a whole range of likely and unlikely excuses.

Someone could have tipped a drink all over her. Or burned the dress with a cigarette. She could have sat in something unmentionable out there on the lawn, for which Pee Wee or Pasha must take the blame; she could have caught the flared skirt on a jagged edge; could have developed a mysterious allergy to silk.

But Laura would know, of course. Laura always knew. And Laura would be sure to spell it out. 'It's your own fault,' she would revile her. 'Because you're so fat.'

When she heard Laura's laugh she half believed she imagined it, chiming as it did with her worst fears. But then there it was again, that mirthless, artificial tinkle which caused Caroline to freeze to the spot.

She threw a look over her shoulder, expecting to see behind her her mother with hands on hips, with head tipped back to reveal her long white throat, as she shared with the ceiling her derision. But there was no one. The landing was deserted, a long corridor of emptiness, with door on closed door to right and left, diminishing into the distance.

Where then. . . ?

Caroline went tentatively forward.

And as she passed the master bedroom, the beautiful balcony room, she heard more laughter. This door stood open, and the French doors beyond (a through draught ushered in the scents of hayseed and honeysuckle). Caroline hesitated. Her gaze was irresistibly drawn.

Her mother was standing a few feet from her, with her back towards her, in the horrible embrace of Rick Sharkey who, while he lifted her skirt with one hand, had clamped on to her bum with the other. Laura's long, brown legs were bare. And, horror upon horror, she wasn't wearing any knickers.

We all have an instinct to deny. If we see something too terrible, we think no, no, it *can't* be, this is some kind of mistake, a hallucination or mere misreading of the situation.

Now, for instance, there had to be a dozen perfectly good reasons why the pair of them should be up here, in the matrimonial suite, in this posture of apparent intimacy. There had to be any number of innocent explanations. Only, hard as she tried, Caroline could think of not a single one. Nor could she co-ordinate mind with body. Move, hissed an urgent voice in her brain, get away. But nothing happened, nothing responded, until . . .

Perhaps she made a sound, caught her breath, gave a little gasp or sob. Or Laura sensed her presence, or Rick Sharkey caught a glimpse of her. Whatever, everyone was suddenly staring, they at her, she at them, Laura with a look of surprise and indignation, Caroline in utter shock and disbelief.

'What the hell. . . ?' Laura found her voice. Something very nasty happened to her face. Almost literally, she turned ugly – in her daughter's eyes at least.

'I didn't . . .' protested Caroline and, feeling she might choke on her own unhappiness – so physical did it seem, like something indigestible, a lump of chewing-gum inadvertently swallowed – she made a dash for it, slammed into her own room and flung herself on the bed.

How could Laura – how *could* she – play so fast, so loose with the feelings of those who loved her? How could she cheat on her husband under his very roof? How could she put so much happiness at risk? An image of Sir John – that tall, kind, noble man – shaped itself like a genie from the smoke that fogged Caroline's brain. And she was all at once overwhelmed by the chill realisation of how very precarious was her position here at Hartwell, entirely dependent upon the good faith of others. All her life she had, of course, been bound to Laura, had belonged only when, where, and for as long as Laura belonged. But seldom had she felt so powerless, so marginal, a mere cipher.

Laura came licking into the room like a flame up a fuse; any minute the situation would go off bang. 'What were you doing, snooping around up here, when you were supposed to be out with your guests?'

She stood over the bed, panting audibly. Caroline did not have to lift her head, to know how anger would be curling the corners of her mother's mouth or pinching her nostrils.

'I wasn't,' she said dully into the pillow. Laura had a

small but lethal arsenal of snipey verbs which she habitually loosed upon her. Caroline could not sit in quiet contemplation of eternal verities but she was 'mooching'. She could not wander lonely as a cloud, but she was 'skulking'. And if she came upon her mother *in flagrante*, why, it naturally followed that she had been 'snooping'!

'You had no business . . .' Laura gripped her by the shoulder very hard. Her nails would leave little indentations, red nips in her white skin. 'Do you hear me? You had no right to come creeping round.'

'I wasn't snooping,' Caroline told the pillow. 'I wasn't creeping.'

'*Look* at me when I'm talking to you.'

'I'd rather not, thank you,' Caroline responded with mumbled contempt.

'You think you're so high and mighty, you sanctimonious little cow. Anyway . . .' Some of the fight went out of Laura. Her grip slackened. 'It's not what you think.'

'Oh isn't it?' Caroline raised herself up, rolled on to her side and lay propped on her elbow. 'I got it all wrong. I suppose? You weren't letting that revolting man grope you?'

Neither of them was surprised when Laura slapped her face. The gesture was stagey, it lacked spontaneity. It was what people did in films, and Laura generally conducted herself as though she were on camera. But Caroline was unprepared for the sting of the blow, or for the way it would sound from the inside, a sharp crack in her head, for the clack of her teeth, or for the feeling of utter affront. Emotionally more than actually, it knocked her sideways.

Yet, for once in her life, she kept calm. For once the tears did not gush. She could not have cried if she'd wanted to. 'I hate you,' she told Laura with conviction. 'I really, truly hate you.'

'Oh, you, do, do you? Well, now listen to me.' Laura half knelt on the bed. And she punctuated her words with a series of little jabs to Caroline's chest. 'I gave you life. I brought you up. Through good times and bad I took care of you, and you tell me you hate me. Well, you've got a bloody nerve, that's all.'

'If you say so.'

'You think it was easy, do you, being a single parent? Providing for you? Raising you on my own?'

'But you never did,' Caroline reminded her coldly. 'Or hardly at all. There was scarcely a time when you didn't have some – ?'

'I could have had you adopted, do you realise that? Do you understand? They brought me the papers, they tried to make me sign. It was *that* close.' Laura tweezed finger and thumb to demonstrate, holding them in front of her eye. A hair's breadth was implied. A mere whisker.

Was any of this true? If so, who had brought the papers? Who tried to make her sign? And – most perplexingly, since she had so very much not wanted a baby – why had Laura refused to do so?

Caroline, who knew by now, by heart, the litany of her mother's goodness to her, and of her own shortcomings, the thousand and one ways in which she failed to measure up, had never until this day heard such a tale.

More surprisingly, it had not occurred to her that Laura had had choice, that it could all have been quite otherwise.

But how extraordinary now to imagine the way things might have been. She could have grown up in the bosom of some very ordinary family (she constructed for herself photofit images of a mother, a father, two faces, one round, one oval, upon which she imposed eyes, noses, mouths, and which she endowed with rosy cheeks, with dimples, with smiley little lines), the sort of people to whom the social workers might happily entrust an infant.

She could have lived in a little semi-detached house, somewhere like Swanley or Shortlands or Surbiton, with a neat back garden with a little lawn and a swing and a creosoted shed full of tools and plant trays and old sacking. She could have taken quite a different name, be it Foster or Farlow or Featherstonehaugh. She could have attended the local state school, travelling there by bus, or in her mother's Volvo estate, with shopping from Sainsbury's spilling from carriers on the back seat, and a labrador called Blackie bouncing about in the luggage compartment behind.

Then Laura, her mother, would have been no more than a figment, an idealised notion, someone who existed only in her dreams. And she would never have heard the name Charteris, never heard of Hartwell, never been accustomed to the wealth or privilege which had fallen to her but which to this day she could not take as her due.

'You should have done,' she said dully.

'What?'

'You should have had me adopted.' A part of her bitterly regretted narrowly missing that unknown other life which seemed at this moment so vivd and so attractive. But then, hadn't she always been an ingrate? Wasn't that what Laura maintained?

'You never wanted me, did you? Wasn't I the accident that cost you your career and ruined your life?'

'Perhaps you're right.' Laura turned away. She folded her arms. Everything about her – her hair, her frock, her body language – was flouncy, quivering with barely contained ire. She looked about eighteen. And she had the air of someone who had been unforgivably wronged.

Caroline dragged herself off the bed. All the energy seemed to have drained from her; her limbs felt leaden. Her ripped side seam, under pressure of her distress, surrendered another few inches. She did not care. What did it matter if her dress fell apart? Her whole world was falling apart.

'Don't you love John?' she asked, addressing the question to her mother's back, and if there was a softer note in her voice it was for him, because of him.

'Oh, sure.'

'Then why. . . ?'

'Why what? Look, I told you. There was nothing . . . . It was nothing. All right,' Laura cast a brief, impatient look over her shoulder, 'just a friendly kiss and a cuddle.'

'In your bedroom?'

'I was showing him the Chinese screen.'

'I see.'

'He's interested in that sort of thing.'

'Uh-huh.'

'And then he said how good it was to see me, and gave me a friendly kiss. What could be more natural?'

'What could? And letting him feel your bottom. What could be more natural than *that*?'

For once Laura was lost for words, though her lips kept working, pursing and parting. And her green eyes, as ever, had a great deal to say for themselves.

Caroline crossed to the window, to look upon the gathering below, upon a noisy swirl of colours. Oh, how she loved this generous and accommodating old house. How she loved the green acres that surrounded it. How loved the family, loved Freckles and Pee Wee and Pasha. It would break her heart to leave it. But she knew what she must do.

She said, 'I'm going away from here. I think that will be best. Yes, that is what I shall do.'

CHAPTER

— • —

3

Inexperience, said Elaine Posner, was not to be regarded as a handicap. Rather it was the blank sheet upon which life had yet to make its mark. She gripped an imaginary pen and mimed some elaborate calligraphy, tilting her head to one side as she considered her invisible handiwork.

Caroline sat across from her and tried to appear at ease. She thought she had never seen such a perfect manicure job, so red or so regular a set of fingernails. They exactly matched the plastic desk furniture – trays for things incoming, trays for things outgoing, trays for matters pending, and a pen tidy from which sprouted a thicket of felt tips, a ruler, a single white rose. Those nails might almost have been office issue, requisitioned from central stores.

Elaine swivelled around on her chair to consider for an instant the London sky beyond her eleventh-floor window. She sighed. Then she came twirling back, faced front. 'What I do ask from my staff is the three Ps. Can you think what they might be?'

Caroline couldn't. She made an effort. But her un-conscious mind, anarchic as ever, threw up piffle and pigswill. It threw up polyunsaturate and priesthole and parachute. She shrugged apologetically.

'First . . .' Elaine lifted an index finger. 'Personality.'

Caroline tried to look vibrant. She tried to look full of life, and at the same time to convey hidden depths.

'Second . . .' Elaine's middle finger joined its neighbour to form a V for victory. 'Punctuality.'

Caroline stiffened, she looked alert.

'Third . . .' Elaine gave the Scouts' salute. 'Perseverance.'

Quite how was one supposed to respond? Caroline fidgeted as she debated. 'I have personality,' she could have volunteered. 'I am punctual. I persevere.' But she somehow could not bring herself to give slavish utterance to those claims.

Still, no matter. For Elaine was off again, turning anticlockwise through two hundred and seventy degrees, to consider the magazine which adorned the partition wall to her right: twenty-four blandly beautiful faces under the distinctive *Donna* logo. Caroline's eyes wandered over the cover lines, which promised month on month to deliver the reader from her dreary workaday existence, to revitalise, remodel, re-educate and redirect her, to pep up her love life, to trim her hips, to tone her thighs, before setting her on the road to an exciting new career. Let There Be Lust! Hip Hooray! Try This For Thighs! Up, Up and Away!

'This will be your first job,' Elaine said. Not would; will. It was as if the matter were already decided. Caroline, who had spoken barely a word since she arrived, felt obscurely cheated. She might not have shone in the interview, but she had hoped at least to emit a faint glow. Should she not have had some opportunity to do so? And what about the things *she* had prepared to ask? Intelligent questions about production schedules, about circulation, about target audience, about the opportunities for advancement.

Elaine completed the circle and studied the letter of application in front of her, speed-reading it under her breath, her eye gliding across the page. 'Dear Ms Posner . . . writing in response to your advertisement for a junior editorial assistant . . . Eighteen years old . . . Passed five O-levels. Sat three As (results awaited) . . . Keen to find work in publishing . . . Welcome the opportunity . . . Warrah, warrah, warrah . . . Yours sinc, Caroline Karasinski.'

She glanced up, seeking confirmation. 'This is you?'

'Yes,' Caroline conceded, though she felt like an impostor. She had had the highest motives in not using the name of Charteris. She was firmly resolved, in seeking a position, that she would not trade on Laura's name. But her father's surname did not sit comfortably upon her; she felt as she had done once at school, when she had mistakenly assumed someone else's blazer, to realise only when she was aboard the bus into town, how poor was the fit, how unfamiliar and not altogether savoury the contents of the pockets.

'Any relation?' Elaine Posner's eyes were the bluest Caroline had ever seen. It did not occur to her that this was an effect of tinted lenses, any more than it occurred to her that the nails were extensions. Free from artifice as she was, she rarely suspected it in others.

'No,' she said hastily, confused, thinking still of Laura, of the Charteris connection. And then, because that made no sense in context, 'I mean, of whom?'

'Of Tony Karasinski. The photographer.'

'Yes, he's my long-lost daddy,' Caroline disclosed. 'He's the dreadful man, the shit who got my mother pregnant and then buggered off. It is to him that I owe my obstinate streak, my thin hair, my fat waist, my lack of grace, and indeed every one of my innumerable faults and flaws.'

No she didn't. Of course she didn't. She was momentarily tempted to do so, curious to witness the effect of the words on this woman, but wiser counsel prevailed, and she merely gave a doubtful shake of the head.

'You've not heard of him?' Elaine Posner misinterpreted. 'He was a big name in the sixties, you know. I worked with him a lot. Now I'm showing my age.' She smiled the complacent smile of a woman who knows that hers is the only age to be. Caroline was invited, by that smile, to rue that she had been born too late, that she had missed *that* decade, was not of *the* generation.

'Well . . .' Caroline spread her hands. 'Vaguely.' It no more occurred to her to think about age than it did to attribute the cornflower blue of Elaine Posner's eyes to gas-permeable perspex. She was just not of that turn of mind. Chewing her lip, she reflected instead on the irony of the situation. She had been so anxious to do this on her own, to know beyond doubt that Laura's name had rung no bells, had opened no doors for her. And it had simply not occurred to her that her father's name would have, if anything, still greater resonance with Ms Posner.

Elaine Posner was tall and straight. Aerobic exercise and sunbed sessions had bestowed upon her a kind of hard, brown woodiness. She wore her hair ruthlessly cropped, unashamedly white, soft as duckdown. She had featured once in the *Sunday Times* supplement, in an article on stylish women, for which she had been photographed in profile, daringly devoid of make-up, in a plain grey shift, and in which she had been quoted as saying that fashion was the handmaiden of style.

Today, however, she was in Lycra, she was sportive. And style was subordinate to fashion.

'I worked with them all, you know,' she confided. 'Bert Stern, Avedon, Penn, Bailey, Donovan, you name it. Karasinski was among the best in his time. But he was one of those who sank without trace. Still, all that is by the way.' She splayed her fingers and, frowning, appeared to study the webbing between. She might have been pausing for effect. Or congratulating herself on how handsomely the years of skin care, of regular moisturising, of lanolin treatments, had paid off.

'Yes,' prompted Caroline, wishing to move the conversation along. She did not care to be reminded of her father, who had been so comprehensively rubbished to her by Laura, and who had shown no interest in her since the day she was born. She had never met him, never spoken to him, and had neither the will nor the curiosity to do so.

But Elaine's thoughts seemed to have snagged on some moment of her youth; a vivid skein of memory was unravelling before her mind's eye. 'We did some great work together, he and I, when I was at *Vogue*. There was one shoot in particular. He was very clever, very talented. And a shocking ladies' man. But I used to wonder if he really liked women. He did have the most extraordinary way of making every girl look like a whore.'

'Would there . . . in this job . . .' Caroline ventured, 'be opportunities for advancement?' And then, fearful that she might sound pushy, 'I mean, after a while, when one had worked at it and learned the ropes?'

'Oh, my dear . . .' Elaine allowed herself to be nudged out of her reverie. 'On *Donna* everyone is encouraged, talent is nurtured, budding geniuses come into bloom. It is my greatest satisfaction to pass on my wealth of expertise to the younger staff members. I think my team – the A Team, as I like to call them – will confirm that I have an open hand, an open heart and, always,' she made a vague gesture, 'an open door.'

'Only, you see . . .' Caroline's grip tightened on the bag in her lap. It was one of those purse types. Clutch bags, they call them; Caroline clutched. She had done it all wrong, she was aware, in the matter of dress. She'd come in what she'd supposed to be appropriate interview attire, a neat suit with a boxy jacket. And she felt faintly ridiculous as well as dated, like an overfed, overdressed Sloane. Her courage faltered, her confidence dipped, she felt the brightness of her cheeks, but she pressed on. 'I have always wanted to write.'

There, the secret was out! All these years she had held it to herself, guarded it from scrutiny, her private dream. And now she had shared it with a preposterous and self-obsessed stranger who seemed, inexplicably, to be on the point of hiring her.

No one had ever had sight of Caroline's notebooks, into which she had poured her very heart. She sensed

that she overwrote, that she was callow in her percep-
tions, that every line betrayed her immaturity, her
insecurity. But she had found such solace in committing
all the stirrings of her psyche, every detail of her day-to-
day existence to the feint-ruled page. And the idea that
some people made a living, that they actually got paid for
doing that thing which in itself was so rewarding,
seemed almost beyond belief.

'*Do* you, now?' Elaine responded. 'Yes, yes, well, of
course . . . At *Donna*, talents are nurtured.'

And, said Caroline wryly to herself, budding geniuses
come into bloom. Aloud, she said, 'So there might be a
chance?'

'My dear, there will be every chance. Though your
duties will in the beginning be what might best be
described as menial.'

'I honestly shan't mind that.'

'Making the coffee. Booking things in for the fashion
department, booking them out. Sending trannies back to
picture libraries. A bit of typing. A bit of filing. Dealing
with readers' enquiries.'

'I'd be quite happy to do any of those things.'

'So . . .' Elaine turned her attention once more to the
letter of application. 'You are Caroline Karasinski. No
relation. You live at number 43 – '

'I've arranged to rent a flat at that address. I've not
moved in yet. But I hope to do so by Monday, when the
contract is signed. Just now I'm staying with a friend.'

'You have A-levels in English, French and History, and
you have completed a short diploma course in . . . Tell
me about that.'

'Oh,' Caroline hedged, 'it was just one of those . . . you know. Where they kind of round you off.' She just hated the word 'finish'. 'Teach you to make *gougère*. Teach you to make small talk.'

'I should have thought,' Elaine smiled her condescension, 'you would receive a better education in the University of Life.'

'Absolutely,' Caroline was ready to agree. 'It was only, really, Granny who wanted me to do it.'

'And you did so to please her? That's most commendable. Now, I expect you would like to know about pay and conditions, that kind of thing.'

'Well . . .'

'This job is graded 8, that's the lowest on the pay scale. And salaries are subject to annual review.'

'I'm sure I should be quite satisfied,' Caroline assured her. 'Do you mean to tell me that the job is mine?'

'It was yours, my sweet, the moment you walked in here. Before you said so much as a good morning. This is how I work, you see. I am intuitive. I act on instinct.'

'Crikey.'

'I can take the measure of a person . . .' Elaine snapped her fingers, 'just like that. I'm an uncanny judge of character. And I'm simply never wrong. I frighten myself, sometimes, with my own perspicacity. Anyway, I spotted something in you as soon as you came through the door. Do you know what that something was?'

Caroline couldn't imagine.

'It's another P, as it happens. Have a guess.'

A rapid computer search came up with Pyrex, prostitute, pusillanimity, prebendary. But no matter. Her role was to listen, not to interject. 'I, er . . .'

'Potential,' declared Elaine in triumph. 'Raw material which I can shape.'

Putty, thought Caroline. Plasticine. Play-Doh.

'I said to myself, "Here is someone with whom I shall be able to work." '

Caroline knew at once, with a dreary sense of certainty, what Elaine was on about. 'Next thing, she'll be telling me I have such a pretty face.'

'You're such a pretty girl.'

Sometimes, Caroline told herself, grimly amused, I frighten myself with my own perspicacity. Now we move on to the subject of weight.

'I can tell you'll fit in and be one of the gang. And I expect you'll want to come with us at lunchtimes to the gym. Then you know what would be marvellous? We could get the fashion department to make you over.'

'Marvellous,' echoed Caroline without conviction. She understood all about magazine make-overs. She had studied the form. It was where you took some poor, unsuspecting wife and mother from Pinner, with boisterous twin sons and a part-time job as a school dinner lady. You chopped off the hair she'd worn long all her life, then set it so stiffly it looked like acrylic, in a style she would never achieve at home. You chose for her the kind of clothes in which she would not be seen dead, and made her up to look like one of those girls who squirt you with perfume as you walk into Selfridge's. You recorded every stage of this ritual humiliation, right down to the victim's protestations (' "Not *too* short," pleaded Penny, as Gavin of Gay Blades got to work on that tousled mop

. . . "I'm not sure about orange," she demurred as we selected for her a linen shift in a daring shade of tangerine'), you plonked her in front of the mirror and assured her that, in spite of the evidence of her eyes, she looked ten years younger, or ten times prettier, or whatever she wanted to be told; then you photographed her wretched and bewildered, half persuaded by the flattery heaped upon her by experts, half hoping it was all a nightmare from which she might at any moment awake.

Well, Caroline would not subject herself to such torture. She would not be so compromised. Nor would she be talked into trying out any of the thin-thighs-by-Thursday diets which were an editorial staple. And no way was Elaine Posner going to remodel, re-educate or redirect her. Better women than she had tried and failed.

If she wanted Ps, Caroline would give her three: she'd give her pig-headed, she'd give her pertinacious, she'd give her perverse.

She would make the coffee, she would correspond with readers, she would book things in and out, she would type and file and return photographic transparencies, she would do everything the job demanded, but she would not allow herself to be manipulated.

Because she had made herself a solemn promise, on her eighteenth birthday, that she would thenceforward be her own person. Finally, the very security of Hartwell had made her insecure. She had been appalled by her own reliance, not just upon her home but upon her mother. For with Laura she had had a relationship so strong, so close and so irrational, that even the arguments, the scoldings, had come to seem essential to her existence.

Perhaps she had become addicted to those little adrenalin rushes she experienced with every confrontation, hooked on the fighting that pushed up her pulse rate and made her blood sing. Rows were like road accidents: you'd see one up ahead, and in spite of yourself you'd feel a thrill of anticipation as you were drawn to the carnage, though you knew it would sicken you to your stomach.

Maybe it was thus for Laura too. Maybe she, in her way, was also hooked. Maybe Caroline had fulfilled some need in her, if not the conventional need of a mother for her child. 'You don't *have* to go,' Laura had said. Not 'I don't *want* you to go', let alone 'I wish you would stay' – and yet, somehow, that had been implicit.

'But I *do*,' Caroline had insisted, though gently, sensing for the first time this curious dependence upon her, and taking strength from it. She had felt very smart then, very wise, and very, very determined. She had called upon the obduracy of which she had so often been accused; she dug in her heels. 'I have to,' she'd said, 'for *my* sake. To find out who I am.'

She had always been there, after all. She had been something exclusive to Laura. She was a living, breathing possession. And Laura never parted willingly with those things she possessed.

'Everyone has to leave at some point. What would you have me do? Should I waste my life away? I ought to have been gone by now, I ought to be earning a living.'

'Why?'

'What?'

'Why ought you?'

'Well, because . . . I mean, how can you ask? It's obvious why.'

'John gives you an allowance. Plenty for your needs.'

'I know, and I'm grateful. You can't imagine how grateful. I thank him from my heart. Only it's not the same as money you earn yourself.'

'You will find that it *is*,' Laura had told her with a disparaging sniff. 'You will find that it spends the same. That it buys the same things. Anyway, what can you do? What kind of work are you suited to?'

'Look, I may not have your advantages. You may not see me on the cover of *Harper's* – or, come to that, of *Canine Monthly*. But I'm quite good at English. And I do have some qualifications. I'm not so stupid. And there must be a million different jobs I can choose from.'

'Where will you stay?'

'With Granny, until I find a flat. After all, she's forever asking me to spend a bit of time with her.'

'Now I *know* you're off your head.'

'No, I'm not. I'm really not. I'm perfectly sane – never more so.'

'Well, rather you than me.'

'I'm sure she'd echo that.'

'She'll drive you barmy.'

'Oh, I dare say.'

'And *you'll* drive *her* barmy. You know you try her patience. You'd try anyone's patience.'

'It won't be for long. Anyway, if I'm so tiresome, why

are you making such an issue of it? I should have thought you'd be glad to get me out of your hair.'

'I shall worry about you. About whether you'll cope.'

'I'm not quite so wet or witless as you suppose.'

'Well, we'll see, then. We'll see what John says.'

What John had said, characteristically, was 'Oh, right ho. If that's what you'd really like to do, I'm sure we're all behind you. Though we'll miss you, of course. You'll have to promise to come and see us often. And this will always be your home, remember that.'

'Thank you,' Caroline had told him, moved to hug him, burying her face in his shirt front, and blinking away the vision which haunted her, of her mother in flagrant delict.

That image returned to mock her now. She screwed up her eyes to shut it out, and of course succeeded only in shutting it in; angrily it bumped against her consciousness like a wasp against a window pane.

'That seems to be settled, then,' said Elaine Posner. 'If you want us, I think we very much want you. When would you be free to start?'

Caroline opened her eyes. She blinked. Exultant, she thought, 'I've done it! I really have done it! I'm all fixed up. I have gainful employment.' And to Elaine she said, in measured tone, 'Would Monday be soon enough?'

———— • ————

'We should have one in on Monday,' said the sales assistant. 'Would that be soon enough?'

Laura did not at once reply. She wanted the blouse and

she wanted it now. She might not wear it this week, or next, but she wanted to own the thing, to know that it was hers, to have it hanging in her wardrobe under a transparent skin of polythene, and she didn't care to wait. So she simply stood there, piqued, staring across the counter, as if at any moment some happier solution might be offered. As if the girl might have second thoughts, and disappear behind the scenes, to return triumphant with the size 10 which she had mistakenly supposed was out of stock.

They had a 12, for heaven's sake. They had a 14. But what use was 12, what use 14, when one was a perfect 10? It seemed to Laura a kind of dereliction of their duty to her, the customer; it seemed unforgivably remiss of them to have sold out. She half suspected that the stupid girl was playing games with her. She wasn't even *trying* to find the blouse to fit her, which Laura suspected might yet be on the premises somewhere.

'Or we have one in blue,' the girl offered with the merest hint of conciliation. She didn't much mind, her tone implied, if Madam bought a blouse or not, and pooh-pooh to a price tag of four hundred pounds.

Laura's fingers curled into her palms. She stapled her lower lip with her top teeth. This was the trouble with the British today. They had no concept of service, and everything was too much trouble. Whereas, if this had been New York, or Paris, or Milan . . . if it had been Fifth Avenue or Faubourg St Honoré . . .

'I don't want it in blue,' she said petulantly.

'In that case, if you wouldn't mind waiting until Monday . . .'

'Oh, don't trouble yourself. Don't put yourself out. I can always go elsewhere.' Huffily, Laura gathered up her packages – a scarf from Hermès, a skirt from Armani, a dress from Chanel, a whole carrier bag of goodies from the Clarins counter at Harvey Nicks – and, with a reproachful clatter of heels on the varnished pine floor, she made for the door, which sprang shut behind her, guillotining some muttered insolence.

It was a blinding London morning. The hard sunlight was mean with shadows, and everything looked edgy. Behind the black lenses of her sunglasses, as she cast a glance to right then left, up and down Sloane Street, Laura's eyes stung. She had conceived this week in town as a means of lifting her spirits. She could spend a day at her health club, have a massage, have a facial, have lunch or dine with friends; she could go to the theatre, take in a movie, she could dance all night, she could shop till she dropped.

But the shopping did not palliate her as she had hoped. In the normal way there was deep satisfaction in scribbling one's signature on a credit card slip. There was the most profound gratification in the writing of a cheque. Laura loved the very act of buying, loved the leathery breath of her purse when its jaws snapped open. She loved the feel and crackle of new bank notes, loved to watch as her purchases were folded for her in layers of tissue, which whispered excitedly of money well spent.

Only today the old magic was missing. She felt mounting dissatisfaction, a wretched emotion experienced more in the bladder than in the heart. Impatience, irritation, always made her want to pee. She would walk around the corner to Harrods, she decided, where she could freshen up and have a coffee, before trying again, at Kenzo, in whose window she had glimpsed a handbag without which she now felt she simply could not *live*. (It was often thus when something caught her eye. She could not rest till she possessed it. For without it, whatever it was, it seemed to her she might never be happy again.)

Neither a visit to the ladies', however, nor a cup of tarry espresso in the coffee bar, did anything to enliven her.

She blamed Caroline. For the past eighteen years, one way or another, she had been blaming Caroline, and on this occasion, it seemed to Laura, she had particular justification. In a funny way she was missing her daughter. She felt rejected by her. She felt judged by her. She felt that all the years of caring for her, of taking responsibility for her, of being as it were her keeper, had been thrown back in her face.

It rankled with her still that Little Miss Piggy, Miss Priggy, should dare to criticise her, when the child knew nothing, *nothing* of the constraints of marriage. For Caroline could not understand – might never understand – how trapped, how frustrated, a woman like her should feel, making love every night (all right, not *every* night) to the same sweet, decent, unexciting man.

It was such a waste, as it seemed to her, of her sexual potential. God – if there was a God (and, frankly, one was bound to ask oneself) – would have had but one purpose in creating Laura Grant. She had been put on this earth to be adored by men, to bask in male admiration. And not to do so was worse than a nonsense; it was against nature.

Monogamy was all very well in its place. It was quite a good system for ordinary men and women, for the public at large – and by golly the public was at large today, out in strength, choking the pavements with its backpacks and baskets, cluttering up Knightsbridge, when it should have gone to Croydon, or to Brent Cross where it belonged – but when one was so very exceptional, marital fidelity just didn't make the same kind of sense.

What particularly needled Laura about the unpleasant scene she had had with Caroline, was the way it had left a kind of stain, left her feeling somehow bad, as though it were *she* and not her daughter who should be mortified. Bloody cheek! This freighting of guilt upon her was both unfair and unacceptable. She was not ashamed – why should she be? – of having one little hug, one little kiss, with an old amour. Yet the feeling was persistent as toothache, it nagged and nagged.

The concentrated dose of caffeine had made her if anything more nervy. She must move on. Back, then, to Sloane Street? To Kenzo? To that tan leather bag which could still be heard calling to her, though ever more faintly, and with nothing like the same insistence, saying merely, insouciantly, 'Take me or leave me.'

Oh, the hell with it! She might just return to her suite at the Dorchester, put her feet up for half an hour. She could soak in the elegant roll-top bath, in water laced with essential oils, sandalwood and lavender, whose aromas were soothing to the soul. She could treat herself to champagne and orange juice from the mini-bar, and sit watching drivel on television. She could spend an hour or two on the telephone, catch up with erstwhile lovers, or bitch with friends. Or chase her agent, threaten him with holy hell if he didn't get off his backside. But for once even this prospect failed to please. Talking wasn't going to help.

Laura didn't properly understand the word lonely. She didn't feel it as most people do, as a wrenching at the heartstrings. She rarely, if ever, experienced that sense of aloneness that assails most of us at certain moments, in the cold darkness of a lofty church or under a canopy of stars. Human companionship had always seemed to her much like any other commodity; it might be had on demand, albeit at some price. Her need for it was more whimsical than emotional – she might occasionally want for it, much as she wanted for a glass of good wine or a smoked salmon sandwich or a new shade of lipstick; she did have these passing fancies – and she took it entirely for granted.

So when there settled on her a sense of isolation too deep to be assuaged by mere chatter, by calls to friends and acquaintances, she was at a loss to know what it signified. She shivered and supposed she was getting a chill.

She had to get out of the store, but her sense of direction had deserted her. She took wrong turn on wrong turn, through marbled halls, past beguiling displays of perfumiers' fanciful conceits. Nina, Gigi, Cassini, Sung . . . their very essences had apparently been distilled and bottled (remove the stopper, went the fallacy, and that individual's quiddity, their special something, refined extract of person, would escape into the air and turn to vapour – *sic transit* Giorgio Armani). All around her, glass winked and dimpled at glass. Mirrors marked her haphazard progress. On every hand she glimpsed herself, Laura here, Laura there, till she felt like a chip of colour in a kaleidoscope.

Eventually, amid the hosiery, the racks of tights and stockings, she got her bearings. She steadied herself against the Pretty Polly stand, waited for her pulse to slow, then headed for the main entrance, for Brompton Road. She barged a couple of bewildered tourists who would try to come in as she was going out, banged her purchases through the double doors, signalled to the green-liveried attendant that she would require a cab.

And even as the taxi door was opened for her, she glimpsed in her mind's eye a sort of after-image of a familiar face. Then, turning back, she saw somebody she knew.

He wasn't the person she would have chosen above all to encounter here, now, when she was feeling so odd, so unlike herself. It even crossed her mind to affect not to notice him, to climb into the cab and be on her way, to spare them both the sheer effort of this meeting.

But his gaze had got hooked up with hers; there was an unseemly struggle, an embarrassing moment of panic, as they tried to disentangle themselves. And they then had no choice but to smile and wave, after which of course he would feel bound to approach her, to exchange with her at the very least a pleasantry or two, to exclaim at the coincidence, the million-to-one odds against their bumping into one another in this way, to remark mindlessly upon how small a world this was.

He was quite exceptionally beautiful. This thought struck her with some force. Seeing him here on the street, among faceless strangers – a tall youth, slightly sway-backed, with a broad, unlined forehead, an uncompromising chin, pale complexion subtly washed with colour – that beauty impressed itself upon her as it had never done before. And something else. He'd had a haircut. It made him look vulnerable, as haircuts can by their newness; it made him look sort of exposed and somehow less supercilious. There was a boyishness about the man which he had been conspicuously lacking in childhood. When he ran a hand across his head, smoothing the shorn locks, and gave a sheepish grin, she felt an unaccustomed fondness for him.

He was swept along a few yards by the tide of humanity eddying around Harrods' doorway, before he was able to swim free, to strike out towards her. 'Laura,' he said.

'Hello.'

'Who'd have thought. . . ?'

'Yes, isn't it bizarre. I've been shopping, you see.'

'Yes.' He took in at a glance the bags and boxes. 'I see.'

She watched for the raggedy lip, which was all too often his response to her. She waited for his nose to crinkle in contempt, for deep grooves of distaste to bracket his mouth. But he betrayed not so much as a flicker of disapproval.

'And you?' she asked.

'Oh, me.' For a second time he smoothed the spiky hair, which bristled disobediently. 'I've been dipped and sheared? Didn't you notice?'

'I noticed. I like it, Jasper. It suits you.'

'Not too drastic?'

'Not at all. I wouldn't say so.'

'Only, you know how it is.'

'I know. They can be very scissor-happy, these stylists.'

'And they simply don't listen. You say "Just a trim".'

'They always think they know better, don't they?'

'Give 'em an inch and they take an 'ell of a lot.'

'Well, in any case, it's terrific. A really good cut.'

'This is how I look at it. It's worth that bit extra, worth coming to town, if you get the job done properly. Better than going to the local butcher, letting some bimbo loose on it.'

'I agree, absolutely.'

'I mean, look what they did to Tobias only last week? I said "What did they attack it with, a meat cleaver?" '

'Not that he would care two hoots, the little scruff.' She gestured with her hand towards the waiting taxi, towards the uniformed man who stood waiting also, with a restraining hand upon the door handle. 'Can I give you a lift somewhere?'

'Where are you off to?'

'Oh, to Park Lane, to my hotel in fact. I've had enough of the crowds. I've had enough of today.'

'That bad, eh? Then let *me* drop *you* off. I can take the cab on to the station.'

'You're off down to Dorset?'

'That's what I planned.'

There was an evil stench in the cab's interior. A blue plastic disc, affixed limpet-fashion above the back shelf,

proved to be the source of noxious odour. It called itself
an air freshener, and claimed to smell of Scots pine. A
notice thanked them for not smoking. The driver slid
back his window and shared with them some racist
sentiment, his personal reaction to the foreign visitors
who spent no money, but merely cluttered the place up.
When he chucked his vehicle around Hyde Park Corner,
they were thrown together on the bench seat. For a
second Laura was looking at the sky. Jasper put out his
arms to steady her, clamping her shoulders with his
hands.

Then he surprised her. He said, 'How about lunch?'

And why not? What could be more civilised, what
more agreeable, than for a woman and her stepson to
have a bite together?

Except . . .

'I . . .' said Laura, whose instinct was to decline. It was
not as if they were pals, the pair of them. On the whole
they barely rubbed along. And the idea of prolonging
this time together, of sitting across a table from one
another, drawing on their last reserves of polite conversation, was not particularly appealing. But then again
. . .

'Go on,' he urged, perhaps reading her mind. 'Let's
risk it for a biscuit. What do you say?'

She read the advertisements on the undersides of the
fold-back seats, one for executive office furniture,
commended to her by a man in a sharp grey suit, the very
model of the thrusting businessman; the other for the
delights of Lebanese cooking, which might be sampled
not half a mile away in Piccadilly.

'Well, all right then,' she consented, sparing him a smile. 'I mean, I'd like that very much. It would be nice.'

Jasper rose smartly to the occasion. 'We've changed our minds,' he called to the driver. 'Turn around, if you would please, and take us to Kensington.' Then he settled back and spread his legs, with an air of satisfaction, and with a feeling that things might after all be under control.

It had been disconcerting for him, running into Laura like that. He'd have walked on by if he'd had half a chance. But then she'd seen him and he'd been snared. Still, almost immediately he'd rallied. He had indeed, after the initial dismay, been almost glad to see her. She would be company at any rate, she would be someone to talk to, and talking just might do the trick.

He'd been having a truly bloody week. He wouldn't put it more strongly than that. He wouldn't entertain the thought that the problem might be more than temporary, a short, dispiriting phase, something to do with biorhythms, with body chemistry (his creative juices had ebbed, but they would flow again, he'd be awash with them).

The trouble was his novel. The novel that wasn't. Or, at least, that had yet to see the light of day. Because it was all there, sapping his emotions, feeding upon him, growing fat within him. It was his baby. And like so many first babies, it seemed in no hurry to be born.

Jasper had a pretty fair idea by now what the novel was going to be. It only remained for him to decide what it would be *about*. There was all this material in his head. Really stirring, powerful stuff. But as yet there was no plot *per se*, there was no structure.

There was the face of a woman at a lighted window, glimpsed in the instant before she drew the curtains against the approach of night. There were stone stairs winding up and up around a central well; the ammonia smell of urine; an echo of footsteps toiling on the topmost flight, the rattle of a key in a lock. There was a Macdonalds on some rainy high street, with red buses swishing by; squashed polystyrene cartons in the gutter, the chuckle of water in the drains. A Belisha beacon flashed monotonously, on, off, on, off, on, off . . . So there you had it. And then again, there you didn't. There were all these ideas, notions, emotions, most of them pretty impressionistic, which thus far had failed to coalesce.

Beyond which there was another little difficulty, there was the small matter of words. For here was the really curious thing: you could have a perfectly coherent thought, one with beginning, middle and end, yet when you went to write it down it was somehow too grand, too exalted to bend to the will of syntax.

It was beginning to seem to Jasper that mere language was not an adequate vehicle for such high thought or such deep sentiment. Fishing expeditions through the thesaurus yielded intellectual tiddlers, most of which he tossed back in disgust.

And yet, without language there might be no novel. In which case he was stuffed. (Or helpless, impotent, inoperative, as Roget would have it; kaput, unstrung and without resource.)

Sitting at the library window for the past seven days, gazing out over the green acres of Hartwell, his stately home, his inheritance, with a sheet of top-quality A4 bond wound into the typewriter on the table in front of him, with the margin widths determined, the spacing optimistically set, he had felt so sick at heart, so bleak, it was as though the inside of his head had been scraped away, his skull hollowed, full of nothing but old scraps of brain and stale air. Like the cold interior of the fridge, when the door was closed and the light went out, and the contents just sat there in various stages of silent decay.

Think, think, *think*. He had tried to conjure that woman's face, flickering candle-pale at the window; to breathe again the earthy smell of rainwater, to hear the ringing of footsteps on the stairs. But the clóser he came to writing these things down, the more they were diminished, shrinking to a dot the way the picture used to do on the television screen, disappearing altogether as he jacked the carriage-return and the typewriter snaffled up the page.

He had heard, of course, of the phenomenon of writer's block which had afflicted most of the great authors at some time in their lives. But to suffer it so early in one's writing career did set one most frightfully back.

On the seventh afternoon, when he'd had nothing to show for his hours of effort but a scrolled sheet of paper, a useless cylinder, the impulse had come to him to have his hair cut. It would take a weight, quite literally, off his mind. More oxygen would circulate around his cranium. Most of all it would be a change. And in some mysterious way, further change might follow hot upon it.

So here he was in London, in a taxi of all things, with

his stepmother of all people, with the promise of at least a decent lunch.

'This will do,' he instructed their driver, as they crested Church Street. The brakes uttered that squeal of protest which is characteristic of London cabs, and they came to a shuddering halt. Then, 'I'll get it,' he told Laura, who in any case had made no sign of searching for the fare, and he dipped in his pocket for a fiver.

'We'll be lucky if they can fit us in,' she said doubtfully, as she passed out her packages and accepted the steadying hand he so gallantly extended.

'Oh, *we'll* get in,' he assured her.

It seemed to her, glancing through the glass front of the restaurant, as she stood behind him, waiting for him to settle their debt, that there was standing room only within. And already there was a press of customers around the curved bar.

To the driver Jasper said, 'Take fifty pence on top.' Then, turning to her as the change was slapped into his palm, as his fingers closed upon the coins and he raised his fist in thanks, he grinned as if drawing her into some kind of conspiracy, inviting her to indulge with him in a schoolboy jape, a piece of harmless fun.

'What are you up to?' she asked him, delighted. Laughter bubbled up inside her. She no longer felt angry or frantic or insecure. She felt inexplicably full of glee.

'Laura.' Jasper relieved her of her baggage, crooked his arm and offered it. She latched on and leant her weight against him, surprised at how stable he felt, how supportive, for someone so slim and willowy. He was wearing a linen jacket of exceptionally fine quality.

He always had had taste, though. He always had had style.

'Charteris,' said Jasper to the female greeter as they walked together through the door. 'Two for one o'clock. We have a reservation.'

The young woman frowned as she ran her pencil down the list of the day's bookings. She tapped the lead on the lined page, an agitated stippling motion. She glanced up, cast around the crowded room, trying vainly to locate an available table, then returned her attentions to the book, to her tap-tap-tapping.

'Who did you speak to, do you know?'

'Good grief,' said Jasper, 'it didn't occur to me to ask.'

'And you rang when, did you say? This morning?'

'I rang last week. I asked for my usual table, by the window. I was quite specific, and I was told there'd be no problem. No one warned me to expect the Third Degree. Look, this is ridiculous. I think we'll go elsewhere.'

'Just a moment.' The woman hesitated in miserable indecision, then inverted the pencil and set to work with the rubber, erasing a name (perhaps by their late arrival, some unfortunate couple had forfeited their table). 'I'm so sorry about this. But we can fit you in, although not by the window. Will that be all right? Good. Would you care to check your bags in? Then, if you'd come this way.'

'If I could come that way,' said Jasper in Laura's ear, as they fell in behind the girl, 'I wouldn't need the relief massage.'

'That was very naughty of you,' she scolded him when they were seated. And how different was this playful

ticking off from the ones he had been used to in the bad
old days, when he had tried by his insolence and his
disobedience to push her to the limit, to drive a wedge
between her and his father, to drive her from Hartwell.

'So, what are you going to do about it?' he teased her.
'Stop my pocket money? I remember when you stopped
my allowance for one whole term for some very minor
transgression. I thought I'd never forgive you.'

'But you *have* forgiven me?' she queried. 'And as for
the "minor", I frankly doubt that. Your transgressions
were generally of a pretty major nature. They were
seldom less than heinous.'

'In fact, now I come to think of it, economic sanctions
were continually in force. Privileges were for ever being
withdrawn.'

'Listen, you asked for it. You *know* you asked for it. You
were unspeakable most of the time – unlike Tobias, who
might have walked mud all through the house, and put
newts in my bath, and been sick at his birthday tea, but
was at least, on the whole, agreeable.'

'Tobias . . .' said Jasper, picking up a roll, pulling it
apart, stuffing a hank of dough in his mouth and working
it over for a moment . . . 'is not such a complex
personality as I.'

'Obviously not.'

Laura felt luscious. She couldn't stop smiling, though
she kept her lips tightly compressed, allowing the
merriment to dance behind her eyes. This was all such a
lark, somehow, and so unexpected. Besides which . . .

Though mirrors tried to claim her look, she kept her
gaze firmly upon Jasper. She knew without the need to

check that they were quite the most beautiful couple in the place, she in her short yellow shift, he in his John Galliano. She knew, too, that they were the focus of envy, of curiosity, of endless speculation. With a caressing motion, with her right hand, she swept back her hair, offering him a profile, a glimpse of a dangly earring. Bangles jingled cheerily at her wrist. 'Are we going to have a drink, do you think?'

'Oh, I think a bottle of something or other.'

'I like white.'

'Do you?'

'At lunchtime, yes.'

'Then white it will be. For Laura must have what Laura will have.' He crooked a finger for the waitress. 'I hated you, you know, with all my heart, in the old days.'

She arranged her elbows on the table, made a flower of her hands, rested her chin prettily within it. 'And you don't now?'

He took time to consider. And the answer, when he found it, evidently surprised him. 'No,' he decided at last. 'No, now I come to think of it, I don't believe I do.'

CHAPTER

•

4

Fish, according to Maudie Grant, was a rich source of nutrients, of iodine and phosphorus, of linoleic acid and Omega-3. The edible bones of tinned varieties provided valuable calcium, they provided fluorine.

Caroline inclined her head as her grandmother offered up a prayer. For what they were about to receive – two sardines, no more, no less, on squares of wholemeal toast, topped off with a sliver of lemon – might the Lord make them truly thankful. She didn't know about fluorine or phosphorus. She didn't know about Omega-3. She only knew that this was not a meal to give a growing girl.

She picked up her knife and fork and took a tiny mouthful. She sipped her Evian water to flush her kidneys, to clean away acidity, to wash contingent impurities, wastes and whatnots out of the system, to keep the bladder April fresh and in the pink.

The clock on the marble mantelpiece chimed six. Maudie very pointedly checked her watch. Her eyebrows shot up a good half-inch. She gave a little tut, a reproach.

The last meal of the day, here in Onslow Gardens, be it high day or holiday, was served promptly at five, to

allow sufficient time for the food to leave the stomach
before the human body moved from the appropriation
phase to the assimilation phase, and thence to the
elimination phase, to the real nitty-gritty of the digestive
cycle, the disposal of toxic debris.

'I'm sorry, Granny,' Caroline apologised meekly, 'but
four-thirty was the only time Elaine Posner could fit me
in. And she did *talk*. I can't tell you. She said it was a
"window" in her day.'

'Very well then,' said Maudie, sounding stiff and
unforgiving.

'And after all, I got the job, so it was worth it. I mean
. . . I don't mean . . . Well, what I'm saying is, at least it
was time well spent.'

'I hope so, dear.'

'Oh, I *think* so. It's a great opportunity for me. A chance
to break into publishing.'

Maudie's eyebrows performed another of those extraordinary *sautés*. Why, she was doubtless wondering, did
the foolish girl wish to 'break' into anything, to go
blundering into the unknown, when she already had an
entrée? She, Maudie, could so easily have spoken with
her dear friend Gerald MacIntyre at the eminently
respectable Murray MacIntyre, publishers of *belles lettres*,
biographies and memoirs, of worthy, wordy academic
and educational texts. A position could have been
created at the firm's headquarters (Caroline envisaged a
draughty house in Bloomsbury, with high moulded
ceilings, and black bakelite telephones, and wooden
filing cabinets, and a pervasive smell of yellowed paper
and tarry pipe tobacco). Maudie could have had a word

in Gerald's ear, in which the hair grew white and whiskery as cress, and he would have taken the child under his wing.

'Anyway,' Caroline persisted, if only to generate a bit of heat, though a voice in her head warned to leave it alone, '*surely* it doesn't matter once in a while if you have your supper a little bit late?'

Maudie did not deign to reply, but her look said it all. It said one would not find this easy-come, easy-go attitude to punctuality or to natural hygiene among the Vilcabambans of Ecuador, the leanest and the longest-living people on earth. One would not hear an Abkhazian centenarian in the USSR, careless of inner cleanliness, saying, 'Put the samovar on, mother, we'll have high tea at seven.' As for the Hunzukuts of Pakistan, in whom cancer and heart disease were simply not known, one would not catch them slipping out for a vindaloo at midnight, now would one, really?

Well, there was no arguing with that. Caroline suppressed a sigh as she addressed herself once more to the meagre rations. Frowning in concentration, she cut a dainty square of toast and, in the stillness, in the absence of small talk which signalled her grandmother's disfavour, tried not to crunch it, but to mash it to pulp between her molars.

She reminded herself that she had invited herself here, that she should respect the rules of the house, that she had no right to disrupt an elderly lady's routine. It would not, after all, be for very much longer. Next week, with luck, she would have a place of her own. For the first time in her life she would have absolute freedom. She could eat what she liked, when she liked. She could have fry-ups, blow-outs, take-aways, to make it up to herself for this deprivation.

One very positive thing at least had come out of her stay in Onslow Gardens: nine days with Maudie, and she had gained a deeper understanding of her mother. Could anyone blame Laura for being so excessive, so self-seeking and unruly, bearing in mind the rigours of her upbringing? What must her childhood have been like? How could she have endured it? No wonder she'd run wild.

And, on the subject of Laura . . .

'You know when I was born,' said Caroline in a rush, before her courage failed. Maudie was not one for heart-to-hearts, for the baring of souls, preferring to make conversation in a lighter vein, to worry that the Princess of Wales was looking peaky, or to remark upon the disgraceful attitude among corporation dustmen. But here was a rare opportunity for the two of them to talk.

'Don't start a sentence with "you know", dear. It's quite redundant, don't you see? Just say "When I was born." '

'Yes, well. When I was born, was there some question of my being put up for adoption? Was that what you wanted? Did you urge it on Laura?'

'Oh, my sweet child.' Maudie was visibly upset. This was scarcely a topic for the dinner table. She set down her knife and fork and reached for her glass of water. 'Whatever makes you. . . ?'

'I'm sorry, Granny, to bring the subject up. Only Mummy said something about it. And it's sort of playing on my mind.'

'I can't imagine . . .' For a moment it seemed Maudie might brush the question aside, decline to answer. That whole sorry episode was surely best forgotten.

But, then again, such curiosity was perfectly natural. Caroline was bound to wonder sometimes about the circumstances of her birth. Perhaps, after all, it was not a good idea to sweep things under the carpet.

So Maudie did her best, she cast her mind back, she relived the terrible disgrace. 'You see, it wasn't easy for me. I'd done my utmost with Laura to instil in her some sense of propriety, to rear her as a lady. But she was always wayward, always restless and flighty, and for-ever in some scrape or other.

'Then there were those frightful days when it seemed half the world had gone quite mad. I mean, can you imagine? Young men with their hair right down their backs, prancing about in the park without so much as a stitch of clothing, chanting and blowing bubbles. Layabouts and drug addicts. All that noise. All that moral laxity, that *laissez-faire*. They called it "Swinging London".' Maudie shuddered to think of it. 'You know what that meant? Everybody jumping in and out of bed with everybody else. And Laura was moving in such circles, going about with the fast set. It quite turned her head.'

'Then my father – '

'That dreadful man! What she ever saw in him I never understood. We fell out about it, to tell the truth, and I didn't hear a word from her for weeks. Then, when she did get in touch, it was to say that she was having a baby.

'Now, you can think me old-fashioned, Caroline. You

can say I don't move with the times (although why one should feel obliged to do so is beyond me, when they move as they do, in quite the wrong direction), but it was a very great blow to me. And, you understand . . .' Maudie looked for an instant quite discomposed. Little spots of red showed through her face powder. 'I had no sense of *you*, d'you see? There wasn't the feeling that any day I should have the most delightful granddaughter.'

It was Caroline's turn to blush.

'It was just such a mess. I couldn't see how Laura could cope with a baby, and *I* certainly wasn't up to the job. I'd had so little success the first time around, as it seemed to me. So I suppose what I felt was . . .'

'That if she were to give me away. . . ?'

'Yes,' confessed Maudie, 'that is how I saw it. Fresh start. Second chance. That sort of thing.'

'I appreciate all that.' Caroline smiled at her. 'I understand why you would have felt as you did. But the thing I *don't* get is, why didn't Laura agree?'

'I imagine it was partly,' said Maudie, picking up her knife and fork once more, 'because I urged it upon her. All her life she'd defied me, almost as a point of principle. And then, of course . . .' She cut a neat tile of toast.

'Then?'

'Well, then, I think she decided she quite liked you.'

'Liked me?'

'Quite loved you. In her fashion. She does love you in her way, I have no doubt, although she may not always show it. Or she'd have whistled you down the wind all those years ago. Which she is capable of doing, as we both know.'

'I guess so,' agreed Caroline, blushing ever more hotly.

'And things turned out for the best. In the end, I mean. After, you know, that other business.'

'Yes, I remember.' Caroline reflected on another time, another place, the first chapter of her life, before Hartwell, before happiness, which had come to seem to her no more real or less remote than the stories she had read in childhood.

'And finally she's settled. She has a charming husband. She has standing in the community. She's very much calmer.'

'Uh-huh,' agreed Caroline again, though 'calm' was not a word she would have chosen to describe her mother. Mostly Laura was frantic. She was driven. 'Oh, Granny, I'm so glad that you and she were reconciled. It would have been rotten if the two of you were still not speaking. For one thing, I should never have known you.'

'She is my daughter, after all. She is my only child. There has to be a bond.'

'And you have forgiven her?'

'I . . .' Maudie, who had a high regard for truth, was forced to look within herself, to consult her conscience, before she answered. 'I don't feel as angry as I did, let's put it that way. Although what has been done may never be undone. At any rate, I no longer have to worry that I shall be reading of her exploits in the *Daily Mail*. I am content to think that she is happily married, that she is no longer racketing around town, getting up to all kinds of mischief. Yes, I'm very thankful for that.'

———————— • ————————

'Aren't you ashamed of us?' he asked, with his mouth fused to her shoulder, so the words tugged at her skin. His short hair tickled her chin. She felt his penis swell again, against her thigh, as he thrilled at their very badness. She felt it leak a little dog-lick of wetness, of excitement.

'No,' she told him in that so-whatish way of hers. 'It's not as if we planned it. We weren't to know.'

And this, simply, was how she saw it: these things happened. She thought in terms, not of choice, of volition, of the exercise of conscience over conduct, but of inevitability and irresistibility. One's sex drive was an utter compulsion. One was a slave to it. Fact of life. Nothing to be done about it. Might as well enjoy it.

She had heard, of course, that shame might attend like some peeping Tom upon illicit coupling. She had heard about remorse, about wives who went weeping to their husbands, about husbands wailing to their wives, confessing all and begging for forgiveness. She had read the anguished letters which people wrote to women's magazines, to the problem pages, those dreary poolings of guilt and regret, testaments to human fallibility. But where was the sense in any of it? What did it achieve? All right, so one committed some minor indiscretion. What earthly point was there in beating oneself up about it? What use in opening a vein?

'You don't feel even the slightest bit. . . ?'

'Why? Do you?'

'I . . .' He lifted his head, and bid with his eyes for

hers, seeking her attention. She seemed like a stranger. He could scarcely remember where he had first seen her, where seen that fine, straight nose, that outrage of red hair, the claret lips, those green eyes now hard as onyx, glazed by lust, returning nothing to him, not even light. In a dream, perhaps? An erotic fantasy? Or in some other life? 'Who *are* you, by the way?'

'If I knew the answer to that, I would save myself a fortune in analyst's fees.'

'Do I know you?'

'I very much doubt it?'

'Have we met before?'

'Just in passing.'

'Laura, Laura, this is *weird*.'

'Go on, now, tell me. Say what it is you feel.'

If he were honest, he was feeling finely balanced between elation and utter horror, like someone walking a high wire, who dare not look down or even contemplate what boiling torrent or fetid swamp lies below. But he sensed that she had something else in her mind, and was moved by something more than duty to supply it.

'I have never,' he told her with sincerity, 'seen anything as beautiful as you.'

She gave a quick, satisfied smile, the ghost of a nod, like one who, on checking the change, finds she has been given no more or less than her due.

'But I love my father.'

'*I* love your father,' she replied, though in a faintly bored, distracted manner, as if she were playing a game of snap with a small child, and had momentarily forgotten that she was not supposed to win.

'Then how can I do this to him?'

'Oh, darling, I don't think he'd expect you to do it to *him*,' she said with a congested, lying-down laugh. 'But you can do it to me one more time if you wish.'

'You're incorrigible,' he told her, impressed. In hindsight Hilary, whom he had taken for the ultimate sexpot, seemed positively prim. For one could not imagine Laura peeking over the quilt, or swathing herself sari-style in a sheet when she wanted to go to the bathroom. And where Hilary had been merely at home in her body, Laura positively luxuriated in hers.

'I'm insatiable.'

'*I'll* sate you,' he boasted.

'We'll see about that.'

He rolled on to his side, seized hold of his prick and wagged it at her. It was very long and springy. When he straddled her it was with such an air of concentration, such a look of grim determination, that she felt quite unstrung, kaput, without resource, she went limp. He might have been contending in some big event, in the puissance, which demanded he push harder, jump higher, than anyone had ever done in history.

And when he dropped his head to nip her breast, she thought she might just *die* of ecstasy. She murmured yes. She murmured no. No, no, Sir Jasper.

Laura was sleeping. Jasper had never seen anyone withdraw so suddenly or so absolutely from the waking world. It was like a . . . not a rejection exactly, but a closing off, a closing out. He sensed that he was nowhere in her consciousness.

Her breathing was shallow, inaudible, the merest ripple in her chest. When he tried to penetrate her from behind with what now passed for an erection, in the position detailed in his sex manual so unpoetically as 'Rear entry, both on side', she did not even stir, and with something like relief he slid out of her and relaxed.

For a while he just lay there, buttressed by one arm, watching her. She was quite without flaw, without the little moles and pocks, the tucks and puckers which are usual features of the human skin, and which are so endearing in a lover. But then, Laura never had endeared.

In repose, she was sort of tight; nothing sagged, nothing gave. Even her face remained much the same, it did not prolapse as faces usually do when subject to gravity, like loosely stuffed cushions with the filling all packed at the bottom. Her mouth, half smiling, did not slew or gape or dribble or distort. And when those green eyes were closed, subtracted as it were from the sum of her charms, the symmetry of her features, the sweet accord between them, was if anything more striking.

She was a living sculpture, a work of art, a credit to her personal trainer, the formidable Dmitri, and to the body-conditioning system which he had devised. Nothing about her aroused tenderness in Jasper. She had none of the usual vulnerability of the sleeper which can be so affecting. But, after today, he was not sure if he could live without her.

'She's my father's wife,' he said to himself. But there was something black behind his eyes, beating like a crow's wing; reality was obscured, to be glimpsed only in bewildering flashes.

'She's so much older than me.'

He found he liked this thought. He liked everything about the situation. He was a writer, after all. He was a novelist. And novelists were meant to live fast, to die young, in penury, of the pox. They were meant to be extreme.

Now what a tale would his biographer have to tell, of youth misspent, of talent squandered! That he should have found time to produce his *oeuvre*, to bequeath to a grateful world such a body of work, when he'd spent half his life in bed with unsuitable women, would be a wonder to students of the written word for generations. His dangerous liaison with his stepmother – the so-called 'Scarlet Woman' – would exercise the finest minds in academe. Had she provided the inspiration for this plot, that character? Had she been his crucible or his cross? His muse or mere amusement? Mentor or tormentor? Was it she who had destroyed him, or had he destroyed himself? Some earnest young man or woman would have to scour his journals, study his letters (he must strike up a lively correspondence with this person and that) for the clues that would be scattered there.

Naturally he felt a pang of guilt, a twinge of self-disgust. But there was pride in there too, there was obscure satisfaction. And it was also true, as Laura had said in mitigation: somehow, this thing just happened.

Jasper had come to town today for a haircut. He had not come to have a fling with a woman whom he had never liked, a woman whom he had resented from the day she invaded his family home. And he was hard put, now, to account for it all, to explain to himself how it had come about.

There had been a moment in the restaurant, with the wine warm in his blood, with laughter on the loose and skittering, when he had looked across the table at this stranger; he'd caught her eye as she spooned into her mouth a fat, ripe strawberry, and she'd winked at him, and he had thought, 'Good grief!'

Isn't this too delicious? that wink had said. And aren't we simply the most gorgeous pair?

'Coffee?' he'd asked her.

'Why not?'

'Brandy?'

'Mm, yes, do let's.'

She had plucked a pink daisy affair from the silly little vase on the table, and proceeded to pull it to pieces, very deliberately to pick it apart. Petals littered the starched cloth.

'He loves me, he loves me not.'

'Do you have to deflower that, er, flower?'

'Does it bother you?' She'd poked the stem, the poor, sad, stripped bloom, back into the vase.

'Well, it doesn't seem kind, somehow.'

'It's only a plant, Jasper. It doesn't *feel*. Or do you think it does?'

'I thought I heard it screaming.' He had reached across like a croupier raking in chips, to sweep the petals into a neat pile. When his hand brushed against the bodice of her dress, there had been a spark between them, a snap and crackle, audible as the scream of a daisy.

'What time is your train?'

'What train?'

'The one which will bear you home to Dorset.'

'Oh, *that* train!'

Then he had been quite unable to take his leave of her. He had rehearsed it over and over, every stage, from the moment of signalling for the bill, to their parting outside the hotel ('Bye bye, it's been nice, let's do it again soon, now really must fly'). With some light-hearted word of farewell he would peck her on the cheek, before she slid out of the taxi, revealing a tantalising length of bare thigh. He would turn for an instant to wave; she would touch two fingers to her lips and waggle them, sending him a kiss. Then she would be spun by some flunkey through the Dorchester's revolving door, and he would be borne away on the ever-rolling stream of Park Lane traffic, racing Daimlers and BMWs to be first away at the lights. And actually, what could be more straightforward? It was really only a matter of making a move, of putting one foot, so to speak, in front of the other.

But he had been weighted by disclination. He had felt like a sleeper who hears the alarm through layer upon layer of exhaustion, and is down too deep to be roused. Then, as the sleeper might decide 'Just five more minutes', so Jasper would decide, 'Just one more coffee. Maybe another brandy. Perhaps one last cigarette.'

The restaurant had emptied slowly, like a sink, leaving behind a kind of human residue. By four o'clock a few stragglers remained, the privileged wealthy with no work to go to; the wildly ambitious with a game plan still to discuss, with options to consider, an agenda to be set; and here and there couples like themselves, immobilised by the booze they'd imbibed, or by their mutual infatuation.

In the end it had been Laura who'd decided. 'This won't do, will it? We ought to get going. Look, why not come back with me for tea?'

And that had been manageable, it had been thinkable. They had only to move from A to B, and might defer a decision about C which, anyway, in the event, had taken care of itself. C, it was, that 'just happened'.

C stood for copulation. For coition. Carnal knowledge. It stood for consummation. For cunni– But never mind that now.

Yawning, stretching, Jasper got up to go to the bathroom, to look in the mirror, to see if he had grown another head.

It was . . . what? Seven, eight o'clock? The sun was going down, taking with it the best of the light, but not the heat in which the city was bundled, as in a smelly, slept-in blanket. You could not so much feel it, in this air-conditioned room, where the atmosphere was thin and wobbly and the walls were washed with shadows, as see it in the grey beyond the window.

Laura opened her eyes. She had a flinty taste in her mouth, and her tongue felt enlarged, it bulged against her teeth. She knew just where she was. She *always* knew. Her return to consciousness was both total and immediate. She had been gone; now she was here.

At once she closed her eyes again, and carried back inside with her an image of the swags of rich fabric with which the bed was hung about, and which created a convincing four-poster effect. She visualised the tall windows under striped awnings, looking across the fugged street to a dry and thirsty Hyde Park, where Londoners might be seen using up the remains of the day, strolling hand in hand with heads bowed against the flurries of dust, or throwing sticks for barky dogs. The traffic roar was filtered through three panes of glass; the noise was thin, but audible and incessant.

From the bathroom across the hall came the sound of water running, and of Jasper clearing his throat, an irritable little hacking, an impatient cough-cough. She imagined him splashing his face, then groping for one of the fleecy white towels, blotting the water which spangled his lashes and dripped off his nose.

What was his mood now? She couldn't guess it. How little she knew him! But then, she had never tried to know him, and with Jasper it would indeed have been an effort. He didn't offer himself the way his brother did. What you saw might be one thing; what you got, quite another.

When he came back into the room she made no move, gave no sign, but waited. She heard him cross to the television, heard him switch it on and flip through the channels like a discontented child – earnest talk, loud music, canned laughter in rapid succession boxed the ears – then switch off.

'Want some champagne?' he asked nonchalantly.

'How did you know I was awake?' she asked, hauling herself up in bed, reclining against the upholstered headboard. He was standing naked in front of the television, holding the handset, watching a flickering picture, some cable programme, with the volume right down low. There was very scant cladding on his bones. She liked the shape of his bum, its squareness; it formed a perfect, inverted 'T'.

'Because you're not snoring.'

'I don't snore,' she said with assurance.

'How do you know?'

'I just *do*, OK?'

'OK. Will I call room service?'

She considered. Already she felt soused in alcohol. But frankly, when one was in that state, there might be no going back. One simply carried on, sustaining an artificial high, or one went right down. It would give her a blinding hangover, of course. But that was tomorrow's problem, not tonight's. 'Oh, go on, then. If you want to.'

'Champagne, yes? And sandwiches?'

'What were you thinking? Beef or something?'

'Caviar.'

'Don't be gross.'

'Oh, come on. Just for a joke.'

'At eighty pounds an ounce, on my bill, the joke would be on me.'

'It will annoy the kitchen. Make them sick with envy. What do you say?'

'Absolutely not. I don't take the pleasure you do in annoying people, you little bastard.' And, as he fiddled with the controls, as the television boomed, 'Turn that bloody set right off, can't you? I've already got somebody clog-dancing inside my skull.'

Obligingly he pressed the 'off' button and laid the handset aside.

Laura got up and went to the bathroom. 'Or we could go out,' she shouted to him, as she sat on the loo.

He appeared in the doorway and stood watching her.

'Do *you* mind?' she protested.

'No,' he said. 'Do you?'

'Actually, not a great deal.'

'Do you *want* to go out, then?'

'I don't know. Are you bothered?'

'Not especially.'

'We shouldn't be seen together, anyway, should we?' she worried aloud. 'I mean, lunch is one thing, but a nightclub rather another. If we went to Tramp or some-where, there'd be bound to be some slimy little toad of a photographer hanging about, and the next thing I knew, my picture would be splashed all over the Sunday papers.'

'*Your* picture. What about *my* picture?'

'Jasper, honey, you're not known the way I am. You forget, I'm still a name. I'm still a face. You can go about incognito, but I can't. Be an angel, now, will you, and run me a bath?'

Obligingly he turned the gold taps, tested the water, made adjustments.

'Can you imagine if the papers got hold of this?' She shuddered to think of it. 'It would be a gift to the tabloids, wouldn't it?'

'Toff has it off with sex-mad stepmum!' Jasper delightedly supplied the headlines. 'Nob knobs his father's wife.'

'Oh, do shut up, Jasper. We're going to have to be the very souls of discretion from now on, aren't we? We're going to have to connive.'

He sat on the rolled edge of the bath-tub and looked at her sharply. He was so nearly pretty. A weaker chin, a snubbier nose, and he'd have been effeminate. 'You don't see this as a one-off?'

'A one night stand? No. Do you?'

'I'm not sure. I'm confused.'

'Wouldn't you like to do it again?' She flushed the loo and leant over the bath with a gratuitous display of fastidiousness, to dabble her hands.

He came to stand behind her, grabbing her hips and guiding her back on to him. (Rear entry, standing, according to the text book, was a very nice way of making love, and easier than face to face. The wife, it said, should bend over, and could if she wished lean against a chair, or some more solid structure. It didn't say *whose* wife she should be.)

'Oh,' he said, 'certainly, I'd like to.'

'I mean, clearly we've no future.'

'No, clearly.'

'But it will be fun while it lasts.'

'It will be that, all right.'

Autumn 1990

CHAPTER

——————— • ———————

5

'Coo,' said Lavinia Pine. 'I wouldn't have thought . . .' She pitchforked an untidy bale of pasta into her mouth and processed it assiduously.

'Wouldn't have thought what?' asked Caroline, at once amused and rather cross. 'That I was capable of it?'

'Frankly, no.' Lavinia dabbed at the corner of her mouth with a linen napkin. Oily spots of tomato sauce glistened on her chin. 'You've certainly been hiding your light under a bushel all these years.'

'You missed some,' Caroline informed her, as she followed with detachment the mopping-up operation. 'Down a bit. Left a bit. There, that's got it.'

'I mean, it isn't as if you did anything very much at school. It isn't as if you wrote anything then.'

'Not so as you would have noticed, at least.'

'Not so *I* ever noticed.'

'I never showed it to anyone, you see. The truly personal stuff.' Caroline reached for the magazine which lay on the table between them, a complimentary copy of *Donna* for Lavinia, riffled the pages, told herself for the umpteenth time, incredulously, *I'm* in here. My words. All my own work.

'Why didn't you?'

'I was shy about it. About revealing too much of myself.'

'No good being shy,' said Lavinia dismissively. 'Well, thanks for the magazine. I must remember to have a read.'

Weren't people funny? Caroline felt she might never understand them. Finally she had achieved something tangible, measurable, entirely for herself. Finally she had realised a lifetime's dream – albeit in a small way. And far from heaping praise upon her, far from showing pleasure or pride, her friends and family were being variously iffy and sniffy about it. Two cheers for Caroline! Hip hoo-bloody-ray!

'I wrote a short story,' she had boasted last weekend, on one of her very occasional visits to Hartwell, finding her mother alone in the drawing room, stretched out on a sofa, staring down at the pattern of the carpet. 'It's to go in the mag. It's being published in the next issue. It comes out this very Thursday.'

'That's nice,' Laura had responded with indifference. Then she had swung herself up, snatched from the table beside her a bottle of perfume, drenched her wrist with it, and snorted it impatiently, her mouth warping with displeasure. 'I'm not sure that I like this scent after all. It's Cassini. What do you think? I don't know that it's really me.'

'I can hardly believe it's actually happening. To see my name in eighteen-point type. And a little photo of me. My first picture by-line. I thought I'd just die of excitement when Elaine told me it was good enough to print.'

'It's a floral chypre fragrance with a heart of jasmine,

Bulgarian rose and oakmoss,' Laura had recited in tones of heavy irony. 'With vibrant, fruity accents of mandarin and osmanthus, and a warm foundation of amber – at any rate, that is what they claim.' And she had let out a cold, bleak laugh, a cynical bark, an expression of her utter disillusionment. Once again, she implied by that laugh, she had been let down. Once again her trust in others had been betrayed. When would she ever learn? 'It's the designer's fragrant tribute to the women he has dressed.'

'What about the women he's *un*dressed?' Caroline asked, very dry, very droll. 'I'll send you a copy. You can read it. You *will* read it, won't you?'

'What? Oh, yes, send it to me. You know, this doesn't even smell like the same stuff as I tried in the store.'

'Perhaps it's gone off.'

'Why should it have done?'

'Goodness, *I* don't know. Because perfume does, doesn't it?' Caroline had plonked herself into an armchair, almost extinguishing Pee Wee, who had been sleeping there, disguised as a cushion. 'Ouch,' she'd protested as his teeth scathed the skin of her arm. And, 'There's no need to be like that,' as, muttering dark and doggy threats, the disgruntled terrier stood up, turned circles and flopped down again.

'What's that smell?' Jasper had demanded, coming into the room at that moment. His eyes, having sought and discarded Caroline, had settled then, almost angrily, upon Laura.

'It's top notes of sheep,' Caroline had supplied, refusing to be cast down, to be affected by other people's moods, though it was disappointing when they refused to listen to one, and it wasn't very nice, actually, or very flattering, to be treated like yesterday's newspaper, subjected to one cursory glance then tossed aside. 'With an undersong of jasmine and Ozymandias and Hungarian rose – or something to that effect.'

She had sensed a tension between her mother and her stepbrother, and had supposed that as usual they'd been squabbling over some inconsequential matter. Well, those two never had got along, had they? If only they would both grow up and stop being so stupid and petty, how much nicer things would be for everybody!

Then, 'Guess what?' she had said brightly to Jasper, more to leaven the atmosphere than in an attempt to impress him.

'What?'

'I wrote this short story – '

'I wrote *a* short story,' Laura had corrected, pained. 'Don't say "this", Caroline, it's so frightfully common.'

'All right, I wrote *a* short story, and it's going to be published this week. *A* week. Isn't it great?'

'*You* did?' He had turned then to look at her in a funny, concentrated manner, as if he were peering into the sun (she had half expected him to shade his eyes with his hand); as if he could not quite make out her features.

'Yes. I. Me. Caroline. The undersigned. Yours truly.'

'Well, well,' he'd sneered, 'whatever next? Foyle's lunches? Public readings? Drinks at the Groucho? The Booker Prize, maybe?'

Caroline had felt her face filling like a wine glass, right to the brim with colour, but she had pressed on. She'd been two years away from here, and in that time she had learned a few tricks of confidence, she had learned to stand her ground.

'I wrote it. And Elaine said it was great, she said she'd feel privileged to publish it.'

'Elaine?' Jasper had crossed to the window and stood there playing with the heavy gold curtain tassel, swinging it, banging it repeatedly against the glass until the pane shivered. The trees beyond had been the same rusty colour as Laura's hair. The sky had been a uniform grey.

'Do stop that, Jasper, you'll break something,' Laura had scolded him tetchily.

'Elaine Posner. My editor,' Caroline had explained. 'At *Donna*.'

'Ah, at the magazine.' In an instant Jasper's attitude had changed. He'd lightened up. He had looked for all the world as if he were relieved, and he had even managed a quirky smile as he ridiculed the genre. 'Women's fiction, eh? Barbara Cartland sort of thing? Mills & Swoon stuff? "Her eyelashes swept the room. Her bosom was on fire. Her breath came in short pants." Isn't that the style?'

'No, Jasper, it is not the style,' Caroline had responded coldly. 'And I don't see why you have to be so beastly.'

'Jasper was quite unpleasant about it,' she confided to Lavinia now. 'He did his best to trivialise it. I thought he was hateful, actually.'

'How *is* the impossibly handsome Jasper?' Lavinia wanted to know, digging her fork into the spaghetti, winding busily, then ducking her head as she crammed in this fresh consignment of carbohydrate (for an embarrasing half-second she had a kind of umbilical attachment to the plate; then with one bite she was free).

'Oh, he's all right, I suppose,' said Caroline, poking at the fish on her plate. Pan-fried fillets of Dover sole with sage, as the menu would have it, as though you might fry in something other than a pan – as though you might use a chamber pot. And she wondered just how all right Jasper really was. He seemed to her more and more like a man with a problem. He never settled to anything. While Toby kept busy running the family farm ('We have a smallholding,' Jasper liked to boast; 'Speak for yourself, Bro,' Toby would retort), Jasper loitered, lone and pale. Or he shut himself away and worked on his novel, which seemed somehow to sap the very soul out of him.

He had even been through a phase – now, thank goodness, over – of writing to her, long, cryptic letters, nicely phrased and apparently full of incident, but really all about nothing, rather as if they were in code, as if there were some subtext which she simply could not discern.

'Watching your calories?' Lavinia enquired, looking smug.

'Aren't I always?' For most of her life, it seemed to Caroline, she had been watching those beastly energy units, counting them in and counting them out, calculating how far and how fast she would have to walk to atone for a finger of KitKat. And for what? So that the odd pound or two might melt off her hips – and never enough to notice.

'I suppose I'm very fortunate, being able to eat what I like.'

'I suppose you are.'

The two girls made a point, every month, of meeting up for lunch, perpetuating a friendship which should have been allowed long ago to die the death, and which was now not even deserving of a decent burial. They chose Orso in Covent Garden for a rendezvous, because, as Lavinia said, there were always some low-cal options on the menu, and because, as Lavinia *didn't* say, it gave her the opportunity to play Spot the Famous Faces.

In this way Caroline, who might be hungering for a pizza, or for garlic bread, and plump Italian sausages with roast potatoes, would feel shamed into choosing some simple fish dish, which she would pick at resentfully, praying all the while that Lavinia would not take off and go table-hopping (for now that she was in the world of showbiz PR. it appeared, Lavinia knew absolutely everyone – everyone, at least, who was anyone).

'On the subject of Jasper . . .' Caroline took a sip of mineral water, took a moment to consider.

'I say, isn't that . . .?' Suddenly Lavinia sat forward intently. Her head shot up on several inches of neck. In her ruffled collar she reminded Caroline of nothing so much as a turkey.

'What?'

'Oh, no, my mistake.' Lavinia subsided. Her head reposed once more between her shoulders. 'I thought that was Sarah Miles just coming in.'

'Where?' Caroline followed her gaze. 'That one by the bar? She doesn't look remotely like Sarah Miles.'

'Not now,' agreed Lavinia, as though the woman had undergone some mysterious transubstantiation, as though Caroline had merely missed the moment. 'If it had been her, I should have had to go across and say hello.'

'Well, naturally.' Caroline took another sip of mineral water. 'About Jasper. He really is dreadfully crabby these days. In fact, now I come to think of it, he's been that way for ages. Probably since he split up with that bolshie girlfriend he had. Hilary somebody. All teeth and no bra. And that was . . . ooh, at least a couple of years ago.'

'You think he's still carrying the can for her.'

'A *torch*, Lavinia. The expression is "to carry a torch". Well, I don't know. It does seem highly unlikely, and yet . . . It's not as if he's had another girlfriend since.'

'Such a waste!'

'Yes, isn't it?'

'A nice boy like that. So you think what he needs is the love of a good woman?'

'Not *too* good, I shouldn't imagine. It's my impression that he's attracted to the bad ones.'

'I shouldn't be in with a chance then?'

'Are you serious?'

'Why not?' Since finding her niche in publicity, finding her métier, Lavinia had amplified her *maquillage*, turned up the volume on her lipstick and blusher, which she now wore very loud indeed. She had also taken to plucking out her eyebrows, to drawing two black arcs above the natural line. The effect was to make her look permanently startled and not a little foolish.

Caroline was at a loss to answer her.

'I mean, here am I, young, free and single . . .' Lavinia picked up the menu and studied it minutely. 'Are you up for a pudding? No, you're probably right. Better not. Just a cappuccino, eh? Now, what was I saying? Oh, yes, about Jasper. What if you were to arrange a little supper, Caroline? Something informal, at your flat, and invite him to spend an evening?'

'Why should I want to do that?' wondered Caroline, mystified. 'I have no ambitions in that direction. And after he's been so unutterably piggish – '

'I mean, so that *I* can come and meet him,' Lavinia explained as to an idiot child, her patience sorely tried. 'Do listen, won't you? Then maybe he and I can get better acquainted. Good wine, soft lights, sweet music . . .' Lavinia began to sway as if such sweet music played now in her ears.

'Dream on, Lavinia. I told you, you're not his type.'

'You're very possessive of him, aren't you?' Lavinia challenged, and she sniffed as though literally smelling a rat, as though she had wind of some subterfuge, some dastardly ploy to keep her and Jasper apart. Caroline, she seemed suddenly to suspect, was deliberately inter-posing herself between them, placing her great, fat bulk in the path of true love.

'Not in the slightest,' Caroline snapped. The red roared up within her. How ironic that she should spend half her life trying not to blush, while Lavinia daubed on the colour.

'You fancy him as well, don't you? Come on, 'fess up. Tell your old auntie.'

'I do not fancy him,' insisted Caroline hotly.

'You've never had a boyfriend, have you Caro?'
Lavinia probed with the deceptive gentleness, the deft-
ness of touch of a vivisector dissecting a live frog to
determine its tolerance of pain.

'Of course I have. Most certainly I have.'

'Who was that, then?'

'There was Nigel.'

'Nigel Barton?'

'To name but one.'

'He wasn't a boyfriend. Not as such.'

'We went out together.'

'You made up a fourth for bridge.'

'We still went out.'

'Only the once.'

'Twice at least. He took me to his school production of
As You Like It. And to Worthing for tea.'

'Not what you might term heavy dating. Now,
Caroline, have I permission to say – '

'No, you jolly well don't,' said Caroline, 'whatever it
is.'

Since she had attended a weekend course on inter-
personal communication, Lavinia had taken to prefacing
her more presumptuous remarks with this permission
nonsense. Still, it made a change from the old days,
when it had always been 'I'm not being nasty, but . . .',
followed, as night follows day, by some personal remark
or other, quite breathtaking in its nastiness.

'Look, what is all this?' Caroline eased her chair out
from the table. 'Can we get the bill, Lavinia? Or I'll leave a
cheque made out to you. I really have to dash. I don't

have time for coffee. I've got proofs to read, pages to press by six o'clock if I'm not to miss the messenger.'

'Hang on a sec, will you? Don't go flying off in a huff. I'll get the waiter, then I'll leave with you. I have work to do as well, you know. I have clients to see. I have releases to write. I have press conferences to organise. And I've a forward planning meeting.'

'Best kind of planning, the forward sort. Oh, all right, very well. I can hold on for a few minutes.'

While the two of them had been below ground, the weather had taken a turn for the worse. A wind had sprung up. Litter bowled by them. Shop awnings slapped about, tugged at their moorings.

'Blast,' complained Lavinia. 'I've got dust under my contact lenses. You're very fortunate, Caroline, not to be short-sighted.'

'Brown eyes are stronger than blue ones,' said Caroline. 'I read that somewhere. The less pigment you have in your eyes, the more weak and watery they are, and the more likely you are to need glasses.'

'Bullshit.'

'It's just what I read. Or heard somewhere. Or something.'

'Well, watery or not, I'd rather have blue eyes than brown, any day.'

'Then *you're* very fortunate.'

They stood and dithered on the corner, each with her hands jammed into her pockets.

'Anyway,' said Lavinia eventually, with transparent insincerity, 'it's been nice.'

'No it hasn't. It's been dire.'

'Well, whose fault was that?'

'Not mine, I'm sure.'

'Listen, let's not quarrel.' Lavinia swooped on Caroline, kissed her cheek. 'I expect it's just PMT or something.'

'I expect so,' conceded Caroline, accepting this as an apology of sorts, almost gracious by Lavinia's standards.

Then, 'Evening primrose,' said Lavinia.

'What?'

'You can take evening primrose for it. Start a few days before you get your next period. Then you won't have these time-of-the-month miseries, these emotional ups and downs, you'll be all sweetness and light, like me.'

'Well. . . !'

Before Caroline could catch her breath or formulate a suitable reply, Lavinia had left a scarlet seal, an endorsement of friendship, upon the other cheek, and was off up the road at a collected trot. She had gone perhaps fifty yards when she stopped and turned to wave, to deliver her parting shot.

'You *could* throw that little dinner party, Caro,' she called, 'and invite Jasper along. Bring the two of us together. Think about it, will you, darling? Toodle-oo.'

Back at her desk, Caroline sat and simmered. And it was a full ten minutes before she could recast the story of that lunch, rewrite it as a comedy, with elements of farce.

But eventually she came to thinking it had all been quite a hoot. A real side-splitter. And she was smiling over her work when Elaine emerged from her office, with page proofs fluttering in her hands.

'Caroline, honey, we seem to have left out the photographer's credit on the women's suits fashion, the Tailor Maids. Will you make certain it gets on there?'

'Oh, sure. Sorry,' said Caroline, keenly aware that – never mind the 'we', the implied sharing of blame; never mind the printed notice on Elaine's desk which declared that here was where the buck stopped – in her new and important position as chief sub-editor, the responsibility for such oversights really lay with her. Elaine had long had a predilection for the plural, which had such a cosy, matey, all-girls-together ring to it. And since she had been named Magazine Editor of the Year at the journalists' annual self-congratulation dinner, where she had accepted the award on behalf of her team (without whom, as she'd said, she would be nothing), 'we' had displaced both 'you' and 'I' altogether in her lexicon.

'And the impotence feature needs a headline. I thought "Going Off At Half Cock". What do you reckon? Or, "When Sex Is A Flop". Oh, and can you be a perfect angel and write a standfirst for the piece? Psychosexual problem, no man alive hasn't suffered it at some time, nothing to worry about, just shows he's sensitive, give him heaps of love and understanding, warrah, warrah, warrah, reassure, reassure . . . You know the sort of thing.'

'Fine,' said Caroline easily, and began at once to draft that introductory paragraph, a few well chosen words of magazine speak, to be set up in bold type, to beguile the reader.

'Ah, Caroline.' Barbara, the features editor, put her head round the door. 'You're back. We need a standfirst writing for impotence. Something a bit sympathetic, mm? No bad-taste floppy willy jokes. Oh, and Patrick called. He said he'd phone back later.'

'Patrick who?'

'Well, he didn't say. Just Patrick. Doesn't that mean anything to you?'

'No,' said Caroline blankly. 'I don't know a Patrick.'

And this was the truly extraordinary thing, this tells us something about the human mind, and the ability we have to repress those things that we find simply too painful to contemplate. At that minute, as she shook her head in puzzlement, she totally, utterly believed it.

Caroline was quite convinced she didn't know a Patrick.

———————— • ————————

Sometimes, Doris too forgot. There might be an hour, two hours, a whole morning, when her mind was taken up with different things, when that other malarkey went clean out of her head. And it was a relief, in a way, to be free of it, for her poor old brain to have a bit of a rest from it, to dwell for a while on domestic and day-to-day concerns, not to have to wrestle with this larger matter.

Like today. She had gone down for her pension, and she'd run into Mrs Mack who'd had the shingles but was definitely on the mend. And Mrs Mack had told her about the new traffic system which they were all going to oppose (someone was getting up a petition; everyone was to sign; must a child be knocked down and killed before the authorities saw sense?). Also, Janet Donovan's girl had had her first, a boy, four weeks before time; he was in an inky-baker but they thought he would be all right.

With her pension money Doris had done a bit of shopping, bought some veg, (though she wasn't paying them prices for tomatoes or a cauli) two nice chops for the weekend, a knuckle of ham, and a copy of *The People's Friend*. And in all that time she hadn't given a passing thought to you-know-what.

Then, back at the flat, she'd got down on her knees and scrubbed the bath, she'd had a good old go with the Vim at the ring of grime around the tub, a sort of slick of body oils and moisturisers which the girl always left behind her. And this had brought the child to mind. And of course Doris could not think of her without thinking of that wretched business.

These days she saw less and less of the kid, who came and went at all hours, who was into everything, and who everywhere left traces of herself. It was like having an infestation of mice, Doris thought with annoyance, as she wrung out a dishcloth and swept crumbs off the kitchen table. You bought bread or biscuits, and the minute you turned your back they would be got at. Packets would be ripped open; half a loaf would disappear. The lid would be off the jam; there'd be fingerprints in the butter. The milk would have been drunk to the last drop. And all this by stealth, without so much as a please or thank you.

Then you'd put up a meal, you'd set good food on the

table, and the girl would just sit and play with it the way a
baby does; she'd say, 'This is lovely,' and leave the lot.

'If you'd lived through the war,' Doris would
admonish her, 'if you could remember rationing, you'd
not turn your nose up at meat and two veg.'

'I'm not turning my nose up. It's really nice, honestly.
I'm just not very hungry.'

'Nor would you be, when you've been at the cornflakes.'

But there was no reasoning with her. She was very
sweet, Doris told herself as she set a pan of cold water on
the stove to boil, she was very good in her way, but it
wasn't easy somehow to get through to her.

Still, she might have been worse, she might have been
more of a handful. She might have been like Dawn,
whose head had been quite turned by ideas.

Doris had a deep, abiding distrust of ideas, which in
her view were responsible for most of the world's ills.
Oh, they'd had their place, she was not denying that.
They'd had their time. Mankind would be in a right old
pickle now, it must be said, if it hadn't invented the
wheel or the water closet. Or the sewing machine. Or the
safety pin. And where would you be without knitting
needles or knicker elastic? But there ought to be an end to
it. The day should have come when someone said
'enough'. In Doris Fairchild's view, there had been no
need for inventions after the twenties or thereabouts.
That's where they should have stopped: with television.
That's where they should have let it lie.

As for books, pray answer her this, and but her no
buts: where was the sense in writing more and more of

them, when no one could hope to get through in a dozen lifetimes the lot that had already been written? Walk into Coulsdon library and what did you find? Section upon section, shelf upon shelf, books on every subject under the sun, from carpentry to cookery, and a novel to suit every taste. If she were Prime Minister, if Doris Fairchild were in Number 10 Downing Street, she would declare a whatsname: no more books till the existing ones were worn out. No more books till this lot had been read. Or at any rate till somebody had something sensible to say, and then they could get special permission to publish it.

It was books, as much as anything, that had been Dawn's downfall. It was from books that she had had her funny notions. When Doris remembered her daughter, it was with a mixture of great sadness and vexation. Stupid, stupid Dawn, to have done for herself the way she did.

Distracted, she cracked an egg into the pan before the water had come to the boil, so it spread like a starburst, a horrible mess.

'What are you doing?'

The girl materialised like a ghost in the kitchen doorway. She was white as a sheet, too, which came of living on chocolate and cornflakes, or not having three square meals. She was wearing a close-fitting, stripey T-shirt dress, broad bands of colour which barely undulated. She really was far too skinny.

'I was poaching an egg, wasn't I? For my tea. Now look what you made me do.'

'*I* made you do that?'

'Creeping up on me that way. Like a will o' the whatsname.'

'I'm sorry.'

'What's that you've got there?'

Oh.' The girl looked at the leaflet in her hand. 'It was stuck through the door. It's about the Green Party.'

Doris sniffed in disapproval. All this Green nonsense. Another silly idea.

Then without knowing why, she made up her mind. Standing there at the stove, with an egg-slice in her hand, she came to her final, irrevocable decision. 'Shell,' she said, 'you must listen to me now. It's about your mum. There is something I have to tell you.'

———————— • ————————

'There's something I have to tell you,' he said urgently.

'No, don't. Don't do a number on me.' She loathed that soulful expression. It meant he was about to get heavy with her. Such a bore.

'I tell you we *have* to talk. You've got to listen.'

'I would very much rather not.'

They had retreated to the fountain garden and were standing in the lee of a high stone wall, where they hoped they might be safe, not only from an angry wind that had sprung up as they all sat down to lunch – there had been a sudden rush of cold air, and on an upper floor a door had slammed; a horrible, portentous crash – but from listening ears, from prying eyes, from the constant comings and goings of the place.

This was the exasperating thing about Hartwell: in no

part of the rambling house or gardens could you
absolutely count on being alone and undisturbed. You'd
sneak up to the library for a secret tryst, and as hand
touched hand, as lip brushed lip, in would drift Sir John
in search of his paper, or his reading glasses, or of a little
human contact, the company of his family which seemed
less and less to be available to him. He would want to
know had anyone seen this or that, and, as he stood there
in a miserable dither, his blue eyes roaming, never
settling, he would seem himself to be somehow lost, to
have mislaid his sense of who or where he was.

Or you'd hole up in the study, only to have – what did
she call herself? – Mary, the elder of the Dowdeswell
girls, barge in on you with an insouciant 'Oops, sorry, I
thought there was no one here. Only it's my day for
doing the brasses.'

So you'd be driven out into the grounds, you'd stroll
far from the house, way, way out of earshot, and just as
you opened your mouth to murmur 'My God, I could *eat*
you raw, I could fuck you from now until Christmas',
Weekes would pop out from among the rhododendrons,
brandishing the secateurs, or the boy Freddie would
come puffing by in a mask and goggles, with a cylinder of
weedkiller strapped to his back. Even now an autumnal
smell of wood smoke, of smouldering logs, signalled that
someone might be tending a bonfire nearby. Little smuts,
blackened leaves like wisps of chiffon, spiralled high in
the shifty air.

Still, the fountain garden was at least enclosed, and at
this time of year didn't need to be gardened. It felt damp
and chill and dead. When she leant against the wall,

shoving her hands sullenly into her pockets, a yellow dust of lichen powdered her soft suede sleeve. There was no sound but the monotonous thrum from the pump house, a melancholy plashing in the pools and porphyry bowls, the sighing of trees, the occasional snap of burning twigs.

He stared long and hard into her face, at her features, all sort of set, except for her green eyes, dark now as pond water, and choppy with emotion. Strands of auburn hair floated loose or whipped against her cheek.

She frightened him when she looked this way. He was afraid she might start shouting. He hated it when she shouted. He hated the way rage and vituperation spilled out of her at the slightest push, as if these were always there within her, as though she were brimming with bad feelings. He hated the name-calling and recriminations in which she would so readily indulge, her vile temper and her vicious tongue. But most of all he hated it when she cried.

Laura Charteris wept very, very rarely and to devastating effect. Her eyes would be all swimmy and shimmery with tears, in the instant before she turned away, as she covered her face, and as the sobs were seemingly wrenched from her.

He would feel for her then an aching tenderness, though with complications, with annoyance and a sense of utter futility. This was the trouble with all women, this was what they did to you. Whatever their age, when they started to cry, they regressed to childhood, they became little girls. And only a complete cad could yell at a little girl.

How genuine was her distress he never knew. At moments he had suspected her of acting, of artifice. But what a performance! It would go right to the heart of him. How could he but be moved, never mind that a part of him knew almost beyond doubt that she was once again manipulating him?

Because he loved her. Or he was obsessed with her. Or something. And one way or another she was screwing up his life. Which was why he must find a way to be free of her.

'You know what we have to do.' He sized his hand against hers, fingertip to fingertip, palm to palm, pressing gently, as though to make a solemn pact, as though each of them had slit a wrist and they were now exchanging blood for blood. And he worked up his sorrowful expression, he worked on it.

'Is that what you want, then? That we should finish this?' She could not accept that he might actually mean it, that he would ever seriously contemplate ending their affair. How could he, when he yearned for her as much as he had ever done? For she had only to catch his eye across the room, to solicit his gaze, to ruche her mouth, to blow a kiss, or to raise her chin and gloss her top lip with the tip of her tongue, rumpling her hair with a careless hand, and she knew he would come running, he would fall at her feet.

Very well, he could have his say now, if he must. He could wank on for a while about decency, about integrity. She would allow him his five minutes of metaphorical hand-wringing, of high-minded claptrap. She'd let him get it off his chest. Then she would go down on her knees on the wet and mossy flagstones. She would unzip him, and with some trepidation – for the fantasy persisted that the snake had fangs – would coax his prick out, take it in her mouth. . . . And she'd raise her eyes to him as if enquiring, 'Now what was it you were saying? About doing the honourable thing?'

'We're destroying each other.'

'Oh, don't be so melodramatic, Jasper.' In an unconscious gesture of impatience, she checked her watch and saw that it said 'Cartier'.

'I'm not being. Really not. It's true. I, at any rate, am being torn apart by all this. By the having and the not having. And the lies, the cheating, the endless, unmitigated guilt. And the ultimate pointlessness of it all.'

'You think everything should have a point? Some tidy resolution? You think that's what life is really like? You believe in happiness ever after?'

'I don't know. Yes. No. Possibly.'

'Well, let me tell you, darling boy, there is no such animal.'

He gripped her lapels, shook her gently, reproachfully, as if the fault were all with her, and yet he could not bring himself to blame her. He turned up the collar of her coat, babied her, bundled her up, then pulled her to him, kissing her with the utmost delicacy on her smooth brow.

'You know, Jasper,' she said, mocking him, 'you always were a mannered little tit.'

'I'm not going to rise to it, Laura. I know what you're trying to do. I'm not going to be provoked into fighting with you and end up making love to you. I said I have something to tell you. I've made up my mind to it. I won't be taunted out of it. I am going away for a while.'

He was serious. He meant it. She received the truth as one might the news of a sudden, violent death; believing and not believing, now ice cool and calm, now close to panic.

So that was the case, was it? These were the facts? Then so be it. She understood. OK, OK, OK. Oh God! Oh, Jesus, no! Her ardent, awkward, vain, self-seeking, tempestuous lover, her sex toy, her plaything, her marvellous boy, was leaving her. After more than two years he was able to resist her: ergo, she was resistible.

Laura remembered then that she was forty, and wished that she were dead.

'Loving you has meant a lot to me.'

'Don't be so goddam patronising.' She could have hit him for that. For being trite.

'I'm not patronising you. How could I? I'm just trying to say . . .'

'Where will you go?' she asked, and as she struggled to maintain her equilibrium, her eyes slid back and forth like the bubble in a spirit level.

'God knows. To France, perhaps. To Paris. I have a friend.'

'A girlfriend?'

'Just a friend friend. He has an apartment. I could maybe stay for a while.'

His plans were not so vague, however, as he would have her understand. They were in fact pretty well firmed up, but he knew better than to tell her that he had already bought the ticket.

For some weeks now, as they had sat in habitual silence together, he and his typewriter, like an old married couple with nothing left to say to one another, the conviction had been growing in him that his circumstances were all wrong.

For how could he hope to evoke the real world when he was stuck here in his stately home? How could he write his devastating commentary on human experience when he scarcely moved from Hartwell to experience it?

He was too rich, that was his trouble, and too privileged. Wealth and social position could be most fearfully handicapping. He needed somehow to get in amongst it. To get down there and grub around. And where better to do so than in Paris? There he could live in a cheap rented bedsit, where he could lie under a candlewick bedspread, listening to productive coughing from the next room, oppressed by the kind of lurid mauve wallpaper that remained with you when you shut your eyes and was a backdrop to your nightmares.

He could stay out till dawn and watch the pale sun come up over the Seine. He could hang out in the Quartier Latin, frequenting bars and bookshops, living on Gauloises and coffee and on Chinese carry-outs. He could shop for clothes not in the eighth *arrondissement*, but in the flea markets around the Porte de Clignancourt (these, after all, were the caring nineties, when the designer label had lost so much of its cachet). He could pick up some syphilitic tart and take her back to live with him. He could drink himself to death on absinthe – though not before he had internalised the city, so his writing was somehow shot through with it and garlicked by it.

He was sorry about Laura, and expected that he would miss her acutely. But missing would be part of it. No gain, as they say, without pain.

'I, meanwhile, am supposed to do what?' She knew she had turned ashen; she felt the drag as the colour went.

'No, Laura, don't be like that. You have your life here. You have your husband.'

'Your father.'

'My father. Who loves you.'

'And *you* don't?'

'I do, but . . . We were never going to be for ever. We always knew there would have to be an end to it. Laura, for heaven's sake, I'm twenty-three years old, I have my whole life to live, I have a novel to write, I have to find out who I am.'

He could not have intended those words to wound so deeply. But had he indeed intended it, the words could hardly have been better chosen. For Laura heard: 'I am young, you are old.' She heard '*Your* life is half over; mine has yet to begin.'

'You want to find out who you are?' she hissed at him. 'Well, no need to go all the way to France for that. You're a lazy, spoilt, snobbish, no-talent streak of piss. You're not half the man your father is. And you're a rotten fuck. Now get lost. I hate you. Go to bloody Paris, and don't come back.'

———— • ————

'Oh, give me a break,' said Caroline wearily, as she

replaced the receiver. And to Barbara, by way of explana-
tion. 'A reader's mother wishing to protest in the
strongest possible terms about our printing the F word
last month in the Edna O'Brien story.'

'I thought the F word *was* the strongest possible term. I
hope you told her to fuck off.'

'Not exactly. I said the word was used legitimately in
context, as a verb to describe standard sexual behaviour.
I told her that until the mid-seventeenth century it was in
common use and was neither dialect nor slang. That it
first appeared in a dictionary in 1598, with its synonyms
jape, sard, swive and occupy. I made the point that,
when society isolates a word and creates a taboo around
it, not only is the language impoverished, but it is a gift to
exhibitionists who will go out of their way to misuse it.'

'Swive me,' said Barbara, laughing her rasping laugh.
She was a good-natured, middle-aged woman with a ripe
sense of humour rather refreshing after Elaine, who
would not recognise a joke if it fell into her lap out of a
Christmas cracker. 'I'm impressed.'

'*She* wasn't. She's thinking of bringing the matter up at
next Tuesday's meeting of the Doncaster Townswomen's Guild. She said we ought to have put a dot, dot,
dot, and that would have made it all right.'

'Well, the best of British L dot, dot, dot to her, I say.
Where did you dig up all that seventeenth-century rot,
anyway? It's utterly convincing. You must write it down
for me, for next time I take a call from Disgusted of
Tunbridge Wells. If you can't beat 'em, bamboozle 'em,
that's what I say.'

'It isn't rot. We did it at school. We had a very

progressive English teacher. We learned among other things that the Nupe of West Africa are the most prudish people on earth – '

'Which was to reckon without the Doncaster Townswomen's Guild.'

'They don't have any native word for sexual intercourse, defecation, menstruation or semen.'

'Who, the Don – '

'No, the Nupe. They favour circumlocution.'

'Well, they say it's more hygenic, especially in a hot climate. You know, I read the other day that the Italians don't have a proper word for privacy.'

'That's like saying we don't have a word for fiasco.'

'Anyway, this won't get the baby bathed. Or the magazine put to bed. Impotence is OK, is it? Done the intro? And have you finished with the health feature? Swim with dolphins to lift depression. I ask you! Can't say I'd fancy it, would you? Still, one woman's meat is another woman's *poisson*.'

'Dolphins aren't fish, they're mammals.'

'I know, I know. Don't let's get bogged down in the details. What shall we call the beastly piece? "Don't Flip. Take A Dip With Flipper"?'

'Now *you're* being flip. You know that's not at all in the spirit of the article. And the dolphin in question is called Fungie.'

'Funny, this thing we have about naming everything,' mused Barbara, perching on the desk and extending one leg, considering a short but shapely calf. 'I mean, when a mother cat has kittens, she doesn't say, "Right, I'll call the white one Snowball, and the tabby one Tiddlypush." '

'We don't know that she doesn't,' Caroline observed, smiling. 'That's a very anthropocentric assumption.'

'It may be anthropo-oojah, Miss Clever Clogs, but I bet it's a fact. Ask any cat what it thinks its name is, and it will say Miaow.'

'Anyway, I think it's nice. It's friendly. I can never think of Pee Wee and Pasha as anything but . . . well, Pee Wee and Pasha.'

'So who are Pee Wee and Pasha when they're at home? And where, while we are on the subject, Caroline Karasinski, *is* home? You are something of a mystery, you realise? You intrigue me, frankly. Where do you "hail from", as we say in the great and glorious world of magazines?'

'Well, my people live in Dorset,' said Caroline vaguely, dissembling, and she mottled horribly with embarrassment when she realised just how posh that 'my people' must sound. A dead give-away, a clue to the social connections she had sought to deny.

To this day, no one at *Donna* knew her background. Had she been a better liar, she might have reinvented herself – she might have written for herself a different story, to satisfy the general curiosity. But she could only really deal in truth and half-truth, so was forced to evade each question as it was fired at her. And her very failure to account for herself, it seemed, made her an object of abiding interest among her colleagues, whose lives and loves – not to speak of their sexual adventures, their cycles, their most intimate secrets – were shared around like sweets. (A nosier or more confiding lot, thought Caroline, you might never hope to meet.)

Her hairiest moment had come just a fortnight ago, in Elaine's office, at the Friday strategy meeting. Caroline had never been very comfortable in these gatherings, in close proximity to her assured, assertive and articulate colleagues. And, with Veronica, the fashion editor, drop-dead chic, smothered in Samsara, on one side of her, and Tina, the art director, smelling of Biagiotti's Roma on the other, she had begun to feel distinctly claustrophobic.

'Right,' Elaine had said when she had welcomed them all and had shared with them the comment from the publisher, Bill Tanner, that their magazine was reaching new heights of excellence (praise being, of course, the greatest motivator, as anyone with the most basic management skills could tell you). 'About the Fortysomethings feature. The glamorous forty-year-olds. "The Big Four-Oh!", I'm calling it. Oh, with an aitch. And a screamer.' She drew in the air with one finger, a giant exclamation mark: stick, spot. 'Now, any nominations? All suggestions welcome. Felicity Kendall? Is she forty? Check, will you, Barbara darling? She'd be ideal.'

'Jean Shrimpton,' offered Tina.

'The Shrimp? Heavens, no! She's pushing fifty. I remember one particular shoot she did for *Vogue* in '65 . . . But I like the way you're thinking. Sixties model. Penelope Tree? How old is she? She wasn't fifteen when she started, but she'd have passed for thirty-five, even then. What ever happened to her?'

'She branched out,' said someone foolishly, and giggled.

'Laura Grant,' put in Veronica. 'She must be about that age.'

'Who's Laura Grant?' queried Kimberly, the fashion department junior, aged seventeen and three-quarters.

'A big name in her time,' enthused Elaine. 'Where is she now?'

'Isn't she running a cats' refuge?' said Tina. 'Or a hotel in Brighton, was it? Or something.'

'Oh, no, she married the Earl of Wherever,' Barbara recalled. 'She has a title. You do hear of her from time to time.'

'They used her,' Veronica reminded everyone, 'on the cover of the launch issue of *Finesse*.'

'Shame about *Finesse*.'

'Not really. It never knew its market. You can't get away with that catch-all approach any more. You have to target.'

'But it's always a bit sad when a magazine folds.'

'Especially after only three issues.'

'Well,' Elaine beamed, 'Laura Grant is a possible, then. A definite maybe. Can I leave you to make the contact, V? Get in touch with her agent. I suppose she still has an agent.'

'She isn't forty!'

Only when she sensed all eyes upon her, had Caroline realised she had shouted. And, feeling her face suffused with colour, she had dropped her head and muttered into her notebook, on which she had doodled a scottie dog, a tree, a house with smoking chimney, 'I don't think Laura Grant is forty yet.'

Because she knew that Laura would have died a

thousand deaths to hear 'Who's Laura Grant?', to hear 'Where is she now?'. Or the crack about the cats' home. She would be mortified if the magazine were to approach her, to propose that she be lumped together with sundry superannuated beauties, actresses, chanteuses and television presenters, under the heading 'The Big Four-Oh!', on the thin pretext that all of them were wearing well.

And, to her own surprise, Caroline, who had always taken on trust Laura's claim to celebrity, to the extent that she had gone to some trouble to distance herself from it, was both indignant on her mother's behalf and almost overwhelmed by pity for her.

Poor Laura. As it had seemed to Caroline, she would never come to terms with ageing, but would always cling by her fingernails, with quite extraordinary tenacity, to the past, continuing to define herself by her success of so many years ago. And here was the most distressing thing: it could only get worse.

'Now, has the Editor of the Year passed these layouts?' asked Barbara, who believed, as deputy editors always do, that she could do the job a thousand times better if the boss would only be persuaded to stand down to make way for her.

'Yes,' said Caroline, glancing up at the clock. It was already a quarter to six. She had better get her skates on. The messenger would be here at any minute. Rather unjustly she blamed Lavinia. If she'd not felt obliged to have lunch with her, but had had a sandwich at her desk as she usually did on a press day, she'd have been finished in plenty of time.

Snatching her clipboard she ticked off those pages that were ready to go, writing 'NTN' against the dolphin piece, meaning 'not tonight'. NTN, Josephine. She would keep it over until tomorrow, hold on to it until lunchtime, late charges notwithstanding. There were facts that ought to be checked, and certain infelicities in the prose which needed her attention.

She was folding proofs and slipping them into the bag when the phone on her desk rang.

'I'll get,' said Barbara, who was still sitting there watching her. Then, '*Donna* editorial,' she said into the mouthpiece. And, 'All right, yes. Yes, it's ready now. Oh, is there? Well, I don't think she's expecting . . . Right you are. I'll tell her.'

'Bike?' enquired Caroline, glancing up as Barbara replaced the receiver.

'Downstairs. And someone else.'

'Who else?' Caroline closed the bag, tugged at the zip.

'Patrick, apparently, is here to see you.'

'Patrick who?'

'Reception didn't say. Just Patrick. The guy who rang earlier, I presume.'

'But . . .'

'Probably some blasted PR. You know what they're like. I had one on to me the other day. "Hi, Barbara, it's Corinne from First Impressions." I said "Hi, Corinne from First Impressions. I don't know you from a bar of soap. And I'm a busy woman. What is it you want?" She said, "Just to let you know that we've taken on the Miss Tress account." I said, "Oh, really. Well, I'm in a fever of indifference." '

'So what is he doing at the office?'

'Who? Oh, PR Pat. I dare say he's one of those pushy buggers, bringing you a sample of some marvellous new product. A gadget that makes your early morning toast while ironing your blouse and playing "God save the Queen"!'

'God save *me* then, from Patrick.'

Caroline tucked the bag under her arm and walked to the lift. She pushed the button and watched as the numbers lit in succession – eight, nine, ten – signalling the imminent arrival of the car.

The bell tinged. The doors rolled back. Caroline stepped into the wobbly conveyance, checked her hair in the tinted mirror, and grimaced at her hated reflection, tantalising herself as always with the fear that the cables would at any second snap and she would go plummeting down the shaft to the basement, that the ground would come rushing up to meet her.

Then, all at once – and the experience was not unlike dropping through space; only it was not the ground but the past that came rushing up, making her stomach lurch – she realised who he was.

Of course Caroline knew a Patrick.

CHAPTER

6

'You haven't changed a bit.'

This was, admittedly, a pretty daft thing to say to someone whom you'd not had sight of since he was four years old, and who now stood six-foot-something in his scuffed trainers. But these were the only words to have suggested themselves to Caroline. And there was this much truth in them: she would have known him anywhere.

She had stepped from the lift feeling only confusion. And she had, in that instant, not so much blacked as whited out: her head had flooded with light; she could scarcely see for dazzle, she could scarcely think.

Then, as she had handed the printers' bag to the leather-clad motorbike courier, muttered 'Thank you', thrown him an oblique smile, grateful for routine, for the familiar, for a formula of sorts, someone had bounded to her side, yelling, 'Carrie, Carrie, it's you. It really *is* you!'

He had seized her arm and shaken it exuberantly. Then he'd grabbed her hand and squeezed and squeezed until finger bruised finger, smiling all the while with unalloyed joy, full into her face. Which was when she had made that dumb remark: 'Patrick? You haven't changed a bit.'

He had grown, of course. He was tall and square. He had a big face, a strong, skewed nose (poor nose, it had been broken at some time), a wide, loose, elastic mouth. And his eyes, which at first glance appeared green, were more grey-blue, flecked with topaz, one noticeably larger than the other, a peculiarly pleasing disparity. Yet he was still the Patrick she had known. *Her* Patrick.

His dark hair looked hacked about and messy, and was no single length, but there were comb stripes through it, some evidence that he had made an effort to subdue it. He was wearing a shell suit – a flimsy nylon tracksuit affair in powder blue, which had been made for someone smaller, someone with shorter arms – and this huge, huge grin.

She loved him. It was that simple. It was perfectly pure, unmixed emotion.

Most of what we feel is complex. Happiness has a taint of tristesse; love is tinged with hatred. Anger is hurt; hurt, anger. Humility is arrogance in heavy disguise. Half the time we don't know *what* is going on within us.

But Caroline knew beyond doubt. Her heart was insistent upon it. She loved Patrick. What was more, she always had done. Only that love had been stored away somewhere unseen, as if on safe deposit, for most of her life.

'What. . . ?' she asked then, laughing, shaking her head, incredulous.

'Look, is there somewhere we can go? Where we can talk? And be together?' He was never still, but jigged around her, hopping from one foot to the other, grinning, nodding, his head bobbing like a balloon.

'There's a very tacky pub on the next corner. The Red Lion. Or the White Horse. Or the Green Man.' She shrugged helplessly. 'Oh, I can't remember. My brain's not working.'

'Then that will do, won't it? If it's the Pink Elephant it will do for us, just so long as it's near.'

'All right. I'll have to dash up and get my coat.'

'Yes,' he said. 'Yes, do that. And be quick, eh?' Now that he had found her he seemed loath to let her go. Her hand was still in the protective custody of his.

'I'll only be a minute,' she told him, and gently she shook him off.

She rode up to the eleventh floor, dashed into the ladies' loo, locked herself in a cubicle, and pressed her face against the metal partition to cool it, waiting for the throbbing in her temples to stop, for her blood to cool to a simmer.

She sat down and tried to pee, but, thought she was dying to go, her bladder seemed to have tied itself in knots. So she pulled up her knickers, adjusted her dress, pushed the flush button, staggered to the basins, lathered her hands under the tap, then yanked at the sodden roller-towel which refused to relinquish so much as one laundered inch. 'Typical.' Wiping her hands on her skirt, Caroline craned across the washbasin to get within an inch of the mirror, to inspect her face through breathy mists, marking the brightness of her eyes, the hectic pinkness of her cheeks.

'Well. . . ?' said Veronica, coming through the door, crossing to stand beside her, decanting on to the tiled shelf the mangled contents of her cosmetics bag, a pile of tiny plastic tubs, of tortured tubes and smeary bottles, dirty wads of cotton wool, a lipstick kiss on a balled-up tissue, a feathery string of false eyelashes . . .

What must it be like to take this almost sensual pleasure in your appearance? To be on such terms with your own face? To love yourself so very much? Ordinary as she was, being both plump and plain, Caroline supposed she might never know.

She did not wear make-up, couldn't see the point. Her eyes were dark, her lashes long and thick; she had no need of mascara. Her skin wasn't bad, either, thought it mantled horribly. Her features were regular, they were nicely proportioned. In theory, on paper, they ought to have worked for her. And if eyes, nose, mouth, chin, the whole caboodle did not somehow, in practice, amount to beauty (as patently it did not), if there was a subtle something, a certain magic missing, then no amount of lipstick or liners would make up for the deficiency.

Just the same . . . 'Do you think,' she asked with diffidence, turning to Veronica, afraid she might be committing some breach of etiquette. 'Would you mind awfully if I borrowed a spot of eyeshadow?'

'Oh, sure.' Veronica did not so much as glance in her direction as she dabbed foundation on her face and smoothed it in.

'Thanks.'

But still Caroline hesitated.

'What's up?' Veronica reached for a sable brush, paused in the act of dusting on powder, noticed Caroline's confusion and naturally enough misunderstood. 'Take what you want. No problem. Don't be shy. Help yourself.'

'It's just that . . . well, I don't know what colour to choose.'

'Ah.' Veronica laid the brush down. She took a moment to look properly at Caroline. Then, 'Taupe,' she decided.

'Taupe?'

'That one there. The browny grey. The Bourjois. Yes, that's it. Hey, hang on though, not like that. You have nice, wide-set eyes. You just need a dusting of it in the mid– Christ, no, you haven't a clue. Oh, honestly, Caroline! Here, do let me.'

Five minutes later, Caroline stood once more waiting for the lift, feeling weird and whiffly in her skin, and very much not herself.

It wasn't the make-up which Veronica had so deftly applied –although she could feel it, every speck of it; she was highly sensitised to it, her face prickled like a peppered steak.

No, it was this other silliness. This flight of fantasy, this self-deceit. You heard of people hallucinating. What were dreams, after all, but hallucinations? And your eyes could of course play tricks on you. She had once, at a distance, across a meadow, mistaken Miss Penwarden for a small horse; and as a young child, when she'd had measles and had been burning up with fever, she'd been convinced there was a chicken on the dressing table.

But visual fallacies were on thing; a waking dream, in which the protagonists walked and talked, and wore shell suits, and grabbed your arm and waggled it, was something rather other. She had always had a vivid imagination, but to have imagined that Patrick – who had been lost to her so utterly, and about whom she'd had no conscious thought in years – had returned to her now, that he was down there waiting for her, large as life and twice as natural, raised some very serious questions about her mental health.

God forbid, but she might end up like that bag lady who was often to be seen in Theobald's Road, haranguing some unseen party, a companion visible only to herself, shouting 'You two-faced little toerag, you poncy-looking reprobate!'

At worst, it seemed to Caroline, she had entirely flipped her lid. At best she must be having some kind of nervous breakdown and should go forthwith to swim with dolphins, whose love of fun, friendly 'smiles', and unconditional friendship were soothing to a soul in torment.

Because of course there was no Patrick. Or, at least, there *was* a Patrick, but not here. He was somewhere far away and had forgotten her.

She would descend to the ground floor, and would find everything in the smart reception area just as it always was, from the uniformed commissionaire with his braids and epaulettes and his Errol Flynn moustache, to the banks of glossy pot plants and the Barcelona chairs.

People would be coming and going. Mostly, since it was pushing six o'clock, they would be going. Some she would know by name, some by sight, some not at all. And she would not spot among their number, try as she might, the big, beaming face that had been so real to her not a quarter of an hour ago.

'Perhaps I've been overdoing it,' she told herself as she stepped once more into the lift. And she began to feel self-pitying and put-upon. She was shouldering too much responsibility in her job. They took advantage of her good nature, her willingness and complaisance.

Well, she had some leave due to her, and it was up to her to take it. She had only to agree it with Elaine, to embody that agreement in a memo, and to mark off the weeks in question, the appropriate squares on the wipe-clean board. She must just instruct her deputy in the matter of work outstanding; of things to be done. And type out lists and schedules, draw a flow-chart, so that in her absence all would go like clockwork.

Then for a while she could do exactly as she pleased. Although there was a problem, obviously, with being able to do that: it meant you were forced to address the question of what exactly it was that pleased you.

She could spend the days in her flat in Battersea, catching up with the washing and ironing, doing the hoovering, the domestic chores which at home were done by servants, and which had been such a novelty when she first arrived in London, when she'd been playing house, but which had long since become a bore.

Or she could go to Hartwell which, in this her favourite season, would be at its richest, with the trees just turning red and gold. She could take Freckles out and ride the boundaries of the estate, with the dogs bickering and snuffling around them. She could go to the ancient orchard and gorge herself on the many varieties of apple that grew there – Kingston Black, Blenheim, Beauty of Bath . . .

It would be good to see the family, to see her stepfather, and Jasper and Toby. And she needed to see Laura, although she could not have said why when their meetings were always so unsatisfactory and so fraught.

Right. That was decided. That was what she would do. Tomorrow morning she would talk to Elaine, tell her she wanted some holiday. She would travel down to Dorset, to Hartwell. And thus, with a bit of luck, would she be restored to sanity.

'So here you are,' said Patrick, bobbing around her once more, absolutely solid, less style than substance.

A second wave of shock and disbelief rolled over her, far more powerful than the first, almost knocking her off her feet. 'Yes,' she responded foolishly. 'Here I am.'

'Come on then,' he cajoled her, sounding very Irish, picking up a battered, zippered hold-all, from which trailed a blue sleeve, as though a shirt had been foiled in a desperate bid to escape. 'Let's get that drink. I guess we're both in need of it.'

Out on the street, in the middle of the busy pavement, in front of an incurious bus queue, he turned, set down his hold-all, and embraced her. Then her arms found their way about his waist. Big, wet tears rolled down her face and dripped off her chin. And there they stood for what felt like minutes, pleached, entwined, as though each were quietly determined never again to be separated.

'At the moment,' she said weepily, 'I can't take any of this in. It's more than I can cope with.'

'Give it a while to settle down,' he counselled her, as though he were the elder and infinitely the wiser of the two of them. 'It'll come good. You see if it doesn't.'

'It's not that I'm not glad. Because I *am*, really. I think probably this is the happiest day of my life. It's just that I'm numb. I can't quite feel it.'

It was a bit like those times when you had a heavy cold, and a plate of appetising food was set in front of you. And you knew it was just the most delicious meal, but the actual taste eluded you.

'Look, I understand. It's the same for me. I'm all at sixes and sevens. And I have to say, I didn't know if I could go through with this. I had to wonder, Shall I? Shan't I? For there's been an awful lot of water flowed under an awful lot of bridges.'

'Yes, an awful lot.'

'But it was only nerves you see. I never really doubted. I knew I had to see you. Hey, Carrie, will we have that drink or what?'

She didn't as a rule like pubs, which were in her view best seen from without, when the lights through leaded windows promised a warmth of welcome, a conviviality, that was rarely to be had within. Most London pubs were full of chauvinist men, presenting a solid wall of backs around the bar. They were beery, noisy, squalid places, and rocked with immoderate laughter. If you were lucky enough to get a seat, it would be on a rickety little stool at a table drenched with lager, right next to the fruit machine and under a speaker, with Dire Straits pounding down on you, so you couldn't hear yourself think.

Yet, 'This is all right,' declared Patrick, as he went

ahead of her through the double doors and stood gazing approvingly around him at an interior done out to evoke the London of Dickens, when the streets were lit by gas and were patrolled by beadles, when the cobbles rang with the clip-clop of horses' hooves, and alleyways echoed with the cries of flower girls selling violets, and ragged old men begged a farthing from you with murmurs of 'Gawd bless yer, guv.'

And this was the funny thing: as she stood at his elbow, as she followed his gaze, taking in the plastic ceiling beams, the sawdust-strewn concrete floors, the wooden booths, partitions with mullioned windows, the sparkling bottles on the shelves and optics, the gleaming ranks of pump handles around the bar, she was caught up in his enthusiasm. Why, there was nothing wrong with this place. She liked it. It was, as Patrick said, all right.

'What will you have?' he asked, crossing to the counter and prospecting in his different pockets for the wherewithal.

'Oh, let me.' She opened her bag, dipped in for her purse.

'No, Carrie, it's on me. You go now and save us a table, there's my girl.'

'Well, if you like.'

'What's it to be?'

'Uhm, a spritzer, please. That is,' she translated for him, 'a dry white wine and soda.'

'You know,' he said unexpectedly, 'you're awfully pretty.'

'I'm *not*. Of course I'm not.'

'Well, sure you are.' He dropped a kiss on the top of her head. 'Now, go and grab that table, eh?'

She slid into a booth and sat there watching him. A nervy, lanky, tremendously appealing youth (the barmaid was attracted to him, Caroline could tell, and she felt a dreadful pang, a real heart-pain, as it came to her that he must have many girlfriends, or, worse, one special girl).

How perplexing it was to think that the Patrick she remembered – the tiny child whose white and stricken face she had last seen in another place and time, through the rear window of his father's Ford Capri, getting smaller, smaller, smaller, till he disappeared completely from her world – must be in there somewhere, under the shell suit, under the skin of the man.

'Here we are.' He was walking very slowly, with a sort of skating motion, sliding one foot then the other, watching the drinks lest they spill. Only when he had set them safely down did he lift his head and treat her to another of his smiles.

'Thank you,' she smiled back, warmed through by his niceness.

'They only had the medium-dry wine,' he explained apologetically. 'But the girl said it's a very nice one, so I figured it would be just fine.'

'I'm sure it's lovely.'

When Patrick eased into the booth, sliding along the bench opposite her, his knee banged the table leg, and drink slopped everywhere.

'There, now look what I've done!'

'But it doesn't matter, does it? What the hell?'

'No, no, it doesn't matter.'

He took the glass of lager and raised it to her. 'Here's looking at you, kid.'

'Cheers.' She sipped the wine. It was disgusting.

'Now, tell me, how is . . . she?' He set the glass down, inclined towards her urgently, with an air of getting down at last to business.

'Laura? She's fine. That is, she's quite well. But moody as ever. In fact more than usually so – or that was how it seemed to me last time I saw her.'

'Is she happy?'

'Not as you or I would understand the word. Laura's different, you know. Do you remember?'

'I don't know, to tell you the God's honest truth,' he said, making a fist and studying it, staring at the bulging knuckles. 'It's hard to say, you see, how much of it is actual memory, and how much is just things I've been told.'

'Are you angry with her?'

'Probably. I mean, if you dug deep enough in the old subconscious, I dare say you'd find some heavy shit. But I don't bear her any ill will. And I don't believe just everything my father's said about her.'

'He's given her a pretty bad press, I guess?'

'Pretty bad.'

'Do you want to see her?' Oh, wouldn't that be horrible? Wouldn't that be just the most upsetting thing? If this had been, from the beginning, the purpose of this exercise. If he were looking to her to be a go-between; if her role were to be no more than that of mediator.

But, 'No,' he said to her intense relief, shaking his

head. 'I'm not in any hurry to open that particular can of worms.'

'Not even, say, for curiosity's sake?'

'Especially not for curiosity's sake. It was *you* Carrie, that I wanted to see.' He rummaged in a pocket and produced a bag of peanuts. 'I reckoned you might like some of these with your wine.'

'That was thoughtful.'

With clumsy fingers he tugged at the bag, but to no avail.

'Shall I. . . ?' she offered, amused.

'No, no, it's all right, I can – Oh, balls almighty!' he swore as the packet came apart and nuts showered all over the tabletop. 'Oops, I'm sorry. Excuse my French.'

'That's all right.'

'And me?' she asked after a moment's hesitation, not raising her eyes to meet his. 'What do you remember about me?' She isolated a peanut and, watching it with close attention, chased it around with her fingertip, playing a kind of table hockey.

'About you, Carrie? Well everything, really.'

'Everything?' She glanced up sharply.

'You were the centre of my world for a while. You made me feel so safe. The way you used to tell me stories. You always could tell a tale.'

'I used to make up fairy tales for you. Your eyes would be round as saucers.'

'And you'd sing me to sleep. I loved the songs you used to sing me. Except for the one that scared the pants off me. I couldn't tell you how it went now, but for this one line . . .' He filled his lungs and sang it lustily, 'And the Lord Mayor of London's going to put him in the Lord's Mayor's show.'

'What was so scary about that?'

'Well, I hadn't a clue, you see, what it meant. Who the Lord Mayor of London was, when he was at home. Or about this show. But I had visions of a great big, wicked man putting a little boy in a cage. Or in a big pit, with bars over it. In some kind of hell hole.'

'Ah, my poor little darling! You were so small then. I should have thought you'd have forgotten the songs.'

'Yet I never did.'

She took another sip of the unpalatable wine.

'Not nice?' he asked solicitously, as she made a wry mouth.

'Not brilliant.'

'Perhaps it doesn't travel well. You should have drunk it at the bar.'

'Will you excuse me a mo? I must slip out to the loo.' For her bladder had unknotted and she was busting to go. 'Any idea where it might be? Did you happen to. . . ? Oh, look, I see the sign, it's over there.'

The ladies' – distinguished from the gents' by a silhouette figure, a kind of Little Bo Peep, in bonnet and crinoline tacked to the door – was windowless and stifling. On one wall a hot-air drier roared and then fell silent (Caroline, entering, heard its dying breath).

'Oh, hi,' said Kimberly, who was on her way out. 'It's you. And who's that dishy bloke you've come with, Caroline, you dark horse? A new boyfriend, huh?'

Perhaps, *perhaps* it was because of Lavinia. Because of the unkind and condescending things she'd said at lunch

– all that hateful you've-never-had-a-boyfriend stuff.
Yes, that must have been the reason why, instead of
putting the facts before Kimberly, Caroline smiled a
secretive little smile and, in saying nothing, by omission
lied.

But then, of course, the truth was not so simply told.
She was hardly going to stand there, was she, and give
chapter and verse? She wasn't going to say, 'No,
actually, he's Patrick Mulryan. My mother's second
child, born of her disastrous marriage to the Irish
playwright, Tom Mulryan. My baby half-brother, whom
I loved to pieces until the day he went away.'

This was not the time or place for Caroline to relate
what really happened. To remember how the infant
Patrick had had such miraculously clear blue eyes, such
dewy skin, such endearing, chubby arms and legs, such
innocence.

She could vividly recall the smell and feel of him on
those deeply gratifying early mornings when the grown-
ups were closeted in their own room (always strictly out
of bounds to children), when Patrick would climb from
his own wet bed and, shedding pyjama trousers along
the way, creep in with her, to snuggle up against her, still
damp with his own urine – warm hands, bony knees,
cold, rubbery little willy. 'Wead to me,' he used to say to
her, before stoppering his soft mouth with his thumb,
making contented little mmmming noises, bumping his
heavy head against her, tickling her with his hair. And
she would read to him about Babar the Elephant, or
would sing to him until his lashes fluttered and he fell
into a doze.

It had been the closest, the most tactile and intimate relationship she had ever enjoyed (Laura, so physical in some ways, was not in other ways a great one for touch). And it had ended brutally.

There were always fights, of course, between the parents, with screams and shouts and objects going crash. There were those times when Tom and Laura grappled together, falling at last, exhausted, in an acrimonious heap. There were rude words, and there were prolonged sulks, whole days when no one spoke, when the silence got into your ears and buzzed there.

Then Caroline had been used, of course, to the idea that things might be taken from you. Ordinary, everyday things. Sweets, because they'd spoil your teeth. A biscuit, because you forgot to say thank you. A doll whose hair you'd very rashly trimmed. But never in her worst dreams had she imagined that they could take away a brother, that any naughtiness on earth could warrant such a punishment.

Laura had always been a great one for denying, for confiscating, for withholding things, for withdrawing even her affections. 'Give that to me, you'll hurt yourself.' 'Put it away, or you'll break it.' 'Play with that nicely or I'll lock it in the drawer.' 'Stop that silly noise or I shan't love you.'

But nothing could have prepared Caroline for the row to end all rows, the final threats and the recriminations. 'He's my son, and he's coming with me. Don't follow us, don't try to contact him. If you make trouble I'm going to the papers, I'll let them have the dirt on you, every detail, you slag bitch.'

Misty early morning. Not yet fully light. Car doors slamming, an engine wheezing, stalling, wheezing, stuttering to life. Patrick in his Paddington T-shirt, bundled into the back seat, still bleary, blinking with sleep.

Then that face, that white and woeful face. Mouth shaped into an O of outrage. And not even a goodbye.

Laura had wept then, saying, 'He's gone, he's gone, he's left me.' Meaning, of course, not her boy child, but her man. Laura never had cared much for boys.

Caroline considered her face – her made-up face – in the freckled mirror. Patrick thought she was pretty. He had actually said as much. 'You know, you're awfully pretty.'

And he had kissed her on the top of her head.

'So,' said Patrick, 'you are something of a writer.'

'I am?'

'The story. Your story. In the magazine.'

'Oh, that story!' said Caroline casually, as if she'd written dozens, as if this were her umpteenth piece of published work. 'You mean you saw it?'

'Saw it? Of course I saw it. Otherwise I shouldn't have known where to come for you.'

'Then that was how . . .'

'I was at the dentist's, see. I mean, I hate the bloody dentist, never go if I can help it. But I had an abscess, I was screaming with pain, so I had to see the guy, I had no choice.

'Anyway, I'm sitting in the waiting room, scared shitless, listening to the whistling of the drill, and for something to do I pick up this magazine. Then I'm turning the pages, when something catches my eye. A face. *Your* face. And I don't recognise the name, the Karasinski bit, but I'd know the face anywhere. I know it just has to be you.'

'It wasn't such a good photo. I don't photograph well, Laura always says. I assume a stupid expression. I remind her of my father.'

'Well, I don't know about that. I thought it was a great photo. Although now that I see you . . . Anyway, I'll tell you Caroline, and it's the God's honest truth, I went into that surgery and I never felt a thing. I'm lying in the chair with all this tackle in my mouth, and he's poking around with a metal pick, and I'm thinking, It's Carrie, it's just got to be. And he could have drilled through the back of my head and I'd not have noticed.'

'Serendipity.'

'Fate, I like to think, taking a hand in my affairs. Because I'd already made my mind up. I was going to track you down.'

'You had? Honestly?'

'Cross my heart and hope to die.' He reached for her hand, which was lying on the table, turned it over and inspected her fingernails. 'Bitten to the quick.'

'I know, they're shocking.' She withdrew her hand, tucking it protectively under one arm. 'It's a dreadful habit.'

'Not so bad. At least it harms no one. Though you should try to grow them, Carrie. For you have lovely hands. And they say it takes the sensitivity out of the fingers, having the nails short like that.'

'Well, I do try, you know. I'm so ashamed of the state of them. I say, did you. . . ?' she ventured. 'That is, did you happen to *read* my story? In the magazine?'

'Read it? Of course I did. I thought I'd die of pride. Laura must have died of pride, I'll bet.'

'You thought it was. . . ?'

'I thought it was tremendous. I thought it showed real talent.'

'And where have you been all this time, Patrick? How have you been?'

'In Dublin's fair city. And fine and dandy. My Dad married a dozen years ago, did you hear about it?'

'I didn't. No, I don't believe so. My mother never mentions Tom.'

'It was in the papers about the wedding. I just thought you might have seen it.'

'No. Sorry. Well, I would have been no more than eight years old then. Too young to take an interest in the newspapers.'

'So I have a stepmother, Josie, who's a great gas.'

'I'm so lucky in that way, too. I have a lovely stepfather. Sir John Charteris.'

'Uh-huh, I've heard. Well, you've been living a high old life by the sound of it, Carrie. Mixing with the aristocracy.'

'They're just like everybody else, of course. My step-father is completely down-to-earth. So is Tobias, the younger of my stepbrothers. Although Jasper – he's the elder one – can be a bit snooty at times.'

'And have you a boyfriend? Are you courting?'

'Not at the moment, no.' She withdrew her hand from under her arm and gave the wine anther try. 'You?'

'No one just now. I'm footloose and fancy free.'

'And you came to London solely. . . ?'

'To look you up. Exactly.'

'You could have written first. Or telephoned. Why didn't you write? Or ring?'

'I guess that's one thing I've had from my father: I've a feeling for the dramatic. I wanted to make a grand entrance. And I wanted most of all to see the look on your face.'

'I hope it wasn't a disappointment, then.'

'It was a picture.'

'That's good. Because I was, you know, thunderstruck. I thought I might just have looked stupid.'

'I don't think you would ever look stupid.'

A shyness settled on the pair of them. For a few long seconds, neither could think of anything to say.

'Would you like another drink?' she offered at last.

'Not unless you want one.'

'When did you arrive in London?'

'This very morning.'

'Where are you staying?'

He made spuds of his fists, hammered one with the other, frowned at a knot in the plank table. 'I was thinking,' he said eventually, 'I might crash out at your place. That is, if it were convenient. If you had a spare couch or something.'

'Well . . .' The idea instantly engaged her. To have someone to sleep in the spare room. Someone to cook for, to make coffee for. Someone to talk with. Someone just to *be* there, a presence around the place. 'That would be fine by me. You can stay for as long as you want.'

'Ugh, there's sticky all over everything.' Caroline, sniffing, licked her fingers. 'The sweet-and-sour sauce. It must have leaked. What a nuisance!' Gingerly she unpacked the contents of the paper carrier, the Chinese meal that they had bought to share, lining up the foil cartons on the worktop. 'Can you get plates? They're in the cupboard on your right.'

Patrick had done all the ordering. 'I'll leave it to you,' she'd said bashfully, and he had gone through the card.

'We'll never eat all that,' she'd protested, laughing, enchanted by him. In truth she wasn't sure that, after so much excitement, she could eat anything at all. But he'd been adamant. 'I will, if you won't. I'll have you know I'm starving. I've not eaten since last night.'

'Even so . . .'

'Now,' she wanted to know, 'are you sure your eyes weren't bigger than your tummy?' And as she glanced at him sidelong, with a hint of coquettishness, her own tummy seemed to flip.

He had not made a move to get the plates, but was standing stone still, staring at her. His mouth opened very slightly – she saw the glint of his teeth – then closed tight. His eyes might after all be green. A deep, sea green. He said, 'Could I just hold you a moment?' So she went to him.

He made a funny, croupy noise in his throat, laid his head on her shoulder, pressed his lips against her neck.

'I'm so happy,' he mumbled, sounding wretched, sounding tortured.

'Me too,' she responded with the same kind of anguish.

It was the most wonderful feeling in the world, to have in her arms this fine, strong, restless, responsive, fidgety human being. This fully grown man. And yet she was frightened because something was afoot. Something was about to happen, and she had not the will to prevent it.

'Jesus, you're so beautiful.'

For once she did not demur. She accepted it. In Patrick's eyes, if in no one else's, she was beautiful.

He backed her against the broom cupboard, pressed against her. She remembered again that cold and rubbery baby willy, which was now so big and hard and terrifying.

He smelled different, too, from the little boy who used to wet the bed. He smelled grown up and masculine and musky and nylony. He smelled of soap and sweat and maleness.

She had read somewhere that smells were not, as she had supposed, purely abstract, but were made up of microscopic particles of the thing in question, and might even be photographed, with the use of a special camera. In this case, then, microscopic particles of Patrick were going up her nose. She was breathing him in.

She felt as if she'd come alive, as if there was a current flowing through her and she needed to be earthed. She felt fizzly.

She used to wonder this about sex: if no one ever told you what to do, how on earth would you ever guess? It

was all so improbable, so absurd. But now she understood completely. Now it was clear to her: the body
knew. It just did.

'Will you kiss me?'

'We shouldn't,' she said without conviction.

'Come on,' he insisted. 'Come on, my darling, kiss me
now.' He smothered her mouth with his and thrust his
tongue between her teeth.

In panic she told herself, This is all wrong. This is
sinful.

But it didn't *feel* wrong. It felt perfect. More perfect,
indeed, than anything she had dreamed of. It was as if
there had been a Patrick-shaped hole in the jigsaw of her
life, and that missing piece had at long last slotted in.

She placed her hands on his arms and felt the bulge of
his muscles. Ducking her head, she said 'Patrick,' in a
very small and squeaky voice. 'Patrick, listen to me. I've
never . . . done anything like this before. That is, I mean
. . . I am a virgin.'

'It's all right,' he promised her, and his voice came out
all mangled. 'I'm not going to hurt you.'

November

CHAPTER

---•---

7

She couldn't eat, she couldn't sleep. If this was love – and she supposed it must be something of the sort – she didn't rate it. Frankly, it stank.

At night she would lie for hours as the dark dragged at her eyes, fretting about the eight hours of which she was being deprived, which she regarded as an entitlement, her inalienable right, and which were essential to the process of body repair, of cell regeneration. The skin was supposed to renew itself every five days; the skeleton every three months. A full 98 per cent of the atoms of the human body, if Dmitri spoke true, were replaced in the course of a year. And the worry was that hers must be falling behind with the job – that five weeks, three months, a whole year would elapse, and she'd be stuck with old skin, old bones, old atoms.

The sky would be white and pearly beyond the windows when finally Laura fell into a fitful doze. And she would awake mid morning unrested, with a psychic hangover, a terrible sense of letdown, of low self-esteem and the feeling that life was ultimately pretty pointless, a joke in poor taste, a waste of everybody's time.

It was all *his* fault, the selfish sod. Who exactly did he think he was to treat her in this fashion? It was true, as he'd said, that they'd always known their affair was not for ever. It was the nature of an affair, after all, to be finite. Either it must end or it must alter, develop into something more enduring, to gain recognition, to be dignified with the title of 'relationship' or even 'marriage'. And there had been no way they were going to relate; no way they would have married.

But it is one thing to expect some kind of resolution, to assume that things will run their course; quite another to find oneself rejected, to be deserted by a stuck-up little tit who fancied himself as the greatest novelist since . . . (Oh, think of a novelist. Proust? Yes, he would do.) To be given the brush-off by a young man so vain that he stole glances at the mirror when they were making love (more than once she had witnessed this self-admiration, had seen how Jasper in the looking-glass clicked with Jasper on the bed).

Laura Charteris was a beautiful, mature woman, a sex goddess, a siren. Any normal, red-blooded male would kill his own mother for the chance to get into the sack with her. Which led to one inescapable conclusion: Jasper was not the normal, red-blooded male he would have the world believe. Jasper must be a closet gay.

If this rationalisation was a salve to her ego – and she had almost convinced herself of it – it did nothing to soothe her aching heart, to ease her loneliness. She missed him with her body and her being. All the colour had drained out of her existence.

Nor was John any bloody help. He just looked at her with hurt and puzzled eyes, and said such stupid, stupid things as 'What's the matter?', and, 'If there's anything I can do . . .', when it should have been obvious to a halfwit that there was no earthly thing to be done.

Yesterday evening, for instance, she'd been sitting at the piano, staring at the keys, so black, so white, so uncompromising, each with its particular function, its own one note. Once upon a time she had played a bit. She had a certificate. But right now she knew the noise would jar her nerves.

'Are you all right, my love?' John had come to stand beside her, massaging her shoulders with his long fingers, digging, kneading, poking, till she squirmed out of his grip.

'Of course I'm all right,' she'd snapped at him. And she'd slammed down the piano lid so hard that the strings sang for uncounted seconds.

'I wish you'd share it with me, whatever it is.'

For a moment she'd had half a mind to do so. Just imagine if she had done! Suppose she'd let him have it, straight from the shoulder? 'It's because of Jasper. For more than two years we'd been lovers. Now he's buggered off and left me and I'm sick about it.' What would he have said? What done? Wept and forgiven her? Banished her for ever from Hartwell? She hadn't dared to test him on it. He was the kindest man on earth, but perhaps not endlessly kind: even he must have his limits.

She stood now on the balcony outside the bedroom, gazing at the silvered waters of the lake. There was a wetness in the atmosphere this morning, and a chill. The long, hot summer had bleached the lawns and crazed the parched soil, but today the ground was weeping moisture and the air was misty with it.

Paris would be lovely at this time of year, with all the winter fashions in the shops. 'I could go there,' she thought. 'John would be glad for me to go. He'd agree to anything to cheer me up.'

She imagined strolling down a wide and tree-lined boulevard, bumping into someone, opening her mouth to mutter a polite '*Pardon*', the word dying on her lips as she registered the so-familiar face. 'Jasper.' 'Laura. What are *you* doing here?' 'Just walking.' 'I've missed you.' '*I've* missed *you*.' 'Should we start again?' 'If you want to.'

She pictured herself chic in a dogtooth check Moschino jacket and matching mini skirt, with her hair in a neat chignon. Then she had herself girlish, gamine, in jeans and a big man's sweater, with her hair loose and wild. She had him a little the worse for wear, looking thinner, older, lined by care. She penalised him heavily for his inconstancy.

She moved the action to the Bois, to the *quais*, and finally, most satisfactorily, to gloomy Père Lachaise, where Oscar Wilde was buried, and Edith Piaf, and Jim Morrison, with whom she had once had a bit of a thing (when Jasper asked what she was doing here she could say she was visiting Jim).

She forgot for the minute her latest theory – the one about Jasper's sexual orientation. For the present, for the purposes of fantasy, he was straight as a die.

The gardens of Hartwell had less reality for her at that moment than the desolate acres of Parisian cemetery that she visualised. She saw herself moving distractedly between ranks of pale gravestones, colliding with a tall youth. 'Oh, *pardon*!'

'Oh, pardon me, your ladyship. I never realised you were out there. I shan't be two ticks. I just came to do the beds.' Mrs Holloway, the housekeeper, appeared at the French windows, clutching to her chest a pile of clean, pressed linen, and by her look defying Laura to send her away.

She was in every sense a stout woman, big, stalwart and dependable, heavy on shoes. She had been with the family for twenty-four years. Lady Jane it was who had engaged her, and it was to Lady Jane that she still answered, or so it sometimes seemed to Laura, who detested the woman though she could not fault her as a worker.

'Oh, sure. Go ahead,' Laura told her dismissively, over her shoulder. And she tried, to no avail, to escape once more into her imagination, to screen out the background noise, the huff and puff, as Mrs Holloway went the distance with the kingsize duvet.

'Lady Jane never could abide these Continental quilts.'

'What?' Laura went snappily indoors to watch this punch-up. The duvet was apparently ahead on points.

'Her ladyship . . . That is, the first Lady Charteris. I was just saying how she never did care for these quilt affairs. Wouldn't have one in the house.'

Lady Jane did not, of course, have to sleep in this bed any more. Laura thought of saying as much, for the pleasure of making Mrs Holloway wince, but she was too depressed to utter; she was too tired and dispirited.

It occurred to her that Lady Jane had no further need of bedclothes, since she was covered by the sod. And this if nothing else they had in common: they'd both been covered by sods.

'What are *you* doing, anyway, making up beds?' she demanded as the thought crossed her mind. 'Isn't that the girl's job? Mary Pushface?'

Mrs Holloway, who had succeeded at last in peeling off one duvet cover, paused in the more challenging task of replacing it with another. When she bit her lip, it was as though she were quite literally biting back a retort. Her bosom rose and fell. 'Mary Dowdeswell,' she said, 'has gone.'

'What do you mean, "gone"?' Laura picked up a silver-backed brush from the dressing table and set about brushing her hair, which crackled in the charged air.

'She no longer works here.'

'She's been dismissed? By whom? Should I not have been consulted?'

'Not dismissed, no. She just walked out. Because of some words she'd had with your ladyship, so far as I could understand.'

'Words? What words? You mean that little altercation yesterday?'

'Something to do with a pair of earrings – '

'But that was all over and done with. It turned out I'd mislaid the wretched things, although just for a minute, when I found they weren't in the drawer . . . Well, naturally enough I quizzed her.'

'She considered that her honesty had been called into question.' Mrs Holloway was visibly upset. She mangled the duvet cover in her hands. Wisps of grey hair had escaped from her bun, lending her a faintly distrait appearance. 'She felt she had been accused of some-thing– '

'I accused her of nothing,' retorted Laura hotly. 'I merely asked her, had she seen a pair of diamond earrings? Was she quite sure she hadn't? That sort of thing.'

'Well, I don't know about that. But she was up on her high horse and away. Said she could earn as much in Safeway where her sister works, and she'd not have to put up with insults. "I'm not staying here to be called a thief," she said. "They can – " And she used a very colourful phrase which I shall not repeat, as to what you might do with the job.'

'Did she indeed?'

Mrs Holloway gathered herself in, she drew herself up, made a neat tuck of her mouth, preparing to speak as she found. 'In my opinion, it's a pity. She was a good little worker. And reliable. And trustworthy.'

'Well, it's too bad of her. She might have given notice. Have you tried to find a replacement?'

'Mr Stevens has been on to the agency. They'll try to send someone in, temporary, though they say they're short-handed.'

'Nonsense. There are millions of people unemployed.'

'That's as maybe, but . . .'

'Look, finish the bed, do. Don't let me delay you. And those flowers in the tall vase. I don't like them. Please take them downstairs.'

'Arum lilies,' said Mrs Holloway, bending, presenting Laura with a backview, plumping pillows. 'Lady Jane was always very fond of Arum lilies.'

———————— • ————————

There were no seats in second class, so Shell went and sat in first. If an inspector came she would pretend to be foreign, shake her head with incomprehension, unman him with an apologetic smile. Or she would make out that she had lost her ticket, rake through her dufflebag, while her huge, slate eyes flicked up and down, now taking in the jumble of her possessions, now gazing helplessly into his face, where she was confident she would find sympathetic response.

That would be all right, then. Having made her plans, she put the problem from her mind. No sense in worrying when a thing might never happen. She wasn't one for looking ahead – or, for that matter, for looking behind – if she could avoid it, but lived in the moment, in a sort of bubble, in the weightless, spinning, iridescent here and now.

Nor was she given to thinking too deeply. She didn't seem to be equipped to do so. At this moment, for instance, there was something of profound importance which she supposed must be addressed. Her life had sort of blown inside out. But although she had a queasy feeling, she could not bring any rationality to bear upon it, she just could not get her head around it.

'Well, that must be some kind of record,' declared the middle-aged man who had plonked himself opposite her, the only other occupant of the compartment, shooting the cuff of his grey jacket, checking his watch, as the train eased out of Waterloo, as trolleys and porters, and piles of that week's colour supplements, and wheeled cages of mail went flying backwards. He had thinning hair and the strawberry complexion of a business luncher who regularly did himself well. 'We're actually leaving on time for once.'

Shell remembered that she was – or might be – a foreign visitor, that she spoke no more than a few words of phrase-book English (Is there a bathroom on this floor? Does the tour leave from here? The washbasin is clogged. This soup is cold. Keep the change).

'Please?'

'I was just saying, we're away on time. *On time.*' He mouthed the words at her, and tapped the glass of his big, gold watch with meaning. 'A triumph for BR. What are you, French? *Français*? Or German? *Sprächen Sie Deutsch*? You're a student, I suppose? Is that it? Oh, never mind. What's the use?' With the ostentation of an origamist shaking out a paper cathedral, he shook out his *Daily Telegraph* and – deprived of his chance to chat up this lovely young girl, to engage in one hour and forty minutes of delightful flirtation – disappeared behind it.

Good! thought Shell, thankful to be left to herself, to be spared a dreary discourse on Disastrous Railway Journeys of Our Time. She'd been stuck with BR bores before, the type who talked you down the line, via Guildford, Godalming, Petersfield, Havant, all the way to Portsmouth Harbour. People who spoke knowingly of investment, and of infrastructure. Who delighted in telling you how doors kept flying open on the Intercity 125s. Who loved to contrast the service in Britain with that in France, with the SNCF, with the TGVs on which you were guaranteed to get a seat, and the staff were unfailingly polite, and the buffets were never crowded, and the food was superb, and the fares were lower, and come wind, come weather, you could leave Paris after breakfast and be in Lyon for elevenses, or all the way to Marseilles for lunch . . .

Then, as if this were not imposition enough, there was always, at the end of such a monologue, some kind of proposition, some kind of pass made at her (you could hear it approaching from afar, the way you could hear the 9.47 from Horsham, by the excited chattering of the electric rails, before it came nosing round the bend).

Sexual harassment was a fact of life for Michele Fairchild. And some people would say that she asked for it, that she deserved all she got, going about as she did with next to nothing on. (Well, look at her now, in that skimpy white stretch-cotton dress, fused to her figure so her nipples, her thighs, her pelvic girdle showed through!) But it was not her extraordinary, aberrant beauty, or what she wore, the way her bony outline showed beneath a thin sketch of clothing, so much as her manner that made men ill with lust for her.

It was a matter of presentation, of her tousle-haired, heavy-eyed look, and her lazy body language. Shell, who was not a great reader, had recently come across the word 'bedraggled', which she had heard in her mind's ear as bed-raggled. And that – though she had only a vague sense of it – was how she herself appeared: she looked as if she'd been raggled in bed.

People mostly assumed she was stupid, which was to miss the point of her. True, she had not excelled academically: she had passed through the state school system to emerge without so much as an O-level in needlework. Her exam marks had told their own tale: E for this, F for that. 'Doesn't try,' her reports had said of her. 'Lazy.' 'Won't make the effort.' But she was not, after all, a fool.

It was just that she cared little for information, for facts. The repeal of the Corn Laws, the return to the Gold Standard, the square on the hypotenuse had seemed irrelevant to her (what, after all, as her nan was fond of asking, had any of this to do with the price of lard?). Thus she had spent long years staring out of the classroom window, her mind as blank as the endless blue sky. And she had done long hours of detention for neglected homework, for inattention, for her failure ever to get to grips with the business of learning.

Even so, she was never quite the bad girl her teachers believed. It was not her fault that school uniform sat like an insolence upon her – that merely by wearing the regulation skirt, blouse and tie, she appeared to be making mock. Nor was she conscious of how her insouciance, her maddening detachment, made the female teachers strangely tetchy, the male teachers sick with desire for her. No doubt she would have been unsurprised to learn how these professional men fantasised about misconducting themselves with her, but she had no notion whatever of the way in which her sleepy eyes, her passivity, her obduracy, quite as much as her face and body, were arousing to them.

It was one of those dissatisfying days which would never come to anything. The sun would never quite show itself; nor would the sky fulfil its halfhearted promise of rain. Though it was nearly noon, through kitchen windows there could be seen the flickering blue whiteness of fluorescent strips. The washing that flapped on rotary driers, cranked around by an irresolute wind, would be gathered in still damp at the end of the short afternoon. In one back garden a dog foraged in the flowerbeds, his tail waving among the late-blooming double dahlias. In another, two young boys with plastic bats beat ruthlessly about the bushes, scything off whole twigs. A downpipe from a bathroom billowed steam.

Dreamy, incurious, Shell watched as whatever it was that bound neighbour to neighbour, the continuous ribbon of human habitation, spun out ever more loosely.

There was a row of shops with flats above. A church. A petrol station. Then dark and oozing farmland. Black copses. Canted fields with black-and-white cows all cluttered at the bottom.

Town born, town bred, she did not understand the countryside, the way it spread about and had no centre. She supposed where she was going it would be very rural. It loomed dauntingly large in her imagination, a rambling house with stables at the side, and one of those drives that went both in and out, a circle of gravel around which horsedrawn carriages would once have rumbled . . .

Why was she going there? What would she do when she got there? How about if she simply turned around, took the next train back to London, and put the whole thing from her mind for ever?

It had been Nanny Fairchild who'd insisted that she make this journey. 'You get yourself down there. You see that woman. Tell her what I told you.' And only now, when she was on her way, did it occur to Shell that, in this matter as in most, there was such a thing as choice.

For as long as she could remember she had done her grandmother's bidding. Nanny was, after all, so knowing, with something to say on every subject under the sun. Mere wishes, she had always told Shell, were silly fishes. Patience was a virtue. The devil danced in an empty pocket. A little learning was a dangerous thing . . . And the more you thought about these things, the more you came to see the wisdom of them. But this trip, this escapade, this errand, might not be quite so wise.

An inspector armed with a ticket-punch appeared in the corridor, stood there swaying behind the glass pane, through which he made prior assessment of these two passengers – one eminently first class, and one rather other – before rolling back the door to usher in the noise of rattling wheels, bounced back off bricked embankments.

'Your tickets, please.' He fixed on Shell, who remembered she was Hungarian. Or Portuguese. Or deaf? She could be deaf. For had she not a remarkable facility for screening out sound? Had she not sat through week upon week of double biology, without hearing one word about photosynthesis, or cross-pollination, or binary fission?

She lifted her eyes to his face in polite enquiry (what could this nice, grandfatherly person be wanting?) Then, as her fellow traveller reached in his pocket to produce a ticket, the light dawned, and she delved into her bag for her own.

'This is for second class, love.'

'Please?'

'French,' explained the businessman smugly. Wasn't he just that type, though? The sort who had to know a thing before the next person. His port-and-stilton face was flushed with its own importance. 'Doesn't speak a word of English. She's a student, as far as I can make out. Here on some kind of exchange.'

'Well, I can't help that. She can't stay in first. She'll have to pay up and look pleasant, or move on down to second.'

'Oh, come now, have a heart. She's just a kid. An innocent abroad.'

'Never mind "have a heart". I have a job to do.'

'But it's jam-packed in second. I happened to see. They're squashed in like sardines. There's not room to swing a cat.'

Michele dropped her head to study her ticket. Was there something wrong with it? Was it in some way invalid? Oh, the British system was so bewildering! When she showed her face again, it had assumed an expression of sheer mystification.

'Look, look, I'll tell you what. *I'll* pay the difference.' Her new friend and ally brought out a fat wallet, extracted a fiver and proffered it. 'Here. Take what you need out of this. Or will it not suffice?'

'Ah, well, wait now . . .' The official was not altogether happy with the turn of events. He raked his peaked cap back on his head, then pulled it down over his eyes to accessorise his frown. It was for him, if anyone, to be magnanimous. 'I suppose, this once . . . though tell no one, mind, or you'll get me shot.'

'Jobsworth,' remarked the businessman as the door rolled closed behind the inspector.

'Please?'

'Little Hitler. That is . . . just a figure of speech, you understand. Did you say you were German? Oh, forget it. Don't worry your pretty head about it.'

He had embarrassed himself. Up went the *Daily Telegraph* again, this time in self-protection, a physical barrier between them.

What would it be like to be French? Or German? To think in some other language. You could not but be a different person – or so it seemed to Shell. She had only once been abroad – with the school, to Versailles, where they'd seen a huge palace, and got drunk in a bar and 'run amok' as the teacher in charge had reported it. And she'd not had seaside holidays or that sort of thing, with her nan – for money did not grow on trees, and anyway, east, west, home was best. Shell had now and then hitched to Brighton, a short run down the A23. But mostly she hung around Croydon. Croydon for a pretty girl, as Nanny would often say. Sutton for mutton. Cheam for roast beef. And Mitcham for a thief.

She stared for a while at the man across from her, at the stubby fingers which held the newspaper aloft, and which now and then chivvied it as it started to collapse under its own weight (and how heavy, how *heavy*, all those long and earnest words must be!).

Two minutes out of Shaftesbury, hearing perhaps the particular song of the rails, and knowing precisely where they were, he finally lowered the paper, regarded her speculatively over the top of it, folded it, set it aside and stood up to heave down his briefcase from the rack.

Shell stretched like a marmalade cat, stood up and slid

into her denim jacket. She hopped off the train ahead of the man, but he closed in on her at the ticket gate (she felt, or fancied she did, his warm breath on the back of her neck).

Turning, she gave him one of her palest smiles. 'Thank you for offering to pay the difference. And you were right about one thing: I am here on some sort of exchange.'

Before he could respond she ran for a taxi, carrying with her the image of his startled face. Then, ducking, she spoke through the cab window to the driver, to tell him her destination.

———— • ————

'Blue ear disease,' said Tobias, of a swine infection which had been hot news in *Farmer's Weekly*, afflicting continental *cochons* and now threatening to cross the channel, to lay low the British porker. He said it twice. 'Blue ear disease.' Then, when he did not receive the courtesy of a reply, he sighed, picked up a stick and threw it for Pasha who, with tongue flapping and spittle flying, went bucketing through the long, drenched grass to retrieve it.

The great thing about dogs, Tobias reflected, or *one* of the great things, was that you knew where you stood with them. They didn't blow hot and cold the way people did.

What was the matter with everyone lately? The wicked stepmother, the old ratbag, had been at her worst in recent weeks, even driving out the delightful Mary Dowdeswell, who had been so decorative, such a joy to see around the place, particularly when she bent to scrub the bathtub, or to tuck in the bedsheets, doing neat, tight hospital corners.

And what of Jasper? In the past few months he had been visibly wasting, not actually physically, but morally; frittering his time, dissipating as a person, so that the move to Paris, his ultimate disappearance from the scene, had seemed no more than the final stage in an attenuated process of disintegration.

Then, most worrying of all, what of Father? Sir John, at the best of times vague and abstracted, seemed to have moved out of his head altogether, to have gone down to live in his boots, leaving the lights ablaze up top, the doors and windows swinging wide.

Tobias was a simple soul, not troubled by temperament. He did not, he liked to think, have his brother's delicate sensibilities or his lack of resilience. So long as he might bonk around like a good'un, and drink flagons of burgundy, and gulp down plates of rare beef, and great lungfuls of country air, Toby Charteris was happy as the proverbial pig in muck whose ears betray not a tinge of blue but are ever a healthy, sprauncy pink.

He had years ago recovered from the death of his mother, the only real tragedy to have touched his life. So he knew about death; he knew that the survivors . . . well, survived.

He had been in love a couple of times, and been given the heave-ho, so he knew about that too; he knew it was getoverable.

He'd had no experience of financial hardship, let alone of poverty, and was eternally thankful for that. A man's wealth, he had heard it said, was his enemy. Well, with enemies like wealth, who needed friends! It was great to be rich; it was such freedom. Until the capitalist system came to a sticky end, as Hilary-with-the-big-boobs had warned that it must, until the day when it would be pulled apart by its own internal thingummyjigs, he intended to thrive under it. And thrive he did.

There was no cloud in his sky, then, except . . .

'I say,' he said, aiming a kick at a tall, spiny thistle, which snapped in half and bled sap. 'Everything all right, is it? I mean, there's nothing wrong, is there?'

'What?' Sir John stood still, listing slightly, turned his face to the sky and hooked his thumbs into the back of his belt. The ghost of something passed behind his eyes.

'You seem a bit pensive. One might even say "worried". I thought there might be something up with you.'

'With me? Oh, no, no, no. Nothing wrong with me.' When Sir John sighed it went right down deep, came right back up again, got caught up in his throat and fluttered there. 'It's just . . .'

'Yes?'

'Well, it's Laura. She doesn't seem quite herself these days.'

Au contraire, Tobias might have said, had not tact prevailed, in his judgement Laura was very much herself, only more so. All right, she was behaving like a first-rate bitch. So what? Laura *was* a bitch. That was the point of her.

He had nothing against his stepmother, or against bitches in general. They had their place in society, they had a function, if only to keep a chap on his toes, to test his mettle. The mistake was to imagine that these women were anything other – either better or worse – than they were.

Sir John, for instance, seemed curiously to have overlooked the fact that his second wife, beautiful though she might be to behold, was at heart a grade-A hellhag, the harpies' harpy.

Meanwhile Jasper, in an opposite way, had her horridness all out of proportion. He was older, of course, he had been closer to and more vividly remembered their mother. Naturally he had always resented her replacement. So had Toby, truth to tell, in the beginning. But while Toby had adjusted, Jasper seemingly could not. Far from growing up and growing out of it, he had if anything been getting worse, to the point where he could not apparently be in the same room as Laura, could not look her in the eye or exchange one civil word with her.

'I expect it's just chemical,' offered Toby, with a lightness which he did not feel. 'You know how women are, they're slaves to their hormones.'

'You might be right.'

'Hey . . .' A smile spread like butter across Tobias's face. 'Why does it take a woman with PMT twenty-four hours to cook a chicken?'

No response.

'Because it fucking does, all right?' he screeched.

'Eh? Oh, a joke, what?'

'Yes, a joke, what? Well, *I* thought it was funny.'

'Oh, yes. Yes, very amusing. The trouble is, you see . . .' There was that stirring there, again, behind John's eyes. 'I don't seem able to talk to her. To help her. I'd move heaven and earth to make her smile again. But it's pretty impossible when she won't even say what's wrong, what?'

'Could be she can't say,' Tobias mused, screwing up his face so his eyes and brows looked like one continuous, heavy-handed scribble. 'I mean, it could be she just feels low for no reason. It could be she's simply depressed. It happens to the best of us – well, not to me, actually, but to most people – at some time. It's episodic. In other words, it should pass of its own accord.'

'And if it doesn't?'

'Well, I'm quite sure it will. Just like that. You never know, you might go back to the house and find her bouncing up and down on the sofa with her knickers on her head, singing "Happy days are here again". You might find her and Holloway and Stevens doing a round-the-house conga, decked in streamers, wearing funny paper hats.'

'You think I should go to her? Try once more to speak to her?'

Tobias shrugged. 'My instinct would be to leave her alone. Give her some space.'

'Space? Oh, right! Space, eh?'

'I mean, be there if she wants you. Just be there. Don't push it.'

'No? No. Right-ho.'

'I remember when Fleur Fordyce was giving me a hard time because – '

'There might be some perfectly simple solution.'

'It's not as if she's too shy to tell you when there's some little thing her heart desires.'

'That's true. Do you suppose she's missing Caroline?'

'I suspect not.' Toby stooped to pick up another stick and chucked it for Pasha. 'No earthly use your worrying yourself silly about it, whatever. That won't help her if she has the blues. Talking of which, I was reading in *Farmer's Weekly*. There's this thing called blue ear disease – '

'Sunshine!'

'Excuse me?'

'What she needs is some sunshine!' Sir John declared excitedly. And, warming to his theme, 'I was reading in the paper the other day about this thing they call SAD. It stands for . . . uhm, for seasonal something disorder. Some people get really down in the dumps if they don't get enough sun.'

'The sun was shining beautifully the day before yesterday. I had my shirt off.'

'Even so, even so . . .' Sir John all at once began to jib like a tethered horse, to dance around as if at the end of a rope. 'I'll leave you to it, what? To check the fences. I'll cut along back to the house and have a word with her. "Book a flight," I'll tell her. "Anywhere in the world you want to go. You name it. We'll jet away, just the two of us. It will be like a second honeymoon. What say?"'

'I honestly think – '

'A little holiday. Just the job. Just what the doctor ordered.'

'If you take my advice – ' ventured Toby. But his father was already off at a canter. He could do nothing but stand there, watching John's retreating back, and feeling for him, fearing for him, till his heart ached.

———————— • ————————

'Drop me here,' said Shell, 'at the gate. I can walk the rest.' For it would not be on, really, to go swishing right up to the door in full view of everyone. Better to do a recce, to get the lie of the land. In any case, she needed time to collect her wits. She was about as nervous as it was in her to be; she felt unwell with it. It wasn't like her to get in a tizz, she was usually pretty laid-back, but this was all so far outside her everyday experience, and she felt such a long, long way from home.

'Mixing with the nobs, are we?' enquired the cab driver affably. When he put his foot on the pedal, the brakes snatched to the right and the car breasted the white line, before he jerked the wheel and drove them at the ditch.

'For all you know, I *am* a nob.'

'And for all *you* know, I'm Queen Nefertiti' (he pronounced it 'titty').

'Well, *are* you?'

'I am, as it happens. Or used to be. I'm her re-incarnation. Trapped on this earthly plane, this mortal coil. Doomed to walk the planet until Kingdom Come, or until Bristol Rovers win the cup, whichever is the sooner. I have been back innumerable times, as you may imagine, down the millennia, once as a Roman Centurion, once – no, I tell a lie, *twice* – as a milkmaid. I was also Cardinal Wolsey, Marie Antoinette, William Tell and Jack the bleedin' Ripper. That will be four pounds fifty to you, beautiful. Or a fiver if you want my autograph.'

'There was no such person as William Tell. He's a made-up character. I saw a programme.'

'I was a different William Tell. William H. Tell, of number three The Parade, Frinton-on-Sea. Now, you got that five pounds?'

'You said four-fifty.'

'It's customary to offer a little thank you to the driver, you know. A modest gratuity, say ten per cent.'

'Oh, here, then.' She thrust a five-pound note at him. 'Now, can I have my fingers back?'

Grinning he loosed his grip and she reclaimed her hand, wiping it ostentatiously on her flank. 'Do keep the change.'

'That's uncommonly decent of you.'

'Put it towards getting the brakes fixed.'

'I'll do that.'

She slid along the seat and opened the nearside door.

'Haven't I seen you somewhere before?'

'Croydon?' she suggested indifferently.

'No, no, at the Pyramids of Giza. In about two thousand BC. Only your hair was different. Very straight. With a long fringe.'

'I don't remember.'

'Well, it was a long time ago.'

When she eased out of the car her skirt rode right up to her nice white Marks and Sparks knickers. 'Yeah,' said the driver, 'I've definitely seen you before.'

'Well, I don't expect you'll see me again. Unless it's in hell.' She slammed the door.

He tooted his horn as he drove away, but she spared him neither wave nor glance. He was just another comedian, one of the countless thousands of dickheads she had met in her time, who liked to have a laugh and a joke with her, who flattered themselves that she was tickled pink by their attentions.

Within two seconds she had forgotten she'd ever met him.

'Bloody hell!' she thought as she stared at the iron gates, at gateposts topped off with lions rampant, at the gravelled drive which, just as she'd imagined, went off to right and left, with a polite notice asking drivers to proceed at no more than five miles an hour.

From here it was not possible to glimpse the house, for enfolded within the two arms of the drive was a thicket of lush, black-green rhododendrons as tall as a block of flats, obscuring all that lay beyond. But when she ventured a few yards, following the curve, there came into view a building so unbelievably big and beautiful, so grand and so gracious, that she declared herself, to herself, gobsmacked.

Blimey, the place must have a hundred rooms. Or at any rate forty or fifty. It was bigger than the Fairfield Halls. As big as Mayday Hospital and twenty times as lovely. It was like Buckingham Palace, only a sort of yellowy gold. And there were lawns, and shrubs, and trees, and fields, and easy, lazy hills on every hand.

She really nearly lost her nerve then. She just stood and stood. Oh, what *was* she doing here? What *had* Nanny Fairchild been thinking of? What had the silly old woman, in her crazy way, let her in for?

It would have been the simplest thing in the world, at that minute, to turn around and beat it to the village, to have a half a shandy in the pub, and a bag of crisps, and to wait for a bus back to the station.

As she hesitated, a tall, rangy man appeared up ahead, hurrying across the rollered grass, his stride uneven, so he pitched to the right the way children do when playing at being horses. He was casually, even scruffily dressed. She supposed he was a gardener.

She waited for him to disappear from view, counted slowly to fifty, then drew in her breath and marched up to the front door. She had come this far, her courage must not fail her now.

'Ye-es?' said the grey-faced, stiff-suited, unsmiling man who answered the summons of the bell.

'I . . .' said Shell. 'I just . . .'

'Are you from the agency? Have you come about the position?'

'I, er . . .'

Inside, behind the man's left shoulder, a brief sound bite, a snatch of argument, signalled that a door had opened abruptly, and had just as abruptly closed. She heard a woman shouting, saying '– me alone, don't keep going on at me, with your stupid, idiotic ideas. Second honeymoo– ' Then there were leaden footsteps on the flagstoned floor, a man's tread getting softer and softer until it died away.

'Kindly call at the side door,' said the butler character, betraying by not so much as a twitch or flicker that any of this had been audible to him. And, 'Yes, that's it,' he confirmed, following her bewildered gaze. 'Round there by the little path, and down the steps. Knock and ask for Mrs Holloway.'

Holloway, said Shell to herself as she followed his directions. Never mind Holloway. I shall be *in* Holloway if I don't watch myself. I shall get myself banged up for blackmail. Or for fraud. Or extortion. Or at the very least trespass. If Nanny's got it wrong – and she *might* have got it wrong; it all sounds so crazy – I'll be in deepest doo-doo, I'll be in shit up to my sodding ears.

Still, there was no law, was there, that said you couldn't go after a job? No law that said you couldn't knock and ask for Mrs Holloway.

So, 'I'm Michele Fairchild,' she said when a big woman with a bun came to open the door. 'The gentleman sent me round here to ask about the job.'

'You're from the agency? Well, I am glad to see you! I've been run ragged since yesterday afternoon. But that was good of them, wasn't it? They said they weren't sure. They were very short-handed. They said not to expect . . . Look, come through, do, and take off your coat. My goodness, are you warm enough? You're dressed for a heatwave.' Mrs Holloway's tongue went trot-trot-trot on the roof of her mouth.

'Oh, yes,' said Shell cheerfully, following her into the extensive kitchen, where a dishwasher grumbled mildly about its lot. 'I have very warm blood.' She felt quite comfortable now, in the presence of the doughty Mrs H. Perhaps it was her upbringing, her being always so close to Nanny Fairchild. Anyway, for whatever reason, she related to older women, who were themselves, usually, oddly protective of her.

'Have you come far? From town?' asked Mrs Holloway through a mouth that bristled with hairpins, as she attended to her bun. 'You're not a local girl, or I'd have seen you about. I *haven't* seen you, have I? And yet . . .'

'Oh, people are always thinking that. Saying don't they know me from somewhere. The taxi driver asked the same thing.'

'You can live in if it suits you. It suits *us*, actually. And what with having to make an early start. Your work day begins at seven sharp. You'll soon find your way around here. What do you think?'

'Mm,' said Shell, sitting down at the long table, resting her chin in her hand. For wasn't this what Nanny had wanted for her? To get a foot in the door. 'I should like to live at Hartwell. Yes. Thanks very much.'

CHAPTER

——— • ———

8

'Surprise!'

For one bewildering moment it seemed to Caroline that Birnam Wood had come to Dunsinane. But it was worse than that. Far worse. For Maudie Grant had come to Battersea. She was here, now, on the threshold, holding in her gloved hands a large, unprepossessing potted plant, crinkly leaves which trembled as if in dreadful anticipation, on a single woody stem, in the up-draught from the stairwell.

'Oh!' said Caroline, appalled, turning puce, plugging her mouth with a bunched fist, biting hard on her knuckles, and peering in agitation past her visitor, as if for an escape, at the low-lit, black-and-rust-tiled landing, where the lift car, having delivered up her maternal grandmother, waited in its wire-mesh cage for whoever should command it.

This was no way, of course, to greet one's aged relative when she dropped by bearing gifts. But the situation was dire. Maudie could not, she *must* not, come in.

'I wasn't expecting . . .' Caroline strait-jacketed herself with her arms, crossing them in front of her, holding hard to her sides. Her bare toes curled, shrimp-like and pink, into the coconut matting. She must not budge, but must stand her ground.

If only she'd not answered the door! But it seemed so rude, somehow, to leave people standing out there knocking and ringing. And how could she have known who it was? Once callers had breached the street door, bypassing the entryphone, as they were too often able to do, the only means to identify them was to open up. Anyway, no one normally came here unannounced, except Jehovah's Witnesses, and ladies collecting the Christian Aid envelopes, and small boys in baseball caps, with comically grimy faces, wanting to know if they could wash your motor.

'It's eleven o'clock,' said Maudie with a strong hint of reproof.

'I know. But it is Sunday.' With something more than ruefulness, Caroline glanced down at herself, at the shirt she had pulled on in haste, and, fumbling, had failed to button. She looked with dislike upon her legs poking out from beneath the hem: upon her dimpled, doughnut knees.

'It's a beautiful morning. Very crisp,' Maudie informed her, very crisp herself.

'Yes, yes. I saw. From the window.' Drawing the shirt tighter around herself, in a spirit more of self-protection than of modesty, Caroline then said in desperation, 'And the wallabies!'

'I beg your pardon?'

'In the park. Just over the road. There are wallabies. Hopping about all over the place. Oh, *do* go now and see them, Granny! They're terribly sweet.'

'Caroline, have you been drinking? Or taking some kind of hallucinogenic drug? Or are you ill? Is that it?'

'Of course not. There *are* wallabies, I swear. Loose in the park. Please go and look if you don't believe me. They're like kangaroos, only just this big.' She spared one hand to demonstrate, measuring, palm downwards, patting the air, two foot, three foot, three foot six from the floor. 'With pockets and everything. If you're quick you'll catch them. Before they move on. They do move around, you see.'

But Maudie Grant had not come all the way across the river to see marsupials, either real or imagined. She had come to visit her granddaughter, and to be given the guided tour of her flat. She would have been here long ago, but she'd been awaiting an invitation – something in writing, on a stiff piece of card – which had simply not forthcome. Allowing a couple of months for sorting out and settling in, she'd been expecting for two years to be formally asked, and that had finally seemed to her to be time enough.

'Well, I'm sure they're quite a feature,' she said sniffily, confirmed in her suspicion that it was all very wild and woolly and bohemian on the southside of the Thames. She thrust the plant at Caroline, forcing her to embrace it, to clutch it to her chest; then turning sideways she slotted herself in, slid between granddaughter and door jamb and, skinning her hands, stripping off the close-fitting gloves, sailed down the narrow hall on a tour of inspection.

'It's just that . . .' protested Caroline, sick with despair, 'I'm in a bit of a mess at the moment.'

Nor did she mean by this the state of the place, the crockery piled high in the greasy sink, the pans of slurry on the stove, which were a sad reflection of the state of her mind, of her emotions in turmoil. She was in it, now, so very deep. She was in it over her head and drowning.

'I shall take you as I find you,' Maudie assured her with patent insincerity, making for the door at the end of the passage, where her instinct assured her the sitting room must be.

Only it wasn't.

Her dominant impression as she barged into the bedroom was one of chaos. A zip-up bag in the middle of the floor would appear to have exploded: its contents had been flung in all directions. Everywhere, there were balled-up socks, odd shoes and tangled T-shirts. There was a pair of blue underpants, forming a faintly indecent figure of eight, as if their occupant had simply dropped and stepped out of them (the picture they brought to mind was not a pretty one). On the bedside table wine glasses had been left to encrust with red sediment. Garments had been piled high upon the dressing table, to suffocate the mirror behind.

The room smelled, too, of overheated humanity, of both the male and the female of the species cooking up together. There was a smack of collusion, something secretive and alienating in the air which made her fastidious nostrils quiver.

For a matter of a second, to Maudie Grant's affronted eye, the young man lying there in bed, jacked up on one elbow, exchanging with her look for aghast look, was not distinct from but mere part of this rough-house, no more out of place than the single capsized stiletto sandal, the black and lacy brassière which strangled a chair leg, the litter of empty envelopes, debris of so many mornings' mail.

'It's not what you think,' offered Caroline in a tiny, childish, pathetic voice, standing at Maudie's elbow, still clutching the waving plant, a housewarming present (as if this house were not already fugged enough with heat). And it wasn't of course – it was not at all what Maudie thought. It was far more serious than she could even hazard.

'Caroline!' With shock, distaste and genuine concern, Maudie turned to gape at her. Was her little girl, her granddaughter, going to the dogs as her daughter had done? Was she more Laura's child than any of them had supposed?

This was perhaps not the time to effect introductions, to say 'Granny, this is Patrick; Patrick, Granny.' Instead, 'I could make some tea,' offered Caroline.

But what *could* she have been thinking of? For tea contains caffeine, which attacks the central nervous system, causing insomnia, depression, headaches and tremors, increasing tension. It overstimulates the adrenal glands, resulting in rebound hypoglycaemia. It inhibits the absorption of iron, zinc and calcium. It is toxic and addictive, brings you out in spots and is a cause of dark circles under the eyes. Tea, particularly in these stressful circumstances, was not the thing at all.

'Just a glass of water,' said Maudie faintly, blindfolding herself with one blue-white hand.

'Look, do please come through to the sitting room and
. . . you know, sit down.'

Caroline went ahead of her, back along the passageway, to the light and airy front room with its green view
of treetops, its pale eau-de-nil walls which, pretty though
they were, made everyone look washed-out half to
death. She set the plant on the table and, backing out,
blushing scarlet, said, 'I'll just make myself decent.'

When Maudie, still shading her eyes, sat down heavily
in a wood-frame chair, a strip of rubbery webbing
snapped under her bony behind with an audible twang.

Down the corridor, a door closed like a cupped hand
on some urgent, whispered conversation. Oh, good
grief, what had she happened in on? Maybe, thought
Maudie, in an effort to be fair, she was too far behind the
times. The world moved on, she must remember this.

She very much did not want to think badly of Caroline,
who, leaving aside her problem, her plumpness, and the
way she played the giddy goat at times, was surely at
heart a good girl, a perfect poppet. But what a worry she
was too! Silly and susceptible. And that young man . . .
Well really! Maudie could not remember when she had
seen a more lascivious mouth. Or such sensual eyes. Or
so vigorous a growth of underarm hair. Or such naked
nakedness. She had looked for not a half a minute upon
his unclothed upper torso, yet the after-image of male
nudity would stay with her for the rest of her days.

And there was one thing more. There was something
about him which touched off a memory. Like yesterday's
dream it was there and not there. It was merged with the
black at the back of the mind, and might only be glimpsed

in the glare of an instant. It was as much a feeling as it was a picture. She felt that she knew him from somewhere.

Then there was the general disarray. The sense that everything here had gone out of control. That Caroline had lost her grip.

Or had she always been this way? When one was rich and attended by servants, untidiness was simply not an issue. Caroline could have been spoiled. She could have become too used to strewing her clothes around the floor, on the arrogant assumption that they would be picked up and laundered for her – that they would somehow, as if by magic, appear on hangers, clean and pressed – as they would doubtless have done back home at Hartwell.

The squalor offended Maudie almost as much as the sex; and each contributed to the general atmosphere of dissoluteness. Perhaps if the whole place had been spruce and neat, if the young man in the bed had had tidy hair, if he'd been wearing monogrammed silk pyjamas, and had shaved off all that nasty stubble, she might not have had this terrible, terrible sense of foreboding.

But it wasn't, and he hadn't, and she had.

'I'm sorry, Granny.' Caroline came quietly back into the room, in stockinged feet, in a demure grey dress done up to the neck. And, 'I'll get you that water,' she offered dully, going through to the kitchen and running the tap. London mains water had of course, at the last count, passed through eight people's bodies, it had flushed the contigent impurities from the kidneys of the good, the bad and the ugly, it had washed out the works of royalty and rogues. But the only bottled water in the fridge was full of fizz; and carbonated water was known to cause wind.

'Well, I don't know what you can be thinking of.' Maudie took the smeary glass from her and sipped it as if it were brandy, to be taken as medicine.

'I'm not thinking of anything.' Caroline squatted, she sat on her haunches, at her grandmother's feet. And the eyes she raised to Maudie's face gave right on to her soul, where all was desolation.

'You see,' Maudie felt she must explain, 'I can't help how I feel.'

'No more can I,' said Caroline bleakly.

'I do realise that I'm out of date. That this behaviour is to be expected nowadays among the younger generation. I do understand that. It's only – '

'You should have rung me. You shouldn't have just come like this.'

'Well, I hoped to surprise you. I hoped you'd be pleased.'

'And I would have been, if – '

'Anyway, the fact remains . . . My knowing about it, changes nothing. Caroline . . .' Maudie extended her hand and, finding no taker for it, let it hang there, upturned as if in supplication. 'I don't want to judge you.'

'No, you mustn't. I don't think you have any business doing that.' Caroline became quite agitated. Still crouching, she started to bob with emotion, to bump up and down. 'I don't believe anybody does have. Any business, I mean. No one has the right to judge. To say this is acceptable, and that isn't. Laying down the law. Who the hell do people think they are? When one is, you know, a consenting adult.' Abruptly she shot up and crossed to the window, where she stood with her arms folded, staring out.

'Most of all I don't want you to be hurt.' Maudie said it as if she meant it. Maybe she *did* mean it. She felt that she did, that this truly was paramount. 'I don't want you to be used, you understand me?'

'Used?' Caroline twisted her head to glance over her shoulder at her grandmother, who saw sudden tear streaks on her cheeks. Then, gazing unseeing across the park, she addressed her words to the window glass. 'Patrick would never use me. He loves me. That's the beauty of it. And the tragedy.' She sucked in her lower lip and bit down on it, as if to stop herself from saying more.

'It's simply that one does hear tales.' Maudie picked up her gloves and eased them on. 'I'm not saying that this boy, this, er, Patrick is a gay deceiver. But you are a wealthy young woman by anyone's standards. And you do have to think – '

'You think he wants my money? Is that what you're saying?' Caroline rounded on her grandmother, turning to her in fury, her brown eyes darting. 'You can't believe he wants me for myself. Because I'm fat or whatever.'

'Oh, now, *please* – '

'No, *you* please. I told you he loves me. And I love him. And we're beautiful to each other. Neither of us meant it to happen, but it did. And there's no way out of it that we can see.'

'Well, frankly,' Maudie shook her head in puzzlement,

'if that really is the case, I can't why should you upset
yourself so much?'

'Upset *myself*? I'm not upsetting myself. It's not me
who's upsetting me. It's . . . well, everyone else.'

When Maudie got to her feet, her knees clicked. She
thought, I'm getting old, and, momentarily at least, she
entertained that possibility. To Caroline she said, 'You're
serious about him, then?'

'Yes.'

'And he about you?'

'Yes.'

'Then where is the problem? Why should you not walk
out together? Provided he's not riff-raff.'

'There's nothing riff-raffy about him.'

'In my day we went in for courtship. For engagement
and marriage, not for these hole-and-corner affairs. We
saved ourselves for our wedding night and gave ourselves to only one man. And, d'you know, I think we
were happier for it? It was all so much simpler, don't you
see? The world was a simpler place.'

'Yes, well . . .' Caroline dropped her head, started
mumbling. She said it would be nice if everything were
simple, or some words to that effect.

'What's that you say? Speak up, child. Lift your chin.
Stand straight and grow good.'

'I said it would be nice if everything could be easy.'

'Then, why is it not? Wherein lies the difficulty?
Darling, once again, please stop muttering. What's that
you say?'

'I said, you wouldn't understand.'

'I wouldn't?' Maudie hesitated. She nearly challenged

'Try me'. But in the end she decided, Caroline was right. Probably, indeed, she wouldn't understand. So she told her instead, 'I'll be off now.'

'OK.'

'Will you see me to the door, at least?' Then, without breaking stride, as she forged ahead, 'Pick your feet up, can't you? It creates such a bad impression when you drag them.'

In the hall Maudie turned and grasped Caroline's elbow. 'You should come to me soon. To have supper. Telephone me, won't you, there's a good girl.' And she pushed out her face to be kissed.

'Gone?' asked Patrick, sitting propped against the pillows, smiling sympathetically.

'Yes. Gone, gone. But not forgotten.' Caroline sat down wearily on the bed, grasped his foot through the sheet and squeezed it. 'Not the happiest introduction to your grandmother, eh?'

'I do remember her. At least I think I do, very vaguely, from when she used to visit. I knew who she was the moment she barged in here. She was a tartar then, as now.'

'She's all right, actually,' Caroline told him. 'I mean, she is what she is. Very rigid. But she can be so kind, too.'

'Will she tell, do you suppose?'

'Tell who? Laura? Why? What's to tell? That she came round and caught me in bed with a boy. So what? There's no law against that, is there? Neither of us is below the age of consent. And Laura can't exactly shout. She's had more men than you and I have had hot dinners.'

'Oh, Carrie, I love your posh accent.' He doubled at the waist, inclined towards her, hooked his hand around her neck and drew her to him. When she rolled on her hip and rested her head against his chest, his heart-thud sounded urgent in her ear. 'You mustn't cry now,' he scolded gently as the tears started again. 'It makes you go all blotchy and your nose runs.'

'I know.' She uttered a sound that was neither a sob nor a laugh, a bleakly humorous sort of coughing noise, and rummaged up her sleeve for a tissue. 'All my life I'd wished I could just shed crystal tears which would make my eyes sparkle, instead of having that horrid puffy look. I cried a lot, of course, as a little girl, which made it worse.'

'Why "of course"?'

'Well, because of the way things were. And the way I am. I'm most terribly wet.'

'*I* don't think you are. I think you're strong and brave.'

'Lavinia – you know, my friend Lavinia Pine? – used to say to me, "You've been booing again, you cry-baby. What's the matter now?" '

'She doesn't sound much of a person, this Lavinia, from all that you tell me about her. She doesn't seem much of a pal.'

'She wasn't. *Isn't*. But she's a sort of habit. Like smoking. I wish I could give her up, but the best I have managed to do is to cut down quite drastically.'

'Well, if you take my advice, you'll kick her altogether,' he told her, rocking her. 'I don't think she does you any good.'

'No, but she doesn't do me harm. Not any more.'

Her head felt as if it had been pumped up to bursting point; the pressure between her ears was unbearable. The veins in her temples throbbed. But it was wonderfully soothing to be held this way, to have Patrick cuddle her, to feel his breath parting her hair. How *can* this be wrong? she asked, but not aloud, because she felt they had exhausted that subject – or, rather, it had exhausted them. They had talked and talked around it and had come up with no answers. Always, it distressed them. Never, ever, could they hope to find salvation.

'We'll find a way to be together,' he would insist, 'no matter what.'

'But to have to make a secret of our love. Or of our true relationship. To go on and on living a lie. How can we endure that for ever?'

'How can we *not*, if there is no other choice?'

'What if we're caught? What then?'

'Who could prove anything? Who could know anything for sure?'

'I always supposed,' she confessed now, because in the end the topic was as irresistible as a damaged tooth to the tongue, 'that I would grow up, and find someone daft enough to marry me, and have his children, and be thoroughly normal.'

'You are thoroughly normal.'

'I'm not sure that's much of a compliment.'

'Oh, it is from me. It's what I most admire: normality. Having seen so little of it. It's the most underrated of virtues, if you ask my opinion.'

'I don't think it even ranks as a virtue in anyone's book

but yours. Or even a trait. It's not about personality. It's more a state of being.'

'It's a great way to be, though, isn't it?' He took hold of her chin and tipped her face up. 'Would you look at you now! All snotty.'

'I'm not.' She dashed her sleeve under her nose and he kissed her. She felt she'd just die without his kisses.

'We're not the first ones ever to have this happen,' he told her.

'I do know that.'

'You read about it in the papers every now and again.'

'*I* used to read about it in the papers. Then I'd think "How disgusting!" I'd think, "Oh, how *could* they? Those terrible people!" And that's what others would think about us.'

'Let them, then. If they must.'

'If it ever gets out. If it comes to be known. If it goes in the – Oh, my God, Patrick, if it went in the papers . . .'

'It won't though. We're too discreet.'

'But it *could*. Somehow it might. I mean, those other couples, brothers and sisters, they all got found out in the end.'

'What's this "all", then? How can you say "all"? There could be thousands and thousands of people like us, living a double life, and nobody – not their friends or families, or their next-door neighbours – ever for one moment imagining it.'

'You don't think we're so freaky, then?'

'We're only half, after all. Half and half.'

'Having different fathers. I'm not sure that makes it any better. In the eyes of the law, at least.'

'We could live abroad. How would that be? Where nobody knew us from Adam.'

'I've thought about that. We could do it, I suppose. If we were driven.'

'You wouldn't want to?'

'I wouldn't mind running *to* something. But I shouldn't want just to run *from*.'

'We're like Lord Byron and Augusta. She had his child, it's said.'

'What happened to that child? Was he all right? Was he healthy?' She was trying to shape a thought, but it proved unthinkable, too enormous for her brain to comprehend.

'He was a she. I don't know anything more.'

'We did Byron at school, for our A-levels,' she remembered. 'There was this poem I loved so much, I copied it down. There was a bit that went: "They name thee before me, A knell to mine ear; A diddly-diddly – Why wert thou so dear?" '

'What's this "diddly-diddly" stuff?'

'Shush. Listen. It goes on: "They know not I knew thee, Who knew thee too well. Long, long shall I rue thee, Too deeply to tell." Now, what do you suppose all that was about? Augusta?'

'Maybe.'

'Do you like it?'

'What I've heard of it. Especially the diddly-diddly.'

'It has special resonance now, though, doesn't it?' she asked mistily.

'It has that all right. Look, Carrie, take that dress off, will you, and come back to bed for half an hour.'

'No. No, not now. I want to tidy up. To get the place a bit straight. I think I shall feel better if I do.'

'Will I help you?'

'Yes, of course. You ought to, oughtn't you? Since so much of this junk is yours.'

'A lot of it is mine. But none of it is junk. Don't you go throwing things away, you hear?'

When she got to her feet he slid out from between the sheets and stood there scratching under his ribs. There was a swirl of dark hair around his navel, like bathwater going down the plughole. He had a huge and persistent erection, a sort of physical manifestation of his enduring optimism. It would all, went his attitude, come good.

'Just sort out everything that wants washing. We'll put a load in the machine.'

'Whatever you say, lady.'

'Come on, Patrick,' she pleaded as he swept aside her blonde hair and planted a kiss on her neck. Her insides seemed to deliquesce and she swayed back against him. And, 'Oh, my God, I do love you,' she said.

'It's love all right,' he agreed.

He'd had girlfriends before, he had told her. Half a dozen or more. But this was different, this was like nothing he had ever known. And she believed him. For when he grabbed her hand and squeezed it, and sought her eyes with his, how could she for a minute doubt it?

It actually seemed – this most unnatural of things – to be the most natural thing in the world. This tall, dark, boyish, exuberant youth was in love with her – naturally. He had been smitten as she had, by the same bolt of lightning, the same *coup de foudre*.

But no one else on earth would condone such love. No one else would ever understand it.

Maudie Grant didn't understand it. Over a solitary Sunday lunch – which at Onslow Gardens was a modest affair, short on protein, rich in lightly cooked, fresh green vegetables – her thoughts kept returning to the matter of Caroline, and to the young man in Caroline's bed.

Who was he, and what did he want?

The truth was – and in the privacy of one's own home, in one's own mind, one frankly had to face it – that a lad like this, with so wide and full a mouth, and a boxer's nose, and sleepy eyes, and such indecent quantities of body hair, was almost certain to be after something.

He might be called good-looking if that was the sort of thing that appealed to you. He might be termed a 'dish', even a 'dreamboat'. He could have his pick, this was the point, of any number of nubile lovelies. In which case, well, why Caroline?

Because, while Caroline Charteris was not without her charms – let nobody say she was without them! – she was also pink-faced and fluttery and afflicted with puppy fat.

She was pretty, of course, that was not to be denied. But to be merely pretty was seldom sufficient. To Maudie, indeed, it was just not conceivable that it would suffice for someone such as . . . what had Caroline called him? Someone such as Patrick.

I don't trust him, Maudie thought darkly, as she sipped a slippery elm tisane to settle her stomach, to aid digestion and, it was to be hoped, to soothe the physical symptoms of her disquiet. There's more to this than meets the eye, she told herself darkly – as if what met the eye were not worrying enough.

'He wouldn't use me,' Caroline had insisted. 'He loves me,' she'd said. And she'd seemed so certain of it. But one must never underestimate the willingness of a woman to be duped by a man. Maudie now and then despaired of her sex, who seemed so often to be drawn to cads and bounders. Look what happened when a fellow was sent to prison. Inevitably, and however heinous his crime, there would be some snivelling wife or girlfriend in the background, declaring to the world that she would wait for him. Then look at all those Members of Parliament, at the Ministers for This and That, caught up in scandalous affairs. Look at Cecil Parkinson, who had been such a disappointment. See how his wife had stood by him.

There was no end, d'you see, to the female capacity for self-delusion. Why, even Laura, with her tremendous advantages, and with a streak of iron running right through her soul, had deceived herself over Karasinski. It was all such a puzzle. For, make no mistake, if her own husband, Monty, had so much as looked at another woman, Maudie would have given him his marching orders.

Call me old-fashioned, she thought as she set cup down in saucer – and as Aggie, for forty years her cook-housekeeper, with her uncanny sense of timing, came creaking in to clear away – but no good has ever come, or ever will, from all this loose morality.

She regretted now, in hindsight, having given Caroline that lovely necklace. Oh, pray she had it somewhere under lock and key! It should be in a safe deposit, or at the very least a safe, beyond the reach of light-fingered philanderers. For suppose this Patrick person turned out to be not just a profligate but a petty thief?

There were times, and this was one of them, when Maudie felt the lack of anyone with whom to share her fears. Thus it was with a certain resentment that she called to mind Monty, who had let her down so badly by dying as he had done, years too soon and without a fight, in the kind of pain that drains the eyes of their colour, leaving her to cope alone with an impossible little girl.

She couldn't help it. Even now she found it hard to forgive him for his shoddy behaviour, for his failure to do the square thing by his wife and his child. Might she not have expected better from one who had been an officer in the Guards? And to what extent had his death been to blame for the way Laura had gone off the rails?

Maudie Grant wanted, not so much for an exchange of ideas – why should she wish to trade those she had, which were thoroughly sound and serviceable, for anyone else's half-baked notions? – as for a chance to speak her mind. The need was so strong in her that she nearly called Laura. But, in the end, it was not *that* strong.

Maudie did not entertain the full range of human emotions, many of which were, in her view, indulgent, soppy, sloppy and self-destructive. She had managed to cut down to a manageable six or seven, which seemed to cover most contingencies (Laura had done a similar thing, though in a much higher register), and ideally she would have liked to reduce even further, to find some kind of set point, to feel every day the same. She didn't have any truck with grief, for instance, or yet with joy. But she was still strong on vexation, and it vexed her to see how life blew through Caroline as a gale might through a house, so all the doors went crashing and bashing, and the lights swung loopily about.

'Foolish child,' she said aloud, reaching for her paper, for the *Sunday Times*, for the review section, which might offer light relief.

On page three, beneath the 'Interview' tag-line, was a photograph which gave her pause. The face was familiar, although rage, elation, passion, depression – all those silly feelings upon which such a man would squander his energies – had sketched in many lines since last she saw him. She knew that dishevelled look, that handsome countenance, knew the big, rude mouth, the ruffled hair, the hirsutism, the snarling sexuality.

Her eye wandered over the text – after a decade in the wilderness, it said, Tom Mulryan was back with a hard-hitting drama for Channel 4 – and then she knew too, with all the force of certainty, who it was that she had seen in Caroline's bed. That young man had been Patrick. Patrick Mulryan. Her other grandchild.

As she got to her feet, all those dreadful emotions which she'd hoped she'd excluded came upon her in one mad rush and knocked her senseless.

It ought not to have happened. It wasn't just. Maudie Grant, who knew all there was to know about free radical scavengers, about trans fatty acids, who could tell her mono from her poly unsaturates, who had given cholesterol no quarter, who had never smoked and who drank only in strict moderation, she who had had not a day's illness in her life, was laid low by the shock.

But then, there is no justice.

CHAPTER

9

'Hartwell'
Dorset

December 3, 1990

Dearest Nan,

Well here I am as you can see at the big house. It was funny how it turned out. I just sort of walked into a job. The last girl went off in a sulk or something as far as I can gather so now I'm the 'skivvy'. I know it's not what we discussed but I'm working round to it in my own way. I'm getting everything sussed before I make a move.

You wouldn't believe this place. You'd die if you saw it. 'Stevens' says that parts of the house go back to the eighteenth century. And the building alone is as big as the 'Whitgift Centre' – no word of a lie. Then there's acres of garden and a farm and everything much as you imagined it would be.

'Stevens' is the butler by the way. He's a bit of a 'dry old stick' but I don't mind him. And 'Mrs

Holloway' the housekeeper likes me. She calls me moppet.

I haven't seen 'her ladyship' yet but I did see 'Sir John' and he smiled and said hello in a nice way. They do say he's a kind man and everybody looks up to him not just because he's very tall. They don't say if 'she' is kind or not but I get the impression she has a temper. Isn't that what you said though – that she had a temper on her? Anyway she went off in a hurry yesterday and it seems her mother has been taken ill so I shall have to wait awhile to put 'Plan A' into operation.

Oh Nanny you really have put me up for it haven't you? I know you have my best interests at heart but I'm not sure if I can go through with all this. We were all right as we were weren't we?

The younger 'Charteris' brother is called 'Tobias' and he has a loud laugh like a horse. You can hear him from right the other end of the house. He looks after the farm and has a good suntan and is very jolly. The older one is away in France writing a book. And the daughter works in London and hasn't been near or by them in an age. See how much I've picked up in so little time!!! That's because they like a good old gossip 'below stairs'.

I have my own room on the top floor with flowery curtains. You'd like it, it's your taste.

I have to go now to catch the post and then I'm to do the silver.

I copied down the family motto which is 'Gloria Virtutis Umbra' but I don't know who it's referring to. I asked 'Mrs H' who this 'Gloria Virtutis' was and she said Run along now, stop your nonsense!

I shall need my cards by the way. Can you ask at the salon for my P45 and send it me soon. Tell them I'm sorry for not coming back and I'll explain 'all' to them later. Say I miss them will you? And give 'Jules' a big wet kiss from me.

Tomorrow I'm going to 'Shaftesbury' with 'Mrs H'. I need a new uniform making as there isn't one in my size. The one I got fits where it touches. I always was a 'skinny lizzie' as you say and I think I'm losing weight through worrying about all this. I hope that doesn't sound ungrateful.

I love you always and I know you meant well.

Luv, Shell.

S.W.A.L.K. xxxxxxooooxxx

When Michele licked the envelope she nicked the corner of her mouth, 'Ouch! Sod it!' she muttered, swabbing it with the tip of her tongue, dabbing at it with her little finger. It was funny when you came to think of it, wasn't it? Looking at a piece of paper, you would never guess that it could cut you. Yet it could hurt more than a knife. It could make you bloody sore.

With rather more care she affixed the stamp and hammered it with her fist. She'd have to dash or she'd miss the midday collection, and meanwhile Nanny would be going mad, wondering if everything was all right, and how she was getting on. She'd spent longer than she'd intended over her letter, chewing the end of her felt-tip pen and staring huge-eyed at the wall as she composed. Now glancing at her watch she saw it was nearly twelve.

She was supposed to use the narrow, winding service stairs, to be as far as possible invisible; Mrs H had been very firm about that. But it would be quicker to go by the main staircase, so she decided to take a chance. There was no danger, at least, that she would run into the famous – and so far elusive – Laura. Nor was Sir John likely to take notice if he saw her. He had this sort of faraway aspect about him, as if he hardly knew what day it was. Of course Mrs H would shout the odds if she caught her, she'd say 'Didn't I tell you to come down the back way?' But Shell wasn't worried about Mrs H.

Now, if a thing was worth doing, Nanny Fairchild always said, it was worth doing well. And on that, she and Mrs Holloway were at one. If the curtains were to be drawn here at Hartwell, they must be drawn just so, to fall in neat and regular pleats. If fresh flowers were called for, they must not simply be jammed into a vase, but must be arranged with care, stem by stem, in fresh water with a tablet of soluble aspirin. If she asked you to clean the toilet, that meant doing under the rim (she carried a little mirror for inspection purposes). And if the great staircase were to be polished, it must be polished to within one inch of its life.

Which was how it was. And that was why Shell, who had grabbed up her shoes and was carrying them, felt her foot slide from under her as she rounded the curve, so she shot all the way down on her bottom.

'Bollocks to that,' she said, shaken, addressing herself to a pair of elegantly shod, size nine feet, 'I could have broke me bleeding back.'

'Are you all right?'

'No, I'm not.' She massaged the base of her spine aggrievedly. 'I'm bruised to buggery. I should probably sue.' And, as her gaze travelled up from the feet to the face, her eyes locked with those of a perfect stranger, a tall, pale young man of ethereal beauty.

'Oh, I beg your pardon,' she said, 'sorry for the swearing. Hush my mouth. Wash it out with soap and water. But it's just that it hurt so fucking much.'

'I'll bet.' He smiled at her with amusement redeemed by sympathy, stooped to ease her skirt down, to make her decent, and offered her his hand. 'Come on, now, upsy-daisy. Let me kiss it better for you.'

He'd have liked to do that. To walk his lips the length of her backbone till she shivered with the pleasure of it and said 'Yes, yes, no, no, o-o-oh.' She was the sexiest creature he had ever seen, with her drowsy eyes and dewy mouth, her amber hair, and that lovely, lovely body, with all the lusciousness of youth. He would have to have her, if not now, then soon, soon.

She was not more than twenty. Would she be a virgin? Please let her be a virgin, please let him have first bite!

He was not a great one for tradition, for the customs of Olde England. You'd not catch him pig-sticking or swan-upping or hoe-downing or first footing or beating the bounds. There had, in his view, to be something wrong with people who played the game of real tennis in the manner of Henry VIII, or who danced around a maypole or got done up as hobby horses. Bank managers and insurance salesmen dressing in cross garters and skipping around ringing bells and banging sticks. And you could keep your Hindle Wakes, your Bristol Mothering Buns, you could keep your Dunmow Flitch.

But there was much to be said, as it now seemed to him, for the feudal custom of *droit du seigneur*. He would have liked to be able to exercise it now, to command this nymphet, to say, 'Take all your clothes off and make love to me here.' Or, as it might be, 'Suck my cock.'

Instead he said cordially, 'I'm Jasper Charteris, by the way. Who are you?'

'Michele Fairchild,' she told him in that dark, sugary voice of hers, and in an endearing gesture of diffidence, she dusted her hand on her dress before offering it to be shaken. 'I've come to work here.'

'How lucky we are then! I say, where *is* everybody, do you know? I go away for a few weeks, and when I get back I find the place like a ghost ship, with no signs of life.'

'Well, I really can't say. Except that Laura – Lady Charteris – has dashed off up to London. Her mother's a bit poorly, apparently.'

'She must be very poorly indeed if Laura has flown to her bedside.'

'What?'

'Is there talk of a will? Is it that bad? Hey, look, sorry. That's not in order. Listen, I was kidding, OK? Forget I said it. I should have phoned ahead, I suppose, to let them know that I was on my way. But father would only have gone and killed the fatted calf – you know how fathers are – and I'm sick to death of fatted calf, I'm up to here with it.' He chopped at his forehead with the side of one hand.

Michele nodded seriously. She was thinking how good-looking was this Jasper. Like an angel, almost; she could imagine him with big white wings all down his back, and with a hoop of light around his head. He didn't *talk* like an angel, though. He talked suggestive. He was coming on to her. And Michele, mightily tired though she was of men coming on to her, felt a keen response, a quickening within her. She could, she told herself, musing upon it . . . She could definitely give Jasper Charteris one.

'How is she?' asked Laura wretchedly, holding off, holding back, hesitating to approach the bed, upon which Maudie lay wired up to the works, a poor, inconsiderable thing, breathing waspily. Laura had never before seen her mother other than perpendicular. Maudie horizontal was a very different proposition, somehow, from Maudie upstanding. She was a stranger the way the dead are strangers; she was both known and unknowable.

'She's had a bit of a near miss, it seems. She gave everyone a fright last night.' The nurse, very brisk, lifted the patient's limp wrist, felt the pulse, frowned in concentration down at the watch she wore pinned to the bib of her apron.

'So I understand.' Laura folded her arms across her chest. She tossed the hair out of her eyes. She parried with her chin. The room spun whitely around her.

Was she supposed to feel guilty? Was that what they wanted? Did they expect that she'd be racked with remorse, just because she'd not been there sooner? Well, she wasn't. She wouldn't be. They weren't going to make her. She had never much cared for nurses, who seemed to her all starch and superiority, and she certainly had no intention of explaining to this one why she had not arrived before now.

'Can she hear me?' she ventured instead, and, absurdly, there rang out in her head, heavily amplified, the voice of the music hall comedian, Sandy Powell, saying 'Can you hear me, mother?'

'She's sleeping. It's the best thing for her. Sleep is the greatest healer.'

'Yes.' Laura drew up a chair and sat near, to study in detail the face of this woman whom she could never love, to gaze in fascination up Maudie's nostrils, and at her closed eyes; at the fine mesh of veins, red and blue, on the lids. She was put in mind of that silly quiz game where one is shown a close-up photograph of a familiar household object – the spout of a teapot, the hole in a flowerpot – and required to identify it. Close up, Maudie's nostrils, Maudie's eyelids, were not identifiable. They looked very strange indeed.

Laura asked herself then what she felt – besides tired, of course, and depressed, and hung over, and so horribly unloved. She did a bit of mental probing to find out where in particular it hurt.

She had been out last night when the call had come. She'd gone for a drive, and for supper with Rick Sharkey who was, after all, an old friend, and who understood her, body and soul. Returning after midnight, she had seen, to her fury, the figure of her husband framed in the lighted doorway like .'. . . well, like a long streak of piss, waiting up, watching out for her.

'What the hell. . . ?' she had demanded angrily, slamming out of her car, swaying up to him, with her head at a dangerous angle, her eyes narrowed to slits through which she loosed small shafts of temper at him.

'Laura, I'm so sorry, it's bad news.'

She had known then, in an instant, what had happened. She had guessed at once the full horror of it. 'Jasper!' Her hands had flown to her face. 'Jasper has had an accident? Jasper is dead?'

'No. No, not Jasper.' John had grasped her by the elbows to steady her, and they'd staggered around like the exhausted finalists in a dance marathon. 'Stand still. Keep calm. *Listen*.' He had actually shaken her, then, though in a gentlemanly, John sort of way, and not at all as she would have liked to be shaken –to be shaken and taken. 'Oh, Laura, you've been drinking. I do wish you hadn't got drunk.'

'I'm not. Listen. The Leith police dismisseth us. Red lorry, yellow lorry. You see, I'm fine.'

'Well, your mother isn't. She's *not* fine. She collapsed. She'd had a . . . transient something attack, like a little stroke, tonight.'

'Me too.' Laura had started to giggle. 'I had a little stroke tonight. And a little coke. And a little poke.'

John had loosed his grip on her then. He had stepped out of the wedge of electric light into the shadows where his face had been invisible to her, as though he were withdrawing not merely his support but his whole self from her. 'Go upstairs. Go to bed and sleep it off,' he'd said in a voice so thick with disgust and so cold that she had shivered and had drawn her coat more closely around her. 'You're in no fit state to travel. I'll have Watkins drive you up to town when you're sober.'

And thus, so far as she remembered, had the evening's entertainments been concluded. Not with a bang, as they say, but with a whimper.

She had woken to find that her husband was not with her, that he was shunning her, and that Misery was her only bedfellow. Oh, God, she had thought, as she rang for service, for sweet tea and Alka Seltzer, what have I done? I've really blown it, haven't I? (Come to think of it, she could use a cup of tea right now, she could use an aspirin, but the nurse, the snotty cow, had melted away, and she could not find the bell to summon her, to place an order.)

She had slept fitfully in the back of the Rolls on the way here, waking briefly as they crossed Salisbury Plain, to see Stonehenge, that looming ring of stones which the Druids must surely have put there for a stupid joke, so that people ever after would wank on about how they might have done it, and what it signified.

They'd been held up in the morning rush, in the quart of traffic which somehow contrives each day to squeeze into the pint pot that is London. And at last, at nearly noon, here she was, at her mother's side, feeling, probably, by far the more frail of the pair of them. It had not for one moment occurred to her that Maudie might die, but she, Laura, at that minute, felt most fearfully mortal.

The question then arose, what to *do*. She seemed to have no function beyond keeping a vigil, which sounded rather fine and noble and touching, but which was in practice intensely dull and surely utterly futile.

Was there any point, actually, in sitting aimlessly here? Would it do a blind bit of good? Sentimentalists might imagine that Maudie would be touched to find, upon opening her eyes, that her only daughter had been there watching over her. Sentimentalists would, however, as so often, be wrong. Her mother's reaction on seeing her, Laura guessed, would be one of irritation. That was how things were between them. It was just the way of it, and could not be helped.

Better, then, to leave the paper cone of flowers which Watkins had picked up for her on the garage forecourt when they'd stopped to fill up with petrol. She could scribble a note to say sorry and all that, to say rotten luck old dear, get better soon, lots of love, kiss, kiss, kiss. She could leave a number where they might contact her, have the car drop her off at the Dorchester, then crawl gratefully into bed and get her head down.

The last time she'd got her head down at the Dorchester, she remembered then with a heart-thump, a great thud of regret, she had been with Jasper. Last night, for a brief instant, she had imagined he was dead. Now she almost wished that he were. For how much greater was the torment of knowing he was alive yet lost to her! How much more deeply hurtful to imagine him, not the other side of the veil which hangs between this world and the next, but just the other side of the channel, a few hours' journey away.

Well, if she could not lay the boy himself, she could at least try to lay his ghost. She stood up and went in search of a nurse, or better still a doctor, someone with authority, to whom she might give her instructions.

Stepping out of the overheated hospital, into the icy wind, she saw Watkins waiting for her with the borrowed arrogance of those who serve the rich and powerful, on a double yellow line. 'Take me to my hotel,' she told him brusquely, 'then you can go back to Hartwell.'

And belatedly the thought came to her, as they moved noiselessly out into the traffic, that Caroline would want to be told about all this. She supposed she'd better phone her.

———————— • ————————

He supposed he should phone Caroline. He'd promised that he would. And he wanted to call her, he needed to speak with her, to feel connected to her by those few magic miles of cable, which would at this time of day be bristling with voices (beneath the grey pavements of London the wires would be chattering with electronic impulses, with I love you, and He's in a meeting, and We must have lunch).

But even as he lifted the receiver, before his brain had so much as summoned up the number, the boy racer on three was unscrewing his filler-cap, the Nissan driver on number ten was parsimoniously tapping the last drops of four-star from the nozzle, and the Sierra driver on eight, a regular, an account customer, was making his way over, feeling in his breast pocket for his fountain pen.

Sighing, Patrick put the phone down. Here was the problem with this job: it demanded so much of your time and so little of your intellect.

He ought to have tried for something better. He ought, as Carrie had told him, to be pursuing some kind of career. He ought, let's admit it, to be at university. If he felt any shame at all it was for this. For having dropped out. For turning his back on his education. For passing up a privilege which others only dreamt of. Otherwise, his situation, the thing with Caroline, just did not seem to him to be shameful. He was besotted; there was no more to it than that. Parts of him that responded to no one else responded to this woman. She was so gentle and tractable and beautiful (above all, to him, she was beautiful). He thought he had never met anyone more quintessentially feminine. At moments, his desire for her was almost overwhelming.

'The love that dare not speak its name,' he said to himself with obscure satisfaction. The phrase referred, of course, to homosexuality. But homosexual love, what with Gay Lib, what with Outrage, and its clubs and pubs and magazines, its pride marches, its own television programme, above all its legal sanction, did not seem to him to be so timid.

No, it was people like them, like Patrick and Caroline, who dare not come out, dare not take to the streets with banners. Theirs was the kind of love that society would abominate for all eternity, that the law would never, ever countenance.

Then, if you were gay you were part of a community, a fellowship; whereas, if you fell hopelessly in love with your half sister, you were well and truly out in the –

'Cold,' said the Sierra driver matily, rubbing his hands together so they made a papery, crackling sound. He masked his face with them and huffed into them, rubbed them again.

'Freezing,' agreed Patrick, punching buttons, waiting impatiently as the cash till rattled out an itemised receipt (dear God, Barbara Cartland could write a novel in less time than it took this machinery to deliver up a tiny slip of paper, detailing the litres bought, the money spent, the percentage attributable to VAT).

'They reckon it might snow.'

'They do?'

'So someone was telling me. We could have a white Christmas, they're saying.'

Christmas? Oh, *Christmas*! He had known, of course, what season this was. He had only to look out on to the windswept forecourt, where in summer would be on display patio furniture and plant troughs, garden umbrellas and barbecues, and where now the winter merchandise had been moved in, the plastic Christmas trees and laurel wreaths, potted poinsettias, and nets of logs and bags of coal stacked shoulder high. Even the bunches of hothouse flowers, sitting forlornly in a bucket, had a taint of frost upon their bronze and umber petals (the chauffeur driver of a Roller, who had bought a bunch this morning would not have got his money's worth, that was for sure).

But none of this really said Christmas to him. None of it evoked that time of year which, for him, back in Ireland, had always been special.

Patrick was an extraordinarily balanced human being. Despite the nervous energy that destabilised him sometimes, he had a very low centre of gravity. It would take a heavy blow indeed to knock him sideways. But he was a romantic, too, with a heart which was forever filling up with song and sentiment. He cared much for his father, his stepmother, his home. The same abiding affection as had brought him here in search of Caroline, he now felt for all that he had left behind.

He thought regretfully of the tall, thin house in Dublin, with lights ablaze in all the windows, and a crust of snow on every sill. He thought of the big basement kitchen with the long plank table. He thought of puddings steaming on the Aga. And Josie, with her hair in a straggling ponytail, stirring something deliciously messy in a pan. And his father, exuberant, uncorking bottle after bottle of wine for the friends who came by in relays, and who never seemed to want to leave.

'I cannot now,' he told himself with anguish, conscious that he was overdramatising, if only slightly, 'ever, ever, go home again.'

Morosely, in a quiet moment, he helped himself from the chilled cabinet to a carton of milk, a tuna and tomato roll in a fuzz of clingwrap. He took a copy of the *Daily Mirror* from the rack, read his stars and, finding no salvation there, just some vague advice on finances, tossed it aside. He thought, 'No one but we can ever understand.'

He was, let's face it – no, *they were* – all adrift. And sooner or later they were going to have to get a grip, to make choices, make decisions.

His coming to work here had involved decision-making of sorts, it had involved choice, albeit of a very low grade. It had been, as he'd perceived it, a kind of first step towards a new normality.

'I shall have to find a job,' he'd told Caroline, when his circumstances, his day-to-day existence with her, had come to feel restricting as a tangled bedsheet. 'I can't just lie about here like a big slug for ever. I ought to pull my weight.'

'Well, you don't have to. Not in a great hurry. It isn't as if we need the money. We have my salary, and my allowance.'

'You don't understand.' For the first time he had experienced the stirrings of annoyance, of frustration; for the first time he had sounded vexed. Precisely because he felt so many things for her, because his very feelings were the problem, he had been tempted in that moment not merely to resent her but to let his resentment show. 'I feel so terribly idle. I have to get cracking or I'll go quietly insane.'

'But what. . . ? I mean, all I'm saying is, find something you will enjoy.'

'It doesn't matter what it is. I can work on a building site. Or clean windows. Or dig gardens. Anything has to be better than nothing. Oh, now look, you're crying. Come here Carrie-Anne, let me hold you. You mustn't take so much upon yourself. Christ, I hate it when you cry!'

'I'm ruining your life,' she had sobbed into his chest. 'You're stuck here with me when you should be having fun going to discos.'

'I don't *want* to go to discos. I don't even *like* discos.'

'And getting some qualifications, learning to be an engineer.'

'I have no desire, in fact, to be an engineer. That was just a phase I went through. I have also, at various times, wanted to drive a fire engine, to be a forest ranger, and to own a wet fish shop. Hey, I'm dead serious. It was for the chance to wear a straw boater and a blue striped apron. All right, laugh if you will then, scorn all my dreams. Now, here, take this hankie and have a good blow.'

Thus had he found himself working at the petrol station, selling anti-freeze and de-icer, and cold snacks and cans of coke, and A-Zs and Zippo lighters, to a public which seemed to be constantly on the move. It wasn't ideal, but it was a start.

'Bit taters,' said the blonde Cockney girl who, having just topped up the tank of her 2CV, was waving a twenty-pound note at him. She had long, gold-blonde hair, and her figure, in tight leggings, was a dream. She looked at him with interest, yet nothing moved within him. Caroline had eclipsed all other women for him. So he simply agreed that it was nippy out, clamped the tuna roll between his teeth as he counted out her change, and bid her a muffled 'oo'ye and 'a' 'ou.

The point was, he decided, not that he might never more go home – well, of *course* he could go home – but that Caroline might not go with him. As he might not go with her to Hartwell. *Especially* he could not afford to go to Hartwell.

Perhaps it would be best if he spent Christmas week in Ireland, while she spent it in Dorset. That way, no suspicions need be aroused. He would have to tell untruths, of course, when they asked what he'd been up to, when Tom got on about the future, or when Josie teased him about girlfriends.

But then, what were a few small untruths when his whole life, from now until forever, would be based on one enormous, single, central lie?

For, let us not delude ourselves, this was how it must be. Like Romeo and Juliet, he and Caroline would have to hide their love. And that was not, actually, a romantic proposition; it was a bloody dire, depressing one, too horrible to contemplate.

He had thought himself into a corner. The only thing that now might cheer him was to call Caroline at once, to hear her smiling down the phone at him.

He grabbed up the receiver and dialled, but her direct line was engaged. Sighing, he replaced the handset. It would keep, it would keep.

———————— • ————————

Doris took the crumpled Co-op carrier bag from the back of the wardrobe, took the large manila envelope from the carrier, and decanted its contents on to the table. This was where she stored the past – in the envelope, in the carrier, in the wardrobe. And it was with a sense of duty to that past, a sense of obligation to those who peopled it, that she would every so often take the lot out and have a sort through.

Old letters, snapshots, bits and bobs. No one but she ever got to look at it. Not, mind you, that she had anything to hide. There were no skelingtons in *her* cupboard, thank you very much. Unless you counted . . . well, you know. Thingummy. It was just that it was personal. It was private. It was all her yesterdays.

At least now, thank goodness, with the girl away, she need not fear that she would be disturbed. 'What are you doing?' Shell had wanted to know, padding up behind her, leaning hard on her shoulder, making chewing-gum noises in her ear, her breath warm and pepperminty, the last time Doris had had the envelope out – what, three, four months ago?

'I'm making lay-o'ers for meddlers and crutches for lame ducks,' Doris had told her crossly, sweeping everything into a heap, shielding it with the crook of her arm.

'What's all them, then?'

'Ask me no questions and I'll tell you no lies. Weren't you supposed to be going bowling?'

'I couldn't be bothered. Anyway, I'm broke. And last time Carly went she got a verruca.'

'How was that then?'

'From the shoes. What's a lay-over?'

'You never heard of a lay-over?'

'I've heard of a *leg*-over.'

'Well, I wouldn't know anything about that.' And Doris had slapped away the hand that had made a pinchy little grab for a slightly dog-eared, black-and-white photograph on the top of the pile.

Here, now, *was* that photograph, taken by Ernest with the boxy old Kodak, of Dawn as a baby, on holiday at Camber, a scowling infant in a frilly bonnet, banging the sand with a spade.

It was funny, when you came to think of it, the way events moved on. It was funny about time. She'd heard some whatsname scientist on the wireless only the other day, saying in all seriousness that – get this! – time might move in either direction, that the universe could go into a kind of reverse, and time would then somehow start to run backwards. Then, if you can imagine this, the glass that you knocked off the table and that broke into smithereens, would gather itself together and hop up on to the table again, right as ninepence. And people would die before they were born, and would remember the future but not the past.

They were all the same, these intellectuals, weren't they, though? They were all jaw, jaw, jaw. And such nonsense! When everyone knew that time went in one direction only, in a straight line from left to right.

Even so, just suppose it were true, suppose the world were to turn topsy-turvy. Then she, Doris, would have to live her days over again, the funeral, the inquest, the police at her door ('Mrs Fairchild, I'm afraid we have bad news . . .'). Dawn dying a sordid death in a filthy squat; then giving birth to an illegitimate child; the shame of her pregnancy; and the teenage years, the sulks, the rebellion. Grammar school, the endless read, read, read. Then juniors, and infants, her first term at kindergarten, the toddler phrase, until finally Doris might hold her again, a babe in arms, and smell her damp and talcumed skin, and have such high, high hopes for her.

Her own parents, first her father then her mother, would be restored to her. And her husband, her Ernest. Then they'd get married, get engaged, he would propose to her, they would walk out together, they would meet and fall in love, and he would write her the letter she held now in her hand, calling her his precious jewel, his buttercup, his only.

She would also know the consequences of her deeds before they were even done, she would know already how things had turned out. Yet, whether they had been for good or ill, she would do the same again, there being no point in *not*.

There was a flaw in the theory, however, and one which the scientist had failed to spot – never mind that he was a Professor of This, and Chair of That, and Head Cook and Bottle Washer at the University of Wherever. Because if everyone lived their lives backwards, they would also have to walk backwards and talk backwards, wouldn't they? They'd talk gobbledegook, so no one would understand a word that anyone else was saying, and a fat lot of good that would be.

Just the same, it was an exercise in time travel, to turn up like patience cards, and always with a small surprise, a series of pictures, of documents, certificates of birth, death, marriage.

Here were Dawn's O-levels, here a school report, showing clearly how very much too clever she had been for her own good. A, B, A, A, B . . . Top marks in English, history, French. Praise for her intelligence, but some questions raised about her attitude.

The one thing Doris would say for Shell: she didn't have an attitude. She had some trying little ways, it must be said. She was the original Dolly Daydream, and no help around the place. She put spent matches back in the box, and left the cap off the toothpaste, and used up the toilet paper. But she was pleasing to the eye in a way that lumpy, grumpy, defiant Dawn had never even tried to be. And she didn't have opinions, she didn't care to argue. 'All right,' she would say. Or, 'If you like.' Or, 'Yes, in a minute.'

Take, for instance, this business with Laura Charteris – or Laura Grant as she had been all those years ago, when their paths had so briefly crossed.

'You go there,' Doris had told her. And Shell, only mildly protesting, had gone. 'You tell her what you know,' she'd said. And Shell might even now be telling.

The die is cast, thought Doris, both thrilled and appalled, as she pored over a photo of her mother. The game is up. The albatross comes home to roost at last.

———————— • ————————

Maudie Grant was awakened by a young man in a white coat standing over her. And no sooner had she opened her eyes than he began to bombard her with the most idiotic questions – what was her name? her date of birth? her address? her telephone number? how many fingers was he holding up? who was the Prime Minister? – as if she were some kind of imbecile, as if she had lost her memory.

Such a lot of silly fuss about so little. She had fainted, that was all. It was an effect of low blood sugar and could happen to anyone. The remedy was quite simple: one had only to eat a piece of fresh fruit on an empty stomach, d'you see, and the fructose would convert at once to glucose and be spirited to the brain and hey presto!

But of course no one had had the wit to bring her fruit. There were some tarnished gold and bronze dahlias in a vase beside her, and a carafe of water, but not so much as an apple or orange, not so much as a grape.

'How are we feeling now?' asked a nurse, fussing with the sorry blooms, rearranging them in an apparently hopeless attempt to make them look attractive.

'*I* am well,' said Maudie tartly. 'I cannot speak for *you*.'

'That's a good girl.'

'Now, do bring me my clothes. And be kind enough to call for a taxi, so I can be on my way.'

'No dear, I don't think that would be such a good idea. Not yet, at least.'

'But this is preposterous. I'm as fit as a fiddle.' Maudie struggled to sit up, but her limbs felt leaden. Her body was strangely unresponsive.

'Your daughter was in earlier.' The nurse abandoned her efforts at flower-arranging. 'She left a hotel number. We're to ring any time.'

'Laura was here? In London? What in heaven's name for?'

'Well, to see you, what else? But you were out like a light. Now you're awake, should I give her a ring?'

'Good grief, no! She'll have gone shopping. She won't want to be bothered with me.'

'Oh, but she was most concerned. Quite, you know, distracted.'

'I dare say she was. Distracted, that is. I dare say she had a thousand other things on her mind. Right. Enough of this. I can't lie around here chatting all day. I have things to do. If you would just give me a hand . . .'

'I'll call the doctor in. You can have a chat with him.' The nurse made swishily for the door, then turned back. 'I was forgetting. Your granddaughter was on the phone. Caroline. Wanting to know how you were. She said she'd be in to visit you the minute she can get away from work.'

Caroline? It would be good to see Caroline, thought Maudie, lying back against the pillows, unaccountably tired. It must be, ooh, months since she saw her. In fact, d'you know – here was a funny thing – she could not even remember the last time.

CHAPTER

10

Shell unscrewed the cap of metal polish, held the bottle to her nostrils and, closing her eyes, took a deep, indulgent sniff. Ahhh, Brasso! She splodged some on a rag and rubbed it over the belly of the coal scuttle on the scullery table, singing as she buffed away with it, that she should be so lucky (lucky, lucky, lucky), she should be so lucky in ler-erv.

Dipping slightly at the knees, she tilted her head, considering her reflection in the distorting mirror of gleaming copper, amused to see how hideous she appeared, a bit like a gonk, sort of jowly, with a great big knocker of a nose, and close-set eyes, and tufty hair, a Neanderthal forehead and no chin.

It was a novelty, when you looked as gorgeous as Shell, to play with the concept of ugliness. Had she been, in reality, even slightly ugly, she would doubtless have found the exercise far less diverting.

She was happy this morning, not just because she had a rare capacity for happiness, because she had an enviable ability to set aside her troubles; or indeed because she liked it down here on her own among the boots and boxes, with no one to get on her back and say 'Do this, do that'. No, she was happy because . . .

'Tu-um, tee-tum, tee tum-tum, tum, tee-tum, teetum-tum, I should be so lucky in ler-erv.'

It was a fortnight to the day since she first set eyes on . . .

She hurr-hurred on the scuttle, wrote a 'J' in the mist with her finger, and watched dreamily as it evanesced.

Jasper Charteris had a thing for . . . hurr-hurr. He had a thing for her. And she? She was wild about him. He aroused such feelings in her, as though her insides had been stirred with a warm spoon.

For the past two weeks they had been playing a tantalising game with one another, coming daily into casual contact, exchanging conversational trifles – a curt 'Good morning', say, if they happened to pass in the hallway, and some mindless remark about the weather – then contradicting these with speaking looks of the profoundest lust and longing.

He had not, since helping her up off the floor, so much as brushed against her, had not laid a finger on her, yet their every encounter had been somehow so intensely physical, it was as if he could actually stroke her with his eyes. And all the little hairs on the back of her neck prickled in response.

The rule, tacitly understood by each of them, was strictly 'hands off'. No patting, petting or pawing, until . . .

And Jasper, like a gentleman, had played by that rule, although there had been one shocking moment, last Friday, when she had fancied that he was in breach of it. She had just finished in the drawing room, dusted, vacuumed, lit the fire that had been laid there earlier (the logs spat irascibly on the huge iron dogs in the grate), and was bending to untangle the Hoover flex, her skirt straining across her bottom, when someone had sneaked up on her and nudged her rudely right between the legs. Gasping, she had spun around to confront whoever it was that had goosed her – only to find there behind her, not the lascivious Jasper, panting with desire for her, but a pleased and puffing Pasha, come to say hello.

'Oh!' she had said then, tugging the dog's ears, laughing at herself, at once disappointed and relieved. Because she ached for Jasper to handle her, she had never in her life felt so touch-hungry; yet a part of her wanted also to prolong this exquisite agony. A part of her was willing to wait. A little voice in her head said 'Not yet.'

Now she wondered how much farther they could stretch themselves before the tension became too great to bear. Another inch, maybe? Or two? Or ten? How long before the twanging of her nerves was unendurable? A day? A week? Not, surely, more than that.

She had done it before, of course. Made love. Yes, dozens of times, if you must know. Well, what would you expect? She was twenty years old, she was eminently desirable, and had had a string of boyfriends (had as in, you know, *had*). She'd gone to bed with them in a spirit of curiosity, or out of laziness, because it was easier to say yes than no ('no' being one of those deceptively little words that can't stand alone, but require endless shoring up with explanations and qualifications). Sex at its best, she had discovered, could be pretty sensational. Such a pity, then, that one so seldom found it at its best!

With Jasper, however, she was absolutely confident, it would be the ultimate. All that waiting and wanting would not have gone to waste; it would have aggregated. It would be there still within them, like the charge in a battery. And they would both light up with it, and bells would ring.

She might not be a virgin, but for her it would be so different from the other times, it would be like the first time. He was so handsome and so fine. It was hard to believe that such a lot of detailed work could have gone into the shaping of a single human being. She closed her eyes and conjured a picture of his face, but it was watery as a dream and ran out through the holes in her consciousness.

These past fourteen days had been the strangest in Shell's life. Half the time, she could scarcely believe what had happened to her. She could scarcely think why she was here. Oh, sure, she had come because Nanny had said to do so. Because she had been sent. She was a messenger on an – no, 'errand' really wasn't the word for it, 'mission' would do better. Her instructions were to speak to Lady Charteris, to talk terms with her.

But how could you talk to someone who was so much not around? Laura was in the house all right – she signalled her presence by ringing the service bell. Delicate little lunches would be specially prepared for her and carried up to her on a tray, to be returned an hour later, untouched, untasted. In the afternoons she would rise and walk in the grounds, where Shell had glimpsed her only fleetingly, in the misty distance. Her Ladyship would then dress for dinner, she would dine with the family in the best traditions of the English country house, before retiring once more, early, to bed.

'What *exactly* is up with her?' Shell had wanted to know, just yesterday, picking at a piece of poached salmon which had found its way back to the kitchen. She was increasingly curious about this woman who was proving so elusive.

'She's very run down, they say.' With a little tush, Mrs Holloway had confiscated the plate of salmon, and her mouth had taken on a sort of stitched-up look, as if her face had been darned. 'Now, you leave things alone, young lady.'

'Why? It will only be thrown away.'

'Don't argue with me, Miss.'

'Well, it will. What did you say was wrong with Laura?'

'I dare say she's worried about her mother, though we hear that Mrs Grant is on the mend. And don't talk so familiar. Remember your place.'

'All right. Are they close, then? She and her mother?' That was not what Shell had heard.

'Why so many questions? I never knew such a girl for questions.'

'Dunno.' Shell had shrugged and turned away. There were so few clues to the real Laura Charteris, in whose past she now had the strangest investment. She knew only that small part of the story which Nanny had told her, and she felt a need to piece together the rest.

But it wasn't like at home, where it was all sort of available, on record, where there were photographs to be peeked at, and letters and documents to be read. There would be no old carrier bag hidden in a wardrobe here at Hartwell, bearing a Co-op logo and containing all the detritus of different people's lives.

Shell had been through every drawer, every cupboard, every scrap of paper back at the flat. She had read the yucky letters that Ernest had written to Doris, calling her his popsy, his sweetie-pie, his dove. She had read Dawn's school reports. And the note Dawn had scribbled about being pregnant ('I know you're going to hit the roof, Mum, but . . .'). And her own birth certificate, identifying Dawn Fairchild as her mother, making no mention of a father, as though it had been some kind of immaculate conception.

You had to feel sorry for Dawn, Shell thought now, setting aside the coal scuttle and starting on a pair of silver candlesticks. All right, granted, she'd not been much of a mother – not much of a daughter, either. But she'd been so brainy, and so tortured. And she'd died so horribly, with her blue needle marks up her arms. She had no memory of her, but she had a strong, strong sense of the woman, for whom she nursed – as children will, in spite of all, for an absent parent – a secret and abiding fondness.

If Dawn Fairchild had been given half the chances Laura Charteris had been given in her life, if she had been half as favoured, half as fortunate, it might all have been so very different for her.

Hmm. Laura's fortune was of prime concern to Nanny Fairchild, who seemed to think they might tap into it, but it was less and less of interest to Michele. She had just one thing on her mind at the moment. And that thing, like fortune, began with the letter F.

———— • ————

'Fuck!' said Toby, awed, as, with a harsh, almost mechanical clattering, two pheasants broke cover. And, as first a dun-coloured hen bird, then a more flamboyant gold, red and blue cock rushed against the slate sky, 'Would you look at those mothers!' Raising an imaginary gun, he took aim and fired. 'Bang,' he yelled. 'Bang-bang. You're dinner.'

'The trouble is,' said Jasper, wincing, lifting one hand to his temple, deciding to share this thing, 'I'm just so bloody blocked.'

But a problem shared with Tobias was a problem doubled. 'Better call in Dyno-Rod,' he counselled blithely.

'Of course, you wouldn't understand.' Jasper's tone was bitter as the midwinter. He plunged his hands into the pockets of the army greatcoat which had been such a find in Camden Market, a seriously wicked garment, with street credibility in the very weave, the warp and woof of it. He kicked at the frozen clods of leaf mulch. His eyes were watering in the stiff breeze, and his face was very white, tipped at the nose with red.

'Sorry, sorry, sorry.' Tobias was at once conciliatory. He did his best to appear serious, to show concern for his brother's predicament, to take an interest in his project, in the novel which had apparently been incubating for so long. 'Still, I expect it will free up, as they say. Just give it a bit more time.'

Jasper shook his head. 'I'm not so sure.'

Yesterday Jasper had seated himself at the typewriter,

pressed the shift lock, and, in a rush of self-confidence, had clapped out CHAPTER ONE. But there was, as it had seemed to him, something most fearfully off-putting about those words. They were so loaded, somehow. They were like the twin barrels of a gun pointing right at your head, defying you to come up with that immortal first line, with words that would echo down the centuries. He'd thought, 'The past is a foreign country.' And 'Last night I dreamt I went to Manderley again.' He'd thought, 'I sing of arms and the man.' And even, 'Once upon a time.' But – wouldn't you know it? – they'd all been done before. Some clever bugger had got there in front of him.

Then he'd had a flash of inspiration. Ripping the page out, he'd fed another into the maw of the typewriter, pressed the shift lock again and rattled away at the keys. CHAPTER TWO, he'd typed.

'How much have you done so far?' Toby enquired.

'Well, you know. A couple of chapters.'

'That's a start, at least. That's something. Want me to look at it, do you? To cast a critical eye? Give you a few pointers? Though of course I should have to charge a small reading fee.'

'No, thank you very much.'

'Suit yourself. If you don't want the benefit of my expert advice.' Toby pretended to pick off a squirrel as it crossed in front of them in a series of loopy dashes. 'Don't say I didn't offer. Anyway, what's it about?'

'What?'

'The book. What's it about?'

'*About?*'

'Yes, you know. What is it concerning? What is its frame of reference? Its main thrust? When you boil the thing down, what have you got? At the end of the day, what *is* it?'

'Oh, really, Tobias! You can't be serious. How can you ask such a question?' Jasper beat on his brow with the heel of his hand. ' "What is it about?" he wants to know. Ye Gods!'

'What's wrong with that?'

'Well, it's just . . . I mean, it's unbelievably simplistic.' Jasper tipped his head back and barked like a seal in derision.

'Why is it? Everything must be about something, after all. It would be a funny kind of book that wasn't. Like *Othello* is about sexual jealousy. And *War and Peace* is about Russia. And *A la Recherche*, as every schoolboy knows, is about a cake.'

Jasper sighed. He said, 'I rest my case.' He closed his eyes against the cold light of day, to find the inside of his head red hot with lust and blazing like a pizza oven.

He wanted the girl, the maid, Michele. He wanted her more than he had wanted anything or anyone. He wanted to seize, to jump on, to ravish her. To ram into her, and turn her inside out. But such impulses were animal, and Jasper Charteris was not an animal, he was the greatest lover in the Western world.

It was all very well for his brother to leap in and out of the sack every five minutes, making the humpy-backed beast with whoever. For Toby had no finesse, no technique, no sexual graces; he would, in Jasper's estimation, be up like a rocket and down like a stick. But when you were as finely tuned sexually and emotionally as he, Jasper, when your soul went layers deep, when you had such delicate sensibilities, and had raised the act of love-making to the level of performance art, you did not just give in to such fleshly exigency.

With faint contempt Jasper watched Tobias, ruddy, doggy, barely housetrained, bounding about in the bracken. What women saw in his younger brother – and they evidently saw *something* – was a continual, unfathomable mystery to him.

'You know,' said Tobias, as the path led them at last on to the road, and he waved vaguely towards the Blacksmith's Arms, 'a glass of beer would be as welcome as the flowers in May right now.'

'You,' Jasper chided him.

'Me?'

'Yes, you.'

'What about me?'

'Can you think of nothing but screws and booze? If you were asked to define a straight line, you'd say it was the shortest distance between two pints.'

'You don't want a drink, yourself, then? You won't join me at the trough?'

'Well . . .' Jasper sighed. 'Oh, go on, if we must.' He actually loathed the village pub. It was an ancient, low-built, white-washed building, with steep-pitched roofs and beamed ceilings. Smoke from the chimneys signalled that fires had been lit in the inglenooks. The place had a certain charm, it had possibilities, but it lacked integrity. The car park was jammed at weekends with newcomers' Volvos and four-wheel-drive jeeps. In summer the small garden was a riot of Cinzano umbrellas, while inside you found yourself, as it were, between a rock and a hard place, forced to choose between the saloon and the public bar. On the one hand you got muzak and basket meals and wheelback chairs and trays of condiments and G and Ts and slices of lemon from a jar. On the other you got guffawing locals, who seemed always to be half-cut, and who made a great show of tugging their forelocks as you came through the door.

Today a sign in the window advertised a 'happy hour'.

'It will be karaoke next,' said Jasper despairingly, as Toby, opting for the public bar, led on.

'Don't be a silly girl, now,' Toby taunted him. And, shouldering his way to the counter, 'Come, landlord, fill the flowing bowl. Best bitter for me and a snowball for my friend Gloria here. Go easy on the Warninks, make free with the R. Whites, top the thing off with a maraschino cherry and give the thing a good swizzle.'

'I'd prefer a small lager, actually,' Jasper cut in icily. He went to stand by the fire, to kick at the logs with the toe of his boot, sending up showers of sparks, ignoring the laughter and catcalls, the cries of 'Lord Snooty' from the rowdies at the dartboard.

'There we are, then.' Toby, the beamish boy, came to join him, bearing two brimming mugs, setting them carefully on a small table. 'Hey, sit here. Want anything to eat? They not only do ploughman's lunch, but – if you can believe it – an executive ploughman's. It comes with extra cholesterol. A coronary special. I could hardly resist it. But then, the way the industry is going, perhaps it's not such a joke. These days Farmer Giles wears a sharp suit, not a straw hat and smock. We're behind the times at Hartwell in many respects. We're going to have to look to our laurels. Anyway, cheers.' He grabbed his drink, took a swig and licked away a foam moustache.

'Cheers.' Moody, self-absorbed, Jasper glared into his glass. He said to himself, Michele Fairchild. Then he played with the name; he said, Michele, fair child. There seemed to him a very real risk that, if he did not make love to her soon, he might burst into flames. Little wonder that he could not write, when his sexual temperature was running so high. And yet it was good to wait, to anticipate, to know – as of course he knew – that she, too, was gasping for it.

How slow and how subtle had been the process of seduction. Every day he had contrived to meet her – in the drawing room, in the library, on the landing. Every day he had fed her the merest morsel of himself – a look, a word, a nod, a smile, his very presence – and by now he was sure she was *ravenous*.

'That new girl . . .' said Toby, and he took another long, thankful draught of beer.

'What girl?'

'The one with the . . .' Toby made an extravagant gesture with his free hand. 'The one with the hair. And the legs. And the eyes and everything.'

'What of her?' Jasper felt his nerves bunch up with irritation.

'There's something about her,' Toby mused mischievously, 'but I can't quite put my finger on it.'

'And you'd better not try. Be warned. Keep your

fingers to yourself. Don't go taking advantage of a member of the domestic staff.'

'Oh, ho, ho! So that's the way it is! You're after her too, you randy bugger. Well, I wouldn't have guessed she was your type. I thought you preferred your women hand-knitted. With big teeth and boobs.'

'You mean Hilly? For Pete's sake, can't we forget about Hilly? I haven't set eyes on her in years.'

'But there's been no one since.'

'Much you know about it!'

'She was your one true love.'

'She was a passing fancy. I was attracted to her mind. She has some interesting ideas. I found her stimulating.'

'And this other one. La belle Michele? You like her mind? Is that what you find stimulating?'

'Now, look, I'm telling you.' Jasper thumped his glass down. Lager slapped on to the table. 'No funny business, d'you hear? No making a pass. Don't abuse your social position.'

'Meaning that that's your prerogative?' Toby was seldom moved to anger. But everyone had been so cranky lately, and the strain of maintaining a bright and cheery countenance was beginning to tell. Things had jolly well better start looking up soon, he told himself now, darkly, or Jesus might no longer count on *him* to be a sunbeam. 'You think you have more right? Some kind of prior claim? Well, that's not how it works, brother. Every man for himself, *I* say. First served, first come. Last one in is a hot potato.'

'When will you ever grow up?'

'Never, I hope. Certainly not till I'm ninety. Look,

there's no need to fall out about this. You fancy her. I fancy her. One or other of us just might get lucky. Well, may the best man win. You could always try telling her about your novel. That way you could bore the pants off her.'

Jasper caught his breath and made a conscious decision not to rise to the bait. Rather, he looked down his nose at Tobias. It was the right sort of nose for looking down: long, straight, aristocratic. And he reminded himself that Shell had eyes only for him. Tobias, no matter what he imagined, was not even in with a chance. 'Would you like another beer?' he asked smoothly.

'No thanks.' Toby's face glowed like a Halloween pumpkin, lit from within. 'From now on I'm in training. No brewer's droop for me!'

———————— • ————————

'The Scorpio woman,' Laura, a Scorpio woman, read, 'can love with abandon and hate with pure venom. She can seem frigid as an iceberg – but when she loses control of her emotions, she erupts like a volcano. Heaven has no rage like her love to hatred turned, nor Hell a fury like a Scorpio woman scorned'

You could say that again! Momentarily losing her grip on her seething emotions, Laura hurled the book across the room. Then with a swish of Thai silk she slid out of bed and walked to the mirror, to see that – yes, even as the book described – she had beautiful, mysterious eyes, a focused, penetrating gaze, piercing with hypnotic intensity, an exterior smooth as black velvet, and a wine-dark, secret soul.

'Sod the lot of them,' she said aloud, for the satisfaction of hearing that husky Scorpio voice, so irresistible to men.

Through the vaporised self-pity that clouded the cold glass, she considered her pale, translucent skin which was absolutely characteristic of Pluto rising. She looked unwell, she told herself, but not peaky. Not sickly or sallow or washed-out or drab. Such whiteness was indeed not unbecoming, particularly in winter when a suntan was not *de rigueur*.

She was thoroughly run down, Doctor Forrest had told her, taking her pulse and sounding her chest and tap-tapping about on her back. She needed to relax, to have bed-rest. It was not to be wondered at. Worry over her mother must have taken its toll.

Forrest was an idiot, of course. A bumpkin. A craggy old man whose eyebrows had bolted. A typical, lum-mocky country GP, woefully out of date, out of touch with current medical thinking. He had seen the Charteris boys through mumps and measles, he doubtless knew his arthritis from his eczema, but he had not the faintest insight into the female condition. Try explaining to him that all the lights had gone out in your life, and he'd have you stick out your tongue and say 'Ah'.

Laura would not have let him near her, had her husband not insisted upon summoning him. 'If you're ill, then see a doctor,' John had told her, though not with his customary kindness and solicitude, rather with sarcasm, nastily, as you might say to a child, 'If you don't want an apple, then you can't be hungry.' It was almost as if he suspected her of valetudinarianism – as if he believed that there was nothing really wrong.

Still, at least Forrest had been persuaded that she was actually poorly: he had agreed that she was under the weather. But he had been out in his diagnosis. He had not put a name to her malaise. Laura alone knew what her problem was: it was an affliction called Other People. And in addition to the R and R which the stupid man prescribed, she needed a large dose of TLC: she needed tender, loving care.

When you had given so much of your loyal devotion (and Scorpio woman is notoriously loyal and devoted: it said so in the book, in black and white), you were entitled to expect some kind of *quid pro quo*.

You gave the best years of your life to your child, to your husband, to your husband's sons, then not unreasonably you looked to them to return to you a little warmth and gratitude and affection. But what did they do? They dumped you, ditched you, showed you the cold shoulder, turned their backs on you. Even John, finally, had turned his back. And this, simply because . . .

Laura recounted to herself, for the thousandth time, the events of that night, a couple of weeks ago, when she and John had had their falling-out. It had been something and nothing, to be frank. A lot of fuss over so very little. She'd been out with an old pal, she'd had a couple of drinks. Well, surely she was allowed just once in a while to let her hair down? Arriving home at around ten, ten-thirty (very well, at the latest, a quarter to eleven), she had found her husband waiting for her, hopping mad, demanding to know where she'd been and what doing till this hour, saying – as if it were *her* fault, as if she'd had any way of knowing – that her mother had been rushed to hospital, that it was thought she'd had a stroke.

Now, ask yourself: was that fair? Was it just? Was it any way for a man to treat his wife? He had shaken her, too. She couldn't forget that. Or the way he had looked at her, so cruel and despising, backing away from her into the darkness, until he was just a voice – a cold, hard, horrible, disembodied voice.

Laura had been shocked at the time by John's rejection of her, when he had always given her to believe that, in his eyes at least, she could do no wrong. But far more painful than the initial hurt had been the growing realisation that this was no mere tiff. He had withdrawn his love from her, as it now seemed, for ever.

What next? Divorce, perhaps. And banishment. She would be sent from Hartwell with, no doubt, a generous settlement. And at the age of . . . Good grief! How old was she? Thirty-six? Thirty-seven? At the age of thirty-something, having sacrificed career for family, she would be forced to start again, to rebuild her life.

She yearned for a reconciliation, even as she knew there might be none. John had set his face against her. He had hardened his heart. And if he had not yet mentioned legal separation, it was only because he was too much of a gentleman to do so while she was ailing.

In which case . . . Laura smoothed back her hair with the flat of her hand and made a quick inventory of her wrinkles. Not bad, she thought, reassured. Not many. Nothing major. Not time to worry yet . . . Now, where was she? Ah, yes. In which case, there was no hurry for her to make a full recovery. Goodness, it could take months and months. Hers could be, if necessary, the most baffling, intractable disease in all of medical history.

The sky beyond the window had turned the colour of bilge. It would probably snow. She felt an unaccountable, infantile glee at the prospect; she hoped for a blizzard, and went quickly to look out upon the afternoon, which was even now being consumed by the dark.

Two figures were walking across the black expanse of lawn towards the house, butting into the blustery wind – Tobias in some kind of shapeless anorak affair, and at his side, in a long flapping overcoat, bloody Jasper.

Oh, why could he not have stayed away? His presence here, now, in the house, was unspeakably offensive, an insult to her, and an irritant. She danced her hands in agitation. What to do, what to *do*? She wanted to slap, to grab, to grasp, to cling. She wanted to hang on tight to someone, and to squeeze and squeeze. She wanted to be held, to be folded into strong male arms – although whether those arms should be John's or Jasper's, she somehow could not decide (these days the two men, like Box and Cox, took turns in the tumbled bed of her fantasies).

At that instant Jasper spoke: a sudden gust of wind smacked his voice against the window pane. And, as Laura stepped back in panic, he lifted his head, seeming to look right up at her, so that fleetingly his gaze met hers.

It came to her then with the full force of revelation. He cared. He truly did. Her spirit had called to his, and his had answered. She had compelled him with her eyes. A thought had passed unmediated from her to him, and he had sent it, like a kiss, winging back to her.

Hope ran warm again in her veins. Her face burned with it. All was not then lost. The legendary Scorpio passions were aroused. And off them sparked new energy, propelling her towards her dressing room, her bathroom, grabbing up, as she went, handfuls of creams and cosmetics. When she went down tonight for dinner, it would be with head held high (she practised the movement, a proud rake of the chin), and in the brilliant shade of red which she had favoured since Rei Kawakubo had pronounced it the new black. The red which shrieked 'danger', which shrieked 'everybody down'.

Below, in the gardens, Jasper stood, his feet planted wide apart, peering sore-eyed up at the length of gutter which flapped loose above the balcony room. The lot of the land-owner, he was thinking, was ever a wearying one, a heavy responsibility. These big old houses simply ate money. And if he noticed how the lights snapped on in window after window, it was purely subconscious. 'You're right,' he said to Toby. 'We shall have to get that seen to. Oh, now look, it's starting to snow.'

———————— • ————————

'It's gone all funny again.' Caroline sat on the sofa, staring at the snowstorm, at the electrical blizzard on the TV screen, the picture in smithereens. Television was still something of a novelty to her. No one at home ever bothered with it. It just hadn't been part of life at Hartwell, where everyone had other preoccupations. Now game shows and chat shows, soap operas and sit coms absorbed her utterly. She was fascinated mainly by their awfulness. They made her jaw drop. 'I shall phone the dealers in the morning. They can send a mechanic.'

'An engineer.'

'That's what I mean. An engineer.'

'Ach, turn the ruddy thing off.' Patrick thumbed the hair back from her cheek, potted a noisy kiss in her ear, and pulled her to him, while with his free hand he prised the remote control unit out of her grip and pressed the 'power' button, sighing with relief as the screen went mercifully blank.

'Perhaps it's the aerial,' she wondered aloud, as she snuggled against him, still seeing a hectic razzle-dazzle in front of her eyes. 'Or atmospheric conditions. Do you think that could be it? The wind blowing the signal about.' She lacked even the most elementary understanding of the workings of the cathode ray tube, and it seemed to her altogether possible that the foul weather might somehow have become caught up with the transmission, to be beamed into her sitting room. In an unthinking way, she half-believed that they had been watching actual snow.

'I guess so. Anyway, who gives a damn? It's chewing-gum for the mind, is telly. Who said that?'

'You did.'

'No, stupido. Who said it *first*?'

'Well, who did?'

'Search me. Some bright spark.' He picked up her hand and counted the fingers, as if to reassure himself that she was still all there, complete, completely his. 'I love you, Missus.'

'I can't think why.'

'No, neither can I. I really cannot.' Patrick refused to indulge her self-deprecation, to be drawn by her put-downs, preferring to tease her out of her diffidence. Didn't she know how adorable she was? It was part of her appeal to him, of course, her very bashfulness. And he was besotted with her squidgy soft-centredness. But it bothered him, too, because it was not appropriate, and because he felt the pain of it, and it made him fearful for her. She would have to toughen up. They both needed to be a bit robust. How else could they hope to come through this?

'Shall I get us some supper?' she offered.

'In a minute, if you like.' He gave her her hand back, placing it in her lap and patting it.

'What do you fancy? I could do a pasta.'

'What sort of pasta?'

'*Alla* tomato. Or *alla* mushrooms.'

'Or *alla* tomato *and* mushroom.'

'If that's what you want.'

'That's what I want. And lots of garlic. And bacon. And cheese.'

'Pig.'

'Hey, listen, I'm starving. I've had nothing all day, except a steak-and-kidney pie at the garage, and that was cack, it made me sick, I chucked it in the bin.'

'You should know better than to eat such stuff,' she fretted, going to work on her nails, gnawing at the pathetic stubs. The mere mention of the petrol station brought her out in a rash of guilt. 'Processed meat products. They're mostly made from slurry. Disgusting. You'll get – what's it called? – spongy cow disease.'

'All right. I hear you. Now get my dinner, you spongy cow. Ouch! Geroff!' Laughing, he raised an arm to shield himself as she set about him with a cushion.

She was at the stove frying onions when he came to stand behind her, to hug her about the waist and to impose the full weight of his head on her shoulder.

'I phoned Laura today,' she told him with false casualness, prodding around in the frying pan with a spatula. And, as her face rinsed red with the shame and confusion she always felt these days in regard to family, she was glad that he could not see it.

'Uh-huh. How is she?'

'She's OK.'

'Just OK.'

'Well, not great. She sounded a bit sort of . . . I don't know . . . a bit querulous.'

'What's her problem, then?' He menaced her neck with his teeth. He was always thus dismissive when he spoke of his mother. Was it possible, Caroline wondered – and this thought had been scratching around in her subconscious – that he could feel so little about his parent? That he had truly cut her down to size? That Laura was no more important to him than – let's be honest – he was to her? Or might there be, as he himself had put it, some heavy shit in there somewhere which must eventually be worked through.

'I'm not certain,' she said distractedly. 'Oh, they've arranged to have Granny to stay. For a rest, kind of thing. So she can convalesce. She's still not quite herself, apparently. So no doubt there'll be some friction there. They've always fought like cats, those two. But I'm not sure what else is going on. If there's some kind of sub-plot.' She drew a breath. And, in a rush, she told him, 'I said I would go for Christmas. Did I do right?'

'I reckon,' he responded neutrally. 'Well, you have to, really, don't you? Or questions will be asked.'

'And you'll go home to Ireland?'

'Yes.'

'Then will you . . . you know . . .' She gazed at the wall, at the pattern of the tiles, at the grouting, at the calendar she had hung there, which showed a picture of Wells Cathedral and claimed that this was July. 'I mean, will you be coming back here?'

'Be coming back?' He laughed incredulously, loosed his hold on her, stepped away from her. 'You think I'd walk out on you? Desert you? Scarper? How can you even. . . ? Jesus Christ!' The skin on his scalp was very slack; his dark hair moved like a wig when he tugged at it.

'I'm sorry.' She turned to him, marking two-four time with the spatula, misery wrenching at her features. 'Only, I wouldn't blame you, that's all.'

'How many times must I tell you, Carrie?'

'I know, but –'

'No buts. I love you. I need you. I can't live without you. I *won't* live without you. I've got you, sort of, in my heart. I've got you here.' In a fury he banged with his fist on his chest.

Dropping her head, she mumbled something into the V of her blouse.

'What's that? What are you saying?'

'I said . . .' She brought her head up again to consider him. He was so *alive*, somehow. This was the wonder of it. That something could live and breathe and run with fluids and have humours, have emotions, and be so much *hers*. At night she would lie awake beside him and cherish the curve between lip and chin, or the way his nose spread across his face as if it had been pasted on, or the sculptural beauty of an ear. She marvelled at his maleness, at the hedgehog coarseness of his pubic hair and the hardness of his penis which was such a satisfying handful. And she was never happier than when she was curled around him, with his bony buttocks pressed against her belly, warm and snug. 'How *can* you love me that way?'

'I can love you that way because . . .' He went to the window, rubbed with his fingertips at the steamy pane. There was nothing but blackness beyond. They were so much alone, the pair of them. They were beleaguered. He sang a few tuneless bars, an unmelodic pa-pom, pa-pom, to relieve his tension. And, for his own benefit as much as Caroline's, he tried to rationalise his feelings. 'There is a part of me that is your brother, that loves you like a sister. But there's another part of me that *isn't* your brother, and that has a passion for the part of you that isn't my sister, do you follow? Do you think that makes sense?'

She shrugged. 'How should I know. I can't tell any more. I don't know *what* makes sense.' She began to stir the onions. Salt tears splashed into the pan. 'Do you wish you'd never got involved? That we'd not met up again?'

'We didn't "meet up". I came to find you. And, no, I most surely don't wish it, though I could wish it wasn't all so fucking complicated. Now, Carrie, don't ask me again what we're going to do, because I don't have any answers for you.'

Sniffing, she used the back of her hand as a handkerchief. 'I wasn't going to ask you. I realise it's hopeless.'

'That's not what I said.'

'But it *is*.'

'No it isn't. Not entirely. Matters could be worse.'

'How could they?'

'You could burn the onions, for a start off, and spoil the spaghetti sauce.'

'Oh, dear, yes. My mind wasn't on it.'

'Well, look, you just pay attention to the cooking. And give me my orders. I'll do a hand's turn. Will I grate some parmesan or what?'

'Or what,' she decided.

'What?'

'Put your arms around me, that's what.'

He came to embrace her. He squeezed very tight. He said, 'Give us a kiss for Christmas.'

———————— • ————————

Laura twirled her wine glass between thumb and first finger, enchanted by the play of electric light upon crystal – and by an interior vision of her enchanted self. Much as mirror trades with mirror, reflections of reflections of reflections, Laura traded with her inward eye, a delightful image of Laura. And in her head she was singing 'Lady in Red' ('Never saw you looking so lovely as you look tonight, never saw you shine so bright'). She felt a tiny bit drunk and absolutely radiant.

She sipped from the glass, set it down, picked up her fork and toyed with the pinkish sliver of duck. 'Caroline phoned,' she said sweetly, conversationally, turning her head to include everyone in the compass of her smile.

'Oh, yes?' John's eyebrows shot up in polite enquiry. Poor John! He could not sustain his hate campaign against her, could not with any commitment remain distant and aloof. His nature was against him. And his upbringing. He was just not a churl. And in spite of everything he loved her. He was visibly thawing as she turned up the heat of her presence.

'Caro? How's she doing?' Tobias piled potatoes on to his plate. 'Still enjoying life in the Smoke? I say, you chaps, fall to, dig in, there's plenty here for everyone. Have a few of these, Laura. They'll make you big and strong. We've got to get you back to your boxing weight.'

'She's coming down for Christmas.' Laura's gaze, like a searchlight, raked around the table and came to rest upon Jasper, who sat with head bowed, his face closed, saying nothing, hunched over his lust. She knew him so well by now, he could keep no secrets from her, least of all that his insides were curdled with sexual desire. If only the table were smaller, their chairs closer! She could slip off her shoe and stroke his thigh with her foot, she could drop it in his lap and tease his throbbing prick with her toe, even as she discussed with her husband the plans they must make for a party.

'That will be nice,' said John, who seemed – dear, kind man –to be mesmerised by her beauty. 'Long time since we saw our girl, what?'

It came to Laura that sooner or later her husband

would seek a reconciliation, he would wish to share her bed again. Well, good. Great. Fine. She could handle that. It was part of the deal that was marriage, and was ultimately what she wanted. Only let it be later rather than sooner. Let it not, above all, be tonight. Laura had other plans for tonight.

'I must say, Wicked Stepmother, you're looking match-fit again at last,' Toby complimented her. 'Are you over the distemper?'

'I think so, yes, thank you Tobias.'

'Glad to hear it. I was getting quite worried. Ah, no thank you, Stevens, not a drop more wine for me, I'm limbering up for the sack race – isn't that right, Jasper?'

Still Jasper said nothing. He seemed almost to have knotted around his ardour. And when he looked momentarily up at his brother, his eyes were dark as coals, and smouldering.

My foolish boy, thought Laura, triumphant. You fancied you were so strong when you walked out on me. You imagined you were so independent. But I knew, always, in my heart, that you'd come running back to me.

'I shall take the Range Rover in the morning,' John said to nobody in particular. 'Cut us a tree.'

'That would be nice,' Laura distantly, dutifully replied. 'I love the smell, don't you? We'll have to get the Holloway character to look out the fairy lights.'

'I can do that if you like,' offered Tobias. 'Cut the tree, I mean. Fairy lights are women's work. I'll take the chainsaw. I say, Jas, you're very quiet. What's up with you? You're sitting there like a smitten sheep. Tongues will start to wag. People might say we're in love.'

'Leave him alone,' said Laura tartly.

'But he's got a face like a pig's bottom. Doesn't he know it's Christmas?'

'Not yet, it isn't.'

'Well, very nearly. We're even now making plans to deck the halls with wreaths of holly, aren't we? To gather around and sing a few fa-la-las, a few ding-dong merrilies, and generally have a good wassail.'

Finally Jasper found his voice. He said, 'Shut your mouth, can't you?'

'Yes, do Toby,' Laura agreed. 'Give us all a break. I say, forgive me everyone, but I think I should go and lie down. I'm feeling a little queer.'

'Anyone we know?'

'I said shut *up*, Tobias.'

'That's right,' said John. 'Shut up, Tobias. And show some respect.'

'Sorry, sorry, sorry.' Hurt and aggrieved, Tobias raised his hands, palms outward, fending them off, shrinking from them. 'It's just my natural exuberance, you see. My jolly old *joie de vivre*, a commodity which, I may say, seems to me to be in short supply round here these days. What the hell is up with the lot of you? You're no fun any more.'

'People have different ideas of fun,' said Laura, with meaning. Jasper would know what she was saying. Jasper would comprehend. She folded her napkin and set it aside, stood up, swayed on her feet, passed a hand across her brow. 'Some of us have a rather more adult view of it than others. Do excuse me, won't you? I just have to go to bed.'

'Will you be all right?' asked John, with at least a hint of his old indulgence. 'Should I send for Forrest?'

'Good gracious, no!' Laura shuddered. 'Please don't concern yourself. I shall be fine.' She spread her fingers on the cloth and studied her nails for a few seconds, allowing her auburn hair to fall about her face. Covertly, she stole a glance at Jasper. She had never seen him so wrought up with passion. No one but she would realise it, though. No one but she knew the signs. 'See you later,' she said softly. And she went then swiftly from the room.

As soon as she was through the bedroom door, she began to shed clothes: a trail of them – the red dress, silk knickers, stockings, suspenders – marked her progress to her dressing room, where she stood before the mirror and considered her nakedness, which was the closest thing she knew to perfection, a work of art made flesh.

She wrapped her arms around herself and caressed her shoulders as a lover might, relishing the satin feel of her skin. It was not surprising that Jasper could no longer resist her. The only surprise was that he'd held out all this time.

What should she say when he came to her, as she had no doubt that he would? She would scold him just a little for his inconstancy, initiate a quarrel, that they might kiss and make up.

She clasped her small breasts and weighed them contemplatively. Then she drew a line between them with one finger, down over her stomach to the depilated triangle which some tasteless creep had named the mound of Venus.

Later, much later, lying in bed, wearing only a gold chain necklace, and soused in Ysatis, she listened impatiently for the sound of footsteps in the hallway, a discreet knock at the door.

Various clocks around the house were striking twelve with their usual bewildering disynchronism, as Jasper slid from his room along the sleeping corridor and placed a foot upon the creaking stairs.

At her door he hesitated, feeling like . . . well, like a thief in the night. He screwed up his eyes and pictured her, her long hair spread about the pillow. He made a fist with which to knock and used it tentatively.

No reply. She might be sleeping. He knocked again, more loudly.

'Come in,' said a voice. And, as he pushed open the door, 'I thought it would be you,' said Shell.

A Merry Christmas

CHAPTER

———— • ————

11

The girl sent a card. It showed three choirboys under a lantern, their freckled faces upturned, their mouths gaping, going 'O'. Oh, little town of Bethlehem, or something of the sort. Inside she had written 'Love and kisses, Shell.' Just that. No other message. No news.

The card stood now on top of the bookcase with three others. On the shelf below were the complete works of Dickens. A set. Ernest had gone in for sets, he had liked things to match, to be uniform, to come in pairs and fours and dozens. There was not a vase in the place, or a chair or a candlestick that hadn't an identical twin. And this straight row of spines with their smart maroon bindings, lettered in gilt, each one just the same as its neighbour, had tickled him half to death. They looked, he had always said, very classy.

'Class, my arse,' thought Doris, dragging her armchair in front of the television ready for the Queen at twelve. Don't talk to her about class. Whoever dreamed up that system, she would happily swing for him.

She never missed the speech, which she found reassuring. Her Majesty, indeed, was reassuring. Under that crown, in her half-moon specs, she looked to be a nice, ordinary, decent human being, a homebody, a grandmother, not so very different, actually, from Doris herself (were they ever to meet – which was not, of course, very likely – Doris felt sure they would hit it off immediately; they would probably have a good old chin-wag).

She went to the oven to look at the half-chicken hissing and spitting in the pan. Nearly done. She'd have the leg today, and the breast cold with mash on Boxing Day. She prodded it with a fork so the juices ran. This would not be the first Christmas she'd spent quite alone, and she didn't much mind it, to be honest. At least she had her health and strength. At least she had her independence, and didn't have to wait around for Meals on Whatsname to bring her stringy turkey in congealed gravy, for stodgy Christmas pud and lumpy custard.

All the same, she could have hoped for something more from Michele. A note, perhaps, to bring her up to date, to let her know the state of play at Hartwell. And, yes, a present. Wouldn't you think she'd have sent a present? A little something – sweets, a hankie, smellies for the bath – a small token of affection, bought out of her wages.

Doris began almost to regret that she didn't have a telephone. She had never held with the infernal apparatus. You paid a lot of money, it seemed to her, to have strangers contruding in your life at all hours of the day and night, badgering you to buy a security alarm or a fitted kitchen, or wanting the Sunlight Laundry, or an emergency plumber, or someone called Jim. Even so, it would have been nice, just this once, to pick up the receiver, to dial a number and to hear the child's voice. It would have been nice to be in touch.

Now, look, listen. Listen to Her Majesty. She had a lovely manner with her, didn't she, never laying down the law, but just taking you through things in a nice way, and was very understandable. She had aged in the last year, Doris thought. That was what grandchildren did for you. Yes, didn't she know it? The Queen would be pushing sixty-five. She was of pensionable age. But of course she would never need a pension, or a bus pass. And why? Because of some accident of birth. Pure chance it was that Elizabeth Windsor got to rule a nation, to ride in a golden coach, and to reside in splendour at Buckingham Palace, while Doris Fairchild had to scratch a living, and to do for herself, and to put up with a leaky toilet because she couldn't afford to get it fixed.

It was one of her major preoccupations, the basic unfairness of it all, the way you were forced to take potluck. Most people never even stood a chance. Her own mother, and her grandmother, and her great, and her great great, and her great great great grandmother . . . they'd all been in the same boat. The same with her daughter and her granddaughter, born as they had been into a long line of losers, with nothing but hardship handed down through generations.

You *could* move up in the world, of course, if you used your loaf. It wasn't easy, but there were ways and ways. Some, like Laura Charteris, got there on their backs. They relied on their looks, on their bodies and their whatsnames to get what they wanted. But they were prostitutes really, there was no other word for it. And they could very easily come unstuck.

Why, this very day, at this very minute, even as Doris

sat watching her old black-and-white television, Laura,
Lady Charteris, might be coming unstuck.

————————— • —————————

'You see,' said Caroline, 'we love each other. That's all
there is to it, really. But it's a terrible problem because
he's half my brother – that is to say, he's my half-brother
– and it's against the law and everything. I wasn't
supposed to breathe a word about it to another living
soul. It had to be our secret, Patrick's and mine. That's
what we agreed. But it's just got bigger and bigger and
bigger, till I can't squash it down inside me any longer. So
I decided I would share it with you because I know I can
trust you. You do understand, don't you? You don't
blame me or anything?'

If he did see, however, if he understood, and whether
or not he blamed her, Freckles wasn't saying. He merely
tossed his head and blew his nose noisily, huffing steam
from his nostrils as he toiled up the steep incline. He
had grown fat since the summer, and lazy; he was
round as a barrel and woolly as a teddy bear in his
spotty winter coat. I've been neglecting him, thought
Caroline who, having supposed that she was brimful
with feelings of guilt, found room in there still for a little
more.

At the top of the hill she wheeled the pony round so
she could look back over the grounds of Hartwell to the
house, dwindled now by distance, a small-scale model of
a stately home. She let the reins fall, and the pony at once
began to crop the frosted turf, moving around like a

Hoover, fussing his bit with the fidgety noise of an old man fielding his false teeth.

I've been happy here, she said to herself, swaying in the saddle, thrown off balance, as Freckles made a sudden lunge at a bush. Perhaps I may be happy here again. But the possibility seemed remote. She'd had it, sort of. It was over.

Nor was she the only one for whom it had gone wrong. The whole household seemed blighted by misery. The atmosphere was so thick with grievance, you could have spooned up great dollops of it with a ladle. The cold outside was bitter, but it was at least an honest-to-goodness, seasonal cold. The cold inside the place was something else, and no coat or sweater or blanket was proof against it.

She had batted down to Dorset in her sporty little Fiat, inwardly determined to make the best of the break. She could survive without her lover for a few days if she had to, though there was not one part of her that didn't miss him. It might even do them good to have this space. And her family still had a call on her affections; she needed now and then to spend some time with them.

But nothing had improved since her last visit. Rather the reverse. She had found Laura sullen, Jasper distant, Sir John distrait, while Maudie, who had been installed in the green room where she spent most of the day, slept for hour after hour after hour, to awake at last crotchety and confused.

As she sat there with her eyes screwed up against the light, Caroline sighted a horse and rider emerging at a trot from the stable block. Tobias, she decided, peering

between cupped hands. Toby on . . . Kia-ora. No, no, on
Bella. She recognised the flighty mare, the way she
crabbed left and right and flicked her tail. In a moment
Toby kicked his mount into a gallop, flying along the
bridleway and up the hill to where Caroline waited.

'What-ho, Caro,' he greeted her, reining in beside her,
flushed and panting with exhilaration. And 'Whoa',' he
soothed, as Bella skittered about.

'Hello there.'

'I hoped I'd catch up with you.'

'Well, we'd not got very far, had we? We've just been
ambling, you know. Hacking around. She all right?'

'Bella? She's fine. She's just spooking herself. Seeing
snakes in the grass. Want to ride over to the ford with
me?'

'If you like.'

'Work up an appetite for the figgy pudding. Get in the
mood for a game of charades.'

'Charades?' Caroline uttered a mirthless laugh. Wasn't
the whole of life one long charade?

'What's funny?' Tobias demanded, as horse fell com-
panionably in step with horse, Freckles exerting a
calming influence over Bella.

'Nothing, actually. I was just thinking.'

'A penny for them.'

'For my thoughts? Goodness, no. They're not worth
even that.'

'Nevertheless . . . Go on, give. Speak. What the hell?
It's only money. I'll write you an IOU.'

'No, it's all right. You can have this one on me. I was
just wondering what on earth was going on here.

Everyone's so dreadfully uptight – apart from you, of course.'

'Of course.'

'So what is it about, do you suppose?'

'I think there must be a curse on the family,' he muttered darkly. 'It's like the Fall of the House of Usher all over again. Any moment I expect the place to split asunder and collapse into the tarn.' Then he chuckled in delight and, as much for his own amusement as for hers, began to chant, 'Usher, Usher, we all fall down!'

'I'm glad you can see a humorous side.'

'You've got to, haven't you? Anyway, Caro, I shouldn't worry. It's probably just the winter. And Old Mother Grant has had a close call, after all. And father has something on his mind, though I'm not sure what. And Laura's just being Laura with brass knobs on. And Jasper's got a bad case of creative constipation.'

'Poor Jasper. He's stuck over his novel?'

'Yes. And also he's in love.'

'Jasper is? Truthfully?'

'That's what I said.'

'With who? *Whom*?'

'Ah, *hah*. I cannot reveal. My lips are sealed. You can pull out my toenails, and gouge out my eyes, and roast me over hot coals, and squeeze my blackheads, and eat my last Rolo, but you won't get me to divulge the lady's name.'

'Very well, then.'

'Very well, what?'

'Very well, don't divulge it.'

'You're not going to poke me with a cattle prod? Or

hang me up by my feet and beat me with birch twigs? Or force feed me Chicken Macnuggets? You don't, in short, *want* me to spill the beans?'

'Not if you've promised that you won't. It wouldn't be fair to Jasper.'

'Cara mia, you're so moral!'

'Do you reckon?'

'Absolutely.'

'I might yet surprise you.'

'Not you. I bet you've never done a bad thing.'

Caroline gazed resolutely ahead of her, at her pony's nodding head, between his swivelling ears. 'That's what you imagine, is it?' And she said to herself, If he did but know!

'I'm convinced of it. And if you *have*, then pray don't disabuse me. Tread softly, for you tread on my dreams. If you've been looking up poo-willy-bum words in the dictionary, and ringing on doorbells and running away, I would rather not be apprised of it. It would destroy for ever my belief in the essential goodness of human nature which you have always seemed to me to embody.'

'A belief which, if I may say so, is sadly misplaced. You must consider me very boring, Toby.'

'Why?'

'Because you're so sure I'm a goodie-goodie. And goodie-goodies always are, aren't they? Boring, that is.'

'Not in the slightest. There's nothing wrong, so far as I'm concerned, with being sound.'

'You think I'm sound?'

'In wind and limb.'

'Not dull?'

'Not remotely.'

The path narrowed and the two horses bumped together for a few strides, before Bella, asserting herself, barged ahead of Freckles. From behind, Tobias looked very square, very secure in the saddle, as if nothing could unseat him. How nice, Caroline thought, to be so sturdy, to be emotionally as well as physically beefy.

'Toby,' she said after a moment, addressing the back of his head.

'Speaking.'

'Have you ever, uh, you know, been in love?'

'Thousands of times.' He twisted in the saddle to grin at her.

'Look, no kidding. I mean, really in love. The way you say Jasper is. Have you ever felt that way?'

The path widened. She came alongside him once more.

'I've been a little in love a lot,' he confessed, deciding to give the question his best shot, 'and a lot in love a little.'

'Who were you a lot in love with, then?'

'Ah, now . . .' He frowned as he recalled. 'I was *quite* a lot in love with Jess. Jessica Bellmaine. You met her, didn't you? At the Clarkes' or somewhere? And I was a *lot* a lot in love with Sophie Picton. You remember old Hugo Farnsbarns-Ftang-Ftang-Upyourbum-Whateverhisnamewas?'

'Hugo Upsall-Wyse?'

'One and the same. AKA Hugo First. Well, he and I had fisticuffs over Sophie. Went the distance. Pistols at dawn style of thing.'

'You did? Who won?'

'Er, me, I believe. On points. A moral victory, at least. After which, for a while, I had a big thing for Arabella Claridge.' In spite of his best efforts to be serious, his face split open as a joke occurred to him.

'Don't say it,' Caroline cautioned him.

'Say what?'

'About the "big thing" you had for her. I'm not interested.'

'Unfortunately, nor was she.'

'Shame!'

'Yes, wasn't it. So, sweet Caroline, when you shall these unlucky deeds relate, then must you speak of one that lov'd not wisely but too well.'

'I must say, I'm surprised. I had this idea that you didn't get involved.'

'You think that I should wear my heart upon my sleeve for daws to peck at?'

'Jasper does.'

'Jasper is Jasper. I'm me.'

'So, are you going to tell me? What's the story? Who is he having an affair with?'

'Oh, ho, ho! You want me to turn Queen's evidence! Well, I shan't, see? You can tie me up and put ferrets down my trousers, and force me to listen to ABBA's greatest hits, and take away my Breakaway –'

'What is all this tying-up stuff? I'm beginning to suspect you've got a fetish for it.'

'Well, you know the old saying?'

'What?'

'Gentlemen prefer bonds. Come on now, I'll race you

to the river.' So saying, he gave Bella her head, and, with
a thunder of hooves, he was gone.

———————— • ————————

'Well, we haven't had that snow they promised us.'
Laura plucked a stray hair from her sleeve – one of her
own hairs, long and lustrous and red still, thanks no
doubt to the high alkaline content of her diet, to her
scrupulous avoidance of corrosive acid foods. She
studied it for an instant, then, with a dismissive little flick
of the fingers, consigned it to the draught of a sigh. 'I
should have liked a white Christmas,' she added lamely.
She hadn't a facility for small talk, and rarely engaged in
it, except flirtatiously, with attractive men, when what
was *not* being said carried so much more freight than
what *was*. And she found it particularly wearing to
converse with Maudie, to whom she had had nothing
really to say since about 1965.

'You remember 1947?' said her mother, picking at the
tartan rug which was spread across her bony knees,
balling the woolly fuzz, milling it between thumb and
forefinger. Maudie Grant might not remember too clearly
the events of yesterday. She might be hazy as to what
month this was. But the memory of that bitter winter
more than half a lifetime ago was all at once crystalline.
'Drifts as high as houses. The coal trains couldn't get
through. The planes couldn't get off the ground. It was a
shocking to-do, an absolute disgrace. People were
stranded in their homes. Everywhere, power cuts. Even
Buckingham Palace was lit up by candles, if you can

imagine it. The Air Force had to fly in supplies to villages.
The people of Widdlescombe nearly starved.'

'Of course I don't remember '47,' Laura snapped at
her. 'I wasn't even born then, was I? And there's no such
place as Widdlescombe. I mean, *is* there? There can't be.
*Widdles*combe! Give me a break.'

'There most certainly is. In Devon.'

'All right, if you say so.'

'You would have been a babe in arms then.'

'I *wouldn't*. I *wasn't*. I just told you, Mother, it was
before I was born. Christ, I could murder for a G and T.'

'You drink too much,' remarked Maudie as her
daughter got up to ring for service. 'You always did. Your
liver must look like a slab of lard.'

Now wasn't that typical of the poisonous old bat? You
had no way of knowing where you stood with her. Either
the woman was gaga or she wasn't, she ought at least to
make up her mind. Instead, she had these tiresome
flashes of lucidity, against which one could never quite
arm oneself. One minute she'd come out with some
remark so sharp it was a wonder that her tongue was not
cut to ribbons; the next minute she'd lapse into retrospec-
tive mood, revealing a sentimental side, of which Laura
had never before caught so much as a glimpse.

She was right about the booze, though, curse her! All
those empty calories sloshing around in the system,
souring the digestion, undermining nutrition, irritating
the intestine wall, threatening the vital organs. It was a
wonder, Laura told herself, that her skin was not
blotchy, her eyes puffy, her hair prematurely grey, a
miracle that she was blessed with so dewy a complexion,

with so fresh and youthful an aspect. Oh, what the hell? Drink was, it seemed, her only remaining vice.

'Ah, Stevens. There you are. I'll have a gin and tonic, please, to take the chill off. And do send someone to bank up the fire. Just look at it, it's burned right down.'

With a drink in her hand, she felt better. Such a cheery sound, the chink of ice cubes.

'Caroline's gone out for a ride on her pony,' she offered, raising the glass and squinting through it at the blur of Christmas-tree lights till she felt quite drunk on the distortions. 'And Tobias, I believe, has gone with her. But look, now, it's nearly a quarter to one. It's time those two were back. It's time they were *all* here.'

'It's time she was married.' Maudie shuffled her feet, so her knees bumped up and down under the blanket. Illness had done something awful to her; she had faded like an old photograph. But her eyes were bright, her gaze keen, and she appeared, for the moment, to be fully commissioned.

'Oh, I don't know. She's young yet.' Laura took a swig of the astringent liquid, which seared its way down behind her ribs. Chance, she privately thought, would be a fine thing. For who would choose to marry tubby little Caroline Charteris, except perhaps some chancer, after her money? This was the problem as Laura saw it – and, goodness knows, she'd warned against it until she was blue in the face. 'Go on a diet,' she'd urged Caroline. 'Shape up. Slim down. Make something of yourself.' But it had been like talking to the proverbial brick wall which, more and more, in Laura's eyes, Caroline was coming to resemble. (No, she wasn't imagining it: the child had actually put *on* weight.) Well, there had to come a time when one washed one's hands of other people. Having done one's best for them, one could simply do no more.

'She doesn't have a beau at all? No one has marked her card?' It was odd. Maudie felt sure she had heard something about a boyfriend, but quite what that had been, she could not recall. It was too, too frustrating. Like trying to tune in a wireless, picking up the faintest of signals from the other side of the world, only to lose it again.

'Not so far as I'm aware. But, you know, she's very secretive.' Laura sniffed. 'If there were someone, I dare say I should be the last to know.'

'Such a shame. If it weren't for her little problem . . . Was that a knock?'

'A knock?'

'At the door. Hark.' Maudie cocked her head and raised her index finger.

'I didn't hear anything, Mother.'

'Yes, there it is again. You heard it then?'

'Mm, yes, you're right. Come,' Laura called out imperiously, and into the sitting room came the funniest rag doll creature, a gawky young woman with big, pale eyes, a white face, an insolent mouth, and unkempt hair the colour of baked earth.

'I've been sent to see to the fire.'

'You have? Very well. Please do, before it goes out entirely.' Laura glared down into her tumbler, at the slice of lemon now beached on rocks of ice. She thirsted for a refill but decided she should wait. Presently, everyone would drift in, and then she'd have another, she'd have a large one. When she glanced up, the girl was standing by the fireplace, idle, gawping at her in the most witless way.

'What are you staring at?'

At once the girl turned her back. 'Nothing,' she said. And, abruptly, as she laid a log across the fire-dogs, 'Sorry.'

'So I should hope.' Laura probed the lemon slice with one finger so it leaked alcoholic juices, which she tossed down her throat like medicine. 'And do hurry up,' she scolded. For this person, by her mere presence, somehow unsettled her. Who was she anyway? What business had she here? Perhaps she was some kind of holiday relief, sent in by the agency. But she didn't look the part, she didn't seem cut out for domestic service. She might have been a model, actually, in these strange times when fashion editors, perversely, preferred the extraordinary, the frankly odd, to the emphatically beautiful (flipping through the latest glossy magazines, Laura would wonder at the changes that had come about since she herself graced the cover of *Vogue*).

'Will there be anything else?' Having heaped up the logs and blown the ashes about with the bellows, the girl now stood before her, dusting her hands on her skirt, sort of staring and not staring, her eyes darting back and forth, snatching – yes, *snatching* – looks at her in a manner which was most unnerving.

'No, there's – Oh, hang on. One thing. Wait. Take this glass. Fill it up for me will you, from the bottle over there on the sideboard? That's it. Good. Right, you may leave us.'

'Thank you,' said the girl. She made for the door, hesitated, then with one more backward glance she was gone.

'Ugly little thing,' remarked Laura, irked, shifting around in her chair.

'Who?'

'That one. Whatever she's called. The maid.'

But this time Maudie did not respond. She had sunk back into herself. She was thinking, rather sadly, of Monty.

'Now!' said John, backing in through the door with armfuls of parcels in colourful wrappings.

'Now, what?' Laura swirled the gin around, took a swig, grimaced.

'What?'

'You said "Now". I said, "Now, what?" '

'Well, nothing really, what?'

Raising her eyes to the ceiling, Laura recited, 'I shot an arrow in the air. It fell to earth I know not where.'

'Oh, quite. Yes. I see what you're saying.' John bent to dump the parcels, with little ceremony, under the tree, then, straightening, fixed her with his desolate gaze. Even if he could forgive his wife – and he had, after all, a forgiving heart –he did not know how to get close to her again. Her mood of chronic self-pity had been replaced these past few days by one of relentless acerbity. He longed at times to fold her in his arms, to feel her warmth and closeness, to nuzzle her hair, to smell her skin, but it would be like hugging a porcupine. 'Well, when I said "Now", I suppose I just meant . . . you know, "Hello". '

'Then why not say that?'

'Very well. Hello. Can I get you a drink?'

'I have one, see?' She held it at arms length in ironic salutation.

'What is that?'

'Why, mother's ruin, what else?'

'I was thinking more of champagne.'

'Why sham pain, when you can have the real thing?'

'What?'

'Oh, nothing. It wasn't even funny. You know, I should never make jokes. Have you heard of a place called Widdlescombe, by any chance?'

'Widdlescombe Fair.'

'That's Widdicombe. This place is Widdles.'

'Oh, well, yes, probably. In Devon or somewhere. Why?'

'No reason.'

'You ask a question like that for no reason?' John ran his fingers through his hair so it stood up in a coxcomb. 'Where is everybody, actually?'

'Well, Caroline and Toby went riding. They ought to be back.'

'And what about Jasper?'

Laura shrugged. What *about* Jasper? What was she to make of him? Did he or did he not want her? Why was he being so shifty? What, in short, was his game?

It had been a mistake, of course, ever to have got involved with the little motherfucker. Except . . . except insofar as he had added substantially to the sum of her sexual adventures, when the big fear, never fully confronted, never expressed, was that she would grow old and die before she had had her fill. Sex for her had always been the ultimate celebration of her youth and beauty, and she had half-formed night-time horrors of herself grown old, still burdened down with un-consumed passion, with unexpended lust.

If Jasper had done nothing else, he had enriched the mixture of sexual experience which was like a pool, a deep, black, oily sump within her. And in that case, why, why, why did she now feel so much the poorer, so depleted, so diminished by it all?

The worst part was not knowing, not understanding. For how was she to interpret the confused messages which he was sending her? Consider the way he so pointedly ignored her – proof, if proof were needed, that she still played upon his mind (for to ignore somebody was a conscious thing, it was a gesture). Then set against this the fact that he had made no move, had not sought her out, or picked a fight, or stolen a kiss, or indeed done anything to bring about a resolution. 'I just don't know where that boy is at,' she thought. And to John she said coolly, 'Jasper? Where is he? Now, *that*, my dear, I really could not tell you.'

He came to stand beside her then, and in a preoccupied way he ruffled her hair.

Laura ducked her head and drew away from him, fending off with a flap of the hand. She hadn't spent half an hour scrunch-drying it just for him to mess it up. 'Don't,' she said crossly. 'Don't do that.'

'Gerroff,' protested Shell, giggling, struggling ineffec-tually, weak with excitement, as two strong hands grabbed her from behind and hauled her into the library. 'Let go of me.'

'Is that what you want?' Jasper spun her around and pinned her against the door as he considered her. That face, that face! He so loved her beautiful, bemused face, endearingly smudged now with wood ash. He loved her wide and smiling mouth, her eyes as green and liquid as Frascati, gazing full into his. 'What have you been doing?'

'Working. What else?'

'At Christmas? It seems a shame.'

'It would be a shame, wouldn't it,' she told him impudently, 'if the likes of us weren't here to serve the likes of you?'

'Worse than that. It would be a tragedy.' He shoved a knee between her thighs, eased them apart, and kissed the throat which she exposed to him as she rolled her head around.

'But I'm not complaining.' She spoke with difficulty, to the ceiling, her voice croaky, the words tugging at the sinews in her neck and chest. Then she dropped her chin and said into her sternum, 'We're having our own Christmas dinner later. After. Downstairs. With wine, and crackers and all.'

'That's nice.'

'Yes, lovely. Listen,' she implored him with those greeny eyes, 'I really have to go.'

'Who says?'

'Mrs Holloway will be after me. She'll be wanting to know where I've got to, won't she?'

'Will she?'

'Of course she will.'

It was curious to think of Shell existing in that shadow world which was domestic service. Jasper had taken for granted, all his life, that unseen hands would make his bed and clean his shoes, that ghostly retainers would come and go, to clean and polish and put to rights, leaving behind them no trace of themselves but a waxy shine and a clingy scent of lavender.

His search for gritty realism had taken him to the inner city, among ordinary people; it had taken him into the home, the very heart of a working-class family. It had taken him, also, to a seedy Parisian hotel, with over-blown flowered wallpaper and scabby lino and a poly-thene bidet on a rickety stand. He had fumbled in the fetid darkness of the landing, as the timer switch clicked and the light cut out as always a few crucial seconds too soon, thinking, I'm here, I'm truly *here*, I'm where it happens. He was proud that he had made those journeys, that he had not been content, as Tobias was, to sit on his backside and feel smug about his lot. He liked the idea that he had grubbed around in the realism and the grit.

Only now did it occur to him that he need not have ranged so far or so wide, when everything he had sought was right here on his doorstep, indeed under his very roof. And it seemed to him, suddenly, that the servants' world, that mysterious nine-tenths, submerged though it was beneath his own, was if anything the more compelling; that it held the greater intrigue. It was almost as if the Charteris family was not after all the point of Hartwell – as if it existed for the other lot, the behind-the-scenes, the below-stairs people, of whom Michele Fairchild was one.

'Marry me.'

'Eh?' She blinked at him.

'Marry me,' he said again, meaning something other. Meaning that he wanted, at this moment – just for the moment – to possess her. He slid his hands up her skirt, hooked his fingers around the elastic of her knickers, and rolled the top down. They were so natural, so cotton, so plain. He loved the lack of artifice, the no-nonsense, unself-conscious honesty of her underwear. He loved its innocence.

'Don't,' she said for a second time, without conviction.

'Michele. Tell me something about yourself.'

'What?'

'Give me one material fact, one secret piece of information. Reveal something to me that you never revealed to another living soul.'

Frowning, she considered the question. 'Well . . .'

'Yes?'

'I'm scared of coat hangers,' she confessed in a rush. And, sounding wounded, 'Go on then, laugh at me, why don't you?' she said, as he shouted with mirth in her face.

'What are you talking about?'

'Coat hangers. The wire ones. They give me the creeps. Ever since I read somewhere about this soldier who ripped up a prostitute with one.' She shuddered, then folded her arms across her chest and glared at him. 'Right, it's your turn. Tell me one of your secrets.'

'My darling, I can't. I can't possibly match that.'

'All right then. Tell me this. Tell me about Laura,' she

challenged, and she was puzzled as his face took on a hunted look. 'What's up with you?'

'Nothing. What about Laura? What should I tell you?'

'I just encountered her.'

'You did? For the first time?'

'Yes. What's she like?'

'Well, what do *you* think?'

'I haven't a clue, have I?'

'But you met – you, er, *encountered* her.' He enjoyed the longer word, rolling it around his tongue, and he made a little note to himself, for his novel, that ordinary people, common people, liked to use such words as encounter, and commence, and purchase, and pardon, they liked a lot of syllables, liked to sound important. 'What do you think?'

'I thought she seemed a real sourpuss.'

He laughed again. 'You could be right at that, my sweet.' And insinuating a hand, he pushed his thumb up inside her and screwed it left and right.

'Geroutofit.'

'You don't want it?'

'It isn't that. You know it isn't.'

'You know what I'd like to do, Michele? Right here. At this very minute.'

There were clouds in his eyes, he was breathing fast through his mouth, and his face was set in a sort of snarl, the nostrils curled. Watching him, she felt dizzy with desire for him. 'Yes,' she said almost inaudibly.

'*Et toi?*'

'Come again?'

'That's kind of what I have in mind.'

'But listen. Ouch. I *have* to go. Before I get it in the neck.'

'In the *neck*?'

'Oh, Jasper, be serious. Stop larking around.'

'You see that table?'

'Which table?'

'Michele, for Pete's sake, there *is* only one.'

'Oh, right. Got you.'

'I want you to sit on it and –'

'But I *can't*. It's all right for you, isn't it? You won't get into trouble if –'

'Am I, or am I not, your lord and master?'

'I suppose so.'

'Well, then, do as I command.'

'But Mrs Holl– Ooh, don't *do* that, Jasper. I mean, please don't.'

He leant his weight against her, whispered 'Cross your legs behind me. Go on, I've got you, that's my girl.' And, wearing her like an apron, he carried her to the table, where he dumped her down. 'Loosen up.' He slapped her thigh and she uncoiled her legs. Yanking up her skirt, he stooped to kiss her. Squeezing her eyes shut, Michele exalted, 'He wants to marry me. He said he wants to marry me.' While Jasper, exultant, congratulated himself, 'Well, Toby, old son, you fancied your chances with this one. But I think I can claim to have won by a head.'

———— • ————

'Heads I win, tails you lose.' Josie flipped a coin, caught it and slapped it down on the back of her hand. 'Tails,' she announced in triumph. 'Right, Thomas, it's you to do the dishes, you hear me? I win, fair and square.'

'You play a funny game, Mrs Mulryan,' Tom accused his wife, and, seizing her from behind, he hugged the breath out of her till she rolled her eyes and lolled her tongue out.

'It's all right. Don't worry. *I'll* do the washing up.' Patrick scraped his chair back from the table. 'I'd like to. I'm so full of turkey, I shall fall asleep if I sit here a moment longer.' And he crossed at once to the old enamel sink, rolling up the sleeves of his new red sweater as he went.

'How domesticated you've become,' said Josie, wondering. 'London has done you that much for you, at least.'

'Yes.' He turned the hot tap with such force that the water splashed up and drenched him. 'Oh, rats!' And he stood there staring through the window at the long, narrow strip of garden, at the black skeleton of a cherry tree, at the brick backs of houses beyond the far wall, refusing to face his parents, to be drawn into discussion of any kind, while he waited for the sink to fill.

Questions hung in the air, unasked, unanswered. What had he been doing, where living, how surviving – that sort of thing. Their anxiety was palpable. They had a sense that he'd been up to something – but they would never in a million years guess what that something was.

'I'll make some coffee.' Josie came to the sink and, nudging him, budging him over with her hip, stuck the kettle under the cold tap. For a matter of seconds they stood side by side, in silence, contemplating the same concrete slab steps, the same scrap of lawn, the same fruit tree, the same forgotten bit of washing, a teatowel or something, starched by frost, on the line, each, if they did but know it, wearing the same unhappy frown. Then, with a little fuffing sound, a vexed puffing of the lips, and a toss of her ponytail, Josie went to set the kettle on the stove.

I love them, Patrick told himself, dunking a plate, holding it up to drip, staring, mesmerised, at the soap bubbles on its glistening surface. It was old and scratched and patterned blue. Josie had a passion for china and was forever buying bits and pieces, oddments from junk shops and market stalls. This one lived on the shelf, on the dresser, part of a motley collection with nothing in common but their chips and cracks and their crazed blue-and-whiteness. He wiped it with a sponge cloth, dunked it again. I love them. And I'm hurting them like hell. They're confused and they're anxious on my account, and *there's nothing I can do about it*. In despair he cast around for something to say, some form of words, some story that would make everything all right again between them and him.

But he could not lie. It was not in his nature. For the first time in his life he saw the point of untruth, he saw the excellent purpose it might fulfil, but he simply would not deal in it. Better, he felt, to say nothing. To lie, if he must, by omission. So he tucked his bottom lip under his top one, and was silent.

Is it always going to be like this? he wondered. And, rhetorically, by way of response, How can it ever be otherwise? There *is* no way. He'd had these thoughts so

many times that they'd worn grooves inside his head.
Thus they ran always the same course, and ended always
absolutely nowhere.

I could just stay here, he realised. Like she said. I could
just not go back to her. But the very idea induced a wave
of nausea, his nerves clamoured, his heart kicked inside
his chest. Life without Caroline would be no kind of life.
He would return to her, or he would die.

He loved her today, at this dreadful distance, quite as
much as he loved her when he held her in his arms. He
could close his eyes and summon her, he could picture
her pretty face, her kind, dark eyes, her soft and rosy
skin, her very . . . Carolineness. There was nothing sick
or unwholesome or perverted about his attraction to her.
It chimed exactly with his past experiences of sexual love,
although much, much louder and with far greater
insistence.

What would she be doing now, this minute, in that big
old house which had been her home? Was she missing
him even half as much as he was missing her? Did her
heart ache the way his did, with loneliness and longing?
Was she subject, as he was, to the disapproving scrutiny
of family? Was she causing them the same intolerable
pain?

It's Laura's fault, he thought bitterly. She was no kind
of wife to my father, no kind of mother to me. And when
she drove him away all those years ago, she sowed the
seeds of her children's destruction.

Because if, *if* they had grown up together as brother
and sister, if they'd played and fought and cared for each
other routinely, as nature intended, there would not

have been this thing between himself and Caroline. There would not have been this *coup de foudre*, and this unholy awful mess.

He should regret, then, the way things had turned out. He should rue it. But he could not, for to do so was to rue his feelings for his lover, and that could not be right either.

A hand on his shoulder. 'You know,' said Josie, 'you can tell me.'

'What?'

He glanced at her, a pretty woman of thirty-seven, with a fine tracery of lines around her eyes and at the corners of her mouth, sketched in by her smile. 'Anything. You can tell me anything. Whatever there is to tell. You were miles away there, Patrick. I wish you'd share it with me. Your Dad's gone upstairs to ring his mother, so we have this little opportunity for a heart to heart.'

'Thanks, Josie, but it's nothing really.'

'Nothing? "Nothing," he says!' She thrust out her chin as the temper flashed inside her. 'You drop out. Disappear. Don't let us know what you're doing, where you're staying. And then you come back here and tell me that it's nothing.'

'All right, all right, all right.' He shrugged her hand from his shoulder. 'It's *something*, OK? But not something I can talk about. It's my own problem, and I have to sort it out in my own way.'

'It's a girl, is that it? It's usually a girl.'

'Yes. Yes. If you must know, that's what it is. How very predictable you must find it. I am in love with a girl.'

'Then why in God's name be so close-mouthed about

it? She's not free, is that it? She has a husband? Am I getting close? Am I warm? As for "predictable", when was love ever that?'

When Patrick turned to her, one of her precious junky plates, all greased with soap, slid from his hand and shattered on the tiled floor.

'I'm sorry,' he said, stricken. 'Josie, I'm sorry. I'm sorry, I'm sorry, I'm sorry.'

'Oh, look now, it's only a silly old plate after all. It's not as if it's important. Patrick, you're crying. My baby, what's the matter? Now, you really have to tell me about it. I know you can't be crying over a plate.'

And a Happy New Year

CHAPTER

————— · —————

12

'Mad hatters,' said Elaine Posner decisively, rapping the desk with her pencil. 'And March hair.'

'Uh-huh,' said Caroline, sitting across from her, signally failing to reciprocate the editor's smile, or to laugh, or nod, or by any other means to render the expected admiration. She merely flapped open her notebook, clicked her ballpoint pen impatiently, and made a few notes. 'Fashion, hats, 3pp,' she wrote. 'Beauty, hair, spread + 1 turn.'

Elaine paused for one pointed moment, pulled a face as if she were sucking on the last tiny pearl of an acid drop, then pressed on with the briefing. 'Diet,' she said. 'We'll call it Slim Pickings. Needs a standfirst. Spring into action. Shape up for summer. Best ever eating plan. Absolutely painless. Body you always dreamed of. Delicious, nutritious. Why delay? Start today. Warrah, warrah, warrah. Now, will you do that for me, dear?'

'Oh, yes,' responded Caroline distantly. 'All right then. Anything else?'

'No. That's it.' Elaine sighed. It was all very well to be *numero uno* in the glamorous world of magazine journalism, to be the editor's editor, *la crème de la crème*. But one could not make all the running. One naturally looked to one's staff for the necessary help and support. One looked to them to be enthused. And – she'd make no bones about it – the A-Team were not the crack troops she'd supposed them to be. The A-Team, indeed, were beginning to look decidedly B. They were looking shoddy. They were not getting behind her as they ought. There was insubordination in the ranks. There was dissension and envy. Perhaps worst of all there was apathy.

Consider Caroline here. Consider Ms Karasinski, who had arrived at *Donna* as an untrained, untried junior, to be given her first big break. In a couple of years she had learned all there was to know about production, from the birth of an idea at one of the weekly brainstorming sessions, through its execution, to its publication. She had been taught all the printer's jargon – she could talk about widows and orphans, about bastard setting, about justification, about ragged right and left, and running turns. She knew her upper from her lower case, knew how to mark up copy, how to correct a proof.

She, Elaine Posner, had shared with Caroline Karasinski her wealth of expertise. She had promoted her to chief sub-editor. Her door had always been open to her, she had always been there for the girl. When Caroline had showed a talent for writing, she had nurtured it, she had brought her on.

Yet now here she sat like a sponge, the very picture of self-absorption, soaking it all in, giving absolutely nothing back. And that first flowering of talent had apparently also been the last.

Then, wouldn't you think that a young woman like

this, daily exposed to a wealth of golden advice, to inspirational beauty tips, to common-sense hints on cosmetics and dress, would have tried to make rather more of herself? *Donna* regularly carried to its grateful readers the very latest diet wisdom, it published up-to-the-minute medical research findings, it dealt in state-of-the-art slimming. And meanwhile its chief sub sat stolidly over her proofs, stuffing her face with salt-and-vinegar crisps and Snickers bars, as week by week her waistline thickened.

'I'll have to have a word,' thought Elaine wearily, as Caroline made for the door. And, 'Close that behind you, will you, darling?' she called after her. 'I don't want all and sundry buzzing in and out at the slightest whim. I have a magazine to produce.'

'So-o, how is the Great I Am this morning?' enquired Barbara malevolently, as Caroline emerged from Elaine's office. 'How is our fair editrix?'

'She's fine,' Caroline responded shortly, going straight to her work station and shuffling papers. She still felt competent to do her job – but only just. She was hanging on by her fingernails. And by tidying her desktop she created for herself an illusion, at least, of control. It gave her a sense that she was coping.

'So what did she want you for?' Barbara hovered at her elbow, hot for intrigue. 'What is that egomaniac cooking up for us now?'

'Nothing, so far as I'm aware,' Caroline shrugged. 'She just wanted to run through the contents for March.' Tugging open her drawer, she began to root through it, searching for a typescale, a pencil, a rubber, indicating as clearly as she could, without being downright rude, her disinclination to gossip. She had no wish to be drawn into Barbara's scheming. For one thing, though Elaine might be ludicrous and silly, she had always been good to her, she had been professionally very generous. For another, Caroline did not share Barbara's growing conviction that she had some kind of right to occupy the editor's chair, let alone that she was more suited to fill it. But most of all, this office politicking seemed to her unbelievably petty in the context of her life right now. And it was a wonder to her that anyone should have the emotional energy for matters so trivial.

'You'll never guess what I heard in the pub last night.' Barbara dragged up a stool and sat near, dropping her voice to a near-whisper.

'No,' said Caroline.

'I was talking to Jennie. You know, Jennie Gould. She was Jennie Fieldgrass till she married. Works in promotions. Anyway, *she'd* been talking to Viv, Bill Tanner's secretary, the one with the black hair. Apparently, she was saying – and this is strictly *entre nous* – that Bill has just about had it with La Posner. He's sick and tired of her. He was mad as hell about the January issue. I mean, genital warts and all. He thought it was in extremely poor taste, incredibly crass. He thinks her ladyship is resting on her laurels.'

'He does?' Caroline sharpened her pencil into the bin, concentrating hard on the frilly wood shaving, trying, in that senseless way, to see how long it would get before, like everything else in her world, it fell to pieces.

'*Absolument*. No word of a lie. He reckons it's about

time she moved on. So what I was thinking . . .' Barbara brought her face close. Caroline dropped her eyes to the proof in front of her. With the fine point of her pencil she crossed out a word, then made a small, neat mark, a 'delete' sign. 'Now would be the time for us to ask for a meeting with Bill. Tell him how things really are. What a prima donna the woman is. Say we can't work with her any longer.'

'Look, Barbara . . .' Caroline laid her pencil down; she lifted her head and sighed as she confronted her colleague. 'If you want to go and talk to the publisher, that's up to you. But if you're planning some kind of putsch, please leave me out of it, do you hear?'

'Really!' Barbara was indignant. 'I must say, I thought I could look to you for some support. I mean, there comes a time when each of us has to stand up and be counted.'

'Very well,' said Caroline coldly. 'I shall be counted. You can count me out, OK?'

'As you wish.' Barbara got to her feet. She shrugged. More in sorrow than in anger, she sighed. And with all the dignity she could muster, she walked away.

'Good,' muttered Caroline to herself, sparing no more than a glance, and she began to race through her afternoon workload, her proofs. She inserted a dash in the text, then in the margin she wrote 'em', and circled it.

Em. The width of a Pica M character. Pica (capital P) being 12-point, the standard size for typographic measurement, equivalent to one-sixth of an inch. Not to be confused with pica (lower-case p), the eating of substances other than normal food, which phenomenon occurs sometimes in pregnancy, when a woman will experience cravings for coal. Or, more comprehensibly, for kippers or cocoa. Or, as it might be, for salt-and-vinegar crisps. Or Snickers bars.

———————— • ————————

'Did you make any resolutions?' Michele lay splayed out like a starfish on Jasper's antique cashmere bed cover, staring at the wall, at the cornice, the elegant plaster moulding, where a cobweb, a floating strand of grime, had somehow survived Mrs Holloway's rigorous weekly tours of inspection.

'What?' Jasper thought he had never seen anyone look more abandoned, like a victim of drowning, washed up on a beach. Sighing, he turned to attend to his hair, smoothed it with matching tortoiseshell brushes, then mated them and set them down on the tall chest of drawers beside the mirror.

'You know. For New Year. Is there anything you've given up?'

'No,' he told her shortly, slipping over his head his half-buttoned shirt, a meagre protection against the cold. Hartwell was scarcely tolerable in winter. Geriatric boilers in the basement groaned under the weight of their collective responsibilities. If you bled one of the stocky, pillared radiators, it would spit and sputter scalding steam, and water would rush in with the sound of the sea. Sometimes, in the bitter months, it seemed the whole house was complaining, room calling to room, timbers to arthritic timbers, like the disappointed inmates of a twilight home.

Then, Oh, *I* give up, Jasper told himself, because this affair seemed to him, suddenly, so utterly futile and so ill-judged. The girl was half daft, she was dippy. You could have no kind of conversation with her, no meaningful dialogue.

He had been enchanted in the beginning by her artlessness, her naivety, and by her odd, intriguing, off-centre beauty. Night after night he had dreamed her into bed, until the time had come to take her there. Sex with her had been beyond fantastic, his most extravagant fantasies with flesh on them. And still his need for her obsessed him. Still he could not sleep for thinking of the dozy little idiot. Yet so soon she was needling him. She was vacuous, and very weird, she was driving him to distraction.

Somehow, he said to himself, I am going to have to extricate myself from this. It has been a mistake. It just cannot go on. The sooner I end it, the less will be the damage. But, boy, is it going to be hard. Because I am totally, absolutely hooked.

She was doing his head in, that was certain. His concentration was shot. Witness the fact that he had written not one word of his novel since he first set eyes upon her. For, remember, he had been at the very point of breaking through, he had been poised for a period of prodigious output, of tumultuous creativity, when this red-headed rapscallion, this sleepy-eyed scullion, had come along and subverted him. It was as if all his talent were being milked out of him with his sperm. As if she were sucking him dry.

He might, it occurred to him, be spilling more than his

seed. Physiologically, actually, he could be depleted of protein, and of essential trace elements, the raw materials which the body requires for the manufacture of semen, and which are clearly not inexhaustible. He shuddered to imagine that, with every coupling, there must be a sort of stripping away of vital stores from his very tissues. To ejaculate was to lose more than generative fluid; microscopic quantities of self, of the genius that he embodied, of the creativity that flowed within him, were being squandered as well.

But it was above all psychically, not chemically, that she was sapping him. To talk with her tired him mentally. Any communication was at heavy cost. In an exchange of ideas he was sure to come off worse. It seemed to him he gave her intellectual meat and drink, he gave her bread, and she gave him, in return, a stone.

Why, even to watch her was to feel a weakening. She moved as if drugged, regarding him from under heavy eyelids, with a smile soft as butter spreading across her face. She laughed at the oddest things. One could never be quite sure what she was thinking, what feeling; her emotions seemed to drift. There was about her, too, a sort of floppiness, not only during sex, but all the time. He had the strangest notion that if he were to shake her – as more than once he had felt an almost overwhelming desire to do – her head would topple off her shoulders, for it seemed only loosely connected, wilting like a flower, this way then that, on the thin stalk of her neck.

'I decided to stop swearing,' she informed him, scooping up one of her breasts, looking it, as it were, in the eye, examining the rosebud nipple, the pink and pimpled areola, the death-white of her skin, the blue-black bruising of his teeth. 'If I'm to be a lady, I can't go effing and blinding.'

Those words, like a shout, hummed on in his ears, seconds after they were spoken, resonant with fearful import. *If I'm to be a lady*. Oh, dear God, no!

It was true that he had mumbled, in an access of passion, 'Marry me,' or something on those lines. But that had been love talk, seductive nonsense, meaning, really, only, 'Get your knickers off.' Surely she didn't for one moment imagine. . . ? She couldn't? Well, *could* she? Panic welled up in him like water in a blocked lavatory (for one horrifying moment it looked as if it might flood over, causing an appalling domestic incident, then mercifully it subsided). Right now, he resolved, he would say nothing either to encourage or to disabuse her. He could let her down gently at some later date. He would choose his moment, preferably not immediately after making love, and tell her he had changed his mind. Or, better still, he would engineer a quarrel, then *she* would dump *him*, with a saving of face on both sides.

'You carry on swearing if you want,' he told her indulgently, fleetingly pitying her, before he was drawn back to the mirror by the question – all at once pressing – as to whether or not a ponytail would suit him. 'You eff, my love, you blind to your heart's content. Hey, tell me, Shell. What do you think? Should I grow my hair?'

'Oh, yes,' she said complaisantly. 'It would look nice.'

'Nice?' He laughed then, that unkind laugh of his, which made her feel thoroughly wretched. And he said it once more, in a funny way, as if the word tasted nasty in his mouth, as if he would have liked to spit it out. '*Nice*.'

Growing one's hair was, of course, Jasper realised, a more passive undertaking than the expression suggested. It wasn't like growing roses or rhubarb, which required some level of intervention, involving planting and watering and the liberal application of well-rotted manure. There was nothing one could *do*, as such, with hair; it was all in the forbearance. He must forbear to make his six-weekly trip to town, to Smile, for a cut and blow-dry. He must just wait, hold back, for the months that it would take, which was frankly a bore, since he had his heart set, suddenly, on this ponytail, which would swing between his shoulder blades and look tremendously outré and arty.

Never mind. So long as he had it in place for the catalogue. For the dust jacket. For the author profile pictures. For the TV appearances, for the promotional tour.

Shell, lying there watching him, saw how he withdrew from her, and wondered at it. He had the hump for some reason, that was obvious. Well, tough titty to him! It was his problem. One minute he was on top of her, breathing like an oxyacetylene lamp in her ear, and the next he was on his feet, standing around in just a shirt, turning his back on her, titivating, talking about haircuts, and snorting at her, and going '*Nice*'.

It made her unhappy when he behaved in such a way, but unhappiness was not something she could work with, so she relegated it, as she did all negative emotions, to the back of her mind, and she told herself a story to cheer herself.

Shell never cried. She just didn't. However awful things were for her – and some days they could be pretty dire – she would not let herself go. Nor did she have tantrums. For she had learned in her cradle, before she could walk or talk or reason, that tears and temper would avail her nothing. No one had ever come to feed her on demand, or to pick her up and cuddle her and go coochie-coo when she was teething. That had not been Nanny Fairchild's way. Not Nanny's way, either, to speak of feelings, except, in a routine way, about a dull ache, or a shooting pain, or about itchy feet or a sore throat, or the varicose veins to which she was a martyr. One's inner life, the responses of one's heart, had always been somehow unmentionable. Thus Shell had developed strategies for dealing with hurt or sadness or upset. She had found that, by filling her head with fancies, with decorative ideas and abstractions, she could effectively crowd out the bad stuff.

'We will be married,' she told herself, rolling on to her front, sinking her chin into the pillow, seeing spooky faces in the wood grain of the walnut bedhead. 'I shan't skivvy any more, I shall be a lady of leisure. And eat little sandwiches with the crusts cut off. And Nanny can come and live in one of the estate cottages. That's what she would like, a bit of a garden, a breath of fresh air. And Jasper . . .'

'Jasper.'

'What?'

'What is it that you do?'

'I beg your pardon?'

She floundered for a second and sat up.

He stood there staring at her, aroused as much by irritation as desire, wanting to jump on her and dance all over her. The tip of his penis peeped angrily from beneath the shirt – like a grumpy old tortoise, she thought, awakened from his winter sleep (she would have liked to stroke it, to pet it, to offer it a lettuce leaf). 'I mean . . .' she pleated the edge of the sheet with her two hands. 'What is it you do for a living?'

He shook his head in disbelief. He gave one of those hateful laughs, a Jasper special. 'You *know* what I do, Shell. I'm a landowner, with all the responsibility that that entails. And I'm a writer. I told you, didn't I, that I'm writing a novel?'

'Oh, yes. I remember.' It was not, in her view, much of a job for a grown man, writing stories. But she understood that it was important to him, so she pretended interest. 'What is it about, actually? The novel.'

'Christ, if anyone else asks me that I shall hit the roof.'

'Now you're cross.'

'No I'm not. Just . . . you know, frustrated.'

'Why?'

'What is all this "why"? Why so many questions?'

She brought her knees up and hugged them. 'Well, because . . .' she said, and she dropped her eyes, then dropped her head on to her knees and snuffed up between her legs the sour, salt, spunk smell of sex, of Jasper running out of her. She did not, *could* not tell him, 'Because I think I love you.' Simply, she did not dare.

'Listen, Shell.' She felt the bedsprings dip as he came to sit by her. He spoke gently, caressingly, as he felt for her a pure and passing tenderness. 'It's not something I can really talk about, OK?'

————— • —————

'It's nothing,' said Caroline, avoiding Elaine's eye, fixing instead upon the displayed magazine covers on the wall above the editor's head, that gallery of immaculately made-up female faces, all smiling in tribute to their orthodontists, all by now so tediously familiar as to inspire contempt. 'Really, nothing at all.'

'Oh, come. Why not tell your big sister? You know, you might actually feel better if you did.' Elaine clasped her smooth, brown hands in her lap, she bent forward with the expectant air of a good listener, she beamed encouragement.

But Caroline merely shook her head. 'No I wouldn't,' she responded flatly. 'I *know* I wouldn't.' Elaine took a deep breath and counted to ten. No sense, she thought, in losing one's cool. Nothing to be gained by getting cross. Indeed, she *wasn't* cross. Just very, very disappointed.

From the start this interview had gone awry. At six o'clock she had summoned her chief sub-editor, ostensibly to hand over a piece of copy ('First person account, "My Fight With A Wasting Illness". Motor-neurone disease of all ghastly things. Rather moving stuff. Quite inspirational. Classic thumbs-up-from-the-wheelchair. Have a read of it, will you? I'd value your opinion. Should we use it in May, huh?')

Then just as Caroline was making for the door, Elaine

had called after her, as though on a whim, 'Oh, by the way, dear, if you could spare me a couple of ticks, I should like a chatette. Have you time? Yes? That's my girl. This won't take a mo. We'll sit over there, shall we, in the strategy area? It's so much less formal when there's not a great big desk between us.'

So, for the past ten minutes, Caroline had sat, sunk deep in black despair, in a black leather armchair, at her most refractory, with her face closed, refusing to be drawn. And Elaine had delivered a prepared speech about the *Donna* philosophy, the *Donna* ideal, about that reputed paragon Donna herself, the magazine personified – leading on at length (and, Elaine felt, seamlessly) to the subject of self-respect, of self-realisation, to everything that Donna stood for (not least, to weight control).

Donna was this, Donna was that. She was a friend, she was a lover, she was a woman, she was a wife. She always worked hard, yet still had time to play. She cooked like an angel, but was not tied to the kitchen sink. She mixed Jasper Conran with jumble-sale bargains to stunning effect. She cared about the Big Issues, but also about individuals . . .

Listening with half an ear to this paean of praise, Caroline had almost been persuaded that Donna actually existed (she amused herself, sourly, by imagining that Elaine and Donna were engaged in a lesbian affair).

'She is concerned about the environment,' Elaine had declaimed.

But, Caroline had silently retorted, she's not so green as she's cabbage-looking.

'She's in her element in the boardroom – and in the bedroom.'

Ah, Caroline had thought, an executive tart!

'She likes to travel, but she – Caroline, darling, are you listening?'

'I'm sorry, Elaine, I'm just a bit distracted.'

'Well, you might do me the courtesy, I feel, of paying attention to me.'

'It's just that . . . Look, I truly am sorry. But I have something on my mind.'

'Well, share it,' Elaine had urged. 'Run it past me. I might just be able to help you.'

'It's not something I can talk about,' Caroline had told her desolately. And her heart had felt like a house-brick in her chest.

Thus had they come to a seeming impasse.

'I can't tell you, Elaine. I honestly can't. Look, forget I mentioned it. It's nothing. Really nothing at all.'

'Well, now . . .'

As Caroline squirmed and looked elsewhere, Elaine subjected her to minute scrutiny through narrowed eyes. And then, at last, she spoke. She said, '*Et tu, Brute.*'

'Eh?' said Caroline.

'You, too, Caroline Karasinski. You are in cahoots with my enemies. You have been plotting behind my back. Guilt is written all over you. *That* is what you have on your mind.'

'But I haven't. I wouldn't,' Caroline protested hotly. 'That is, I mean, what enemies?'

'What enemies?' Elaine drew her fingers across her brow. 'You think I'm deaf, you think I'm blind? You

think I don't see or hear what is going on behind my
back, right under my nose?' Then, 'What's so funny?' she
demanded, as Caroline hooted with mirthless laughter.
'I'm so glad you're tickled by this. You imagine I don't
sense a mood of insurrection? You think I don't know
who is behind it? Who has been whipping it up.'

'No, but – '

'I brought you in, remember that. I brought you on. It
was I, and not Barbara Horton, who gave you a chance. It
was I who nurtured your talent.'

'Elaine, I *realise* that. And I'm grateful. Truly, truly. I
always will be. I would never scheme against you, or
speak ill of you. I have no reason to feel guilty unless you
count . . . Forgive me,' Caroline implored, as the tears
bubbled up. And 'Thank you,' as Elaine thrust into her
hand a sheaf of tissues. 'I have no reason to feel guilty,'
she repeated mumbling into a wad of Kleenex, once she
had regained a degree of composure, 'unless you count
the fact that I'm expecting a baby.'

Ah! Now! *Now* Elaine Posner was on *terra firma*. Now
she knew where she stood. Here she was playing at
home. She could draw on her wealth of experience, and
on her native wisdom, to come to the aid of the party. The
foolish girl had gone and got herself preggy. She was up
the spout. In an interesting condition. In the jolly old
pudding club. And she was not – oh, very much not –
happy about it.

Well, well, well. Elaine drew herself up, she sat tall,
she rose magnificently to the occasion, she assumed the
aspect of a tower of strength. 'I think, first,' she said,
'you'd better fill me in. It was an accident, of course.

These things happen. Do dry your eyes, darling, and stop that silly noise. The question is, what's to be done?'

'Done?'

'Well, you don't want it, do you? Or else, why the tears?'

'No,' said Caroline, sobbing. 'At least, yes. I'm not sure.'

'Let's take it one step at a time.' Elaine reached for more tissues. 'Do you know who the father is?'

'Do I . . . ? Of course I do.' Caroline shook her head in a vain attempt to clear it. For days now, since the awful truth had dawned, she'd had this buzzing in her brain.

'And is he prepared to help you?'

'To help . . . ? Well, yes, naturally.'

'Most importantly, how much time have we got?'

'We? Time?'

'How far gone are you, sweetie? Because it does make a difference. Do you know when you conceived?'

Caroline blew her nose frothily on packed shreds of wet hankie. 'Three months, maybe. Oh, Elaine, I feel such a fool.'

A fool because, on that first night, she had taken no precautions. Because, when most girls her age were on the pill, or carried condoms, or had been fitted with caps or coils, Caroline, an innocent, a retard, had had no protection.

It had all been so unexpected. So unlooked for. Unplanned. Neither she nor Patrick could have known what would happen, neither could have guessed how they would be seized. Sex made you crazy, didn't it? It made you lose your head. It came on with such force, it was irresistible, it seemed worth any risk, however dire. Besides, no one got pregnant the very first time . . . did they?

'Three months? You're sure?'

'Yes, I think so. Just over.' It had to have been that night, hadn't it? Unless a condom had let them down (for condoms had, she'd read, a theoretical failure rate of three per cent per annum, whatever that meant, and an actual failure rate somewhat higher).

'You've missed two periods? Three?'

'A couple. Yes, maybe three. I'm not absolutely certain. My cycle is so very irregular. I kind of lose track.'

Elaine picked up her pen and tapped her teeth with it. She said, 'I know this marvellous man.' Then she reached for her personal organiser, for her Filofax, flipped the pages, looked up a name, a number, scribbled it down on her pad and passed it over.

'Are you suggesting. . . ?' asked Caroline is disbelief. The paper fluttered in her hand.

'Precisely.'

'An abortion?'

'A termination, my sweet. Well, a D and C, let's call it. A tiny scrape. All over in a jiffy. Wouldn't that be best?'

'I don't know.'

'Of course you do. You have your whole life in front of you. You have your career. And the father won't marry you – am I right, or am I right?'

'It's not that he won't. He can't.'

'Oh, tell me the old, old story. I should have thought you'd have more sense, Caroline, than to get involved with a married man.'

'Donna would never do that, would she?' asked Caroline with leaden irony and a stupid, sickly grin.

'She would not.'

'Donna would never be so foolish.'

'No.'

'But, of course, I was forgetting, there's no such person as Donna, is there?'

'There most certainly is.' Elaine raised her head. She shook her hair like a feather duster. She spoke with pride. She said, '*I* am Donna.'

'Er, I suppose you are,' agreed Caroline. 'In a way.' And she glanced down at the paper in her hand, which was headed 'Memo'.

Memo to Caroline Charteris: get rid of the baby. Have an abortion. All over in a jiffy. Bob's your uncle.

'Be guided by me.' Elaine spoke gently but, she hoped, firmly. 'It will be for the best, you'll see. Goodness, Caroline, do try to stop that sobbing. I never saw so many tears.'

'Well, you see,' said Caroline, mangling the Kleenex, 'I'm crying for two.'

———————— • ————————

'You know,' said Laura, 'you are absolutely right. Alcohol is a poison. And a depressant. It's deadly. So I've decided to give it up.'

The minute she'd declared herself, she felt so much better, so much sharper, more clear-headed. All at once she was focused. Her new determination galvanised her: she wanted to get on with *not* drinking, she was impatient for an opportunity to abstain. She wanted this to be February, or March, or April, to have behind her all those booze-free weeks.

She envisaged herself waking early, bright of eye, leaping from her bed and going out for a run in the grounds of Hartwell while the rest of the household slumbered. Then she saw herself seated at the long dining table, covering her wine glass with her hand, motioning butler and bottle away ('Just Badoit, Stevens, if you would'), as she enchanted guests with her scintillating repartee. In a week, maybe two, she would feel like a new woman. She would be reborn.

When she looked to her mother for approbation, however, she found none. Maudie sat motionless, staring out at the winter garden, at the silvered lawns, the frozen lake, the shivering trees, and gave no sign that she had even heard her.

Never mind. 1990 was a bummer, Laura told herself. But 1991 will be the best so far. It was such a great arrangement, this year business, the way one might at the end of every twelve months turn an imagined corner, the way time had been broken down into manageable segments. Whoever came up with the idea of the calendar (and she vaguely recalled it had been someone called Julian), she would have liked to shake his hand.

She knew beyond a shadow of doubt that she would stick to her resolution. Not just her brain but her whole body was committed to it. Heart and mind were as one. She felt it in her fingers and toes and in the pit of her stomach. She felt it everywhere. She tingled with the excitement of it, and with a powerful sense of self-determination. She'd been down in the dumps for far too long. She'd allowed herself to be put upon by the men in her life. Well, let this be an end to it! And from that end might come a new beginning.

'I'll leave you now.' Moved by unwonted affection, by a fit of daughterly devotion, she reached out and patted Maudie's hand, which was curled into the blanket like a claw. 'Will you be all right? I'll have them send you up a cup of mint tea and an oat cake.'

There was a spring in her step as she hastened down the passageway towards the stairhead, and through her brain ran the words of a song ('Oh, no not me, I will survive . . .'). She longed to get started. Or, rather, stopped. To be detoxed. She'd ring Dmitri and tell him of her plans. He'd be pleased with her, for wasn't he always urging her to optimise her nutrition? And perhaps, by way of a reward, she would treat herself to a week at Champneys, from where she would return, glowing with health. That would show her vindictive old husband, and his posturing, perverse elder son! Laura Charteris would be back with a vengeance.

When Jasper's door flew open ahead of her, she hesitated for a fraction of a second, to adjust the set of her head, to tilt her nose up, to lead with the chin. When he stepped into the passageway and saw her there, he would find –

It was not Jasper, though, who emerged from his bedroom, but the skinny piece, the ginger one with the taunting eyes, whose presence in the house was somehow such an irritant.

'Oh!' said the girl, startled. And she stood there like a

halfwit, hanging on to the door handle, staring and staring, with her big mouth hanging open, until Laura, impatient, dismissed her with a nod.

'Sorry,' the girl said then. And she clicked the door shut behind her and made at once for the service stairs.

There was, Laura told herself, something not quite right with that one. Her behaviour was distinctly odd, and her attitude left much to be desired. What was she doing up here, anyway, on the upper floor, in the middle of the afternoon? Not cleaning, surely? For the bedrooms should all have been finished hours ago. In any case, she'd been carrying no broom or duster, no bucket or cloth. Her empty hands had taken flight like fluttering birds and scrabbled at her throat.

Good grief! Had she been stealing? Had they, in their midst, another thief? She must have strong words with Holloway on the matter of standards. This untrustworthy little miss would have to be given her cards.

Convinced that the girl had been up to no good, and thinking to find evidence of it, Laura barged without knocking into Jasper's room.

He was stretched out on the bed, naked, with one knee drawn up, with his hand clamped over his penis, cherishing it. On his face he wore an expression of post-coital smugness – you could always tell, couldn't you, when people had been doing it? – which drained down into his neck when he saw her.

'Laura?' he said, sitting up, dismayed. And then, was it 'Oh, Lor' ', or 'Oh, Laur!'?

CHAPTER

13

Doctor Fellows was a marvellous man. His kindly manner was marvellous. And his smooth way of talking, with all expression nicely ironed out. And his immaculate pink nails. And his Val d'Isère tan. And his black, beetle eyebrows, which contrasted so strikingly with his bushy white hair.

He wore a Jermyn Street shirt with crisp, starched cuffs, and a gold Rolex watch, and these, also, were marvellous, marvellous. He had, Caroline remembered, been warmly recommended to her. Elaine Posner could not speak too highly of him. So it would be just too silly if she were to take against him.

She tried to cross her legs, but was constrained by her tight skirt, and by her full thighs, and by a sense that she should not fidget. If she sat very still and quiet, she felt, and did nothing to draw attention to herself, the good doctor might cease to notice her. She longed to efface herself to the point of invisibility. She longed to rub herself out, to disappear (raising his eyes from his note-pad he would see, across from him, nothing but an empty chair).

But then he asked her a question. He said, 'You are quite, quite sure about it?' And she had no choice but to speak up in response.

She played nervously with *Elle* magazine, the slim post-Christmas issue, which she had brought to read in the waiting room. She rolled it very tightly into a cosh, and imagined she might bash him on the head with it. 'I'm sure,' she heard herself say. 'Yes.'

Doctor Fellows set aside his Mont Blanc fountain pen. He rested his elbows on the desk. He matched up his fingers and examined them for a moment. He pressed his palms together and brought his steepled hands up to his lips in an attitude of prayer. He made a soft poof-poof-poofing noise, measured expulsions of breath, indicating that the matter was receiving his full and fair consideration – or that some question lingered yet about his lunch (had there been, in those *moules*, just a mite too much garlic?)

Caroline's tongue seemed to have fused to the roof of her mouth. She swallowed, and it peeled off drily. She licked her lips. She drew breath. 'You see,' she said 'it's really for the best.'

Because that, after all, was what they'd agreed, she and Patrick, finally, in the early hours of this morning, though everything in them screamed against it. It was, it had to be, the best thing all round. It was the *only* thing.

What had they done, they had asked each other over and over, not in words, but with glance and gesture. What havoc had they wrought? What mortal sin committed? Their guilt was huge, it was inexpiable. And to share it was not to diminish it; rather, they saw it magnified in one another's eyes.

Out of their love had come something insupportable. And because of it, though they could not yet say it, still less face up to it, such love was surely doomed. How could they be together, when the spectre of the life that they'd destroyed would always be between them, an image of the baby that was not to be?

The pain they felt would be nourished by their closeness, it would thrive on the shame they must share. Already she saw in Patrick's dear, sweet face, grief more profound than she could bear to look upon.

Loss was supposed to unite people, but it didn't, of course. It left one, if anything, more then ever alone.

'In the end we would come to blame each other,' she had realised with a wisdom she would have wished not to possess. 'However much we tried, we would be bound to.'

'It might be all right,' he had said in desperation, crossing from the window to the sofa, sitting down, rebounding, returning to the window, wheeling round once more to face the room.

'I know,' she had agreed.

And so it might. It might be that there grew within her a perfect, healthy, viable infant. She could be incubating a normal baby. Or it could be a human catastrophe.

'I'm not against abortion altogether, are you? In principle, at any rate.'

'To tell the truth,' he'd said, 'it's not something I've thought about. It hasn't somehow cropped up.'

'Oh, *I* have.' Staring at the carpet, she had confessed to him, 'I've thought about it. I've often wondered why it was that Laura didn't have one. Why she chose to have me when she didn't need to. I've wondered if it was in fact a very close-run thing. And just supposing she had, you know, terminated me, so what?'

'What do you mean, "So what?" '

'Well,' she had shrugged, 'just that. So what? I shouldn't have minded, should I?'

'That's a ridiculous thing to say.' His wretchedness made him angry. He had started to shout and thresh his arms. 'You wouldn't be able to say it, would you, if you weren't here today?'

'Shush. Don't yell at me.'

'I'm not yelling at you. Not at *you*.'

'Yes you are. Oh, Patrick, darling, *don't*.'

When she held her arms out to him, he had gone to kneel by her, burying his head in her lap, to mumble 'I'm sorry,' as she stroked his uncombed hair.

'So am I.' She had debated with herself for a minute, then, with only a little wobble in her voice, she had asked him, 'What if we were to go abroad? Go somewhere new. To Australia, say, or America, where nobody would recognise us. I know what we agreed before – that we wouldn't run away, that we'd only run *to* something. Well, all right, this would be running *to*. We could set up home there and have our baby, and love it whatever.' This had sounded rather fine to her, though she'd shrunk from defining for herself just what 'whatever' might imply.

He had lifted his head to regard her sharply. His cheek was rubbed red and his hair stood in spikes. His jaw dropped open. 'We couldn't,' he'd demurred. 'Er, *could* we?'

'I suppose so. I don't see why not.'

'How would we get by?'

'Very comfortably, actually.' For the first time in a long

time she had afforded herself the luxury of a real smile, albeit a thin one. 'You see, we have thousands in the bank now. I have made certain dispositions.'

'I don't know what you're talking about.'

'I have raised a large amount of money. Enough to take us anywhere we want to go. To set ourselves up. To have our child. If that's what we determine we should do.'

'What have you been up to, Carrie? Please explain.'

'I sold something.' She had covered her face with her hand and said through spread fingers, 'I sold my granny's necklace.'

'You *didn't*!'

'I did.'

'Oh, Carrie, *no*!'

'It's not as if I ever wore it, is it?'

'That isn't the point. It was a family treasure. It had sentimental value to you. It must have done.'

'The way I looked at it, there it was, already in the bank, just sitting there. I wasn't going to get it out, I didn't have a use for it. So I sort of . . . what's the term? Liquidated?'

'Liquidised. And you're supposed to be the words person around here.'

'I'm not thinking straight. I liquid*ised* it. I cashed it in. So that we should have more options.'

'It would be practical then?'

'I believe so.'

'There'd be no way anyone would connect us? No way they could guess we were related?'

'I don't see how they could.'

'And the baby might be fine.'

'It might be. Or . . .'

Or it might be very slightly disabled. Or grossly deformed. Or insane. It might have the chance of a few short years of pain. It might be stillborn. What lethal cocktail might their recessive genes produce!

Then even were the baby not damaged, its parents would still be half-brother, half-sister. And they would be exiles. And their life would be a sham.

'It's no good, is it?' she had asked, when they had sat a while, mute, over their respective sorrows.

'I don't think so.'

'We would just be compounding this terrible lie that we've lived.'

'Not such a terrible lie, Carrie.'

'In society's eyes, a terrible one.'

'In society's eyes, maybe. But not in yours. Not in mine.'

'Not in yours or mine.'

'I still love you, you know. More than I can tell you.'

'And I. I love you. Till I die.'

Dawn had come on like a sick headache, to find them still awake, and up and dressed, their double bed not slept in.

'I'll make tea,' Patrick had offered, going to the kitchen, ashen-faced, rumpled, raw around the eyes.

'That's nice. I'd like some.'

'Then you should have a bath and try to get some sleep, my darling.'

'I don't think I could.'

'At least give it a go.'

'Well, only if you come with me.'

They had crept fully clothed between the sheets, and Patrick, flinging out a hand, had sent the alarm clock flying.

'Leave it.'

'No, I have to set it. What time can you ring that Doctor Fell?'

'Fellows. At nine, I should think.'

'We really don't have any options.'

'No.'

'Can I hold you?'

'Yes. Oh, yes, please hold me.'

Even through the fabric of her skirt, his hand felt cold as ice against her. And as she dozed fitfully, around and around in her head went two teasing lines. 'I do not love you, Doctor Fell. But why I cannot tell.'

Ah, but he was, beyond question, a marvellous man. Marvellously manicured. And he was going to help her. For here he was telling her what she must do, explaining the formalities, the legal niceties, which had to be observed. It was clear to him, he was saying, that to proceed with this pregnancy would be seriously detrimental to her health, it would jeopardise her psychological well-being. Here was the address of an eminent colleague. She should seek from him a second opinion. Doctor Fellows felt confident that he would concur.

Now, since time was of the essence, they must make a date. He referred to his diary. How would Friday afternoon suit her? All right? Splendid. Just the ticket!

On the desktop, in a silver frame, was a photograph of a young girl, perhaps Caroline's age, perhaps younger, her long, dark hair swept back and secured with an Alice band. 'Ah,' said the doctor with manifest love and pride, following Caroline's gaze. 'Yes. My daughter Genevieve. She's at Oxford, you know. A very bright girl. Very gifted.'

'Mm,' said Caroline thoughtfully. She got up and buttoned her coat. It was, she reflected – and this was about the best you could say for it – a funny old world.

———————— • ————————

The boy done good. And then, after a year or two – for his had been a precarious business – the boy done bloody awful. Those fickle, star-fucking fashion editors, and up-their-own-orifices art directors, and limp-wristed fairy frock-designers, had feted and flattered him, they had wined and dined him, he'd been the toast of Langan's, the talk of the town – then, as was their whimsical way, they had dumped him.

But, hey, he was cool about it. He wasn't bitter. Let no one say that Tony Knapp was nursing a grievance. He was too big a guy for that, right? You'd not catch *him* crying into his cocoa over the caprices of magazine editors and advertisers. The whole lot put together weren't, after all, worth a wank.

When, some time in 1972, his phone had stopped ringing, and all of London, it seemed, was in a meeting, or at a session, or out to lunch, when it had been borne in on him that he was Outsville, Arizona, he had taken a philosophical view of the situation. So the party, for him at least, was over? That was just too bad. *Che sera sera*.

He'd had a ball, he'd been, like, up all night, he'd done kilos of drugs, he'd driven a flash red Alfa Romeo, he'd shagged the pretty arses off the top models of the day, he'd been a legendary humping machine. Not bad, when you reckoned it up, for a boy from the Elephant, whose mum had a fruit and veg stall in East Street market, whose dad ran a greasy spoon down the Old Kent Road. All good things must come to an end, mustn't they? It had been time to hang up his Pentax, and to get on with real life.

So, nineteen years later, a dreary January afternoon found him listening to Capital Radio, which advised him that it was exactly four o'clock (at the top of the hour, here was the latest national and international news). A glance out at the inky sky confirmed that the day, which had barely begun for him, was already almost over. Yawning, Tony reached to switch off the radio (what interest had he in the exploits of Johnnie Saddam?). In the best-regulated households, up and down the country, civilised people would now be taking tea. He dropped a teabag into a Union Jack mug, filled it from the cold tap and put it in the microwave to boil.

Marvellous invention, the microwave. Sodding wonderful little box of tricks, a boon and a blessing to mankind. These days you could buy a whole range of fancy ready-made dishes, from spaghetti to sweet and sour, stick 'em on the turntable, and in four or five minutes, ping, there was dinner! Since the new Marks and Spencer opened in the King's Road, a short stroll from his bachelor pad, he had been able to streamline his shopping and cooking operation. Then, by eating with a disposable picnic fork, straight from the container, he had reduced to a minimum the need to wash up.

When he opened the fridge it glared at him and offered nothing but a couple of eggs and a carton of milk. He took the milk, swirled some into his tea, spooned in three sugars, and carried the mug through to the darkened front room, which was a shrine to his success.

Through the window he saw, passing by the iron railings at street level, a pair of stout and stockinged legs, white in the pool of tungsten light, and a pair of smart black court shoes. The legs, the feet, the hem of a coat, came to a halt, turned in through his gate and started hesitantly down the basement steps. A tubby blonde sort, a young girl with an appealing, flustered face, dithered a moment in the area, looked doubtfully up at the scabby facade of the house, blundered into the dustbin, then was swallowed up by the shadows.

A few seconds later the bell rang. Should he or should he not answer it? The girl didn't look like an evangelist, come to see if he was saved. For a start, she wasn't wearing a hat. Or clutching a bible. Nor, since she carried no big wicker basket, was she likely to thrust at him some doubtful ID, to claim to be on a job-creation initiative, and to press him to buy a sponge cloth or a dish mop or a card of plastic clothes pegs at exorbitant cost, on the iffy proposition that he'd be doing the decent thing by the unemployed. (No one, Tony would respond to these people, could be less employed than he, so they had better bugger off.)

She might, he supposed, be from the council; it could be about poll tax which, as a matter of principle, he had decided to withhold. And in that case, he did not want to know.

But when the bell rang again, longer and louder, with firmness of purpose, as though, whoever she was, she had come to a decision, he was moved by idle curiosity to open the door.

'Yes?'

'Oh,' said the girl, mangling a magazine in her hands, rolling and unrolling it, her face stained with embarrassment.

'Can I help you?'

'Er, I hope so.' Despite her evident confusion, and a nervous vibrato, she spoke clearly, with a posh, county accent. 'Yes. I was looking for someone. A Mr Karasinski. Mr Tony Karasinski. I was given this address by a friend of a friend. Only I see on the bell it says "Knapp".'

This was a turn-up for the books. He leant his shoulder against the door jamb, folded his arms in front of his chest, and subjected her to his arrogant scrutiny (who was she, and what did she want?). Then, 'Tony Karasinski is dead,' he informed her indifferently, taking a packet of Wrigley's from his pocket, wadding his mouth with chewing-gum, working it over with his molars.

Nothing had prepared him for the impact that these words would have upon her. Shock and disbelief scudded across her face like clouds across the face of the sun: dark, light, dark.

'Dead?' she echoed him with dismay. She looked, indeed, as if she might burst into tears. 'You mean . . . ?'

'Yup,' he told her with an odd kind of relish. 'He died nearly twenty years ago. He died the death. He disappeared. Sank without trace.'

'Then he's not, you know, *dead* dead? That's not what you're telling me?'

'I'm telling you that Tony Karasinski is no more. Happily, however, his alter ego, Tony Knapp, is alive and well and living in London South-West. *I* am Tony Knapp. Now, whose little girl are you?'

She made a funny flitting gesture, offering then immediately withdrawing a hand, hiding it behind her back. She butted the air, raised her head, and said, 'Actually, yours.'

'I beg your pudding?'

'I'm your daughter Caroline.'

'But I don't *have* a daughter Caroline.'

'Yes you do. I am she.'

Tony sucked his lower lip, nonplussed. He shook his head. 'You had better come in,' he said to her at last.

———— • ————

'You must take me as you find me,' said Doris Fairchild grudgingly to the young man in the clerical collar, who stood out on the walkway, very ill at ease, shuffling his polished shoes on the coconut matting, smiling an unconvincing smile, while his blue eyes looked warily past her, into the flat. And she could have kicked herself for ever having opened her mouth.

Because she knew how this had come about, all right.

She knew why it had happened, and she had no one but herself to blame for it.

She'd gone down for her pension the other week. For her widow's whatsname. And for the Christmas bonus, which was frankly an insult (she had half a mind to write in and say as much). And she'd been a bit surprised to see Mrs Gentle there, because whereas hers was a Thursday book, Mrs Gentle had always been Friday.

She'd mentioned this to Mrs G, who'd said no, she was a Thursday now, too, which was better for her actually, because Fridays she had sewing circle. Then she'd wanted to know if Doris had met the new vicar yet, who was a charming young man, a real breath of fresh air, so progressive in his thinking, and so energetic (her way, you see, of letting the whole queue know that she was in at the vicarage, that she had a foot in the door, and was thick with the vicar's wife).

So Doris had said no, which was no less than the truth, she had said she'd seen hide nor hair of the chap. And she had added that you would think, wouldn't you, that this man of the cloth might take the trouble to call in on his elderly parishioners once in a while? He might drop by to see if there was anything they were needing in the way of spiritual comfort or succour. Was it any wonder that the pews were empty, when your vicar didn't visit you from one year to the next, as he was paid by the church to do?

Well, of course, it had got back, hadn't it? Mrs Teacup Whisper had gone running off to tell the vicar's wife, who had told the vicar, who had come barging round here, bothering her, when she was up to her eyes in her cleaning and had no wish to be disturbed.

But what could you do? You had to show willing. So, 'You'd better come in,' she offered. And, a shade resentfully. 'I'll make us a pot of tea.'

'Super,' said the charming, progressive, new young vicar, his smile guttering like a candle before drowning in its own grease, as he followed her through into the lounge.

'Chilly enough for you?' she asked over her shoulder, trundling the Ewbank in front of her, parking it behind the kitchen door.

'It is a bit fresh, isn't it?'

'Freezing, I'd call it. A lot of old people will be catching their death from hypochondria if it carries on. There'll be standing room only, down in that cemetery of yours. Still, it's good for business, I dare say. Sit down do. You make the place look untidy.'

'And how was your Christmas, Mrs, er, Fairchild?' he enquired, lowering himself into a chair, trapping his hands between his legs, jigging his feet about, looking like an overgrown schoolboy with ants in his pants.

'It was quiet.'

'Ah, yes, well . . .' His eyes roamed the room as if in search of an escape. 'We prefer a quiet Christmas ourselves, Pat and I. Although of course, it's such a hectic time. And such a joyful one.'

'All right for some, I dare say.'

'Well, especially for children.'

'Oh, yes. Children.'

'Now, can we hope to see you among our congregation one of these fine days? Perhaps when the weather is kinder?'

'You can always *hope*.'

She set the tray. And she opened a packet of Highland Shorties. And she thought that perhaps, *perhaps*, seeing as he was here . . .

You know, vicar, she could say to him, I once done something very wrong. But was 'wrong' the word she wanted? Was 'wrong' right? Vicar, I once done something a bit improper. No, that implied, well, rudeness, it implied *you know what*, S-E-X. Vicar, I once done something rather naughty. Something slightly irregular. Something a bit rash. Something headstrong.

Then, how was he going to reply? Was he going to have to know the ins and outs, the whys and wherefores, chapter and verse? Would he need to be in possession of the full facts before he could give her an official pardon and, as it were, square things with God?

Did she, in any case, want a pardon? Did she want to listen to a lot of platitudes about the Lord being merciful and forgiving poor sinners? On the whole, she thought not.

She'd been a bit down in the dumps lately. That was what all this was about. Things had been playing on her mind. She'd had trouble sleeping. She was worrying herself about Shell. (What *was* the girl playing at? Why didn't she get in touch?) No reason to go pouring her heart out to a complete stranger. Nevertheless, there was in her now an aching need to confide, to open her heart to somebody.

'Vicar.' She popped her head round the kitchen door. 'I was wondering . . .'

'Ye-es?' He sat forward attentively.

'Do you,' she asked, 'take sugar?'

———————— • ————————

'Sugar?' called Tony from the kitchen.

'What? Oh, no. No thank you.' It was so *cold* in this
room, she was blue with it. Caroline sniffed with self-pity
and dabbed her eyes with her knuckle. And she
wondered if she could possibly accommodate another jot
or iota of pain. Because there had to be a limit. Well,
didn't there? A point at which you were full up with it?
When more could make no difference? In the same way
as you could only be so happy (and there *was* a sort of
ultimate, she knew because she had been there, she had
bought the T-shirt), maybe you could only be so sad.

If she were to have news now that Freckles had died, or
Pasha, or her mother or stepfather, could she be any
more forlorn? Would her heart burst, as she felt it might,
or would all the other sorrows just squeeze up to make
room for another one?

Also, wasn't it strange the way you could stand
outside yourself and intellectualise about your anguish?
Strange, the way you could not only live it, but witness
yourself living it? Was this, perhaps, the way that you
stayed sane? And if ever you lost the ability to do it, if
ever you got trapped in there with all your suffering, and
it ceased to seem to you at least in part fictitious, would
you lose your mind?

She should not, of course, have come here. God *knows*
what had brought her to this horrid, dank Chelsea flat,
with its gloomy furnishings, its smell of joss sticks and

tom cats, its atmosphere of despair. It had been sort of a spur-of-the-moment decision. Something to do with Genevieve, the fell doctor's daughter, who was up at Oxford, and who was her daddy's pride and joy.

'She's a very bright girl. Very gifted.' How must it be to have a father of one's own? To be so loved by him, so wanted? She had never set eyes on hers. And what did she know of him?

She had heard that he was a shit. That he was a dreadful man. That he had been a great photographer in his day, though he had had this most extraordinary way of making all women look like whores. He had bequeathed to her, if Laura was to be believed, a weight problem and a wilful streak – so, like her, he must be weighty and wilful.

But these were just discarded scraps of opinion, the leavings from old relationships, other people's trash. It had added up to very little – though enough, in the past, to have persuaded her that she did not wish to meet the man. Not ever, ever, ever.

Then, today, for the first time really, unaccountably, she had felt a need to know. To see and judge for herself. To make her own assessments. This need, indeed, had been so pressing that she could not wait to get started, could not spare the time to travel home before she began. She must find him without delay.

She had been all at once obsessed by the nature of parenthood, by bonds that held, and bonds that were severed, and by bonds that had never been forged, but which must remain loose ends for ever after. If she could see her father, and speak with him a while, it could help

her to tie things up. It could help her . . . not to choose
what she should do, since the die was already cast, the
choice already made, but at least to face up to it, and to
live with it after.

Whether they liked it or not, they were related, she and
Tony Karasinski. She was flesh of his flesh, his child, his
issue. She had his genes in some proportion, she was his
blood type, his bloody-minded type.

There had been moments, as she made call upon call
from a pay phone on the third floor in Selfridges, when
she wondered if she had, as seemed all too probable, lost
the plot. Moments when she feared for her own sanity. A
constant stream of women had passed her, clutching
their carrier bags and baskets, on their way to the ladies'
loos, whence they would emerge minutes later
(Caroline, wild-eyed, marked their comings and goings),
looking lacquered and less fraught and more pleased
with themselves.

A girl with blank eyes rocked a squalling baby in its
pram. Next to her, three young men with Oriental eyes
and big, unstinted smiles, crowded around the receiver,
to speak in turn, in distracting Cantonese.

'Hello, hello, is this Bailey's number?' Caroline had
clamped the receiver between her shoulder and right ear,
screwed a finger into her left ear, and, even as she leafed
with her free hand through her contacts book, she had
kept one anxious eye on the digital display, as the
machine swallowed up and metabolised more and more
of her money.

'Hello, is that Terence Don– ? Oh, I see. Well, thank
you very much.'

'Hi, is this the right number for Terry O– ? Oh, right then. Not to worry. No, no message. Thanks.'

'Er, Brian Duffy. . . ?'

'Uhm, may I speak with. . . ?'

'Tim Marlborough? Oh, great. Look, you don't know me, but it's possible you will remember Tony Karasinski. Yes, yes, it *is* a bit of a "blast from the past". Only I do need to speak to him, and I thought you just *might* have an idea where I could . . .'

She had always hated celebrity ring-rounds, hated the task which had too often fallen to her at *Donna*, when a page needed filling, or when Elaine had had one of her brilliant wheezes, of phoning up famous personalities, cold-calling them to put to them the fatuous question of the day ('What is your favourite food?', 'Which was your finest hour?', 'Your most embarrassing moment?', 'Your biggest break?' 'Your lowest ebb?', 'Your best ever birthday surprise?'). Now, in disbelief, she had heard herself asking the most foolish question ever, asking, 'When did you last see my father?'

'How did you find me?' Tony Knapp came into the room, concentrating grimly on the mug in his hand, on the insipid tea which threatened to slop over.

'With enormous difficulty. No, actually, it wasn't that bad. I made a few calls. Spoke to your friend Tim.'

'How is that scoundrel? I've not seen him since the old king died.'

'He's all right. That is, I have no idea. I just asked if he had your address. Thank you.' She accepted the mug from him. The tea looked grey and was flecked with film, but it was not really the sight of it, or the sour-milk smell, that induced a wave of nausea. Rather, it was, or so it seemed to her, nature's way of reminding her of her condition, of the tenuous life within her. 'Aren't *you* having any?'

'I've got one. Although, where I put the bugger . . .' His eyes wandered the room, trailing over every dusty surface, until he located the Union Jack mug. 'Ah, there!'

He was a tall man – six foot, maybe six-one – but saggy, as if gravity exerted over him a more powerful pull than over other people. His hipster jeans, which cried out to be washed, and which stayed sitting when he stood up, were belted below a pronounced paunch, but he was not otherwise overweight. His hair was unfashionably long, it covered his ears and was kind of wiggly, as though it were too tired to hold a proper curl. His eyes, if they were anything, were grey (she was struck, when she looked into them, by the fact that colour is an illusion, it is a trick of the light – and in those eyes there *was* no light).

Dated fashion posters, blow-up photographs, striking images of stick-thin, wind-tossed women, adorned the walls, attesting to the talent that had been Tony Karasinski's. He had indeed been someone. And his face would have been quite fine, had it not bloated and run over at the chin.

Caroline, who had expected to feel, if not recognition, at least an inkling of kinship, felt only utterly foolish. This had been the most appalling mistake. There was no correspondence between them, no spark, no ring of bells, not even faintly.

'So . . .' Tony flopped into an armchair, regarded her incuriously for an instant, then turned his attention to a whitlow, biting his finger, inspecting it, biting it again. 'What is all this about?'

'It's not *about* anything.' Caroline warmed her hands on her mug, and stared down at the liver-spotted surface of the tea. 'I was curious, I suppose, that's all. I wanted finally, for once in my life, to meet you.'

'Because you say that I'm your father. Well, my lovely, I wouldn't know about that.'

'My mother is – *was* – Laura Grant. She got married, you know, after . . .'

'Laura, Laura, Laura?' Tony seemed to have some trouble placing her. 'The red-haired one?'

'You don't even remember?'

'Sure I do. Bad-tempered bitch. Great tits, but a vicious streak. She once went for me with a stiletto shoe, you know. I needed stitches.'

'Can you blame her?'

Tony shrugged. He spread his hands, not in apology, but in an infuriating, taunting gesture.

'Why did you change your name from Karasinski?'

'*To*. I changed it *to* Karasinski. And then I reverted. You know these poncy art editors, they're suckers for a foreign-sounding monicker.'

'Did you know Laura was pregnant?'

'I forget. Well, there were so many.'

'Look, I'm sorry if this . . . if *I* have come as a shock to you.'

He gave another of his irritating shrugs, as if to say Who, frankly, gives a stuff?

'I say, do you think I could use your bathroom?'

'Oh, be my guest. First on the right.'

Caroline leant her face against the cold tiled wall until her heart stopped battering and the sensation of faintness subsided. She sat on the side of the bath and looked around her. The tub itself was ringed with grime. In it, in plastic bowls and buckets, shirts were steeping (soaking back up the dirt that had soaked out). An Ali Baba basket sicked laundry on to the floor. Black cracks ran through a bar of Camay. On the windowsill there was a razor and what had once been a pot plant, a dry stick embedded in caked soil. Beyond the bubbled glass of the window the day was navy blue.

She could make no claims, herself, of course, to be the world's most orderly person. But there was something worse than mere untidiness at work here, which revolted her, even as it moved her to pity. The air of disenchantment which pervaded the flat had seeped into her bones. She found she was breathing through her mouth to screen out smells. 'This,' she thought, '*this* is my father?' And she shuddered.

When she returned she saw that he had slid down in his armchair. His legs were untidily splayed. A tattered, one-eyed black cat with a torn ear was curled up on the soft cushion of his gut.

'Find it, all right?' enquired Tony, very cor blimey, overplaying the Cockney.

'Thank you, yes. Well, I'll be going now.'

'You haven't had your tea.'

'I know. I'm sorry. I mean, I truly am.'

'No need.'

'Maybe not.'

'If I'd known you were coming, I'd have baked a cake.

Well, it's been nice.' His tone was thick with irony. He yawned, not troubling to cover his mouth. 'We must do it again sometime. You'll excuse me if I don't see you to the door. I'd hate to disturb Cassius here.'

His voice followed her out into the hall and up on to the street. It howled in her head for minutes and minutes like an attack alarm. 'If you're ever down this way again,' he said, '*do* be a stranger, *don't* drop in.'

Friday Morning

CHAPTER

14

'I must know where I stand,' said Shell, for practice, in front of the mirror. 'Jasper, I'm entitled.' She combed her hair with her fingers, scraping it up at the sides and letting it fall in disarray about her face, contriving to appear at once very lovely and very slightly deranged. He should know what he was doing to her. She wanted him to see it, to look at her and to realise with shame that he was sending her – well, ever so slightly – round the bleeding twist. 'You're using me. You've led me on. I don't know what you take me for. It isn't fair.'

Then, dress rehearsal over, she snatched up her hairspray and squirted it, as though to fix the visual impact, to hold the effect, to gel the mood, and she was wafted by the familiar smell – a chemical cloud of methyl alcohol, panthenol, dimethicone copolyol, amino methyl propanol and, most mysteriously, 'fragrance' – back to Croydon, to the salon, to a time not long ago when she'd been happy and among her own.

I wish, she thought. I wish, I wish . . .

The day she had qualified as a stylist it had been, not the fulfilment of a lifelong ambition (she had never been big on ambition), but at least a source of satisfaction to her. That, she had felt, was that. She was sorted. Her future was decided. Now she could relax.

And she had had some great times at Hairs and Graces. She had felt at home there. She'd loved the atmosphere of the place, the cool green-and-white interior, she'd loved the busyness, the larking, the flirting, the sense of belonging.

She had looked forward to Fridays when she picked up her brown wages envelope and skipped off for a half an hour to the Whitgift Centre, to blue most of it on make-up and T-shirts, and tapes for her Walkman, and on patterned tights, and on fun fandangle earrings. She'd even enjoyed sweeping up the shearings, chasing all the different coloured coils of hair in front of her broom.

'Shell, your three o'clock client has been delayed.' 'Shell, your lady is about to expire under that lamp.' 'Shell, can you fit in a body wave before eleven?' 'Can you do a shampoo for me?' 'Have you seen my tail-comb?' 'Put the kettle on, you lazy cow, if you've nothing better to do.'

For a moment she seemed to melt into her own reflection, to move out of her body and to pass through the glass. Then she blinked and returned to the room.

It was probably best, when you came to consider it, to be with your own sort, with people who could have a giggle with you, and didn't ever mimic your accent, or give you funny, piercing looks, or laugh at you for no apparent reason, or try to bamboozle you with big, long words. It had been some kind of craziness that had brought her here in the first place, on an errand for Nanny, possessed of a most dreadful secret which she would honestly have preferred not to share.

And she supposed she had been more crazy still to get involved with Jasper, who was one minute being all shirty with her, and the next minute jumping on her bones. Was it any wonder that she was confused? That she needed to know where she stood? She was supposed to be getting engaged, for Pete's sake. That was what he'd said. Yet there had been no talk of a ring, or a party, no talk of an announcement, or of marking it in any way. And their affair must remain, as he had stressed, a closely guarded secret.

Christ, it was like ice, up here on the attic floor of the house. Jasper should moan about the cold in his room! He was in heaven compared with this.

The winter weather always made her frail. The freezing blasts knifed right through her. She fumbled with the buttons on her overall, with the fastening of her belt.

'One day,' she told herself, 'I shall be able to lie in till eleven, I shall have breakfast brought up to me on a tray.' But she believed less and less in that particular fantasy. Cinderella was, after all, just a fairy story. And as for Jasper Charteris, besotted though she was with him, he was coming more and more to seem a most unlikely Prince Charming.

Sniffing, she tried to squeeze out a few tears of self-pity, but as usual none would come. Well, it was hardly surprising. Six o-fucking-clock. No one could cry at this time of the morning. No one, if they had any sense, was even awake.

———— • ————

'Are you awake?'

'Mm. Yes. What time is it?'

'Early. Not quite six o'clock.' Caroline had somehow wound herself in the top sheet. Patrick tugged at it to unwrap her and rolled her into his arms. She was warm. She was always so warm. And soft and bosomy. And now, sadly, so pregnant.

'Give us a hug,' he said with aching tenderness. Then – because her cheek felt wet with tears as he laid his own against it – 'Oh, please, my Carrie, *please* don't cry. I don't think I can bear it.'

'I'm not crying. Not really.'

'Bad night?'

'A bit.'

'Never mind, angel. By this evening . . .' But he checked himself and did not say, as he had been about to do, that it would all be over. Because of course it wouldn't. It wouldn't. It would barely have begun.

He drew a snorting breath, and scrunched his eyes, and told himself sternly that he must not break down. He must be strong for her. If he could just be half as strong as she . . .

He knew Caroline so well, he knew her thoroughly. He was so close to her sometimes, he could hear the workings of her mind (a sweet and soothing hum when she was happy, but now all clash and clang and grate and grind), while her emotional responses, her joys and sadnesses, her triumphs and disappointments, were almost more vivid to him than his own.

She was such a *round* person, he thought, and he did not mean by that her physical presentation. He had always been drawn to real women, to the pretty and not the prettified. He was lost in admiration for her. She had such a noble heart. She had this approach to the world which Laura apparently called stubbornness, but which Patrick recognised as fierce pride. He thought her brave beyond words, he thought her fine.

So often he had seen that she was dying inside – her scarlet face, her troubled eye, revealing all about her state of mind – and yet she pushed and pushed herself, refusing to be walked on, as people were so quick to try to do. Up would go her chin, and back would go her shoulders, and in she would wade to defend her rights, or to protect what was hers, or to speak up for the underdog, or to tell the truth when the truth needed to be told, when the Devil needed to be shamed.

She had stood up to her terrifying grandmother (to *their* terrifying grandmother) out in the hall, as he lay beneath the covers in dismay. And when a taxi driver had refused to take them south of the Thames, she had cited the six-mile rule and bundled in anyway. And when a man on a scaffolding had yelled out that you'd not get many of *those* thighs to the pound, why, before Patrick could stop her, Caroline had marched across the road and, risking further ridicule, had confronted him; she'd ticked him off and faced him down.

Patrick knew that she fought her corner at work, that she would not let herself be used by her editor (she had regaled him with stories of Elaine; he felt he *knew* the woman). Nor would she be drawn by her colleagues into anything underhand or malicious or base (of course, yes, she had told him about Barbara too).

He knew how, all her life, she had been belittled by Laura, and yet somehow had maintained her sense of self. He was in awe of her spirit, her guts and intelligence. And he knew above all how she would have to call upon those qualities today as never before.

'Carrie.'

'Yes.'

'I feel so . . . inadequate.'

'You mustn't. Please don't. You're everything to me.'

'If there was something more that I could do.'

'Just cuddle me.'

'It's real, isn't it, what we have? It's not some kind of . . . misreading?'

'No, it isn't. It's very real.'

He wished she knew how beautiful she was, not just on the inside, in her soul, but on the outside too. He hoped he might yet have time persuade her of it. But it tore at him that this would be the end of them. That their relationship could not recover, that what followed would be emotional meltdown.

'Shouldn't you,' she said, 'be getting ready for work?'

'For *work*?'

'You must go in.' She sounded calm and slightly distant.

'Why must I?'

'Because you must. It's right that you should.'

'But I want to be with you.'

'Well, I don't want you to.'

Oh, that *hurt*! It was a horrible kind of casting out. He had known, of course, that he could not go all the way with her, that he could not share the worst of it (a lonely-making realisation in itself). But he had supposed she had wanted him to go as far as possible, to hold her hand before, and to be waiting for her after.

'Patrick,' she said, 'I'm sorry. But it's what I prefer. In any case, you shouldn't let them down at the garage.'

'Why not?' He sounded peevish, choked. 'You say you hate the garage. You're always telling me to pack it in. All right, well I shall do so. I shan't go back there ever.'

'You will.'

'I won't.'

'This morning you will. *Please*, Patrick, if you love me . . .'

'What is this "if"?'

'Then *as*. As you love me . . .'

'You're closing me out. I knew you would.'

'I'm not. I'm trying not to. But I'll do this better on my own. It will somehow be more do-able. Patrick, I implore you, get up and dressed, go to your job, and I shall see you here this evening.'

'If that's what you honestly prefer, then.' But he did not immediately get out of bed. He lay with her and breathed her in and was infused with feeling for her. It was easier to endure your own pain, wasn't it, than to endure the pain of somebody you cared for? Because at least you could grapple with your own feelings, whereas another person's were beyond your reach, you could not get a hold on them. All you could do, in that case, was to offer support, to offer solace, and these, it seemed, were being returned to sender.

'Trust me,' pleaded Caroline. And, though she pitied him profoundly, she was resolute. She had to go this last mile alone. He must not come with her today to Doctor Fellows.

Still, 'Oh,' she told herself. 'Oh, woe!'

———————— • ————————

'Whoa!' said Toby as a cup went flying. And, as fragments of Royal Doulton shot across the flagstoned floor, he stooped to help to gather them up.

'Blimey!' said Shell, who just stood there, transfixed, tray in hands, and looked stricken. 'Mrs H will do her nut if she finds out.'

'No reason why she should. Find out, I mean. In any case, it was an accident.' Tobias surfaced smiling, affable, flushed from the effort of bending. 'Could happen to anyone. Probably time of the month. A girlfriend once told me she always knew if her period was coming, because she'd smash a piece of her parents' Spode dinner service.'

He had meant only to console and cheer the girl, to tell her it was no big deal. What was one little cup between friends? *Non fa niente.* But she seemed positively affronted. Perhaps now was not the moment to ask, as he had been on the point of doing, why it took a woman with pre-menstrual tension twenty-four hours to cook a chicken.

Instead, 'I think these days they eat off paper plates,' he finished rather lamely. 'Oh, I say. There isn't any need for tears. You tell the dreaded Holloway it was I who broke the cup. If she wants to send me to bed without any supper, I shall go like a man.'

'I'm sorry,' said Shell, averting her face. 'I don't normally. Not ever. Perhaps it *is*, you know, what you said. That time of the month. Because I'm not usually a cry-baby.'

'Now, now.' Toby deposited the broken china on the tray, eased it out of her grasp, set it on the long pine table, patted his flanks and produced at last, with a small flourish, a clean but crumpled handkerchief. 'Have a good blow and you'll feel better.'

'Thanks.' Shell took the handkerchief from him and examined it. 'We have tissues at home,' she informed him. Then she blew her nose loudly, before solemnly returning it to him.

'You do?' said Tobias, pocketing it, highly amused. 'Well, they're more hygienic, I'll allow. But one does have to think of the wider issues. The rainforests and everything.'

'I suppose so,' she conceded, baffled.

It was a couple of weeks, if that, since Toby had last set eyes on the eminently desirable Michele. And, seeing her now, at close quarters, he was shocked to perceive the difference in her, the damage done to her. She was thinner than was healthy, and her face was too white, and her eyes were huge and full of trouble.

Within him he felt a stirring of compassion and a strong desire to crush her to his heaving breast. Then he was violently angry, he was inwardly incandescent with rage, he was up in arms. He was – if you can imagine it – madder than a wet hen. Jasper, he told himself, was responsible for this. And it really wasn't on. It wasn't cricket.

It was true, they had had a laugh and a joke together, he and Jasp, they had laid bets as to which of them could bed the beautiful girl. But, for all his bravado, he, Toby, would not have taken such advantage. She was not fair game, for goodness sake, she was terribly vulnerable – and not just because of her position here, for there was about her something of the *ingénue*, there was a guilelessness and a gullibility. His elder brother, he decided, was the worst kind of cad. He was a low-down bastard, a slimy toad, a blackguard, a bad hat – and he would take the earliest opportunity to inform him of the fact.

But he couldn't talk to *her* about it, more was the pity. He must not embarrass her by enquiring what was going on. He dare not ask her, 'Why so pale and wan, fond lover?' He dare not ask, 'What's shaking?' Ah, well. If she needs me, he decided with a resolution that surprised him, as he eyed the sorry heap of cup, the shards of china on the tray, I shall make sure I'm there to pick up the pieces.

'Anyway, was there something?' She binned the broken cup and brought another, all at once brisk, as though the tears had never been. 'I mean, can I do something for you?'

No wisecracks, now, Toby cautioned himself. Then, 'Er, maybe,' he said. 'I came down in search of some stuff to clean a plastic feed bowl.'

'Washing-up liquid.'

'That's the fellow.'

'Fairy.'

'I beg your pardon.'

'Here.' She fetched a bottle from the sink. 'For hands

that do dishes,' she smiled at him, and was unexpectedly pleased when she made him laugh (a small happiness, but she tingled with it). It must be lovely, she thought, to be able to crack jokes the way he did, to have an answer for everything. He was much nicer than Jasper in that way. These days, Jasper only made her wretched.

'Dried-on bran mash,' he told her confidingly, 'is always such a problem, don't you find?'

'Well, if it's anything like porridge.'

'In fact, it is a bit. Yes, it's very like porridge. Only for horses.'

She picked up the tray once more, weighed it experimentally in her hands, then said, 'I must take this to Jas– take this upstairs.'

So that was the deal! Toby sighed. What a shame! What a waste! What a cock-up! There was no justice. While he'd been up for hours, mucking in, mucking out, helping with the day-to-day running of the farm which was their livelihood, that lazy git lay around and waited for an auburn-haired nymphet to come twinkling in with toast and coffee – and almost certainly more besides.

Nodding towards the bottle of liquid in his hand, Michele advised him, 'You'll want a good squeeze, I dare say.'

In spite of his chagrin, Toby had to see the funny side. 'I thought you'd never ask,' he said.

'Wake up,' said Michele, 'I want a word with you.'

'What? What is it? Oh, go away.' Jasper was, he always maintained, a night-time person. While some people liked to get up at sparrow's fart and go dabbling in the dew, or (as in the case of Tobias) grubbing in the manure, he preferred to be in bed, putting in his full eight hours.

One, two in the morning would find him at his best and brightest; three, four, and he'd be up on the table, dancing, with a rose between his teeth; so it was scarcely reasonable to expect a sighting of him much before eleven, was it? Well, what was wrong with that? God, how he hated the smug, self-righteous, rise-and-shine, early-to-bed, up-with-the-lark brigade, hated the puritans and their crummy work ethic.

Last night he'd been out with pals, they'd had a bit of a hooley. Champagne had flowed like water, with the result that, today, he felt a little less than special. Oh, it was nothing that another hour or two of the deep and dreamless would not fix . . . but that, apparently, was to be denied him.

Clink, clank went a tray beside his head. A wafting smell of fresh-baked bread affronted him. Whoever said that there was no rest for the wicked had been possessed of singular insight.

'I won't go away. And I won't be spoken too like that.' Michele seized the sheet and tried to tear it off him, as Jasper, glaring, hung on for grim death.

'If it's my manhood you're after, you know, you only have to ask nicely. Oh, Jesus, God, Michele, do give me a break. My body thinks my head's a transplant and it's trying to reject it.'

'I'm going to ask you a straight question.' Michele, panting, abandoned the fruitless tug of war, she relinquished her hold on the sheet and stood with hands on hips. 'Then what I want from you is a straight answer.

You owe me that, at least. And *look* at me when I'm talking to you.'

'Do I have to?'

'Yes.'

'But it's so *bright* in here. It's all that beastly daylight. How's it getting in? Close the curtains, will you, there's my girl?'

'I said, *look* at me.'

He opened one eye. A compromise. And he thought of coaxing her to join him (he had often found that, for some reason, you could have the most fantastic sex with a hangover, when your limbs were loose, and your head was light, and everything was touched with unreality). But what he saw did not please him, and her way of speaking, her turn of phrase was so coarse, somehow, it roughed up his consciousness.

'Now, listen, Jasper, this thing can't go on. It's just too stupid.'

He hated the way she pronounced it, as if it was spelt with an h (a 'haitch' as she would have it): shtupid.

'What's shtupid, Michele?' he enquired with supreme condescension. 'Please enlighten me. You are, I admit, well qualified to speak on the subject of shtupidity.'

'You asked me to marry you.'

'I did?'

'I s'pose you've conveniently forgotten all about it?'

'Er, not entirely. No, I do recall saying something to that effect. In the heat of the moment, you understand. In an access of passion.'

'Oh, I get it.'

'You do.'

'Too right, I do. You used me, Jasper Charteris. You took me for a ride.'

'I did no such thing.'

'You seduced me.'

'And you did not, so far as I remember, raise any objections. You were a . . . I think the term is "push-over".'

'Then you're a pig!'

'Michele, Michele . . .' He squinted at her, shielding his eyes with his hand. 'Must we have this out right now? Couldn't you let it lie a while? Can it not wait until I'm on the mend, when I'm sitting up and taking nourishment?'

Finally, everything was beginning to get to her; it was beginning to get her down. She felt horribly alone, displaced, misplaced. But more especially she felt angry. She'd not be in this dreadful situation were it not for Nanny Fairchild and her crackpot schemes. She should never have agreed to do Nanny's dirty work, to come here among hateful strangers, to expose herself to hurt. But she *had* agreed to come, and here she *was*, and the sooner she got down to business, the better all round.

'It's OK, Jasper. You go back to sleep if you want. I've finished with you. You've told me all I want to know, you, you . . . wanker.'

Whether or not that struck a chord, or rang a bell, it made him wince, it made him flinch. 'Ouch,' he complained self-pityingly. 'Don't shout.'

'Well,' Michele sighed, and there was a catch in her voice. 'At least now I know where I stand. At least I know at last what I am going to have to do.'

'Do? What do you mean *do*?' Jasper hauled himself up

and peered after her, for the words sounded strangely ominous. 'Hey, don't run out on me like that. I'm sorry, honestly I am, I'm just feeling a bit ropey. Don't be a silly little duffer. Stay here and tell me what you're planning, will you? Hop in with me and we'll have a quickie.'

'No.' At the door she paused with her back towards him, holding fast to the handle – hanging on, indeed, for support – as she seemed to consider. Then, over her shoulder, with a composure that surprised him, and with a coldness that froze him, she told him, *'You'll* find out, Jasper, soon enough. You just wait and see, eh?'

———————— • ————————

Laura took a slug of gin and rolled it around on her tongue with satisfaction. 'First one today,' she announced defiantly, and she raised her glass arm-high in private toast to Dmitri, her po-faced personal trainer, that sanctimonious sod, that joyless physical jerk, who was always on at her to give it up, to cleanse her system of the poisons, to be free at last from her addictions.

Not that she didn't plan to cut down a bit, some time soon, when she was feeling more on top of things. It was very much on the agenda. She had, indeed, toyed with the idea of cutting it out altogether, she had turned it over in her mind. But then, to add to all her other problems, she had had the most terrible shock, what with Jasper and the . . . What with him and that girl. And she'd reached for a brandy. And that had been that, she'd been undone. So in a sense you could say it was all Jasper's fault. He had driven her back to the bottle.

Still, she was not – this was the great thing – actually an alcoholic. She could take drink or she could leave it. And it just so happened that today, this morning, she was taking it. Had she been a real alco, a complete soak, she'd have knocked back a whisky on waking. She'd have had a cognac with her morning coffee. She would not have sat through until eleven o'clock, when the sun was well and truly over the yard-arm, before calling out for a couple of shots of Gordon's to set her up for the day.

'You wouldn't remember Livia Langrish,' her mother said, out of the blue.

'Wouldn't I? No. There's no such person, surely? She's a character in a play.'

'I'm not talking about Sheridan, you foolish child.' Gimlet-eyed, Maudie regarded her. 'With all the money we spent on your education . . .'

'We're not going to go through all that again, are we, Mother? I left school a very long time ago. And I never let a lack of O-levels stand in my way.'

'Livia always claimed to have second sight, if you ever heard such silly nonsense. Then they moved to Torquay.'

'Really?' said Laura indifferently, stifling a yawn. Her mother often spoke now in such *non sequiturs*. On the whole, Laura took no notice, though she made dutiful responses, 'Yes' and 'No' and 'Good gracious, is that so?'

She found Maudie's generally uncensorious company, and her undemanding conversation, oddly soothing after all those years of scolding, to the point where she felt herself drawn to her. For the most part the old lady just rambled.

But she was with it, after all, this morning, she was on the ball. 'Well, if she *had* had the gift, you know, if she *had* been psychic, she would never have gone there, would she?'

'She wouldn't?'

'Dear me, not on your life!'

'Why not?'

'She hadn't been there a month when a tree fell on her head and smashed her skull in like an egg. Which goes to prove what I've always said – that clairvoyance is a lot of tommyrot.'

'Mother,' Laura laughed delightedly, 'you know, you're simply priceless.'

It could have been word association, Maudie's brain straining to make connections (it was, when you came to think of it, but a short step from priceless as in a hoot, as in a scream, a caution, to priceless as in very, very valuable, as in worth a fortune). Anyway, 'Laura,' she said, 'there is something you ought to have.'

'There is?'

'Yes, certainly. My grandmother's necklace. The emerald collar. I always intended that it should be yours.'

'But, Mother, you – '

'No, no,' Maudie raised two hands to silence her. 'Don't thank me. It is simply my dearest wish to see you wearing it. It will look very well with your complexion. You will find it over there, in the bureau. In the secret drawer.'

'Oh.' Laura found herself following Maudie's gaze, although she knew of course there wasn't any bureau, she knew there wasn't any necklace – at least, not here at Hartwell – in any secret drawer.

'You gave it to Caroline,' she reminded Maudie. And she could not launder the bitterness out of her voice.

'Caroline?'

'Yes.'

'How is she? We never hear, do we? Ah, well, I suppose she's a busy bee.'

'She's fine, as far as I know. Doing well in her work. She even had an article published, I seem to recall. With her picture at the top. Now look, about the necklace – '

'It was my mother's, d'you see? And her mother's before that? So it ought to come to you. That's right and proper.'

'Quite.'

Yes, it *was*, Laura told herself. It was absolutely right, it was absolutely proper. And if Maudie had come rather late to this realisation, well, better late, she told herself, than never.

What she must do, Laura decided, was to write to Caroline at once, to say – not in an aggressive way, but with impeccable reasoning, with inescapable logic, and with the emphasis on propriety – that Granny had had a change of heart, and that the necklace must now be returned.

She did not anticipate any difficulties. The girl could be an obstinate little madam, but she was not acquisitive, and she had simple tastes, with no real feeling for fine things. She also had – for Laura had dinned it in to her – a highly developed sense of fair play; she had scruples.

Besides, it looked ridiculous around the child's fat neck. And she hadn't the colouring. Or the bearing. She would not carry it off.

'Dear Caroline, I hope this letter finds you well and happy. We are all fine here at Hartwell, and would love to see you when you have the time to visit . . .' A little bit of local news, a bit of family news (how Pasha had been ill, and they had feared it was his liver; how Tobias was talking more and more of going organic; how John had had a bit of a throat, and that ludicrous old fart Forrest had said it was stress-related), then smartly down to business.

Or she could phone. Yes, why not? The telephone was more personal, she always found. And so much more immediate. 'Hi, my darling? How are you doing. Now, your Granny's just been saying about her necklace . . . Yes . . . Yes, I knew you'd see it that way . . . No, no great panic. Next time you're down. Or we could send Securicor. Have them collect it. Mm, on second thoughts, I think that would be safest.'

'Is there anything you need, Mother?'

'What should I need, Laura?'

'Well, I don't know. A pot of camomile tea? A glass of Evian? Only I'm going to leave you for a bit. I've got a couple of calls to make. You'll be all right, will you? You'll ring for service if there's anything you want?'

Laura stood up. She smoothed her skirt. She clasped her hands behind her neck and stretched it out. And she closed her eyes for an instant, the better to picture the green of the emeralds, mischievously conspiring with the green of her eyes.

'Back soon,' she promised, as she made for the door. And she was singing as she stepped out into the corridor.

*

Shell had had a nice bath. A lovely bath, in a tub so long and luxurious that, even when she stretched her leg, she could scarcely reach to turn the gold tap with her toe, to top up the scented water.

Feeling properly warm for the first time in weeks, she had dried herself with a fleecy towel the size of a blanket, and then wandered, stark naked, into the dressing room, to riffle through the racks and shelves, pulling out garments at random (no nasty wire hangers here, but lovely padded ones for delicate materials; solid wood for suits and jackets).

She had tried on, oh, dozens of clothes, holding them up in front of her, smoothing them against her, considering them in the mirror, twirling around to see how they fell, how they moved, before struggling into one thing, then another, then another . . .

They were a bit big, as she had expected, they were baggy on her. But the fabric! The quality! The cut! Discarded shantung blouses, linen skirts, soft cashmere sweaters littered the deep-pile bedroom carpet.

She had chosen, in the end, in keeping with her mood of reckless defiance – two fingers up to the lot of them! – an undulating, sugar-pink satin number, a frivolous fantasy of a frock, sleeveless, strapless, with a stiff gauze petticoat, and with a wired bodice which moved against rather than with her (when she sat down at the dressing table, it rode up, stiff as a breastplate). 'You look like a fairy on a rock cake,' she had told herself wryly. 'But it shows off your legs.'

Tights? She yanked open drawer upon drawer, sorted through, pulled out a pair of silky Dior (nineteen pounds a throw, she reckoned, none of your one-ninety-nine touch).

Make-up, make-up . . . With one finger she went dip, dip, my little ship, selected a pale foundation and smoothed it on, delighting in how beautifully it blended with her complexion, her natural alabaster colouring.

Now what? Blusher. She sucked in her cheeks and brushed bronzing powder into the hollows. Mascara? She decided on charcoal, a fine wand brush sheathed in elegant black. And lipstick. She had to try a lipstick. She fancied a luscious, big, bilberry mouth, a shock of colour offset by her pallor.

What next? A spot of perfume. She unstoppered a series of bottles, sniffed them in turn, and splashed on, at last, one called Cassini, an exotic mix which made her head spin.

Mind you, it would not have taken much. She was dizzy, anyway, with her own daring. She was trembling with it. Without the anger which ran right through her like an electric current and lit up her eyes, she would not have been able to do what she must, to see it through to its conclusion. It was this that drove her now, sheer, smouldering rage.

She was raking around in a jewellery box, in search of a suitably eye-catching necklace, at the heart-stopping moment when Laura breezed in through the door.

One split second before she saw the girl, Laura smelled a presence. She smelled a rat. With a curious dislocation of senses, she was first aware of a scent (a floral fragrance of chypre, with a heart of jasmine, Bulgarian rose and oakmoss, heightened by accents of osmanthus and marigold), and then of someone sitting there, at *her* dressing table, wearing *her* perfume, *her* make-up, *her* witty little Valentino dress.

Rarely was she rendered speechless, robbed of words. In the ordinary way she had plenty to say, particularly in the matter of staff, who (the old faithfuls, the family retainers excepted) were an idle, untrustworthy bunch, and would take advantage of you soon as look at you.

Her thoughts flashed back to the other female, the Dowdeswell girl, whom she had been forced to dismiss for pilfering. (Something – a necklace, a brooch, she could not now remember – had gone missing; some item of hers had been purloined.) But this was on an altogether different scale. This was monumental insolence. It quite took her breath away.

'Oh, hello,' said the girl off-handedly, sparing her a glance, then returning to her maquillage, to the application of a little kohl around the eyes. Laura saw in the mirror her look of concentration, the way her jaw dropped as she drew a neat line, revealing a pearly row of bottom teeth, the snaking tip of a tongue.

'What the hell. . . ?'

Laura strode across the room. She seized the girl by her naked shoulders, digging her fingers in like crampons, and tried to haul her off the stool. But Shell, clinging like grim death to the corner of the dressing table, resisted being unseated. Twisting, she offered up to Laura a face so clownishly made up it was pathetic. She looked like a child who had been let loose with the finger paints. She looked ridiculous.

Yet something in her look, in her expression, caused

Laura to recoil. It crossed her mind that this cheeky miss might actually be demented. What did they know of her, anyway? Of where she had come from? Of who she was? She might, for all that anybody was aware, have escaped from an asylum. She might be criminally insane.

'This is too much,' she said, as calmly as she could, and firmly, speaking as she imagined one should when confronted with a dangerous lunatic. 'Take off my things at once. You will leave this house today.'

'I don't think so,' said the girl with great bravado, though a faint husk in her voice betrayed her tension.

Then, of course, Laura saw the light. She saw what all this was about. Folding her arms across her chest, hugging herself for comfort, she began to pace the room, looking up, looking down, tossing her head like a filly. She laughed in scorn at the carpet. She laughed at the ceiling. Dear God, this was rich! This was simply too preposterous. It was beyond belief.

'You think that Jasper will protect you?' she challenged, coming to a halt at the girl's elbow. 'You think that he will intercede on your behalf? Well, let me tell you, young lady, there is no way. Not if I know Jasper. He won't cross me on this one. He hasn't the guts.'

'Ah,' said Shell.

'I suppose you think that he's in love with you? I suppose you think you've got him where you want him?'

'No,' Shell told her levelly. 'Nothing like that. I'm quite sure he would let you send me away. In fact, I think he would be glad. Yes, I'm sure of it. He would be grateful if you did. He would probably thank you. But I shan't go, you see. You won't make me.'

'And why not. *Why* should I not make you? Tell me one good reason, if you can, why I should not send you packing.'

'Well, because . . .' Shell turned once more to the mirror. She dipped into a glass jar for a hank of cotton wool, and dabbed at the corner of her mouth. She pursed her lips to smudge the lipstick. She puckered up. She studied her profiles, left and right.

'Because . . .' she said again, as it were through the mirror, to Laura's angry reflection. 'Because you are my mother.'

Vicar, I done something naughty.

There was, as Doris Fairchild always said, one law for the rich, and another for the poor. There was no justice. Anyone who doubted this should try walking out of Sainsbury's one of these fine mornings with a half a pound of pork chipolatas tucked under their raincoat. And then they should get themselves a job as a whatsname stockbroker, as a city analyst, or a chartered accountant, and cook the books. Because it was a well-known fact that, while little old ladies who shoplifted were up before the beak so fast their feet didn't touch the ground, your high financiers, your insider traders, your scribes and Faradays were all getting away with murder, they were getting away with millions, bleeding the country white.

So, when you talked about doing something wrong, you had to put it in its true perspective. You had to remember that that 'something', that misdemeanour, in certain circles, would be considered a mere nothing, it would be dismissed as a trifle. ('Not to worry, old boy, we're none of us perfect, what? We all make mistakes.')

In any case, it wasn't like she'd robbed a bank, or held up a building society, or swindled someone out of their

life savings. She hadn't *killed* anyone, for heaven's sake.
She hadn't gone around murdering folk in their beds.
You could open your newspaper any day of the week,
and read of people who'd done far, far worse than she.

Besides which, there had been extenuating circumstances. There had been Dawn.

They always told you, didn't they, that you would love
your child, jewel of your womb? And that your child
would love you in return? Blood, you were assured, was
thicker than water. And no one ever let on that it might
be otherwise, that your only daughter, far from being a
joy to you through the growing years, a comfort in your
old age, would be a blight on your life for ever.

Mind you, it had been fine in the beginning. It had
been lovely. If Dawn could just have stayed a baby, small
and manageable, things might have worked out very
differently, they might not have ended in tears. Doris still
smiled to remember what a picture she had been, her
bouncing bubba, pink from the bath, and dry and
powdered, in a clean terry nappy, waving her arms and
paddling her chubby legs as she was lifted into her cot.

Oh, she'd always had a temper on her, and the sort of
face that coloured up with it. But it was only later that the
real trouble started. When Dawn began to get clever, to
get clever-clever, always cheeking you, and backchatting
and talking down, talking a lot of high-flown nonsense, a
lot of I-know-best.

She would have been no more than thirteen when she
decided to become a vegetarian; then no amount of
reasoning would change her mind. 'None of that for me,
Mum. I refuse to eat dead animals.' 'But Dawn, this is

chicken. A chicken's not an animal, it's a bird.' 'A bird *is* an animal, surely you know that?' 'A bird is a bird, young lady, no matter what your intellectual friends might tell you. And a fish is a fish. And an animal has four legs and fur. Besides, I paid good money for it, so you'll eat it and like it.' 'Uh-uh. I'd rather eat vomit.'

Next she announces she's going to do her own thing, she will live her own life, she will look her own look. She starts wearing beads and feathers and loose, flappy garments, so you're embarrassed to be seen with her in the street.

Half the time she doesn't bother to turn up at school, so her reports say she's bright, they say she's *very* bright, but disobedient. And she locks herself in the bedroom and stays there all day, all night, so that when you *do* get in to clean, the place stinks of stale tobacco smoke and sweat.

She tells you she's a Marxist, and hangs out with undesirables, with long-haired louts who look like they need disinfecting. Then she moves into a 'commune', if you ever heard such nonsense, and from there it's downhill all the way.

Dawn's mind had been poisoned, of course, by the things she had read and by the things people told her (she would listen to anyone, you see, except her poor old mum). And then it had been poisoned by drugs.

She used to show up on the doorstep like a ragamuffin, with dark rings round her eyes. She'd be bloated and blotchy, and her hair would need washing, and all pride, all self-respect had gone.

And guess whose fault this was, apparently. Guess

who was to blame. Not, as you might imagine, her leftie teachers or her layabout friends. Not the people with whom she shared a squat, shared a bed, shared funny cigarettes, or a syringe. Oh, bless me, no! It was all down to her mother, to Doris. It was she who must carry the can.

Well, look, how would *you* feel if you'd worked every hour God sent, to bring up your little girl after her father passed on, only to have it thrown in your face, to be told that you'd made a pig's ear of the job of parent?

And here's another question: how come, if she'd been such a bad mum, it was to Doris that Dawn had turned when she found herself in the family way? How come she had been presented – no, *lumbered* – with a grand-child, and required to do the lot all over again? Where, in short, had Dawn's fine friends been when she needed them?

It was a very different world, don't forget, twenty years ago. Then the fruits of adultery, babies born out of wedlock, brought disgrace upon a household. These days no one seemed to bother with small formalities such as marriage, they didn't trouble to tie the knot. Film stars boasted quite openly to the newspapers about their 'love children', rather as if they'd been terribly clever, as if they were superior to decent married couples.

But the summer of 1970, when Dawn had been in that whatsname home, that hostel for unmarried mothers, had been a distressing time for Doris; it had scarred her.

The place itself had been all right, she would give it that. It had been bright and cheery, and the floors so clean you could have eaten your dinner off them. But the staff, though brisk and efficient, had been stiff with disapproval, they'd been sniffy and curt. The inmates, the mothers, had been treated like school-children, who must be scolded and punished for their misdeeds. And no one rejoiced in the birth of a baby. And everyone spoke in near-whispers.

Not that Dawn had cared. She had lain there like a lump, with the blankets drawn up, refusing to move, refusing to speak.

'Oh, she's a laugh a minute, I can tell you,' Dawn's room-mate had drawled, refusing to drop her voice, to speak in the hushed undertone which seemed to be expected of a fallen woman, sitting up to do her make-up, to white out her face and to black her eyes. 'I haven't had so much fun since I don't know when.' She had got out of bed, rammed her hands into the small of her back, and eased over to the door to shout for service. 'Where is everybody? My contractions have started. I need a painkiller. Christ, I shall be glad to get this over with! It's been weeks since I could get into any of my clothes. Such a frightful nuisance! Utterly tedious!'

'Would you rather it was a little boy,' Doris had asked her, by way of conversation, although the young woman had been very posh, very loud, very Knightsbridge, very much not her sort, 'or a little girl?'

'Why should I care?' The girl had shrugged. 'I never meant to have either. If I'd known I was pregnant . . . I suppressed it, you see. It happens, apparently. Mind over matter. I could still zip myself into my jeans when I was five months gone. I was having periods of a sort. I tell you, I had no *idea*. Not till it was too late. Then, pow!

'My dear Mama is beside herself. I have been banished from home for the duration. And the father's a shit, he's refused to take responsibility for any of it. So, frankly, it's a balls-up all round.'

'Will you keep it or have it adopted?'

'Keep it, I suppose.' The girl had yawned. 'I mean, I did a shoot the other week – the only work I've had in months, for obvious reasons. Maternity clothes. And a mini-interview about how great it is to be pregnant. How gorgeous and female and fecund I feel. Almost mystical experience. In sweet harmony with nature. Bonds forming like nobody's business, and baby still *in utero*. Crap like that. So I'm a bit stuffed, aren't I, publicity wise? I'm kind of stuck with it now.'

'I see.' Doris had sat a moment fiddling with her handbag, opening and closing it, snapping the clasp till her thumb was sore. Rich bitch, she had thought, close to tears. Stuck-up, spoilt little so-and-so. Had she no shame?

'My own fault, of course. I only did it to get back at my mother. The photo session, I mean, and the interview. I knew she'd just *die* to see me splashed all over *Queen*. Well, she hit the roof, natch. She was *mortified*.'

Smiling in small triumph, the girl had picked up a brush and run it caressingly through her luxuriant red hair. 'One thing I will say for being up the spout, it does wonders for the condition. And my skin's never been better. It seems to have a special bloom, don't you think?'

Doris had said nothing, but her eyes had been drawn to her daughter, of whom nothing was visible but a tuft of hair protruding from beneath a breathing pile of bedclothes. Dawn had not in this, or any way, been so blessed. Dawn was not blooming.

'She snores, you know,' the girl had confided. 'Like a pig, actually. I haven't had a wink of sleep for two nights. I've asked them to move her but there isn't a bed. It's too bad, it really is.'

'Mm.' Doris wondered if she was expected to apologise, to take this, too, upon herself, to say she was sorry. Well, she wouldn't, so there!

'What time is it? Gone seven? My boyfriend should be here at any min with my supper. I asked him to bring fruit and cheese and yoghurt. The food in this place is disgusting. Not fit for human consumption. With a bit of luck, he'll bring wine as well. Strictly against the rules, but who cares? A nice bottle of Beaujolais to drown my sorrows.'

'Your boyfriend? But I thought. . . ?'

'Oh, not *that* boyfriend. Not the shit. I have a new one now, who's a perfect sweetheart. I only hope the baby isn't going to put him off. He has a romantic view of motherhood right this moment, but that's because he's so smitten with me. A few sleepless nights, a few shitty nappies, and he might take a more jaundiced view.'

'He might at that.'

'Is it unspeakably painful, the actual birth? I shall scream the place down, if so. To be truthful I'd prefer a Caesar, but I can't be doing with a scar.'

'Yes,' Doris had told her, getting up to go (it was obvious she would get no change out of Dawn today, though she knew she was awake and had been listening). 'Yes,' she had said again, with malice, 'it really is unspeakably painful.'

*

Two nights later, the girl had had her baby, with all the unspeakable pain that that entails. And a few hours later, Dawn had had hers. Both were girls.

'What will you call it?' Doris had asked the superior redhead, bending over the cot.

'I don't know. Sprog. I haven't thought.'

'She's beautiful,' Doris had offered, gazing at the sleeping infant.

'She's all right, I suppose. All babies look the same to me. You know what they say, they all look like Winston Churchill. Listen, I'm going to make a break for the bathroom, though if matron catches me she'll do her nut. We're supposed to stay in bed like invalids.' The girl had thrown back the bedclothes and considered her flat stomach. 'I refuse, absolutely to use a bedpan. Well, wouldn't *you*? So degrading. That's the intention, so far as I can see, to put us in our place, to make us feel humble. We're to be forced to pay for our sins. That's the kind of place this is. Hey, it's better out than in, I will say that. I was sick of the bulge. Keep an eye here, won't you? Cover for me if you have to. Say I've been called away urgently. I shan't be long. But I have to put my face on, don't I?'

Vain, conceited, selfish cow. Snotty piece. Who did she think she was? Just because she had money. And looks. Because she was supposedly 'somebody', a fashion plate, a face. And . . .

Doris had gone to stand by Dawn's bed, to offer a finger, consideringly, to Dawn's baby. She had known even then that she was going to have to do it all again, she was going to have to bring it up, to be a mother to the child.

'She looks,' she said sadly, thoughtfully, to her daughter's hostile back, 'just the way you did. She's the very spit of you, you know that, Dawn?' Then such love for the child had swelled in her breast, such overwhelming emotion, that she had had to sob to relieve it.

She had been assailed by a sense of injustice, of the essential unfairness of life. What could she offer this little mite, this defenceless scrap of humanity? It would grow up in hardship to be plump and charmless like its mother. She would be able to give it nothing, not even, in the end, if history were to repeat itself, her affections. I can't, she had told herself, despairing. I really *can't* bear it.

The other child, meanwhile, had been born into wealth. She had been born to be beautiful like her mother; she would have long legs, long eyelashes, long red hair. She would not be a lump. Well, look, what kind of deal was it, in which one child would have so very much, and the other so very little?

'Don't seem right,' she'd muttered.

Dawn, grunting, turning in the bed, had glowered at her, and turned again to watch the wall. And then, *then* Doris had decided. 'This is for you, my angel,' she'd whispered to Dawn's baby, lifting her, holding her close for a hug. 'You may not be beautiful, but you can at least be rich.'

And, to the other one, 'Never worry, my precious. No, never you fret. Nanny will look after you. You'll grow up to be a bobby-dazzler. And then one day . . .'

'Everything all right?' the red-haired girl had asked, swanning back into the room, peering down her nose at her, or so it had seemed to Doris as she sat there. And she did not check on, did not spare a glance for, the baby in the cot. The baby in the cot marked 'Grant'.

'Yes,' Doris had told her, with only a faint tremor. 'Yes. There's not been a peep out of either of them.'

Friday Afternoon

CHAPTER

————— • —————

16

'. . . Of course the rule misfires in domestic
or farm situations when a hen is made to sit on eggs
not her own, even turkey or duck eggs.
But neither the hen nor her chicks can be expected
to realise this. Their behaviour has been shaped under
the conditions that normally prevail in nature,
and in nature strangers are not
normally found in your nest.'

Richard Dawkins, *The Selfish Gene*

Laura lay back against the leather upholstery and closed
her eyes. Pale winter sunlight washed her eyelids. She
breathed in wobbly air, warmed by the engine, feeling
slightly nauseous and utterly heartsick. When, briefly,
she rested her face against the cold pane of the window,
her brain rattled in her skull. And she thought, 'It can't be
so, it *isn't* so. I simply can't accept it.' But more and more
she was coming to do so. More and more the truth crept
in upon her.

Then she thought, 'I can't handle this. It's more than I
can bear. It's insupportable.'

What grotesque prank had been played upon her?

What had that vile old woman done? At first she had
assumed it was some kind of elaborate subterfuge, a
hoax, a ruse on the part of the girl to blackmail her, to lay
false claim to an inheritance, or – though to what obscure
end? – to worm her way into her affections.

Michele was, it must be said, well informed, she had
done her homework diligently. She could relate where
she, Laura, had been twenty-odd years ago, she could
tell about the ghastly hostel, and her reason for being
there. She could describe in detail the twin-bedded
room, the mustard colour of the curtains, the view from
the window across a playing field edged with wind-bent
trees. She could invoke the formidable matron, all stiff
bib and outrage. She could even describe Laura's night-
dresses, the shades of oyster and peach, the lace trim.
'You had a boyfriend at the time called Gerry. He drove a
red sports car. He brought you strawberries and wine
and wanted to marry you, it seems, though presumably
nothing ever came of it.'

Yes, but look, there must be literally dozens of people –
other mothers, former inmates, nurses, visitors – who
could be possessed of this knowledge, who might indeed
have stored it up for later use against her. What did any
of it prove, one way or the other?

'Shut up,' Laura had shouted, her composure
slipping. 'Be quiet this instant. I will not listen to another
word. Go now, at once, before I call the police.'

Yet in the end she had had no choice but to hear
Michele out, as, relentlessly, the girl went on. 'My Nan –
well, I *thought* she was my Nan . . . She said to say you
will remember her. She wore a blue hat.'

'A blue – ' Laura had shrilled with maniacal laughter. 'Some dowdy little body with sunken tits expects me to remember, two decades later, what kind of hat she wore.'

'You *do* remember her then? That "dowdy little body", who happens to be my grandmother. Or, at least . . .'

'She is behind this, is she? This confidence trick. This bizarre attempt at extortion.'

'She kept up with you, you see, so far as she was able. She read about you in the papers. She liked to know what you were getting up to. To know you were doing very nicely for yourself.'

'This is abominable. It's an outrage.' Laura had clawed at her cheeks to reveal, momentarily, the white rims of her eyes.

'Well, it was for Caroline, you see. Her real grandchild. It was *her* best interests Nanny had at heart.'

'Oh, she did? How touching! And what about *my* interests? What about *me*?'

'I think she felt it was time you knew the facts. And that I . . .'

'Yes, what about you?'

'Well, how d'you think *I* feel? I mean to say. Listen, none of this is my fault, is it? You can't go blaming me.' As she got to her feet, with her long, thin legs, and in that silly, frilly pink dress, Michele had resembled a carnation, wilting slightly on its stem. 'I was just a baby, wasn't I? I had no say in anything. *You* were the careless one, if it comes right down to it. You were the one who didn't give a toss. You're as much in the wrong as Nanny, if you ask me. And I'm the muggins, aren't I,

who missed out on . . .?' She had waved her arms
around extravagantly. '*I* missed out on all this – though
much I care, now that I've seen the way you people live.
Because, with all your money, you're still as miserable as
sin, the lot of you.'

'My God, you've got a nerve!'

'You're spoilt, that's obvious to me. Nanny says you
ought to make same kind of settlement, right? She says
you ought to give me something. But, frankly, if this is
what being rich does for you, I don't want a penny from
you.'

'Nor shall you have. This is monstrous. Ah, now,
though, we get to it, don't we? Now we get to the motive.
The reason for this foul play, this ludicrous charade.'

'I shouldn't have come, probably,' Michele had
allowed, dropping her head, scrunching the skirt of the
Valentino dress, as if to wring it out. 'Only I couldn't
think *what* to do. I was dead confused. And Nanny
insisted. And I suppose I wanted to . . . you know. To
find out about my parents. Not ever having had any to
speak of.'

'Well, your father is a has-been photographer. That is,
he would be if you were who you claim, which you are
not. And I . . . Oh, my God, this is a nightmare! I can't
believe it. I *won't*.'

'Ah, but you will,' the girl had told her, not rudely or
tauntingly, but quietly, with resignation. 'The same as I
do. I didn't at first, you see. I thought Nanny had gone
bonkers or something. It was too much to take in at one
go. Because it was the first I'd heard of it. And I'd never
for one moment suspected. (Well, why should I?) But in a

little while, when I came to think about it . . . You see, it all fits, doesn't it? I mean, I even *look* like you.'

'Then where . . .' Laura had buried her face in her hands as she tried to get a grip, to get her mind around this. 'Where,' she had asked hopelessly, 'does that leave Caroline?'

'I dunno.' The girl had sighed. '*I* wondered about that.'

'She is, you see . . .' Laura, appalled, had felt her eyes smart, she'd felt the sting of tears. She had walked the room as she tried to compose herself, and she'd hammered her fist into the palm of her hand. 'She's my child. She's my little girl. What should I tell her?' A fierce protectiveness and pity – two alien emotions – had then assailed her. 'Poor Caroline,' she'd thought. 'Oh, my poor Caroline!'

'Maybe,' Shell had suggested indulgently, with her head on one side, watching her, 'you don't have to tell her anything. It might just be better if she didn't know. There's not much in it for her, after all. No mother. No father, neither, so far as anybody is aware. Just Nanny, who's not everybody's cup of tea.'

'That woman? She's a criminal. A kidnapper. A baby-snatcher. I shall drag her through every court in the land.'

'Oh, I wouldn't,' Shell had counselled wearily. 'It would only cause more upset. There's nothing to be gained. And you wouldn't exactly come up smelling of roses yourself.'

'Look, what is it you want?' Laura had stopped pacing and turned to confront her. 'What are you expecting from me? You mentioned money. A financial settlement. Very well. How large? How much? What will it take to resolve this?'

'You just don't get it, do you?' Shell had balanced on her left leg, swivelled her right foot, performed a very deliberate little heel-toe, heel-toe, frowning all the while at the carpet. 'I *told* you, didn't I? I don't want nothing from you now. Nanny said I should insist on something. She said it was my right. And it would have been great if it had worked out different. We could have done with a bob or two. But all I really want – all I *wanted* – was for you to look at me, and recognise me, and be pleased to meet me, which I can see you are not, so there it is.'

'Hang on, hang on, hang on.' Laura had brought up her hands either side of her face. 'Give me a moment. Let me sort this out.'

'Sure,' Michele had told her, shrugging, indifferent. 'You take your time. Take all the time you need.'

'Right.' Laura had made a guillotining movement. 'You say you are my natural daughter.'

'Right.'

'In which case, Caroline is *not* my daughter.' Chop went her hands.

'Right.'

'And *you* know.' Chop. 'And *I* know.' Chop. 'But so far she doesn't.' Chop, chop.

'You got it! And it's up to you, isn't it, whether or not you tell her? Whether you feel it would be better.'

'*You* won't tell her? Or that . . . that old witch?'

'Nanny won't. I don't think so. Not if I ask her not to. And I've no intention of it. I wish I'd never fetched up here in the first place. I certainly never intended to stay for so long. To get, er, involved. The job came about by accident, actually. I sort of walked into it. I expected to be found out any day. And then there was Jasper.'

'Oh, yes. Him.' Laura had clasped her hands and borne down with them, as though she were plunging a dagger into her heart. 'Then shall we. . .?'

'Make it our secret?' Michele had tapped the side of her nose conspiratorially. 'Mum's the word,' she had said. And no pun had been intended.

'All the same . . .' She must go to see Caroline. Just to see. To look upon her and perhaps to understand. Laura had crossed swiftly to the door, where she had turned. 'Wait here,' she instructed, 'and say nothing of this to anyone. I shall be back tonight. We shall discuss this further.' She had caught her breath. And then she had added tersely, as a mother might to her trying daughter, 'Please take off that dress, Michele, and make yourself respectable. You look like something left over from the weekend.'

'Where are we?' She opened her eyes and addressed the liveried back of her chauffeur.

'Just past Andover,' he told her.

'Really?' Laura pressed the button to lower the electric window, let the bitter wind assault her for a second or two, then closed it again. 'How long will it take us to get there?'

'Well, now . . .' He considered. 'Friday dinner time, the bulk of the traffic will be coming this way. Out of town. For the weekend.'

'Yes, yes. So how long, would you say?'

'An hour. Maybe more if there's roadworks on the motorway.'

Laura checked her watch. It was just past one o'clock. What a morning, what a morning! It seemed that in the space of half a day her whole life had been turned upside-down.

Oh, let Caroline be at home when she arrived! (A call to the office had elicited the information that Caroline Karasinski – *Karasinski*! – was on a week's leave. A call to her Battersea flat had gone unanswered; the wires had sung of absence and of emptiness; a dreary dring-dring.)

Then, what should she say to the girl if she *was* there? How to explain her visit? Caroline would be more than a little surprised to find Laura on her doorstep, and was unlikely to believe the I-was-passing-so-I-thought-I-would-drop-in routine which she had been rather desperately rehearsing.

'Well, do your best,' she said faintly to her driver, closing her eyes again, blinkering herself with her hand, sliding down in the seat. 'Get me there as quickly as you can.' And, again to herself, or to God, or to the Fates or to someone, Don't let me screw this up, now, will you? *Will* you?

'Is Caroline here?' Laura scarcely seemed to notice the tall youth with the ruffled hair and ashen face, whose voice she had heard on the intercom, who had presumably buzzed her in, and who now stood waiting, watching, in the doorway of the flat, with his head against the door jamb. Indeed, she craned to look past him, to peer behind him, to seek out her daughter. (To seek out, that is, the person she had always thought . . .)

'She's not here,' he said, and his voice had a crack, it had a fault line right through it.

'Not. . . ?' Laura darted a look at him. Who was he? A boyfriend? Caroline had not spoken of a romantic attachment. He was quite attractive, actually, in a slightly rough-and-ready, a sort of slept-in way. He had very nice grey eyes, rimmed now with red, as though he had been rubbing them. And a generous mouth. And a large, flat nose. And loquacious body language, an intense physicality. 'I shall come in and wait for her. When do you expect her back?'

'It's rather difficult, actually.' Patrick did his best to baulk her. That Laura should choose now, of all times, to turn up here, seemed to him beyond belief. The sight of his mother, after so long, and at so inauspicious an hour, nearly unhinged him. Was it possible that she knew. . . ? But, no, he saw not a flicker of recognition in her eyes.

He had left for work this morning, because Caroline had implored him to, but with every minute he had felt more and more tormented, until at one-thirty he had been climbing the walls with worry, so he'd pleaded a migraine and come home. She might not want him to be there with her at the doctor's, metaphorically to hold her hand, but here at least, with her possessions around him, with all the things she owned and touched and wore, the bath towel still damp from her body, and the dent of her face in her pillow, he had felt that much closer to her.

For perhaps the fiftieth time in a quarter of an hour, he checked his watch, and he saw that the moment was approaching. What must her thoughts be right now? And later, when it was over, what would she feel then?

Laura, seeing his distraction, seized her opportunity and shoved past him. 'Who are you, anyway?' she demanded, as she went ahead of him down the corridor.

'I . . .' The obvious thing was of course to lie. To say that he was just a friend. Or had come to mend the washing machine. Or to measure up for new curtains. But he was emotionally done in, he hadn't the strength of will to dissemble. He would tell her the truth and she could make what she liked of it. Indeed, he relished the idea of her shock and confusion. 'I, Laura,' he said vindictively, and for the first time she detected an Irish lilt, 'am Patrick. Patrick Mulryan. I'm your son.'

Well, for goodness sake! Suddenly it seemed that everybody wished to claim her for a mother. And why not? Come one, she thought, come all! The more the merrier! It was a wonder, actually, that Watkins, the chauffeur, hadn't doffed his cap down in the street there, and declared himself as a long-lost child. He was sixty if he was a day, but so what? It would scarcely have seemed less probable than . . .

'You. . . ?' She turned abruptly to stare hard at the boy, who jigged around with anxiety and tugged at the hem of his sweater (he shouldn't have said it, he shouldn't, he shouldn't). And she knew in an instant of course that it was true. Because she saw herself in him, in some small measure. And, with a rush of regret, she saw Tom.

'It's all right,' Patrick reassured her coldly. 'Don't say "Come to my arms, my beloved boy!", or anything like that. It would be so out of character. Listen, I'm sorry. I guess this is a shock to you. Would you like a cup of coffee?'

'A shock?' Laura sank down in an armchair. 'A coffee?' She passed a hand over her eyes. 'Have you,' she asked in a small, strained voice, 'anything a little stronger?'

'So . . .' said Patrick when he'd fixed her a drink, and he dodged about as if to evade her scrutiny.

'So.' She rolled the glass between her palms, then slugged back a mouthful of neat scotch. 'I wouldn't have let him take you, you know,' she said querulously. 'But I had no choice. He'd have fought me every step of the way. He'd have battled it out in court. Or he'd have talked to the press, he'd have blackened my name. That's what he threatened to do.'

'Well, we couldn't have that, could we? Laura Grant's reputation muddied by the media? Oh, look, don't apologise. Don't try to explain. I've had a good life so far. I've been fine.'

'I'm very glad. I hope you can believe that. I'm not such a wicked old bitch as Tom may have led you to believe. Anyway, Patrick, what are you doing here?'

'What am I doing here?' He pulled a funny face. A succession of funny faces, stretching his mouth, squeezing his eyes, going eeeagh. (Lady wants to know what I'm doing here. Well, now . . .)

'Well?'

'I am Caroline's half-brother, after all.'

'No you're not,' Laura told him flatly.

'Eh?'

'Easy mistake. Anyone could make it. Went into hospital.' Laura took another swig of whisky. 'Gave birth. Came out with the wrong baby. Doesn't say much for my observation, does it? Or for any theory of kin recognition? Never noticed a thing.'

Patrick said nothing for a moment, just stared and stared at her. Then, with a shake of the head, he asked her, almost shouting, 'What is it that you're telling me?'

'Ah. It's a long story.'

'Make it short. Make it quick. Make it *very* quick. It's terribly important. You have no idea.'

'First I have to have your promise. I don't want Caroline to hear about this.'

'To hear *what*, Laura? About *what*?'

'Oy, oy, oy.' Laura sighed to relieve her tension. 'It seems she's not actually my daughter. I mean, I *feel* that she is. And in most senses she is. Except she's not flesh of my flesh. I brought the wrong baby home from the hospital, if you can believe it. Hey. I say. What's going on?'

For the boy, Patrick, her tall, good-looking son, was scrabbling around among the telephone directories, snatching up and discarding sheets of paper, tearing – yes, literally tearing – at his hair. He had not the grace to answer her, but, finding what he sought, began frantically to punch in a number. 'Rats!' he murmured as, in haste, he misdialled. Then he tried once more.

'Hello. Hello. May I speak with Doctor Fellows, please? It's extremely urgent.'

Laura watching, wondered at his agitation, at the way he wound the telephone flex around and around his hand.

'What do you mean, he can't be disturbed? Did I not say it was urgent? It's a matter of life and . . .' Distraught, he clapped his free hand to his brow. 'Well, get him *out* of his surgery,' he yelled. And then, dully, 'Oh. Oh, I see.' When he glanced again at his watch it was twenty minutes to three. All was surely lost. He replaced the receiver.

With sudden, extraordinary venom, he rounded on his mother. 'It's no use,' he said perplexingly, 'the guy is operating. Damn you, Laura! Oh, damn you. Why couldn't you have got here sooner? Why did you leave it too late?'

'I. . . ? I don't know what you're talking about.'

'You don't? No, of course. You wouldn't. Oh, sweet Jesus, what a mess!' He flopped on the sofa, laid his head on the arm and cradled it. There was no joy for him, or solace, even in the realisation, now slowly dawning on him, that the two of them were free to be together. They'd had it, he told himself, desolated. It was that simple. They would not survive as a couple united in guilt.

A key turned in the latch. The front door opened, closed. Caroline came quietly into the room with a strange, set look about her. With the merest glance she noted Laura's presence ('Oh, *you're* here,' she seemed to say), then she shook her hair about, and thrust her chin forward, cleared her throat and said to Patrick, 'I didn't go.'

'You . . .' He raised his head from the crook of his arm to gaze at her.

'I'm sorry. I thought I'd do it. Right up until the last minute, I thought I would. But I couldn't go through with it. I'm not sure if I ever truly meant to. Are you angry with me?'

'Angry? Oh, no, no.' Then, to Laura's bemusement –
and, God knows, this had been for her a most bemusing
day – they fell into one another's arms, and, with great
gulps of air, and shaking shoulders, Patrick began to sob.

Saturday

CHAPTER

17

They sent the car for Doris. A big white whatsname with an embolism on the front.

She hadn't been expecting it. Never dreamt. First she knew of it was when a knock came at her door, and out there on the gangway stood a man in uniform, with his peaked cap under his arm, telling her politely that her presence was requested down in Dorset.

'Now, you mean? Right this minute?'

'If you would be so good. It is – I am instructed to impress upon you – a matter of some importance.'

'Oh, well, if you put it like that . . .'

She went at once to the wardrobe for her coat, and for the blue hat, and the Co-op carrier with all the gubbins, the snapshots and whatnot, in it. Then she nipped into the bathroom, to run a comb through her hair, and to have a tiddly-beaujolais. And if you had asked her at that minute what she was feeling, she would have been bound to confess she was a bag of nerves.

It was a relief, of course, in a way, that it was finally over, bar the shouting. But she was anxious, too, about that shouting. About the hard things that might be said. The Charteris characters, she supposed – and that Laura female in particular – might not be best pleased with her. They might take a dim view of her actions.

Then what of Michele? How had she been getting on? And what, indeed, of the other one? At the prospect of seeing again, after so many years, her daughter's daughter, her Dawnie's child, Doris went all hot, she went all cold, she came over quite peculiar.

For a few seconds she entertained the funny idea that they were about to swap back, to effect a fair exchange, to return each girl to her family. Shell would remain at Hartwell, while Caroline would be given into her care, to return with her to Purley, to the flat. But that was plain daft. That wouldn't be the way of it. Not now the girls were grown.

'I meant no harm,' she said aloud, justifying herself to the bathroom mirror, to hear how it sounded. 'I done it on the spur of the moment, sort of thing. Anyway, I looked after your baby all right. I brought her up decent. She wanted for nothing.' Strange, though, how these words, so persuasive in her head, lacked a certain conviction when they were given utterance.

Down in the street, the chauffeur stood waiting, with his cap now on his head, and with a pair of big leather gauntlets on his hands. And – get this! – as she approached the car, he opened the rear door for her, he stood stiff and straight and double-breasted as if she were a VIP, as if she were the Queen of Sheba, waiting to see her safely in.

Comfy, thought Doris, admiring the plush interior, the hide upholstery, the walnut dashboard, as, with the merest murmur of compliance from the engine, the vehicle moved away. Then, to crown it all, as they headed out of the close, Doris Fairchild, glancing through the side window, saw Mrs Teacup Whisper, she saw Mrs Gentle, hurrying along, very full of herself, puffed with self-importance, on her way to do the flowers for the church. Catching the woman's eye, seeing how her mouth gaped in amazement, Doris raised a hand in salutation. She twirled it graciously at the wrist. She gave a very regal wave.

'If you are Laura's daughter,' said Toby, tickled half to death by the notion, 'that means that we are sisters.'

'No it doesn't,' Shell responded with a giggle, 'not exactly.'

He adored it when she smiled. It did something wonderful to her face, it sort of crystallised her beauty. And it was particularly thrilling when it was he who elicited the smile. It made his toes curl inside his cold, damp wellington boots.

Oh, and the tip of her nose moved when she talked. He loved that about her, too.

'Well, as good as.' He waved aside her objections. 'Hey, come on over here and meet Freckles. He's Caro's. I say, what about our Caro, then?'

'What *about* her?'

'Being in the pudding club, for one thing. And we never knew she had it in her.'

'That's not very funny.'

'Blame my scriptwriter.'

'Who's he?'

'Dorothy Parker.'

'Never heard of her.' Timidly, Shell reached up to pat

the pony's head, snatching her hand away when he snaffled up her fingers, hiding it protectively behind her back.

'Don't be scared. He won't hurt you. His bark is worse than his bite.'

'Maybe. But I never got this close to a horse before.'

'You poor little deprived urban person. Duppie, as we call your type. Would you like me to teach you to ride?'

'I don't know.'

'What don't you know?'

She shrugged. 'You might not have the opportunity,' she said ruefully. 'I could be sent packing any minute.' And, after a moment's thought, 'Tobias?'

'Yo?'

'What do you think they are saying about me right now? What do you suppose they'll *do*?'

It was an intensely serious question. He considered it gravely. What *would* they be saying to each other, John and Laura and Caroline, and Jasper, not to mention this Patrick fellow, the latest skeleton to come clattering out of Laura's closet (and you had to wonder, frankly, that she found room in there for so much Armani).

They had all gathered in the drawing room, drawn to the fire, to the heart of the house, where they had begun to pool their bewilderment. Toby, ambling in, had found them standing about in attitudes of upset and confusion, and would have wished to stay, to watch as the drama unfolded.

Only then he'd noticed Shell. She had been standing apart from the rest, standing back, hugging herself, an outsider, an Orphan Annie, ignored, disregarded by them all. Poor kid! he had thought with the huge compassion of which he was capable, a billowing of sympathy which blew out his ribs. And he had gone to her and had drawn her gently to the door, saying, 'I'll show you the stables. A breath of fresh air will buck you up no end.'

'What should they do?' he replied at last. 'You're Laura's child. They will acknowledge you, I hope and trust. They will welcome you to the fold. You will be one of us. They're just a bit stunned at the moment. All the implications have yet to sink in.'

'Are they angry with me?'

'Angry with *you*? I don't see how they could be. It wasn't your fault, was it? Though I doubt if anyone is very thrilled with that grandmother of yours, or very amused by the baby-swapping sketch.'

'They wouldn't go to the police?'

'Not a chance of it.'

'Phew. I was worried sick, you see. Everybody looked so grim. Freckles is sweet, isn't he? I wish I had a lump of sugar to give him.'

'He's not allowed sugar. It would rot his teeth. In any case, he's roly-poly enough as it is. You know, Shell . . .' Tobias regarded her for a moment, his head on one side. 'Now we learn that you are Laura's daughter, it seems so glaringly obvious, it's a wonder none of us spotted the likeness before.'

'Although I'm nowhere near as beautiful.'

'You what? You must be joking. You're a thousand times more beautiful than she. But don't tell her I said so, or I'll put spiders down your neck, and frogs in your

underwear drawer, I'll make you apple-pie beds and all
those other larky things that big brothers are supposed to
do to little sisters.'

'Is that what you used to do to Caroline?'

'Not exactly. Though we teased her without mercy and
called her Dumpling.'

'That wasn't kind.'

'I suppose not.'

'She's very pretty, actually. I think she looks sweet.'

'She is sweet.'

'If she lost a bit of weight she'd be gorgeous. Has she
ever tried to?'

'Has she ever? I should think Laura tried everything on
her. Poor old Caro! She was always, you see, more
slimmed against than slimming.'

'She had a tough time of it, hmm?' Shell sucked in her
cheeks, considering. 'In a way I suppose she had it
harder than me.'

'In a way. Yes, oddly enough, she may have done.'

'She's not exactly maternal, is she? Laura, I mean.'

'Not what you'd describe as an earth mother. Not a
Ceres.'

'A series?'

'Ceres with a C.'

'Eh?'

'No, no A. You know . . . Roman goddess personage.
Big old sort. Double D cup. Sheaves of corn under the
arm.'

'No, that doesn't sound like Laura. I can't *imagine* how
she and I would have got along.'

'As to that, there's no saying.'

'I s'pose not. It could be that we're too alike.'

'Only in appearance. You're a different sort of person.'

'Am I?'

'Absolutely.' He whistled a few bars, tunelessly. 'Boggles the mind, rather, doesn't it, all this?'

'You could say that.'

'Caroline looks like your mother, does she? Or, I should say, like *hers*.'

'A bit. So far as I can tell, that is. From old photographs. Dawn was certainly, well, plump.'

'Bane of Caro's life, her weight problem – though she would never admit it. She does have this kind of . . . resistance to things. She digs her little heels in. The more Laura got on to her about it, the more she hung on to her surplus.'

'She'll do better now she's happy, the weight will just fall off her. She *does* look happy, doesn't she? In spite of it all? I haven't ruined her life by coming here?'

'Ruined? No, I don't imagine so. She's resilient. She has a lot of bounce. As to happy, I couldn't say. She looked pretty dazed to me. Like someone in a trance.'

'Oh, *that*,' said Shell dismissively. 'That's just love.'

'Ah.' Toby frowned. 'That's what it does to you, does it? You go into a trance?'

'Yeah, I reckon. Oy, where are you off to?' She was giggling again, full of mirth, as Toby did a hammy imitation of a sleep-walker, floating off round the stable yard with his arms outstretched. When he'd gone a few paces he said, without turning back, without looking at her, 'I'm falling in love with you, Michele.'

'No you're not. Don't be daft.'

'Yes I am.'

One complete circuit of the yard brought him eventually to her side again. 'Are you still in love with Jasper?'

'That little toe– How did you know about Jasper?'

'I asked first. Are you still – '

'No, I'm not,' she said rather too quickly, and she shook her head vehemently. 'I'd like to kick him in the goolies, that's all.'

'Sounds fair enough to me. Oh, richly deserved, I dare say. Put one in for me, while you're about it.'

She gave him another of her precious smiles. 'You're nice,' she told him warmly. He loved to listen to her voice, to let it run over him. It made him feel scrumptious, like a castle pudding coated in hot golden syrup.

'You like me, at least?'

'Yes, I do. Er, Tobias.'

'Still here.'

'I'm not really a domestic, you know.'

'So I understand. Well, I suspected all along. I even thought of putting a pea under your mattress to see if you were actually a princess.'

'That's not what I meant. I'm not talking about class and all that crap. I just meant, I'm a hairdresser.'

'What luck!' He snapped his fingers. 'Just when I was thinking of having a short back and sides.'

'You could go for something a little more trendy. I could give you a flat-top.' She reached up to ruffle it, to consider it. 'Shave the sides, and gel the rest and – '

'You can do what you like with me, Michele. I shall put myself in your hands entirely. Only promise that you'll be gentle with me.'

'You're crazy.'

'Crazy about you, at least. Michele.'

'Mm.'

'Will you stay around? Whatever the committee decides, will you stop here with me? And be my girlfriend? Ah, no, I see in your eyes, you think it's a rotten idea, you think it's a stinker.'

'It isn't that.' Michele dropped her head. She looked for a while at her feet, at the cobbled floor of the yard, so thoroughly swept and clean. 'But I know you Charteris guys. You say that sort of thing at the drop of a hat. And you don't mean a word of it.'

'I do, I do, I do.' He jumped up and down so the air squeaked in his wellingtons, and he slapped his arms against his sides. 'Cross my heart and hope to die. Look, don't say yes or no. But maybe say maybe.'

'Well, Toby . . .' Then she gave him her most ravishing smile yet. 'Yes,' she decided, 'all right. Maybe.'

There was an old woman who lived in a shoe . . .

Only yesterday, Laura Charteris had had a single child, a girl named Caroline. Now, suddenly, not twenty-four hours later, she had so many children she didn't know what to do.

She had a son, Patrick. She had a daughter, Michele. And she still, somehow, had Caroline, who was, indeed, in one way, more truly 'hers' than any of them.

'Well, this really takes the biscuit,' Laura said to nobody in particular, and she bounded out of her armchair and strode to the sideboard, thinking that a stiff scotch and soda would be just what the doctor ordered. 'It beggars belief.'

From the wall above the fireplace, the first Lady Charteris, the superior Jane, looked down upon her (and, boy, did she look *down*!). Laura, reaching for the decanter, and catching her predecessor's eye, thought better of it. She returned unrefreshed to her seat, encircling her neck with her hands as if to throttle herself.

Across from her, and side by side, sat Caroline and Patrick, saying nothing. They were, the pair of them, Laura realised with a mix of feelings, positively besotted. People in love were, at the best of times, difficult to be with, they shut you out. And there was something conspiratorial about these two, about their muteness; they appeared to be communing wordlessly. As she drew breath for a further rant, Laura saw Caroline slip her hand into Patrick's, saw him give her a reassuring squeeze. She let the breath escape with a sigh, and with it the expected tirade.

They looked good together, she acknowledged, not without difficulty. They looked . . . what? Complete. They looked whole. It struck her for the first time ever how pretty Caroline was, how pleasing that softness of face and figure. And Patrick was terribly attractive; he had that same dark appeal as his father, though without the glint of danger.

Jasper, meanwhile, and Sir John stood right and left of the fireplace, father and son, like bookends, a nearly-matching pair (John was the taller, and if anything the more handsome; John was in fact very handsome indeed).

'There's something else,' ventured Caroline, then, moistening her lips with the tip of her tongue, betraying apprehension. 'Something I haven't yet told you.'

There was *more*? Caroline was a changeling, she was someone else's child. The thin girl was Laura's daughter. Patrick and Caroline were lovers. Caroline was pregnant by Patrick. And there was *something else*? Dear God in Heaven what next?

Laura raised an eyebrow in enquiry.

'Please don't be angry.' Caroline held tighter than ever to Patrick's hand. Out darted her tongue again. 'It was force of circumstance, you see.'

'It was?' asked Laura, mystified.

'Panic, really. I did something out of sheer desperation. I sold the emerald necklace.'

Silence.

'I'm sorry,' offered Caroline. 'Truly. Deeply.'

Silence.

'I know it was wrong,' she blundered on. 'But I supposed it was mine to sell. It was given to me, after all, on the presumption that I was, well, family.'

Under some odd compulsion, Laura turned her head once more to look at Lady Jane, at the patrician countenance, a portrait of a goodie-goodie. 'It doesn't matter,' she said at length, unconvincingly, with an explosive, crackerjack sort of laugh, as if at some private joke. 'Ha-ha. Never mind. Who cares? It was only a *thing*.'

And, at last, she began to weep.

'There, now. Come on, come on.' John crossed to stand beside her, to lay a hand upon her shoulder with a tenderness that tore at her. 'This has all been such a shock to you. To each of us. A body blow. But look at it this way, Laura, Caroline. We *are* still a family. Nothing need change. We are not so much losing a daughter, as, er . . .' he floundered for an instant . . . 'gaining a daughter.'

'Well, I know that, don't I?' Laura responded sniffily. But she made no attempt to shrug him off, to brush his hand away. She rather liked the touch of it, she found it steadying. Warmth and strength flowed from him into her. When she lifted her head, and her gaze met Jasper's, she felt nothing for the boy, not even contempt.

The big oak door swung open just wide enough to admit Stevens, edgeways, with ostentatious tact and discretion, to deliver the news, *sotto voce*, that Mrs Fairchild had arrived.

'Show her in, will you?' commanded Sir John, and, as all eyes turned expectantly in her direction, a shabby little lady in a blue hat, a scrappy, bird-like creature, was ushered into their presence.

For several seconds Doris stood and looked about her appraisingly. (A great barn of a house, this was, she thought, with all them girdles in the roof. And so old-fashioned. Not her taste at all.) Then, eventually, she spoke. She said, 'Nice place you have here.'

Nobody responded. Everyone just stared. The log fire spat sparks on to the hearth.

Gamely, the little lady tried again (Doris had never lacked spirit). Clutching tight to a tatty carrier bag, she sought out Laura. 'You've not changed that much since we last met,' she tendered conversationally. 'How has life been treating you, eh?'

'You!' Laura shot up, making fists, and would have advanced on their visitor had not John hauled her back into her chair. 'You evil old crone. I'd like to slap your face.'

'Come right in, Mrs er . . .' said Sir John, benignly, shushing his wife with the flat of one hand, for he hated unpleasantness, hated scenes of any kind. 'Please sit down. Make yourself at, uhm . . . That's right. I'll have them send up some tea. I dare say we should all be glad of it.'

'Ooh, yes, I could do with a cuppa.' Doris made for the chair next to Laura's. She was very drawn, whey-faced. One of those unhealthy, ill-nourished, wizened people who are nevertheless incredibly tenacious. Only ever half alive, she would probably yet live to be a hundred.

Caroline watched, mesmerised, as their visitor perched on the edge of a seat, resting the bag on her bony knee. *This* was her grandmother? But it was not possible! It was not thinkable! The old lady (perhaps not, after all, so old?) appeared harmless enough, yet such havoc she had caused! Caroline's hand, in Patrick's, flexing, sought support; with a tighter-still squeeze he supplied it.

Since yesterday, her thoughts had been churning like smalls in a tumble-drier, so that first this item, then that, was thrown up. The devastating realisation that she was not her mother's daughter was jumbled with inexpressible joy that she was not, in that case, Patrick's sister. And in there too was anxiety about her pregnancy, as well as ineffable relief that she was still indeed pregnant. Whenever she closed her eyes she saw her whole life in a tangle, and felt queasy. (Or was the sickness, after all, just an effect of her physical condition?)

'You . . .' Doris now sought her out, she addressed her directly, with a familiarity which was curiously coercive. 'You might not understand it, my dove, you might not believe it, but it was for your sake that I done what I done.'

'For my. . . ?'

'So that you should have a chance in life. To give you a bit of a leg-up.'

'Tell me,' Caroline heard herself say. Her mouth felt dry. Her tongue bulged. With difficulty she swallowed. 'I want to know about my mother.'

'Well, now . . .' Doris drew a manila envelope from the carrier and, dipping in, brought out a photograph. 'This was the last photo of my Dawn. I think you will spot the likeness.'

She made no attempt to hand it over, but sat a moment, without expression, gazing at it. And it was Patrick who got up at last, to take it from her, to hand it deferentially to Caroline, who looked at it, and, looking, understood.

This was her mother at . . . what? Fourteen? Fifteen? A round-faced girl with mid-brown hair. No great beauty, though with an air of fierce intelligence, and of defiance. Clever, recalcitrant Dawn, with her astute brown eyes, her thrust-out chin, her hectic complexion and her dissident heart.

I know her, thought Caroline. I know this person. How she hates to have her picture taken, just as I do!

'She had a mind of her own, you see,' said Doris, rather as if this explained everything – which, in a funny way, for Caroline at any rate, it did.

'And my father. . . ?'

Discomfited, Doris fidgeted with the envelope. 'There was a lot of argy-bargy,' she supplied. 'A lot of how's-your-father.'

'A lot of *who's* your father,' put in Jasper, crassly, laughing. Then he shivered in the frost of Laura's glare.

'Oh, right,' said Caroline. Intuitively she comprehended all. Proud, rebellious Dawn was no stranger, after all, to her. She was a soul mate.

It all fitted, she told herself. In a senseless way, it all made sense. And it came to her with the force of certainty that everything was going to be all right.

'I've been a rotten wife,' said Laura, staring distractedly at Pasha, who lay sprawled by the fire, his tail curled up to reveal the neat little configuration of his doghood, his rubbery black balls. Exercised by a dream, he whimpered and scrabbled with his paws.

'No you haven't.' John straddled the arm of the chair, and he clasped her about her shoulders.

The two of them had the room to themselves now. Everyone else had melted away – Doris despatched to a guest suite, where she would stay for this one night, on sufferance, while certain decisions were made; the others to find some space, to be together, or to be alone.

'But I *have*,' Laura insisted. She tried to twist around, to raise beseeching eyes to him (she was good at beseeching eyes; they were a speciality). She was restricted, however, by his embrace, she was restrained. 'Worse than you know.'

'No,' he responded definitely. Meaning what? That he

knew just how bad she was? Or that she was not as bad as she imagined? Squeezing her still tighter, squashing her into herself, sort of bundling her, he said, 'No more of this kind of talk, now, you hear? I don't want you to put yourself down.'

'Very well.'

She lowered her head and enchanted him with a glimpse of her long neck. The knobs of her spine, thus exposed, beneath her pale skin, made her seem strangely vulnerable. And he noticed with a pang that among the rich red hair were some strands of white. Laura, he well understood, would never learn to grow old gracefully. Nor did he *want* her to. He loved her spirit. 'I married you for who you are,' he told her truthfully. And whatever wrong she had done, he absolved her.

'This is all a hopeless mess, isn't it?'

'Not hopeless, no. It will all come out in the wash, what?'

'Well, I guess.'

'That necklace, Laura.'

'My great grandmother's emeralds?'

'We could probably buy it back.'

'No,' said Laura, very much to her own amazement. 'It's honestly not important.'

'It isn't?'

Given this opportunity to reconsider, she might have changed her mind. But, 'No,' she decided, with a rush of blood to the brain, with a singing in her ears like choirs of angels, 'I really don't think it matters a hoot.'

'That boy of yours.'

'Patrick.'

'He's a fine lad.'

'Yes, isn't he? It still seems all wrong, though, somehow, him and Caro.'

'You'll get used to the idea. The pieces will fall into place.'

'I'm not sure of that.'

'Oh, I am.'

'John?'

'Yes?'

She studied her fingernails, neat pink ovals, lustrous as pearl. 'Do you love me?'

'Of course,' he said. And he dredged the air out of his lungs. 'Of course I love you, Laura, my, er love. With all my . . .' (His whole heart, his whole being were implied.)

'We'll have to take care of Michele.'

'Ah. Naturally.'

'Though I simply cannot regard her as my daughter.'

'These things can't be rushed.'

'Uh-huh. When Caroline has her baby . . .' she went on.

'Mm?' he prompted.

But Laura did not answer him. She sank, instead, into herself. And she realised, with no small relief, that she was to be spared one gross indignity at least. Because she was not to be, as she might have been, a maternal grandmother.

'Are you happy?' asked Patrick, as they walked together to the lake, glazed now with ice, and palely gilded.

'I think I am,' answered Caroline.

'Only "think"?'

'Well, of course I am. About us.'

'That's all right then. Hey, did you ever skate on this?'

'No. It was never frozen hard enough to take a person's weight. But Tobias fell in it more than once, I remember, when he was a little boy.'

'Some childhood you must have had here, Caroline, among all this.'

'Well, I did, yes. In many ways I was very spoilt. And I have Hartwell in my bones. But in other ways . . . Well, it could be uncomfortable. It was years before I felt I belonged. And Laura was always so cross with me for being fat and awkward.'

'You're not fat. Not *fat* fat. Just a bit . . . round.'

'Then I *am* awkward, huh?'

'Oh, you're awkward as hell.' He took her hand. 'Your fingers are like icicles.'

'I know. Look, the sun is going. We should turn back.'

'In a minute.' He sighed. 'I still can't take it in, can you?'

'Not properly.'

'It's like the answer to a prayer. I thought there had to be a way – then there was.'

'But who would have guessed it? Who would ever have dreamed it would turn out like this?'

'Who indeed?' He blew out his cheeks, huffed and puffed, as he turned matters over in his mind. 'A bit of a body blow to you, just the same.'

'You're not kidding. But the most peculiar part was to look at that photograph and to see . . . well, *me*.'

'To see *something* of you. You are not her spit and image.'

'I just sort of recognised her. And I had this flash of . . . I kind of knew what her life had been. How it had all gone so wrong for her. I'm sure if she'd found someone nice to love her, it would have taken a different turn entirely.'

'We've been lucky, haven't we, in that respect?'

'I think we have. More than most.'

'You'll be knocked out by Ireland, you know. I can't wait to show you Dublin.'

'Mm-hm.'

'And Josie and Dad. You'll like them.'

'But what will *they* think of *me*?'

'They'll think you're a cracker.'

'I'm nervous about meeting them. About seeing Tom again after so long.'

'There's no need to be, I promise.'

'Just the same . . .'

'Listen, there is nothing to be nervous about. We're *free*, Carrie. And young and fit. We have a whole world of possibilities. And nothing and nobody in our way.' He opened wide his coat and grinned at her. 'Come inside here with us, will you, Missus, and give us a cuddle?'

Jasper stood at the library window in moody contemplation of the frost-bitten gardens. He ached with regret, and – regret being his favourite mode – he was more than content. He had loved Michele, and he had lost her. And it was *all his fault*. If to do is to be, he was doing being. He was doing being heartsick.

Idly he watched as Caroline and her lover, Laura's boy, the lanky, amiable Patrick, strolled hand in hand like a pair of smitten teenagers, towards the lake and into the sunset. All right for some, he thought acidly, as Patrick bundled Caroline up into his windcheater.

What a turn-up this had been, what with Michele being Laura's daughter, and Caroline *not*. And Patrick being Laura's son. And Caroline being . . . Jasper hated the word 'pregnant', it made him feel quite nauseous. He groped for an instant for an acceptable term for that faintly repellent condition, and came up at last with *enceinte*.

To think it might have been her half-brother's child she was carrying! And to think that, after all, it wasn't!

What a mix-up. Such strange events. Daughters that weren't. Incest that wasn't. Lovers caught up in a web of intrigue. It sounded to him like the plot of a novel. In fact . . .

All at once galvanised, he went to his typewriter. He wound in a sheet of A4. He tapped away at the space bar to centre. He depressed the shift key. And he rattled out two golden words.

He typed CHAPTER ONE.

———————— • ————————

Michele's position in the Charteris household was still somehow ambiguous. But, then, she could be pretty ambiguous herself. She was a wafter. She was slow to commit herself. She had found that, in this life, you need take no decisions; someone else will always take them for you.

Very well. On this occasion too, let others decide. She would leave it to Laura and her husband. She'd leave it to

Nanny. And to Toby. Between the lot of them they'd soon sort something out. She could rely upon them absolutely.

Meanwhile, for want of anything better to do, she would go about her business, she would get on with the duties as a housemaid for which she was paid.

At this time of the afternoon she must turn down the beds. And she must take peppermint tea to the old lady.

Maudie Grant was dozing as the girl came softly into the room and set down the tray. She awoke to see a familiar figure stretching up, to see her drawing the curtains to close out the same grey dusk which had enfolded the young lovers. She saw a tall, slim young woman with a mass of red-gold hair, with a pale oval face and an insolent backside.

'Ah,' she said with a touch of impatience, and with a little tush of reproach. 'So *there* you are, Laura, at last!'

A Selected List of Fiction Available from Mandarin

While every effort is made to keep prices low, it is sometimes necessary to increase prices at short notice. Mandarin Paperbacks reserves the right to show new retail prices on covers which may differ from those previously advertised in the text or elsewhere.

The prices shown below were correct at the time of going to press.

☐	7493 0576 2	**Tandia**	Bryce Courtenay	£4.99
☐	7493 0122 8	**Power of One**	Bryce Courtenay	£4.99
☐	7493 0581 9	**Daddy's Girls**	Zoe Fairbairns	£4.99
☐	7493 0942 3	**Silence of the Lambs**	Thomas Harris	£4.99
☐	7493 0530 4	**Armalite Maiden**	Jonathan Kebbe	£4.99
☐	7493 0134 1	**To Kill a Mockingbird**	Harper Lee	£3.99
☐	7493 1017 0	**War in 2020**	Ralph Peters	£4.99
☐	7493 0946 6	**Godfather**	Mario Puzo	£4.99
☐	7493 0381 6	**Loves & Journeys of Revolving Jones**	Leslie Thomas	£4.99
☐	7493 0381 6	**Rush**	Kim Wozencraft	£4.99

All these books are available at your bookshop or newsagent, or can be ordered direct from the publisher. Just tick the titles you want and fill in the form below.

Mandarin Paperbacks, Cash Sales Department, PO Box 11, Falmouth, Cornwall TR10 9EN.

Please send cheque or postal order, no currency, for purchase price quoted and allow the following for postage and packing:

UK including BFPO — £1.00 for the first book, 50p for the second and 30p for each additional book ordered to a maximum charge of £3.00.

Overseas including Eire — £2 for the first book, £1.00 for the second and 50p for each additional book thereafter.

NAME (Block letters) ....

ADDRESS ....

....

☐ I enclose my remittance for ....

☐ I wish to pay by Access/Visa Card Number ☐☐☐☐☐☐☐☐☐☐☐☐☐☐☐☐

Expiry Date ☐☐☐☐